MW01175071

Praise for A.P. Fuchs's *Axiom-man*™

"Axiom-man is that unique breed of superhero that seems almost lost amid today's gaggle of the dark and tormented. He's nice, he cares, and his strength comes not from his fantastic powers, but from his soul. A.P. Fuchs has written a defining superhero novel."

> - Frank Dirscherl, author/creator of *The Wraith*

"Reading *Axiom-man* is refreshing, like reading about the early days of Peter Parker, but with a cooler villain as well."

> - Jon Klement, author/creator of *Rush and the Grey Fox*

"*Axiom-man* was well worth reading and recommending. The broad appeal is amazing—from youth to adult, guys and girls. Superheroes might just become my thing."

> - Susan Kirkland, reviewer, *Calhoun Times*

"Fuchs brings to life a wonderfully imaginative hero we can all relate to . . . . If you're looking for something different, something truly creative, yet filled with action, look no further. *Axiom-man* is the end of your search."

> - David Brollier, author of *The 3rd Covenant*

"I found myself picking the book up at various points in the day, just to read a little more."

> - Darryl Sloan, author of *Ulterior* and *Chion*

"Plenty of surprising twists and turns in this highly enjoyable story. It'll leave you wanting more. Axiom-man is a delightfully human superhero with true depth and spirituality."

> - Grace Bridges, author of *Faith Awakened*

"If you're an action fan with moral sensibilities you'll not just enjoy *Axiom-man*, you'll wish you were he."

> - Frank Creed, author of *Flashpoint*

Axiom-Man™
Doorway of Darkness

by

A.P. Fuchs

'20

COSCOM ENTERTAINMENT
WINNIPEG

COSCOM ENTERTAINMENT
Suite 16, 317 Edison Avenue
Winnipeg, MB R2G 0L9 Canada

ISBN 978-1-897217-69-6

PUBLISHED BY COSCOM ENTERTAINMENT
www.coscomentertainment.com
Text set in Garamond; Printed and bound in the USA
COVER PENCILS AND INKS BY JUSTIN SHAUF
COVER COLORS BY KYLE ZAJAC
EDITED BY RYAN C. THOMAS
INTERIOR AUTHOR PHOTO BY ROXANNE FUCHS

Library and Archives Canada Cataloguing in
Publication

    Fuchs, A. P. (Adam Peter), 1980-
        Axiom-man : doorway of darkness / A.P.
Fuchs.

    ISBN 978-1-897217-69-6 (pbk.)

        I. Title.

PS8611.U34A943 2007   C813'.6   C2007-903381-4

For my younger bother, Jordie, who, growing up, always played my sidekick. Today, my friend, I'm yours.

———

Special thanks to my wife, Roxanne, for her support during the writing of this project and for putting up with me staying up till 3:00, sometimes 4:00, in the morning as I worked on it. Likewise, thank you, dear, for driving me around the city as I researched the various locations portrayed in this book.

Thank you to my oldest friend, Ian Sunderland, M.D., for always being available to answer the slew of medical questions I have.

And thank you to Sergeant Kelly Dennison for providing insight into the workings of the Winnipeg Police Department.

AXIOM-MAN™
DOORWAY OF DARKNESS

PROLOGUE

AXIOM-MAN COULDN'T BELIEVE it.

He stood in the front landing of his apartment, holding the letter that had been waiting for him on the rug where, as Gabriel Garrison, he left his shoes. At first he thought it might have been a note from his caretaker, informing him he was late on rent again, but when he reminded himself that his payment wasn't due yet, he had no idea what he might find within the envelope.

He read the letter again, making sure he had read it correctly the first time. He couldn't have, could he? How could—

Shifting inside, he powered down, sending his abilities deep within himself. The crackle of blue power that was always present while he was Axiom-man left him and for the first time since ever donning the suit, he no longer felt strong beneath the blue tights. It was as if he was nine years old again and realized that pretending to be a superhero and wearing a towel around your neck was stupid.

Gabriel peeled down his mask, thinking that maybe the rims of the eyeholes were somehow obstructing his vision and he wasn't really seeing all that was on the page. But when he read the letter again, his stomach went hollow when he realized his eyes weren't fooling him.

The typed letter read:

Dear Mr. Garrison:

Please forgive me for writing you. For the longest time, four months now, I wasn't sure if I should. But now, it seems, I don't have a choice.

I know who you are, Gabriel. Who you really are. And, no, this isn't a prank. Let's just say that, like you, this knowledge has left me feeling . . . blue.

Please don't fret, as for the time being, your secret is safe with me. But only if you help me. If you don't . . .

If you thought Redsaw's reputation was sullied due to what happened at the Forks, his murdering someone, then think again.

I'll be in touch.

The letter wasn't signed. It wasn't dated but was obviously written within the past day or two given the reference to Redsaw's revealing of his true self when he killed Gene Nemek by throwing a car into him.

Gabriel sank to his knees and, as another first, wanted to get out of his costume and tuck it away as if whoever wrote this letter was watching him right now.

———

"You must build it," the voice said.

It was Sunday night; Oscar Owen was on his knees and he wasn't talking to God. Nor was it God talking back to him.

"It is the only way for you to know the truth." The voice's tone was low, careful and smooth.

Hands on his knees, Oscar flashed to a week ago when his life hadn't been like this. No power, no costume . . . no murder.

It had been a Monday when the black cloud came to him. Lying in bed, unable to sleep, watching the shadows from the trees lining his window outside dance along his bedroom wall—he'd never forget the jolt that shot through him when the room suddenly went black and something blocked the moon. He'd never forget the rain of glass as a smoky cloud burst through his bedroom window, the black wisps of cotton-like fingers searching him out. The cloud had hovered above him that night, coating the room from wall to wall, floor to ceiling, allowing only enough room around him so he could see it in all its enormity, all its monstrousness. He lay there, stiff, wanting to move but unable to budge. He glanced to his right, where his open bedroom door should be. Nothing but billowy black cloud coated the entrance. There was no entrance. There wasn't anything. It was as if the cloud had snuffed out all that was tangible. Just pure . . . blackness.

The cloud looked at him. At least, it seemed to. Though it was featureless, perhaps it was the way its puffy contours moved about in a wind that could not be felt, but for an instant, it seemed as if it had eyes. Then it gathered itself into a long, smoking funnel and drilled itself into his chest like a spike. The second it pierced his skin, his body locked as the cloud found its way through his body, filling out his torso, neck and head; arms, hands, fingers; hips, legs, feet. And even when his body was full, it still poured in to him, *expanded* within him till he felt he was going to burst. Yet even then, the cloud pressed itself into him. Unable to move, only able to *receive*, Oscar let the thing take him. What choice did he have? He didn't know what this thing was never mind what it was doing to him. The cloudy funnel spun counterclockwise to a wind that only it could sense. Gathering up speed, it drilled into him and filled him completely until he could no longer move beneath the weight this thing placed within him.

Drilling.

Spinning.

Filling.

Swwaahhm!

A door slammed, its sound thunderous and all-encompassing. Instinctively, Oscar glanced toward his bedroom door. It was still open.

He shuddered to think of what was locked inside him.

Now, nearly a week later, he knew what that thing was. What *happened*. The cloud gave him great power and for a short time, the city of Winnipeg loved him when he became its greatest champion.

Then the darkness took him, opened itself up. *Revealed* itself to him. It began to speak to him, first as a light buzzing in his ears and mind. Now, tonight, as a voice.

Murder.

Anger.

Death.

Axiom-man.

Rage.

Despair.

Murder.

Axiom-man.

Blood.

Destruction.

Murder.

Axiom—

"You must build it," the voice said. "It is the only way for you to know the truth. It is the only way to receive the power you deserve. You must build it. It cannot be done from here. It must be done from there. You must build it."

"I understand," Oscar said.

"Good. Get it done."

"As you wish."

———

"Let me just lock up, Trav," Mark Headley said. He slid his key into the backdoor at Citytv News and locked it. It was one in the morning. He and Travis Hagen had finally finished for the day after doing a follow up on what had been dubbed around the studio—and the city—as "Black Saturday," the day Axiom-man and Redsaw had gone head-to-head tearing up Portage and Main. They were the best camera team Citytv had. The reporter, Gavin James, had already gone home.

Mark jogged back to his car, a '03 Civic, where Travis sat in the passenger seat, hitching a ride home.

Climbing in behind the wheel, Mark started the car and said, "Got everything?"

Travis checked his thin and wiry self over. "Yeah. Well, left my hat in my camera bag but I can always pick that up tomorrow."

"You sure?"

"Yup. Thanks."

Setting the car in drive, Mark drove past the studio, turned right then left and headed toward Main Street.

Yawning, Travis said, "Thanks for the lift."

"Don't mention it. And stop thanking me. You've thanked me eight times since we left the mess downtown."

"Seven, but who's counting." He offered Mark a toothy grin.

The two rode in silence for a few minutes, both too tired after such a long day to really talk about anything.

Cra-lunk. Something hit the rear driver's side door. At first Mark thought it was a stone the back tire threw up, but when something knocked against the door again, he glanced over his shoulder to see what it was. Nothing. He checked the rearview mirror to see if he had gone over anything lying on the road that he hadn't noticed. The pavement was clear.

Fwamm! The car rocked to the right and a quick image of the car hopping up on its right side wheels then slamming back down again flashed before his eyes.

"What was that?" Travis asked, looking around.

"Don't know." He sped up then slowed down as he turned onto Main Street. Hardly any cars were out at this hour and the ones that were, were far away, mere headlights on vacant city streets. Mark supposed that after what happened Saturday between Axiom-man and Redsaw, not too many folks wanted to be outdoors if it could be helped. At least, not until things calmed down and the lingering tension in the air from that day subsided.

A dark . . . something . . . flickered in the rearview mirror. Before Mark could check what it was, it was gone.

Ka-fraam! The car went at an almost forty-five-degree angle, riding on its right front and back wheels. Travis swore as he hung on to the dashboard. Thinking it'd help bring the car back down, Mark turned the wheel to the left. The tires swiveled and the vehicle turned sharply . . . and rolled. The world went upside down, then right side up again three times before the Civic skidded to a stop, sitting perpendicular on the road.

Dazed, Mark glanced out his window. Red and black streaked toward him and a battering ram made of pure steel slammed into the side of the car, sending it flipping over onto its roof. Travis shouted just as Mark's head slammed into his; a dull smack echoed throughout Mark's skull. The car spun on its roof; his stomach twisted in nausea.

Something dug into his leg. Checking, he saw that whatever had smashed into the car door had forced the inside handle into his thigh. Muscles aching, he tried to wriggle his leg so it wouldn't hurt so bad.

"Trav, you okay?" he asked.

Travis just groaned.

The pressure from the handle suddenly lifted as something tore the door off its hinges. The pavement ran parallel to the roof of the car, the street lights—from the angle he was at—casting a sallow glow on the rough cement. Black upside down boots with red saw-like blades running up the sides appeared before him, then red and black material whirled about the boots like a curtain in the wind before gloved hands reach in and grabbed him, ripping him from the seatbelt and throwing him out onto the street.

The pavement and clouded-over night sky changed places a couple of times before Mark stopped his rolling and skid across the ground.

"Mark!" Travis called after him.

Head throbbing, Mark lay on his back. He tried to look around but the dull banging against the back of his head kept him looking straight up. Footsteps. Someone was behind him. He didn't have to look to know who it was. The black cape that had whirled in his face before he was removed from the car told him everything.

Redsaw.

"Pl-please don't . . ." he said, bringing his hands to his face, palms outward like a shield.

Black-gloved hands reached past his and grabbed him by the collar. Quickly, his body was in the air and was turned around as Redsaw adjusted his grip on him.

"I didn't do anything!" Mark said.

"What's going on out there? I'm stuck. Help me!" Travis said.

Beneath the mask, Redsaw's fiery eyes were tensed around the edges as if he harbored a secret hatred for him. Mark tried to examine Redsaw's face, see who was behind the black mask that covered the man's head, eyes and nose but not his mouth. He didn't recognize him.

Two powerful sets of knuckles plowed into Mark's collar bone and he flew backwards. He slammed into the overturned car, his back letting go a sharp crack when his spine hit the wheel well. Falling to his knees, he stopped his face from hitting the pavement with his hands.

"Mark, get out of here! Run!" Travis shouted from behind.

Mark glanced up to where Redsaw had been standing. The man in the black cape was gone.

Glass shattered behind him and Travis screamed.

Back aching, thinking something might be broken or at least out of place, Mark forced himself to his feet. Slowly, he turned around. Redsaw held Travis aloft by the neck with one hand, his other glowing red.

Legs shaking, adrenaline taking over, Mark rounded the front of the vehicle and came at Redsaw from behind. Before he connected, Redsaw let loose a blast of red energy into Travis's face, incinerating the man's head. Redsaw dropped Travis's limp form to the ground. Spinning around, the masked man stopped Mark's advance with an open palm to the forehead. *Thwump!* The blow sent him to the ground. Head swimming, Mark thought he might be on his knees again and tried getting to his feet. That's when he realized he was lying flat on his back.

The last thing he saw was the black sole of Redsaw's boot coming for his face.

CHAPTER ONE

ON MONDAY MORNING, Gabriel had the TV on while preparing for work. As he stood in front of his bathroom mirror knotting his tie, he thought it might be best not to go in today despite his supervisor, Rod Hunter's, stern warnings about never coming in again late or being absent without a valid reason. Already, he knew, he was probably kissing his job at Dolla-card goodbye after leaving work Friday without notice so he could take care of the Forks situation that led to Redsaw's murder of Gene Nemek.

Gene, Gabriel thought. He had barely known the guy. Only a few days. Gene had been kind, silly and a huge nerd. But Gabriel understood the guy when, it seemed, no one else had. Gene had been naturally clumsy, a bad dresser, snorted when he laughed—things Gabriel made a conscious effort to do while at the office to help safeguard his Axiom-man identity. And for a short time he had thought Gene *was* Redsaw. The geeky guy with the nerdy glasses was never around when Redsaw was and always seemed to vanish just before Redsaw popped up on the scene. Though Gabriel had never felt Redsaw's presence when around the kid—that sick swimming feeling in his stomach, the nerve-wracking sense of dread and darkness that poured off Redsaw like smoke from a bush fire—perhaps, he had thought, Redsaw was able to turn his powers on and off like him. There was no real way to know other than banking on the fact they were very similar, the only discrepancies being Redsaw's energy blasts—red instead of blue—came from his hands instead of his eyes and that he was stronger and faster. It was a serious possibility. Perhaps one

9

day he'd find out. Hopefully the messenger, the strange powerful being made of blue light that gave Gabriel his abilities, would let him know. After all, it was the messenger who told him Redsaw was created to counter Axiom-man's presence on the planet.

Placing his hands on the edge of the sink, Gabriel took a deep breath. Sleeping last night had been difficult, his mind racing about who had sent that letter, with what he was going to say to Rod as an excuse for Friday and what he'd say to others when they asked where his glasses were. He cursed himself for not having a spare pair. Should he take the day off and get a new set?

"If I did Rod would can me," Gabriel whispered. He grabbed his cardigan off the edge of the counter and put it on. Between the yellow-and-black-checkered tie, white shirt and black cardigan, he thought he looked like a bumble bee.

What else is new? he thought. *Folks think I'm a goof anyway.*

Brushing a few stray spots of lint from his black dress pants, he went to the living room to turn off the TV.

Did he just see something about Redsaw on the morning news? The screen had switched to the next story so fast he couldn't be sure. Standing there, remote in hand, he told himself he should get going but the grimness on the newscaster's face said he should watch a few more moments. That's when the aerial shot of a downtown bank filled the screen.

Someone had taken the bank hostage.

———

Oscar Owen ran the faucet in the bathroom off the master bedroom. Cupping his hands under the cold water, he let it pool in his palms for a few moments before bringing it to his face. He had tried washing with warm water seconds before but after last night . . . it was as if his skin was on fire. The shock of the icy water hitting his skin brought refreshment and for a brief instant, washed away the memory of last night.

Those men . . .

It had to be done. Not only had the two young fellows videotaped the aftermath of Black Saturday, they also would, no doubt, ensure that Gavin James branded Redsaw a menace on the morning news. Oscar had seen Gavin's reports before and more than once had Gavin thanked his cameramen on air for reminding him of what *really* happened during a particular event, reminding him of the information gleaned from interviewing bystanders who saw whatever event occurred.

"Everyone already hates you," Oscar said, removing his hands from his face. He placed them under the water again, its coolness stimulating yet calming to his skin.

But removing those two guys' opinions from the news was only one of the reasons for killing them.

He had to build it—the doorway. His master wished it. The master said that if the doorway was built, Oscar would find out who he was and what his recently-acquired power meant.

It wasn't supposed to be this way, Oscar thought, reaching for the towel. He kept the water running in case he felt the need to cool down again. Bringing the towel to his face, shutting out the light of the bathroom, he was reminded of the flash of darkness he saw right after hurling that car into the young man Friday at the Forks. The darkness appeared for only a split second, a blotch of pitch nothingness against a blue sky. It looked just like the cloud that had invaded him a few days before. Then the buzzing filled his ears, the same buzzing that gave way to the master's voice.

The power that surged through him after ending that young man's life, the same power that filled him doubly so last night—the power needed to build the doorway. It was the power that healed his burnt face after fighting Axiom-man Saturday. The power that woke him before Axiom-man could remove his mask.

Last night, after the killings, the master said that the barrier that separated him from Oscar was too dense to be breached by any means created by man. Only power from the cosmos could breach its seal and the only way to acquire that power was to make the deposit that was already within him greater than what it was. The power grew after that first death on Friday. And it was growing now. Soon, Oscar felt, he'd have enough to open the doorway, but when that would be, he didn't know and his heart sank at the uncertainty.

"How many innocent lives?" he asked. "How many? I can't do this forever."

The master's voice returned. "You must be willing to do so for an eternity if you wish to learn the truth. If you don't, you'll be left to wallow in self-pity and darkness until you leave this earth. And that would be soon, for things are changing in my realm and I've received news that Axiom-man is on the verge of a great discovery. Should that discovery take place, he will overcome you. Nay, he will *kill* you."

Furrowing his brow, Oscar felt his skin heat up. He set the towel down, rinsed his hands then brought the water to his face. "Get out of my head," he said. "How do I know you're not just me going crazy? I killed three people! I'm not a fool. I know this is me talking to myself."

"Don't insult me!" The volume of the voice reverberated all around him, forcing Oscar to take a quick step back from the sink. "Do you honestly believe that the black cloud, the source of your power, is something that was merely conjured up in your imagination? And if so, that the powers manifested from the encounter are all in your mind?"

"I wasn't talking about the cloud, I was talking about—"

"Silence! The cloud was a conduit to me. I chose you, Oscar. Do not make me regret it."

Oscar stepped back to the sink, yearning to touch the cold water again. "Why me?"

But the master was silent. He'd either left or was choosing not to respond.

"Answer me!" Oscar slammed his fist down on the countertop. Before his fist made contact, he felt his power *switch* on. His fist smashed through the pressboard to the right of the sink and into the hollow of the cabinet below. He scraped his hand along the wood's jagged edges as he pulled it out, drawing blood. "Tell me! Why me?"

No answer.

Just then his cat, Rolly, entered. He looked up at Oscar with his deep green eyes. Rolly's smooth gray fur reflected the bathroom's yellow light. His dark pupils . . . . The black cloud!

Oscar snatched Rolly up by the scruff of the neck and slammed him down to the left of the sink. Rolly squealed. Oscar silenced him with a quick twist to the neck.

The clear water quickly ran red.

———

Great! I'm going to be late and there's nothing I can do about it, Axiom-man thought as he flew quickly downtown. He was there in under five minutes and made certain to stay in the air over five hundred feet from the scene so that those who looked up would think him only a black spot against the clear morning sky. A bird, perhaps. From up here, he could see everything. Far below, a host of squad cars surrounded the bank. Traffic was backed up far down Main Street and anyone part of the morning rush hour would surely be late for work. Like him. Perhaps he could use traffic as his excuse when he made it into the office. *If* he made it in today at all. He only caught a bit of the details of what was going on at home while he tore off his work clothes and stuffed them into the backpack he wore beneath his cape. The silent alarm had been triggered, presumably by one of the bank's workers. Only one robber was speaking with the police but most likely he wasn't working alone. If any of the workers were still alive, it was unknown.

Emerging out of the cluster of traffic below was a big vehicle, most likely the E.R.U., Winnipeg's Emergency Response Unit for special circumstances. It was too difficult to tell from this high up but at least he now had an idea of how things looked from the outside.

If those guys try anything too soon . . . He had seen enough cop and robber movies to know that whoever held up a bank and had hostages were usually intelligent enough to keep an upper hand over the police.

Axiom-man dove downward, cutting through the air, watching the ground get closer. He veered to the right and headed toward a pack of cars about twenty-five feet from the scene, out of view from the bank's windows. He didn't want the robbers within to see him.

Touching down, he received stares from those both in and out of their vehicles. One guy, who was half-in-half-out of his car said, "You gonna clear this thing up or what? What the heck is going on in there anyway? I gotta get to work."

Raising a hand, Axiom-man said, "Don't worry. Everything is going to be fine."

Bending at the waist, he made sure his head and body were below roof-level of the cars, anything to hide himself from the robbers inside the bank who might be looking out the window. He kept as far away from the direct line-of-sight to the bank as possible and, ignoring questions from pedestrians, made his way to the nearest squad car. A cop stood beside the vehicle, one foot on the inner running board, one arm resting on the top of the open door. With his other hand he held a radio to his lips.

"Haven't heard anything from inside for about ten minutes. Things should be all right but you never know. The last time this happened . . . yeah, well, you heard about it. So did half the city."

Axiom-man couldn't recall the last time a bank had been seized. Then again, he hadn't ever really paid serious attention to the news until recently.

"Excuse me, Officer?" he said, coming up behind him but remaining crouched by the rear side door of the vehicle.

The cop glanced over his shoulder then looked down. "Geez, you scared me." Then into his radio, "I'll keep you posted. Over." He looked down at Axiom-man. "You shouldn't be here. You'll bungle this up if you try anything. Besides, you've caused enough problems already."

"I'm here to help," he replied, ensuring an edge of confidence to his tone. *Can I really help? How would I be able to get inside? Wait till it comes to that.*

"Last time you tried to help, you and Redsaw destroyed Portage and Main. In case you haven't heard, there are civilians inside and—"

He was sure to maintain eye contact. "How many?"

"I'm not at liberty to say."

"Who's in charge here?"

"What, you come in here and try and tell me how to do my job?"

"No, I asked a question. How many are inside and who's leading you guys on the ground floor?"

The cop turned away from him, removed his hat and ran his fingers through his short, dirty blond hair. He set the cap back on his head then returned his gaze to Axiom-man. "Sergeant Jack Gunn," he said hesitantly.

Finally, they were getting somewhere.

"Jack Gunn," Axiom-man said.

"Yeah, I know, the most 'cop name' you've ever heard." He eyed Axiom-man steadily. "Look, I'll get him over here if you want but *only* if you stay put. You screw this up—"

"I'll stay right here. There are innocent people inside. If I can help in any way to get them out, you bet I'll follow procedure."

"Procedure hardly ever works for situations like this. 'Least from what I heard. I'll get Gunn for you." He spoke into his radio and summoned his superior.

Gunn came through the radio's speaker. "What? I'm busy here, Franklin. You're supposed to be controlling traffic not yapping to your girlfriend in dispatch."

"I wasn't—"

"You think I can't tune in?"

"Sorry. Listen, I have—"

"Watch your tone, Franklin, or you'll be wearing the Idiot Apron and bringing me coffee for a month."

"I'm sorry, sir. Axiom-man is here and he wants to—"

"I'll be right there. Over."

Franklin huffed. "He'll be right here."

Axiom-man let a small amount of blue energy coat his eyes. "I heard him."

Grimacing, Franklin turned and stared at the bank.

Axiom-man smiled beneath his mask. *Serves him right.*

———

Valerie Vaughan started when the ear-piercing tone of her alarm clock jarred her out of sleep. She glanced at the clock. It was 7:30.

Why do I always set this thing for so early? she thought, pushing her long, dark brown hair from over her eyes. She turned it off and rolled over onto her side. If today were any other day, she would have reset the alarm till nine.

But that wasn't the plan.

———

"All right, where is he?" Jack Gunn said as he rounded the front of Franklin's squad car and stopped on the other side of the open door.

Franklin nodded toward the ground where Axiom-man sat on his haunches, his cape wrapped around him.

Sergeant Gunn moved from behind the door and stood before him. Stocky and solid, Gunn looked to weigh in at around two-fifty or two-sixty, carrying most of his weight in his upper body. He crouched down and pushed the length of his brown leather overcoat out to the sides, revealing a gaudy white-with-pink-striped shirt beneath. He didn't wear a tie but wore his badge on his belt. The fabric of his black dress pants strained against his large knees, the black somehow bringing out the gray streaks in his brown hair. Touching his short-trimmed beard once, he then put his palms on his knees and scrutinized Axiom-man up and down, as if sizing him up.

"What can I do for you?" he said with a hint of fine-I'll-talk-to-you-for-a-moment in his voice.

"From the looks of things, you're at a standstill."

"You could say that. Listen, before we go any further, know that I don't like you. I appreciate what you do but you have no formal training and just because you run around helping people, it doesn't make you an officer of the law or even a hero. Got it?" It wasn't even a question.

"Got it." And with a small grin beneath his mask, he added, "But you also realize I can do things you cannot do and it is because of those things I've been able to assist you where others have fallen short."

The muscles around Gunn's brown eyes tightened. He rolled his lips inward, as if biting his tongue.

Axiom-man waited for the official tell-off. Did he just screw up his chances of helping out? If he did and someone inside the bank died because he couldn't do anything to help them . . . he wouldn't be able to forgive himself. He already didn't forgive himself for what happened to Gene. To add more deaths to the mix . . . . Axiom-man couldn't bear the thought and was about to apologize but Gunn spoke first.

"Glad we understand each other," he said.

A wave of relief came over him. "What's happening inside?"

Gunn waddled closer, his large knees nearly pressing into Axiom-man's. "Workers came in this morning. Twelve of them when another branch faxed us the staff count. The branches keep tabs on who shows up and who doesn't in case someone's a man short. Anyway, they come in only to find the perps inside—six, from what is known—the safe open, bags stuffed. Seems the job wasn't finished due to misinformation regarding when the morning shift started. One of the tellers managed to hit the silent alarm, tipping us off. Next thing I know, I personally get a phone call from a guy dubbing himself 'Mr. Safe.' He's got them all at gunpoint. A shot was fired when I was on the horn with him. Sounded like someone bought it but there's no way to know for sure."

"Any demands?" Axiom-man found it strange "Mr. Safe" was talking to Gunn, a police sergeant, instead of a hostage negotiator. He could only assume Mr. Safe had asked for Gunn specifically. He just didn't know why.

"Just like on TV. They want safe passage out of here. Thing is, they haven't said *how* they want to get out of here. When I told him I was willing to comply, he disconnected, obviously letting me know he's the one who wants to be in charge."

"Is he?"

Gunn bent his head back and gazed skyward for a moment. When he lowered his head, his face was solemn. "As of now, yeah."

CHAPTER TWO

"HELLO, MR. GUNN," came a voice through the radio on Jack's belt. The police sergeant snatched it up.

"Hello, Mr. Safe," he said. "Have you come to a decision?"

How did Mr. Safe patch in to the police's radio band? Axiom-man wondered.

"Now, now, don't rush me," Mr. Safe said. "You wouldn't want me ending up standing on a mound of bodies, now, would you?"

Jack sighed. "No, I guess not."

"Guess not?"

"No."

Axiom-man wondered why Jack was being so easy-going and could only assume that Mr. Safe had somehow gotten the upper hand before he flew onto the scene.

"Good," Mr. Safe said. "Listen, I'm just 'calling' to let you know it's growing awfully cramped in here. I suddenly feel like there's no room to do anything. Can't move around without bumping into someone. I'm thinking I'm going to have to clear some room."

"I appreciate the position you're in. It must be tight in there, but wouldn't that be a good thing? If room suddenly freed up, you'd then be leaving room for me to come in there so we could talk."

Mr. Safe chuckled softly on the other end. "Maybe. But I also may not want to talk, which leaves you at a disadvantage."

The police sergeant turned his back on Axiom-man. Now standing by the hood of the car, Franklin put his hands on his hips as he listened in on the conversation. Axiom-man remained low despite how much he wanted to stand next to Gunn. Despite how much he wanted to rip the radio from Gunn's hand and try and talk some sense into Mr. Safe.

"Then why don't we keep things level? You tell me what it is you want and I'll try and accommodate," Jack said.

"Try?" Mr. Safe was obviously toying with him and the confidence in the robber's voice made Axiom-man cringe inside.

"Will."

"That's better. As I said, I'm not sure just yet what else I want from you, but what I do want in here is some space." Gun blasts echoed through the radio followed by the panicked screams from the people within.

"Safe!"

"Toodle-oo." The radio went dead.

"Get me Sergeant Hedgewick," Jack told Franklin.

Franklin just stood there.

Grumbling, Jack stormed past him.

Those people . . . Axiom-man thought. *Jack's being played and who knows how many innocent people inside have already died. I know this is a delicate situation, but there's gotta be something I can do.*

Axiom-man stood, raised his arms shoulder level and kicked off from the ground.

———

"That useless, good-for-nothing . . ." Jack turned on his heels with the intent of coolly eyeing Franklin. When this was over, the officer *would* spend a month bringing him coffee.

Jack smiled when he saw Axiom-man fly up to the side of the bank.

Finally, they were getting somewhere.

———

Axiom-man flew up to the bank's side wall, staying out of view of the front windows. About three stories below, he heard the squawk of a bullhorn that was quickly cut off by Gunn saying something like, "Stop. You'll tip them off."

Hovering against the wall, Axiom-man kept to the left of the window beside him. Then he realized that if he did manage to get inside, he had no idea how he was going to get the hostages—never mind Mr. Safe and his crew—out.

But if I fly back down and regroup with the police, I'll look like an amateur who doesn't know what he's doing. Which was also true. Bank robberies, hostages—this was why Winnipeg had a specially trained department for such things. *Have to better plan ahead next time,* he thought. *Hopefully there won't be a next time. Stupid, stupid, stupid.* A part of him did want to fly back down; another wanted to fly away and pretend like he hadn't arrived on the scene at all. Despite four months of crime fighting experience, he still was, admittedly, a novice. *Too bad the messenger couldn't have also bestowed upon me the gift of wisdom and insight. It would have made everything, especially the last week, much easier.* He sighed. *No sense adding to my worry now. Better get on with it and just hope everything works out.*

Cautiously, he peered into the window next to him while also making an effort not to glance below to the police officers who were no doubt watching his every move. On the other side of the glass was an office suite, presumably one for a personal banker, complete with a mahogany desk, computer, plush leather chairs for the clients and some poorly-done nature watercolors that the bank no doubt rented by the month. No one was inside.

I hate going into those, he thought absentmindedly. *They always turn me down for a loan. Okay, stop it! Focus.*

He touched the glass, as if to sense where the robbers were inside. *Most likely downstairs by the vault, if I remember the interior correctly.* But where were the hostages? Were they still alive? Did Mr. Safe and his crew kill them while the radio was turned off?

Better get in.

He considered just pummeling through the wall but as was his policy, he didn't want to destroy any property if he could help it. Yet in a situation like this . . .

Noting that the office door was closed, he floated over in front of the window, ready to duck out of sight should anybody suddenly come in.

"Wait," he said. *Never mind. If the alarm was already triggered once, I doubt it'll be triggered again.*

He drew himself about three feet from the glass and let the brilliant blue of crackling energy fill his eyes, the source of his power. Careful to maintain visual with the glass through the bluey haze, he squinted his eyes and focused a beam of energy into the glass, cutting out a hole large enough for him to fit through.

The loose piece of glass fell inward, shattering on the burnt sienna-carpeted floor just behind the desk. Axiom-man froze, expecting to hear the shrill sound of an alarm, or worse, the sight of two large men with Uzis barreling in to see what the ruckus was about. He quickly retreated alongside the wall and waited to see if anyone would come. A full minute passed and he didn't hear anything from inside. They mustn't have heard.

Giving a friendly nod to Sergeant Gunn below, he straightened his body and flew through the hole, and touched down once inside.

Slowly, he made his way over to the door and gripped the door handle. Gently, he turned the knob and opened the door just a crack to see what was on the other side.

A large balcony with brass railings bordered the main service floor in a huge square. Offices ran off the balcony about twelve feet apart. At first Axiom-man thought the coast was clear but when he opened the door a bit more, he saw each of the four corners of the balcony was guarded by a man in a pale blue jumpsuit, a black balaclava, gardeners mitts and a long, dark rifle.

Okay, think. Four guys. One me. I can do this. He only wished the confidence in his heart matched that of his brain. There had to be a way to . . . *Move. Quickly!*

Axiom-man dove out from behind the door and tackled the nearest gunman at the waist, taking him over the edge of the balcony. The man's arms immediately went up, one hand hanging onto his rifle. A shot rang out, bringing down a spray of plaster from the ceiling. Axiom-man flew him straight for the ground and slowed their decent at the last second before delivering a swift punch to the base of the guy's neck, rendering him unconscious. His three cohorts already had their guns aimed; the main floor to the bank was empty.

Where's . . . Before Axiom-man could finish the thought, bullets whizzed past him. He dropped the gunman's unconscious form to the floor and flew up toward the ceiling, twisting his body left and right, making it difficult for the other three to lock a shot on him. Flying up in a large arc, he came down hard on the second gunman, bringing him down. The guy was still conscious so, planting his feet firmly, he lifted the guy up then smashed his head into the balcony's brass railing, sending the gunman to nighty-nightland.

Bang! Bang! One bullet punctured a hole in the wall across from him, the second grazed his shoulder, tearing the fabric of his costume. *Great. I just fixed this,* he thought. Should he switch to bulletproof armor? Then there'd be no way to wear his outfit under his clothes unless he wanted to look like an Arnold Schwarzenegger-wannabe.

Flying back up, he torqued his body to the left, swooping down along the main floor then arcing back up along the opposite wall and flew belly-up against the ceiling. He almost flew too close to it, but before he could dwell on what an embarrassment that would have been, he bent to the right and landed on the balcony in behind the third gunman. The man spun around and aimed the rifle at his chest. Axiom-man tore it from the man's hands and used it as a baseball bat to the side of the man's head. The gunman dropped to his knees then toppled face first to the floor.

"Huge trouble up here!" the fourth screamed into his walkie-talkie.

Axiom-man dropped the rifle and hopped up onto the railing, then pushed off it, soaring through the air. *Boom!* A bullet whistled past his ear. Hands forward, he dove into the fourth man and pressed the rifle up against the gunman's stocky body. The guy fell backward, the rear of his skull smacking against the balcony floor. With a quick fist to the face, Axiom-man ensured the man wouldn't be any more trouble.

He turned and was stopped short when he saw another gunman clad in the same pale blue jumpsuit and black balaclava at the edge of a hallway below. Axiom-man flew down after him. The guy did an about face and ran off down the hall, heading for the stairwell.

Touching down, Axiom-man ran after him, somewhat amazed at how effortlessly the gunman took the stairs two at a time. The gunman reached the bottom and tore off. When Axiom-man reached the bottom floor, the man was gone. Surveying the narrow hallway lined with office doors, he wondered if he was too late, if the ruckus above provoked Mr. Safe or whoever else to murder the hostages.

"Please, no," Axiom-man whispered.

Cautiously, he walked down the hall, stopping before each door, straining to hear movement or voices from anyone who might be on the other side. Each door greeted him with silence. At the last door on the right, he thought he heard someone whimpering within. About to grab the door handle, Axiom-man stopped when cold gun metal was suddenly pressed up against the back of his head.

"Welcome." The voice belonged to Mr. Safe. "Come with me."

The Past . . .

1504 A.D.

Jeremiah Garir glanced up at the clear night sky, the stars bright pin pricks against a matte of black, and took a deep breath. His wife, Rebekah, had complained of the sharp pains again. It was to be expected, he supposed. She had just begun her ninth month of pregnancy of their first child. The Peraton Village doctor said that she could be due any day now. Rebekah had been thirsty and so had woke him in the middle of the night to go and draw water from the well. He didn't mind getting up. He was thirsty, too. Wearing only his nightclothes—loose-fitting light gray pants and matching top—he slipped on his shoes, grabbed the pottered urn by the door and went outside.

Now, out here in the cool night air, he felt invigorated and wondered if he'd be able to return to sleep easily once he was back indoors. Placing a palm to the edge of the well, Jeremiah took yet another deep breath and wondered why he was suddenly so restless. He had had nine months, after all, to prepare for the arrival of what he hoped would be a son. He had had all this time to go over in his head how he and Rebekah would parent the child, and if they would do well by him or her. Hopefully they would be everything this child could ask for in a set of parents and more. Hopefully. They were young and still somewhat inexperienced at life. He was twenty-eight, she twenty-three. But now, reflecting on it, it wasn't the unease of questioning their potential parenting skills that set his stomach swirling with butterflies.

It was the type of world they would be bringing the child into.

Peraton Village wasn't a terrible place at first glance. Normally, it was actually quite beautiful during the day, with small scattered patches of flowers and shrubs lining the streets, a small forest at its center with an area cleared out for children to run and play. But that's where its idealness *ended. Peraton was wasting away. The majority of the families barely earned enough from their trades or farming to keep a roof over their heads. Many of the children had been wearing the same set of clothes for the better part of the year. And many, adult and child alike, were forced to eat only every other day as a result of the severe drought this past summer, ruining most of the crops. Both Jeremiah's and Rebekah's once filled-out bodies were now mere cloaks of skin over skeletal frames. What was once a simple town with struggling settlers was quickly becoming a breeding ground for the starved and poor. Several of Jeremiah's friends had to sell their small homes and move into makeshift shacks so they could afford to eat. He and Rebekah had contemplated doing the same just after the drought hit; only a small corner of his farm and a tiny vegetable garden Rebekah kept just out back of their tiny home remained. Even if next year brought good weather, Jeremiah doubted he would have enough money to get the farm started again.*

To bring a child into a world where it couldn't eat once breastfeeding was over made Jeremiah shudder with guilt. Who was he to force an innocent babe to live a life of poverty and starvation? He and Rebekah were adults; they would be able to take care of themselves. But a baby? Who was he kidding?

"I'm sorry, dear," he said, looking toward his small home.

Under the light of the moon, his heart sank when he saw the left side of the roof was caving in. He had never noticed it before and now he couldn't afford the supplies to fix it himself. He could do a patch job with some lumber he had kicking around the property, but that was about it.

He ran his fingers through his dark brown hair, the top so long he reminded himself he needed a trim.

Jeremiah took hold of the bucket on the well's outer rim with one hand and the well's rope with the other. Hopefully the water down below was still okay. He had heard rumors in town that morning that some of the folks were having problems with the drinking water and a few of them were getting sick because of it.

I pray to the God of Heaven things will work out, whether for me or for those to come after me. Namely the child my dear wife and I are about to bring into the world, *he thought.*

As he slowly lowered the bucket down into the well, the roll of thunder off in the distance made him straighten.

He looked up. *"There's not a single cloud. How—"*

The thunder rolled again, this time finishing with a resounding BOOM!

The pitch black sky brightened, the stars suddenly muted as startling bright blue clouds formed in the distance. They grew and grew and began tumbling forward from the four corners of the earth. The thunder rolled and grew louder with each advance of the clouds until the entire sky was a gorgeous mixture of light and dark blues. When the clouds finished coming in from all sides and reached the center, the thunder roared as if God Himself had shouted at the earth. Then there, at the center of the sky, a bright blue light appeared and grew larger and larger until it bloomed into a kind of flower that covered the skies from north to south and east to west.

The sky flashed white, followed by another thunder clap.

Then the lightning poured forth and spikes of raw power shot forth from thousands of places in the heavens. Shrieks and screams came from the village not far from Jeremiah's land.

A spire of light zapped from above and, as if it were alive, snaked its way into the window of his home.

"Rebekah!" he shouted, letting go of the rope.

As he darted for the house, a beam of light struck him, too.

CHAPTER THREE

MR. SAFE SLAMMED the butt of the rifle between Axiom-man's shoulder blades and pushed him into the office, then reset the barrel to the back of his head. A metal-framed desk with a fake wood-paneling top was up against the far right wall. Filing cabinets lined the wall to the left. Bodies covered the floor like a carpet. Axiom-man counted fifteen; more than what was reported. Four men in the same pale blue jumpsuits and black masks stood guard over the prisoners, rifles aimed at the people's heads and backs.

"Ladies and gentlemen," Mr. Safe said, "I give you your savior."

A few of the folks raised their heads off the floor.

"Did we tell you to move?" one of the gunmen shouted. With a quick *thwack* from the rifle, he firmly set a young man back to kissing the floor.

The gun barrel still pressed up against the back of his skull, Axiom-man wondered what his next move should be. Mr. Safe solved the dilemma for him and dragged the barrel around the side of his head so it was set squarely between his eyes. Backing away a couple of steps, rifle still trained on him, Mr. Safe said, "Welcome to our little abode."

"You don't need to do this," Axiom-man said. "We can work this out."

"Oh please," he replied. "Don't come in here all nice and pretend like you want to talk. I've seen the movies, too. Cop comes in arms open, promises the world, says the robber doesn't need to execute a host of people to prove his point. The robber gets distracted and, taking the opportunity, the cop arrests him. Disney ending. La la la." He raised the gun and his cold eyes stared down the barrel. "Let's give this a new ending. I cap ya right here and me and my mates finish our dealings with Mr. Gunn. Or" —he snapped his fingers and one of the gunmen cocked a rifle— "we off everyone here save one for insurance and you're left with the blood of fourteen individuals on your hands. What's it gonna be, hero?"

Axiom-man surveyed the bodies. From what he could tell, no one was hurt. Another door was in the far corner. Was anybody dead behind there?

"Is this everyone?" Axiom-man asked.

"Sorry. My secret," Mr. Safe said.

Fine, he thought. "So—"

"So what do we do from here? Man, Dad really knows how to pick 'em." Mr. Safe cut himself short as if he just said something he wasn't supposed to.

"Your dad?"

The rifle lowered slightly. "The cat's outta the bag now, isn't it? Yeah, my dad. The brave Sergeant Gunn of the Winnipeg Police."

Axiom-man wanted to tell him that since he had revealed his identity, it would only be a matter of time before he would be caught if he and his cronies got away. But he didn't. *Let him talk. Who knows what else he might tell you?*

Mr. Safe changed the subject. "Tell you what: I'll make you a deal. I removed my mask, now you do the same. If you don't—" He snapped his fingers again and the gunman shot one of the people in the leg. The room erupted in screams.

"Shut up! Shut up! Shut up!" the gunman screamed and cocked the rifle again.

The older woman with the bullet wound to her calf brought her hands to her face and forced herself to grunt and moan without raising her head.

Axiom-man threw out his hands, palms out. "Okay, okay. Stop. No more. Just . . . stop."

"That's more like it."

So it's come to this, Axiom-man thought. *All that work maintaining a secret identity, all the sacrifices I've made trying to hide who I am and I'm taken out by some low-blow punk who's mad at his dad for some reason.*

Mr. Safe must've expected him to remove his mask right away because he said, "Today or tomorrow, Sweetheart? I'm hoping for today unless you want to force me to stain the rug red."

A gunman came up beside Axiom-man and reached for the mask.

"Let me do it," Axiom-man said. "There's only one way to take it off." Which wasn't true at all but hopefully it would buy him a few more seconds to think of a way out of this. *How can I be so selfish? These people will die if I don't obey.* Then as a thought that didn't quite seem his own: *Well, it was fun while it lasted. Besides, someone else already sent you a note saying they know who you are. But they also said my secret was safe. For now.* Yet if he did take off his mask, odds were no one would recognize him anyway. With his powers still shifted on, his hair held a blue sheen and the whites of his eyes along with his normally-brown irises were glazed over with bright blue energy. That in and of itself was a disguise. The mask was almost a failsafe.

The people whimpered and moaned, their tones clearly indicating they needed help.

By any means necessary even if that meant exposing himself.

Slowly, he reached up to the top of the mask and curled his fingers around the fabric's edges.

So it ends.

———

Valerie headed down Portage Avenue. Walking briskly, her heart raced at what she was about to do.

It could only mean good things, she thought.

She was dressed a bit fancier than what she was used to: black slacks, a blue collared shirt, a black blazer and matching high-heeled shoes. A gust of wind blew at her and she was thankful she had tied her dark brown hair back in a tight ponytail. If there was one thing she hated, it was being unable to see as strands of hair blew in her face. Especially on days she tried to look good.

She hefted her attaché case in her left hand then stopped her stride. "Wait a minute." No one on the sidewalk was walking toward her. They were all heading down to Portage and Main.

The area's blocked off after Saturday. What's the deal? She looked across the street and the same thing was happening on the parallel sidewalk.

"Did this city suddenly just get jobs all at the same place?" she said. Then with a sigh: "Always something happening." She checked her watch, seeing if she still had time before her appointment. She did.

Valerie headed off down the sidewalk to see what was going on.

———

Axiom-man winced beneath his mask as he slowly peeled the fabric down his forehead.

Shots rang out from somewhere upstairs and a loud *WABOOM* shook the building. Plaster rained down, the prickly white shards landing on his knuckles and hair.

The people laying on the floor screamed. A couple of the gunmen swore and Mr. Safe said something, too, but Axiom-man couldn't hear what over the echo from the ceiling crashing down.

Something hit the floor and his body quaked with dread. Then, "Don't let me stop you."

That voice. That *voice*. How could he forget it: that low, edgy tone filled with a bravado that made him cringe inside every time he heard it? Mask still over his eyes, Axiom-man quickly replaced the fabric over his forehead.

Redsaw stood before him.

Insides buckling, stomach suddenly doing loop-de-loops, Axiom-man backed away then stumbled onto his knees. Instinctively, his eyes glazed over with brilliant blue, building and building and—he let loose, sending a stream of blue energy into Redsaw's chest. The man in the black cape flew back over the people and into the drywall across the way. The wall crumbled behind him and fell on top of him as he hit the ground.

A gunman off in the corner got to his feet and aimed his rifle at Redsaw. A wave of red energy quickly removed the man's head from his body.

The helpless people on the floor yelped and whimpered.

Mr. Safe removed a handgun from one of the pockets in his jumpsuit and cocked the hammer. A red energy beam knocked the gun from his hand. Collapsing to his knees, Mr. Safe cradled his hand.

Movement to his right. Axiom-man spun around and grabbed the rifle from the gunman nearest him and, using the gun like a sling, hurled the man into the side wall. The body dropped like a sack of flour. Axiom-man glanced to the destroyed drywall to see what Redsaw would do next but the man was gone.

Two screams whirled Axiom-man to the right, just in time to see Redsaw's fists light fiery red then send that energy into the gunmen on either side of the room, the hot blasts searing a hole through each man's chest.

Mr. Safe tried crawling past Axiom-man and was quickly stopped by a dark blue boot to the small of his back. Grunting, Mr. Safe collapsed to the floor.

A flash of red went off to the side and when Axiom-man looked, he saw Redsaw dumping the body of the gunman he had just thrown into the wall. Another beam of red came at him before he had time to react and the next thing he knew, the floor and the ceiling changed places and he landed on top of a row of hostages.

Weeping, Mr. Safe said, "No, no, come on. I didn't do anything."

Without a word, Redsaw clasped his hands on either side of Mr. Safe's head. A red glow surrounded Redsaw's black gloves and the smell of cooking flesh and burnt fabric filled the room.

"No!" Axiom-man screamed and got to his feet, accidentally stepping on one of the hostage's hands.

"Hey!" the chubby woman said.

Without time to apologize, Axiom-man dove at Redsaw from behind and the two landed on Mr. Safe's lifeless body.

"Get off me!" Redsaw growled and with a single shot of the back of his elbow to Axiom-man's ribs, sent him flying back but not before a loud *crack* sent a fiery dart up Axiom-man's side.

On his back, Axiom-man tried to sit up . . . but couldn't. Redsaw stood, turned and surveyed the room.

Folks raised their heads, checking to see who was still standing. Some lay face down in fear, their faces pressed into their hands as if to hide from the mayhem around them. Two tried to escape on hands and knees.

Redsaw's fists lit up and sent those two aflame.

"Redsaw!" Axiom-man screamed and pushed himself into a sitting position. A blaze of pain raced through his ribcage and more than anything he wanted to lie back down again. But he couldn't. Not with so many peop—

Redsaw turned and faced those lying on the floor.

The room went red.

———

There was something she wasn't seeing, Valerie knew. She just didn't know what. Cop cars lined the road before her, a throng of people on the other side. Yet there was still enough distance between the crowd and the bank so there had to be something else she couldn't see from her position.

Pushing her way through the crowd, she was quickly reminded of the last time she forced her way through a mass of people—The Forks. The accident. Gene Nemek's death. She hadn't known it was him until she saw the paper the next day. Though she hadn't originally thought much of him during the brief time they worked together, seeing his murder reported in the paper made her heart ache.

"Excuse me, excuse me," she said, making her way through.

"Hey!" a man said, grabbing her arm.

When she turned around and yanked her arm away, her words caught in her throat. Joel Taylor stared back.

———

The corpses—all of them—were aflame. The stench of burning meat and burnt hair made Axiom-man's stomach swim even more.

"How could . . . how could . . ." he started.

Redsaw cut him off. "You think this is bad, you should see what I did outside."

"Out-outside." He wanted to say more but his head was aching and his stomach was still dancing. *Have to get away from him. Back up, make some room between him and*—Grimacing, he forced himself to his feet, about to tear Redsaw apart for murdering all these people. Instead, Redsaw merely grinned then reached for the sky.

The man in the black cape flew through the hole in the roof before Axiom-man could reach him.

———

A swarm of cops rushed through the crowd gathered outside the bank as Axiom-man flew to the front doors. When he set his feet down, the strength ran from his legs and he grabbed the door handle to keep from falling over. All those people . . .

What could he do? What could he *say*?

They're all dead, he thought. *I could have saved them but . . . but . . . I didn't. Couldn't. I tried and . . .* He took a deep breath, his head woozy. Glancing up, he saw a huge hole in the concrete just above the front door where Redsaw had made his escape. If Redsaw wasn't so fast—and if *he* hadn't been so slow—maybe he could have caught up to him and . . . stopped him.

Outside the cops were still coming forward, a huge mass of dark blue uniforms covering the area like a blanket.

You can't go out there unsure of yourself. Take what you saw and tuck it away. You can grieve later. This is too important. You need to be out there.

He opened the door and walked outside. A hot pang of electricity slugged him in the chest.

The bodies were everywhere, row upon chaotic row of corpses like a river of death running past the front of the bank. The stench of burnt meat hit his nostrils and it was all he could to keep from gagging. Smoke drifted off the smoldering bodies—police officers, the E.R.U., emergency workers and those who were just unfortunate to be around when Redsaw did whatever he did. What *had* he done? To the right, a police car was lying on its roof on top of another. To Axiom-man's left, another squad car was sticking out of the E.R.U. vehicle like an arrow out of its target.

The cops who had just come onto the scene circled the bodies, guns drawn. Some carefully tiptoed through the throng of the dead like one would step around broken glass. A few gawking civilians left their places in the crowd and came forward, offering to help. The cops shooed them away, telling them to "Get back" and "Go home." Ambulance sirens filled the air and grew louder the closer they neared.

The people. So many. All just laid out as if on display, a trophy to . . . what? Murder? Death?

"Redsaw," Axiom-man said through gritted teeth. He took in the sight of the dead again, as if for the first time.

How could he have missed it when he stood behind the front doors just moments ago? Had he been so distraught over the deaths of so many within that he was blinded to the mass of bodies outside?

Am I that *out of it?* he wondered. Though his emotions were human, he couldn't help but feel they should be something more. That *he* should be something more. *But I'm not, am I?*

To the right, he noticed Franklin, lying on his back, eyes wide, mouth open, smoke swirling up and out from his chest like a smoking hole in a burning log.

Axiom-man scanned the skies, hoping he'd see Redsaw.

But Redsaw was gone and nothing but blue mixed with a few thin, misty clouds stared back.

A middle-aged cop came up to him. His nametag read SIMONS. "What happened here?"

Keep it calm. Axiom-man forced an edge to his voice. "Isn't it obvious?" He didn't mean to come off so cold and the way Simons gave him a sidelong glance told him he had been.

"You weren't here for this?"

"No," he said. "I was inside and, to tell you the truth, it's not much better in there than out here. But at least inside there weren't as many people."

"How many?"

"Around twenty. Perhaps one or two more." He honestly didn't know how many were dead inside. The hostages, the gunmen—it all happened so fast. All the people, as much as he hated to admit it, had become just a group of faces without identity.

"Man . . ." Simons said, removing his cap and running a hand over his bald head.

"Yeah."

They were at the bottom of the stairs. The other officers were checking the bodies of their fallen comrades for pulses. Some were speaking with the emergency workers and firemen who had just arrived. Some just stood there with blank expressions, trying to get a handle on what they were seeing.

"What can I do to help?" Axiom-man said.

Simons replaced his gun back in its holster then put his hands on his hips. "Honestly, I don't know. I've never seen anything like this. What I do know is we—that is the force—

are not done with you. You're going to have to talk to somebody and shed some light on what happened. Anyone else who might have been able to do that . . ." He didn't finish.

Axiom-man put a hand on Simons's shoulder and for a second thought the officer was going to cry. Though the cop's eyes were glazed over, Simons didn't shed a tear.

At the base of the steps, one of the bodies stirred.

CHAPTER FOUR

PUTTING A HAND to Simons's chest, Axiom-man held him back. "I'll handle this." He stepped over to where one of the limp uniformed bodies was rocking side to side, and upon further inspection saw there was someone underneath. Careful to maintain respect for the dead, Axiom-man gently lifted the smoldering corpse and laid it to the side.

Sergeant Jack Gunn lay beneath. A second later the stocky man was on his hands and knees, coughing. Axiom-man went down on one knee beside him and placed a hand on either shoulder. "Easy. It's okay. I've got you."

Gunn shrugged Axiom-man's hands off him. "Get off me!"

Axiom-man backed away as Gunn shakily got to his feet. Simons rushed up beside his superior but Gunn turned away from him and told him to aid his fellow officers.

"Yes, sir," Simons said quietly and left.

The police sergeant kept his back turned on Axiom-man, the man's brown leather overcoat covered in soot and specks of charred flesh. Approaching him, Axiom-man wanted to see if he was all right. Jack spun around, his gun drawn, both hands holding it firmly.

"Tell me why I shouldn't knock you right here," Gunn said, his voice low and like iron.

Around them the police officers stopped their work. When Gunn saw this, he said, "What are you looking at? You tell me I'm doing the wrong thing. If it weren't for this guy right here, your brothers would still be alive!" Then back at Axiom-man, "And I'm willing to bet dollars to donuts that there's an ugly mess waiting for me inside, too." When Axiom-man didn't say anything, Gunn spat, "Well?"

Axiom-man nodded. *Jack, I'm sorry.* Tears pinched the corners of his eyes and he was thankful he was wearing a mask. *Why do I have to be so weak? But it's human, isn't it?* Maybe he wasn't cut out to be a *human being* never mind a superhero.

"Sir—Jack—" Axiom-man said.

"Don't 'Jack' me." To his men: "What did I just say? Come on, look alive!"

The men hesitated a moment then got back to work. A part of Axiom-man wished he was facing the crowd so he could see how they were reacting to this. A couple of hecklers telling Jack to pull the trigger answered the question.

"Sorry. Listen, let me explain. I don't know what happened out here. I wasn't here," Axiom-man said.

"Exactly. You weren't here and I'm not sure if I should be thankful for that. You might have made it worse, if you could imagine. Redsaw came out of the sky so fast it took us all a moment to realize we'd even seen something. His hands were already ablaze with that red energy garbage he's got. Suddenly the area lights up and my men are flying all over the place, getting cut in half, others losing their faces, some with huge gaping holes through them . . . . Sick." He took a step closer. "How are we supposed to recover from that?"

"I don't—"

"And what's inside?" Jack's eyes did a dance. "More are dead, right?"

"Yes."

"I'm going to kill you."

That's it. "If you kill me, I can assure you Redsaw will attack again. You can't stop him."

"And you can?"

What should he say? Sure, he stopped him one time before but Redsaw still got away. And he hadn't stopped him just now. Yet at the same time, there was nothing the police could do. Granted, Redsaw blindsided them with a surprise attack, but what would it take to bring him down? Machines guns? A

A.P. FUCHS

tank? *Careful. Don't make him bigger than he really is.* "Yes, I can. I will find him. I will stop him. You have my word."

"Not good enough." Jack's eyes narrowed behind the gun. Axiom-man moved in and knocked Jack's arms skyward as a shot boomed in the air. At such close proximity, Axiom-man's ears rang and he could only assume Jack's were, too. He ripped the gun from the police sergeant's hand and held it away.

Jack took a swing, slugging Axiom-man in his already-broken ribs. With a grunt, he staggered back, cradling his side. "Don't . . . don't do this . . ."

"Too late," Jack said, coming at him, fist cocked. He lashed out with a left hook. With a quick duck, Axiom-man dodged to the right, sending his left palm hard into Gunn's solar plexus. The cop flew backward and landed several feet away.

Glancing at the gun once, Axiom-man threw it down then took to the sky, his ribcage screaming as hot pain raced through his bones.

———

Shouts came from up ahead.

"What's going on?" Valerie asked.

"Axiom-man just left," Joel said, "and I don't think his being here went over well."

Axiom-man . . . Valerie thought. Had she been wrong about him? Their flight together, that moment on the viewing tower at the Forks, the way he looked at her on her balcony . . . . It all added up to someone who genuinely cared not just for her, but for everyone. *I hope he's all right.*

Joel stood on his toes, trying to see over the crowd. His mouth clamped shut and his eyes widened. Setting his heels back on the pavement, he said, "Come on, we should go."

"Why?"

"You don't want to see this, Val."

'Val,' huh? It was what he used to call her. Back then. Back when things were perfect.

40

Valerie went on her toes as well, trying to get a glimpse of the scene. She was too short and cursed her five-foot-four stature.

Very faint from somewhere up ahead: "Come on, make some room and get these . . . these bodies out of here."

Bodies? How—how many? "Can you see anything?"

Standing six feet tall, Joel had an easier time peering over everyone but even his height wasn't enough. "Not really. It doesn't look good, kiddo. We really should go."

Now it's "kiddo." Is he deliberately trying to tick me off? She wanted to see what had happened. She wanted to know what was so bad that Axiom-man's being there caused such an issue. Yet she also *didn't* want to know. Her memory of him—the ideal he represented and who he was to her—she didn't want that sullied. But she also wanted the truth. If Axiom-man had done something that warranted changing her opinion of him— wasn't that worth discovering?

Joel checked his watch. "I got to get going. Do you really want to stick around?"

She shielded her watch's face from the glare of the sun. She had about fifteen minutes till her appointment. *Guess I'll have to find out on tonight's news.* "I'd like to, yes, but you're right. We—I—should go."

He smiled at her and it was only then that she took him all in. His jet black hair was combed perfectly to the side, left to right, not a strand out of place and without the use of any gel or hairspray. But it was his blue eyes, just now, that really got to her. So blue-blue with a sheen to them that made pictures of the Pacific pale in comparison. It was those eyes that got her hooked three years ago. It was those eyes that were drawing her in now. Joel took a step closer and the scent of his black leather coat reminded her of the comfort of climbing into a new car. Coming through strong and clear from beneath the leather was his athletic frame and she didn't doubt it had only improved in the years since they'd been together.

Purposefully, she drew her eyes away from him, reminding herself that bumping into him today was a mere fluke and not some moment pre-determined by who knew who.

"Where you off to?" he asked.

Sirens blared up somewhere close. They began to fade as the emergency vehicle drove away.

"I have an interview with Owen Enterprises. It's for a secretarial position for Owen Tower."

"Is it nearby?" His voice was so soft. How could he so easily make her forget what he did to her?

"They have a small office just off Portage, about five minutes away." Why did she give him the distance? *Watch what you say.* "From what I hear, it's only a temporary thing till the tower's completed. Not sure if I'd start there or have to wait a year until construction is done." *Now you're getting into too much detail.*

"Would you like me to walk you?"

"No!" she snapped without meaning to. "I mean, no. I'm okay. Thanks though."

He gave a wry grin. "Still going to stick it to me, eh, even after all these years?"

"You know exactly why, Joel. After what you pulled, you're lucky I'm even talking to you right now."

"Why *are* you talking to me?"

Grumbling, she turned away from him but try as she might, she couldn't will herself to walk away. "Just trying to be civil. We're all people, right?" That was lame but it was the first thing she could think of to say. It was also true. She never quite understood how exes couldn't even give each other a courtesy smile or wave when they ran into each other in public.

A hand reached over her shoulder, holding a white business card. It read: JOEL TAYLOR, ATTORNEY-AT-LAW. Though she didn't know why she noticed it, she saw he ran his own firm and, oddly enough, she recognized the name: Taylor, Fox and Gordon. They had handled a big case for the city last year, something to do with the mayor, Charles Jones, taking under-the-table deals from street gangs. One of Joel's partners—she couldn't remember who—won on behalf of the mayor's defense.

She took the card, complete with phone number.

"Good, then," he said. "I like that. We're all people." He stepped in front of her and looked deep into her eyes. Valerie couldn't help but look into his. So beauti— "I'd honestly like us to square this away, Val. It makes me sick inside every time I think of what went down. I'd like to make peace, put it to rest, let it go—you know what I mean. If you'd like to do the same, give me a call." A pause. "You know what? Better yet: I'm going to be at Moxies later, the one attached to the MTS Centre. I'll be there at six. If you can make it, I'd love to have dinner with you. My treat. Just show up. If not, no hard feelings. My cell number's on my card if you wish to confirm, okay?"

"Okay." Her voice squeaked. She cleared her throat. "O-okay." *No, don't say that!*

He gave her a smile and gently touched the side of her arm. "Okay. I hope to see you then."

Joel turned and made his way through the crowd. Even if she wanted to chase after him to cancel, she couldn't.

Once more, she couldn't get her feet to move.

———

In the middle of a forest just outside the city, Redsaw sat on his haunches, hugging his knees, rocking back and forth. Forehead pressed up tight against his kneecaps, he wondered if he'd yet shed a tear. Focusing, he noticed the corners of his eyes were wet . . . but that was the extent of it. Yet inside, he was broken. Something had . . . snapped. Something had given way but he wasn't sure what it was. He kept getting a mental image of an iron pipe running through his body from head to foot. It was this "pipe" that was his strength, his pride, his *drive* to be the better of all human beings. It was this core desire to do great things not just for himself but for the world that had kept him going ever since starting his empire four years earlier.

Now . . . it was broken. He didn't know when it broke—other than recently—but the idea that it *was* broken was destroying him now.

They all died. So many people. I-I— "I killed them. Me." Though his voice was hardly a whisper, it sounded as if he were shouting it at the top of his lungs. He perked his ears, wondering if anyone around might have heard him. But no one was around, he knew. This forest was empty save for a few deer and some birds.

Mark Headley and Travis Hagen from last night. Though they hadn't deserved to die—they had to. And after he killed them, the power surged through his body, a newfound strength unlike any he had encountered before. A strength that was even sweeter than that which the black cloud bestowed upon him. But to kill innocents, he knew, would be going too far. Just to pick people at random or people who hadn't done anything wrong—No, he couldn't bring himself to murdering them. However those who did evil, they deserved it. At least with them gone, they'd never hurt another.

The bank. Those men holding those people hostage. They deserved death. The police outside, sitting there, doing nothing instead of bringing the perpetrators to justice—that was just as dangerous as executing the crime.

"But I killed those people. They were just lying there, waiting to be rescued. I . . . I slaughtered them." He closed his eyes, thinking a tear would fall. None did. Heart aching, he recalled the moment after killing the gunmen, remembered how the dark power growing within him took hold of his will and emotions, forcing his hands to decimate the innocents on the floor. "I didn't mean to." The voice. Whoever or whatever it was, *it* had forced him to do it. "You made me do it. You. Not me. You!" Redsaw's rocking increased, his breathing becoming shallow and labored. He had *enjoyed* it. The murders. Guilty or innocent, pleasure abounded and euphoria filled him each time he blasted a hole through a person's body. And after . . . after, he caught a glimpse of something: a fleeting shadow, there one second, gone the next. The shadow was huge, like a hole in the air, its inky abyss calling to him and tugging at his heart, overwhelming him—all in the span of a second. A second that seemed like an hour. A second that seemed like a day.

"How many more have to die?" he asked. He hoped the voice would answer him, but no answer came. He also wasn't sure if he wanted an answer. If the voice gave him a number of how many more victims, that would mean that once that number was reached, the killing would stop. And if the killing stopped, so would the post-kill elation that brought temporary peace and pleasure to his entire being.

Redsaw stopped rocking and hugged his knees even tighter. Squeezing his eyes shut, he said softly, "Tell me what I'm supposed to do. Tell me what this is all for, or is it all for 'understanding,' like you said? Please answer me. I can't do this." Then, "I can't do this much longer. I need to know, why me? I need to know what it is you want. I need to . . . I need to . . . I need to know."

Silence greeted him. A breeze swept by, rustling the leaves on the trees. A bird chirped. The voice didn't speak.

"Tell me!" he screamed and shot to his feet.

A few paces over to his right loomed a large oak tree with a wide trunk. He stormed over to it and plowed his fist into the bark. The wood snapped and groaned. He withdrew his fist, the broken rim of wood gouging through the fabric of his glove and into his flesh. Ignoring the blood running from the wound, he slammed his other fist into the tree, creating another hole beside its kin. He jerked his hand back, scratching the skin beneath the glove. Growling, he stuck a hand into each hole and yanked up, tearing the tree from its trunk with a loud *crack*. He threw it several feet in the air. The tree tumbled back and crashed into others, tearing down the branches of several before it finally settled.

Blood ran from his hands. Grimacing, he brought the red energy forth, coating his hands in its fiery brilliance, the heat from the energy forcing the wounds to seal shut with a smoking sizzle. Redsaw ignored the pain. Hands ablaze, he spun around and sent forth a crimson wave of light into a thicket of bush around the base of another huge tree. The bush immediately went up in flame, a fiery dance of yellow and orange before him.

Redsaw took a deep breath, trying to still his stampeding heart. It was no use. Peace would not come. The voice did not speak.

Murder was on his mind.

He needed an outlet.

———

Axiom-man landed atop CanWest Global Place and walked to the center of the roof, out of view from the edge so anyone looking up from the street over thirty stories below would not see him. He needed to be alone. Yet he also didn't want to be completely isolated. If someone needed him . . .

He stumbled a few steps, his left side blazing. Cradling it, he glanced up to the sky and winced against the sun. "Ow . . . aw, man . . . ow . . ." How bad was it? He had never had his ribs broken before but by the way the bones cried out, they had to be snapped. "Am I . . . am I bleeding inside?" He didn't know. He checked the side of his uniform, imagining sharp tips of bone protruding out the side, the material a dark purple, the red of blood mixing with the deep blue of his uniform.

No blood. Just pain. Just pure, pure—

Shouting, he spun a circle on his heels as if the exertion would somehow make the pain go away. It didn't.

It only made it worse.

I can't go to work like this. He checked his watch. It was 8:42. He was supposed to be at work nearly three quarters of an hour ago. *I'm going to get fired.* Of all things to think of at that moment, if he lost his job, he had no way to support himself and would have to move back in with his parents inside of a couple weeks. Being Axiom-man *and* living at home—*Come on, you have to think of an excuse. A good one. Something plausible. Something that isn't . . . something that isn't stupid.*

The bank. The people. Redsaw and the fiery blaze set forth from the man's hands. Murder.

I let them die. All of them. The cops, those people—No, not the cops. Redsaw got to them before . . . before . . . ". . . before I could do anything." The thought sent a blade through his heart, slashing through the tissue and making him bleed with remorse and . . . regret. "I could have stopped him. I should have. But he had me. He just . . . *had* me. I wish—" He caught his breath. When he inhaled, his lungs filling and pressing up against his ribcage set the bones alight with a hot ache. "I wish he would have killed me. At least then I could have gone down fighting." *But you didn't fight, did you? He just beat you down. The guy's so strong and he just . . . beat you down like you were nothing. But I can't be nothing. I've held my ground against him before.* Axiom-man began walking toward the roof's edge. *I can't even remember how I did. I just . . . did.* He stepped up on the roof's edge and stared at the windows of the Richardson Building across the way. *Last time . . .* "Last time it was an issue of power. Me shooting my energy beams against his. But strength-wise he's still my better. So strong." *Why didn't Redsaw kill me? He probably could have.* He turned his attention to the street below, the intersection where two days before he and Redsaw had had it out. Below, the street was torn up, the area taped off, construction workers and a couple of pieces of large machinery working here and there. Several of the construction workers were just standing around "supervising," whereas only a few were doing real, actual work. *Standard*, he thought absentmindedly. The thought of Winnipeg's frontline of repair "hardly working" made him feel a little better. When he chuckled, the pain in his ribs told him it really wasn't that funny at all.

Turning away from the edge, he went back toward the roof's middle.

"Redsaw should have killed me," he said once at the roof's center. The statement was meant not as a slight against himself but rather one of mere fact. Redsaw *could* have killed him—but he didn't. "Why didn't he? Why keep me alive? There has to be a reason. The messenger said Redsaw was created to counterbalance me, someone to ensure that I wouldn't bring the planet out of the chaos it was sinking in. If this is all part of some big cosmic, I don't know—thing—then there has to be more to it than what I'm seeing. How much does Redsaw know? Does he know *why* he's here or why he has his abilities? Or is he just driven by anger and hate and it's as simple as that?" *I've got to find out who that guy is. I need to talk to him. Wait, you already tried that and he shut you down pretty quick. Didn't want to talk other than a word here or there.* "I wish the messenger would have told me more. He told me enough, but not *more*." *Man, this sucks. Big time. Bigger than big time. Humongous time is more like it. Sheesh, my ribs hurt.* He had to get them fixed. What was he supposed to do: go into the E.R. and say, "Hey, I was in a fight with Redsaw this morning and he beat me up pretty bad. Can you help me?" Would they be willing to help if he did go to the hospital as Axiom-man and asked for assistance, or would that paint him as weak? Last he heard, heroes were supposed to take care of themselves and all had secret ways of healing up before their next encounter with a villain.

And work. What was he supposed to do about that? He couldn't call up his boss and tell him what happened. He also didn't want to lie to him. Right from the get-go he had decided that even though he had chosen to lead a double life, he'd do everything within his power not to lie to anyone about it if it could be helped. If he did, he wouldn't be much better than those he brought to justice.

There had to be . . . something . . . he could do.

An idea hit him.

He couldn't believe he was going to do it.

The Past . . .

"REBEKAH!" JEREMIAH SCREAMED as his body hit the ground. He expected himself to be dead but instead found himself very much alive.

More *than alive.*

Body pulsing with vigor, he scrambled to his feet and was at the door in a flash. He gripped the handle and pulled with all his might. It was only when he was two steps in the door did he realize he had pulled the door straight off its hinges and sent it flying back over forty feet.

How—? Rebekah. *Jeremiah ran to the tiny room off the kitchen and found her floating above the bed, the room bathed in the blue light streaming in through the window. Nay, the whole house was filled with this brilliant blue.*

"Rebekah!" *he said, coming to her side. She was awake but lay hovering above the mattress with wide eyes and uneasy breathing. What was going on? The baby! Jeremiah put a hand to her stomach. Repeatedly, the baby kicked against her tummy, over and over as if it, too, was suddenly filled with this inexplicable surge of energy.* "Darling?"

She glanced over at him. "Jeremiah? What is it? What is happening?"

"I do not know," *he said.* "I was outside, fetching your water, when the sky became as bright as day with light blue clouds. Then lightning came from the sky. Not flashes, but bright blue lines as if God was mad at us and wanted to teach us something."

"I hope He does not take our child." *Her voice was thick with tears.*

"I pray not either. I pray not."

The house suddenly became dark, the blue vanishing as though a candle flame had blown out.

As his eyes adjusted to the dark, he saw his wife's body still wasn't touching their thin mattress. "Rebekah, you are floating."

49

A.P. FUCHS

Rebekah awkwardly sat up as if she were sitting on something. She felt beneath her legs and bottom, feeling the air between her and the mattress. "Help! Get me down!"

Quickly, Jeremiah took her in his arms—she felt incredibly light, as if she weighed no more than a dinner plate, especially for a pregnant woman—and removed her from above the bed.

"Let us go to the kitchen," he said. Once there, he pulled a chair away from the table and sat her down.

His wife's hands immediately went to her stomach.

"It is kicking," she said. "Hard." She winced. "It has stopped. I . . . its feet hit my hands then suddenly . . . it stopped."

He knelt down beside her and lifted up her nightgown so her tummy was exposed. He put an ear to her stomach and listened. The baby's fast heartbeat rang loud and clear.

"It is okay," he said. "I can hear it."

"Thank the Lord."

"Yes, indeed."

"And outside?"

"I do not know." He stood and went to the small fireplace he kept burning most of the year. He took a candle from atop the mantle and lit it, then brought it over to her so they would have light. He set it in its holder atop the table, and wondered what they should do next.

Jeremiah remembered the screams from the village. Perhaps he should walk over there and see if anyone else was up and around—not that he doubted they wouldn't be—and perhaps together they could discover what just happened.

"If I left for a moment, would you be all right?" he asked.

"How long?"

"Perhaps an hour, maybe less. I want to go into town and see who else witnessed this."

"Please, do not go. I am scared. I was floating, Jeremiah. Floating!" She pressed her lips together, remembering it wasn't wise to get wound up while pregnant. "You remember four years ago when they found that young witch? She had been floating, too. I do not want to die on the pyre like she had."

50

Rebekah had a point. Not only would he lose her, should she be discovered, but he would lose the child as well. He couldn't have that. Wouldn't.

"I will not say anything," he said. "I promise. Besides, you are not a witch."

Her eyes grew hard. "No, I am not. But I also do not want to be possessed either."

Jeremiah hadn't thought of that. What if there was an evil at work in his wife? What if some dark spirit had decided to take over her body? What about the baby?

"Then we shall pray," he said and took her hands in his.

Rebekah bowed her head.

"Dear God," he said, squeezing his eyes shut, "we do not know what has just transpired. Are You angry with us? Was that You who rained light from the sky? Only You could do such a thing. We are scared, Father, and my wife is especially scared. I ask in the Name of Jesus Christ Your Son to rid her of the evil spirit within her, should there be one. Do not let Your servant be taken by the evil one, and do not let our baby be taken either." *Rebekah broke down crying at that last statement.* "Deliver us, save us and help us. Please do it now. Please."

He waited, Rebekah's small hands trembling within his own. He half-expected her body to jerk and twist as the evil spirit left her. Instead, she remained perfectly still on the chair.

The minutes passed and eventually Jeremiah gave up waiting for something to happen.

He opened his eyes and asked, "How do you feel?"

He took her hands from his and wiped her eyes. "Fine. The baby feels fine, too."

Breathing deep, he stood and noticed that his knees didn't creak like they normally did. They felt . . . stronger . . . somehow. Both his legs did.

"I am going to go into town," he said. *Rebekah nodded silently.* "I will not be far away, should you need anything." *He stepped passed her, stopped, and placed a hand on her shoulder.* "I will be right back."

He hated himself for leaving her sitting there in the chair, the door to their home no longer in its frame, the night air pouring in. But he needed answers. What he saw in the sky wasn't natural. Not once had he ever seen anything like it and he doubted anyone ever had.

51

Jeremiah jogged to the edge of his property, half-noticing he was running with an ease he had not experienced since he was younger, then turned right onto the road that led into town. He counted his steps in his head to help keep himself calm, each slap of his foot against the dirt road sending a little jolt throughout his body.

He reached nineteen steps when the jolts stopped and his feet were touching nothing but air.

CHAPTER FIVE

"I TELL YA, Garrison, you're going to be the death of me." The disappointment in Rod's voice pierced Gabriel's heart almost as badly as the hot sting in his ribs. Gabriel's job was everything to him. Sure, being a customer service representative at Dolla-card wasn't his dream job—he wasn't even sure what his dream job would be if could choose—but without it, well, the idea of having to go back home and live with his folks sent his stomach into a knot.

"I'm s-sorry, Mr. Hunter. Truly. It wasn't my fault. Honest." *Sound apologetic, which you are anyway. Just keep up appearances.* He sat on his sofa at home, powers *shifted* off, mask rolled down around his collar. "I-I, well, like I said, I was on my way to work and I saw the commotion in front of the bank. Did you hear the morning news?" He waited a moment for Rod to reply but Rod didn't. "So I went to see what was happening and got hurt in the Axiom-man and Redsaw scuffle. I haven't been to a doctor yet but that's what I plan on doing today. I can barely move."

"Always something with you. Like I told you before, you were doing real good for a while attendance-wise. One of the best. But then you started to slip. We can't have that here." Rod took a breath. "Look, you're one of the best employees I have. Stars across the board and all that. I'd really like to keep you around but not if you're gonna always be late for work or missing hours. You just took off Friday. What happened, by the way?"

"Well . . ."

"Listen, it doesn't matter. I'll do you a favor and not raise a stink about it as long as you don't tell anybody. Besides . . ."

Gabriel covered the receiver and breathed a sigh of relief. When his posture slouched, his ribs objected and he had to straighten his back again. "Thank you. Uh, besides . . . ?"

"I'll tell you about it when you come in. Tomorrow, I'm assuming?"

"Yes, sir. Tomorrow. Again, I'm truly sorry." *Tomorrow? Can I really make tomorrow? How long does it take broken ribs to heal? More than twenty-four hours.*

"Okay, then. You rest up today, bring a doctor's note and we'll start over. Deal?"

"Deal. I mean, yes, sir. Absolutely."

"Good-bye."

"Good—" But Rod had already hung up.

Gabriel opened the mini black velvet-covered book by the phone and looked up Dr. Ruben's number. "Wait a minute. What am I doing? Gotta go to the emergency room instead. Not sure what Ruben could do for me at his office." Groaning at the thought of going all the way to St. Boniface Hospital— though it really wasn't all that far from where he lived—he set the mini phonebook down and placed a hand on his ribs, easing the pain.

Beside the phone was an envelope. *The* envelope. He had nearly forgotten about it in all the excitement this morning. His fingers hovered above it, hesitant to pick it up. Should he really add to his misery by re-reading the letter within?

Be strong. He picked up the envelope, removed the letter and read it over.

Let's just say that, like you, this knowledge has left me feeling . . . blue. The words really jumped out at him now. Slowly, he leaned his head against the back of the couch.

This person knows, he thought. *They* really *know.* What was he supposed to do?

Nothing.

Not until this person contacted him again. He just hoped it wouldn't be soon.

———

That evening, Redsaw flew above the city, scouring the streets below for anyone who might be traveling alone in a back alley or someone causing some sort of disturbance. For a moment he thought this was how Axiom-man must feel patrolling night after night in his blue uniform, just waiting for someone to break the law or cry for help.

Bor-ring, he thought. You could only fly in circles for so long before you were tempted to head off elsewhere. But then if you *were* gone and something happened in the area you just left . . . "But he does do it," Redsaw said quietly. "A man of patience, a man of virtue." He grimaced and added, "Disgusting." The people loved Axiom-man, Redsaw knew. And the people hated *him. You're a murderer. What do you expect?*

After years of trying to rise as someone respectable in the public eye, after trying so hard to benefit humanity as Oscar Owen, after trying to emulate Axiom-man's character by donning a costume and putting others before himself—all had been quickly dashed when that young man died at the Forks. It had been an accident, an act of rage and frustration. It hadn't been intentional. Not in the least. But after. After the young man's death, the buzzing, the voice—the power!

"Too late to turn back. I am only at the beginning of my journey. Something lurks around the corner, something incredible. It's there. I know it. I can *feel* it. Just need to embrace it when it comes."

It wasn't all a total loss. No one knew that Oscar Owen and Redsaw were one and the same. As Oscar, he could still rise to power. And as Redsaw, he could help Oscar get there, like he had after he first got his powers and sped up work on Owen Tower. That was only a start. If Redsaw could somehow covertly aid his daytime counterpart—there was no end to what he could achieve.

He had to be careful. He had to be precise.

Below, downtown traffic was thick, the cars bathed in a yellow glow from the streetlights; people milled about on the sidewalks.

There had to be somebody down there he could use to bring him closer to his goal. There had to be somebody who would be a sacrifice for the greater good.

There was always somebody and Redsaw grinned at the thought that he would decide who.

———

As usual, Moxies was busy this evening. Valerie stood to the side of the doors enough to let in others who were stopping for dinner. Hands folded politely around her purse, she caught herself glancing out the doors' windows more often than she meant to.

What is it with this guy, she wondered, *that I'm making such a big stink out of this?* She hadn't *meant* to wreak havoc in her closet the moment she got home from work and find the perfect outfit nor had she *meant* to pay careful attention to her hair and makeup, but a smooth-fitting ivory dress with the shoulders revealed and her hair done up except for the bangs, the maroon hair clips complimenting her dark lipstick, had to do. She had used Joel's business card during her lunch break, informing him she couldn't make dinner this evening. But, as was his way, he had talked her into it and she had somehow let it slip she was off at 7:00 so he said he'd move his original request from 6:00 to 9:00 and asked if that was enough time for her to get ready. *Get ready?* she had thought. *As in a date?* Joel then suggested 9:15 if that made it easier and she agreed. He was off the line before she had the chance to really think about what she'd said.

Now, she couldn't wait to get this over with and toyed with the idea of leaving. As always, she once again found herself at his mercy.

Face it, girl, you've got it bad. This guy did a number on you and you're still willing to give him another go. Can't believe this. She checked her watch and at nine-fifteen on the dot, Joel appeared on the other side of the glass, a caring smile on his face. He opened the door and entered.

"Hi, Val," he said, stepping right up to her.

Boy, did he smell good, and she knew him better than to reveal what cologne he was wearing. It was one of the things— his little secrets—that had driven her nuts before. Now . . . now that didn't really seem to matter. At least not yet. She found herself wishing not *ever*.

"Let's get one thing straight," she said before she realized the words were even out of her mouth. "This is not a date. Nope. You asked to meet me here so here I am. Deal?"

His bright blue eyes did a gentle dance. "Deal." He stuck out his hand. She looked at it, unsure if she should take it or not. The way he stood there, all casual, wearing a different outfit than he had earlier in the day. His deep blue collared shirt, red tie and black suit jacket and matching pants said he thought tonight *was* a date. She took his hand hesitantly and shook it. The way his fingers wrapped around hers . . .

"Shall we get a table?" he asked. She pulled her hand away, more forcefully than she meant to. He raised his hands. "Relax, Val, I'm not going to bite."

"Says you," she muttered and walked on past him.

Once they were seated at a corner booth and menus were set before them, Valerie wondered who was going to pick up the check. Joel could certainly afford it, big time firm owner that he was, but if she let him pay then this would definitely become a date. She tried to remember how much she had in her bank account.

The waitress took their drink order—a Blue for him, Coke for her—and left them alone to decide on the main course.

"So?" he breathed and undid the button to his suit jacket.

"So?"

Joel leaned forward, hands on the table. Valerie leaned back against her seat, as if he was going to pounce on her.

"Look, why not just do this now and get it over with, 'kay?" he said.

A.P. FUCHS

"Get what over with?"

"I asked you here tonight because I wanted to ask you to forgive me for what happened."

Was she seeing things or were his eyes slightly glazed over?

"Joel, what you did—"

"Let me finish." He pressed his lips together as if quickly going over a rehearsed speech in his head (which was probably true). "I'm sorry, Val. Truly and deeply sorry. I have no excuse for treating you the way I did. Earlier, when I told you it makes me sick inside when I think about what happened, I was telling the truth. Not a day goes by without regret." She must have flashed him an incredulous look because he added, "It's true. No lie. So many times I've had those clichéd 'do over' thoughts, the 'what ifs' and all that. Many times I've wished for the chance for . . . for me to just go back in time and talk to myself and tell myself that what I was about to do would ruin not only your life but mine as well."

"My life's not ruined, Joel. I was hurt. Destroyed for a time. Who could blame me? You cheated on me." And there it was. She hadn't revealed what he'd done to her to anyone, not even right after it happened, and the person she was telling for the first time . . . was him.

"I know. And I feel awful. I've felt awful for two and a half years. Every day. After we broke up . . . I broke up with her, too, you know? I saw her right after you found us in my apartment. And when I looked at her, all I saw was your heart breaking, the way you looked at me with tears running down your face. I had to let her go. I *chose* to. And as sad as it is to say, I don't even remember why I did that. Hurt you, I mean. Her father was a partner in a firm I wanted to break in to at the time. Perhaps that was why. Perhaps I felt she was able to offer me more. It was selfish and stupid and I hate myself for it. I'm sorry, Val. I'm so sorry." He cleared his throat softly. "Will you forgive me?"

The waitress came and delivered their drinks, then asked if they'd decided on anything.

"No, not yet," Valerie said.

58

———

Gabriel popped back two Tylenol 3s and washed them down with a glass of water the moment he got home. He'd already taken two at the E.R. but if he did decide to go out tonight, he wanted to be sure the pain was absent. He just hoped he wouldn't get all loopy from the drug.

Walking slowly to his bedroom, he carefully removed his sweater, being sure not to raise his arm too high lest he risk aggravating his ribs. There really was nothing they could do, the doctor told him, other than for him to mind his movements and not partake in any strenuous physical activity until it healed.

I always thought they put a cast around your midsection or something, Gabriel thought. *Guess not.* He just wished there wasn't a sharp pain at the end of each breath. Thankfully, those pains should only last for the next day or two till things settled down to a dull ache.

He went to his closet, knelt down, and pulled away the stack of folded sweatshirts, T-shirts and towels lining its bottom. Beneath these was a Sears box. He took the box, put it on the bed and opened it, revealing his Axiom-man uniform. Pulling out the cape and setting it to the side, he placed a hand atop the dark blue fabric of his suit and wondered if going out tonight was really a good idea after all.

"But if I stay in," he said, "and there is someone out there who needs me . . ." He grinned. "I guess my mind's already made up."

Gabriel took out the remainder of his suit then went to work removing his civilian clothes.

Ribs aching, he could hardly wait for the latest round of painkillers to kick in.

———

Shortly after ordering, Valerie felt the urge to just up and leave. She couldn't, she knew. Well, she could but what would that say about her? That she couldn't—*wouldn't*—forgive this guy? That he had scarred her so badly she lacked the resolve to make peace with it? She honestly didn't know if she ever would, yet if she ever wanted to be the strong independent woman she knew she could be, the first step would be to accept his apology and work on healing what he'd done to her heart.

They didn't speak for a while, she sipping on her Coke, Joel sipping on his beer, his question hanging in the air like smoke.

Eventually, Joel set his beer down and asked, "I don't want to beat a dead horse, but you haven't said anything yet. I was hoping we could settle this before dinner."

"Why?"

"Why not?" he said. "I'm just looking for peace, Val. Aren't you?"

The comment hit her hard because that was exactly what she was looking for, and not just between them, but also in a more general sense. For a long time she'd been longing for a feeling of place, a feeling of peace, both professionally and personally. This weekend she thought perhaps, personally, she'd find a place with Axiom-man. She still wanted to know what went on behind those glowing blue eyes of his and if, even now, he was thinking about her.

The interview today went well and though she wasn't informed straight away if she got the job (despite her expectations), she left feeling that she had landed it and that she'd find out soon.

She didn't reply to Joel's question. "You have to understand something," she said. "You hurt me. And I'm not just talking about you being with some bimbo behind my back. Our whole relationship hurt me, Joel. The unreturned phone calls, the times when I poured my heart out to you and you seemed a million miles away, the times you said you'd meet me somewhere and you never did—Now that I think about it, it was those things that hurt the most. The little things. Matters of the heart. The important stuff. How am I supposed to know you really mean what you say? How can I take your word for it when history dictates your word is worth absolutely zero?"

"I've changed, Val. Really changed. What happened between us was a wake up call. Like I was suddenly pulled outside of myself and could see clearly for the first time what I was doing to you. And to me. But when I finally realized it, it was too late. It was over between us. I'm asking to try again. There, it's out there. I said it." He put up his hands. "Wait, I'm not talking about a commitment or anything like that. I'm talking about just seeing each other now and then and going from there."

It all came rushing at her, everything he said. Was he serious? Was *she* being serious by sitting here listening to him?

"I don't think that's a good idea," she said.

"Why not?"

"Why not?"

"Yeah."

"Because . . ."

"Because?"

If she told him the truth, if she confessed her fear, it would all be over for her. The walls had been up for so long. No one was allowed in. Even Axiom-man, as much as he had somehow been able to lower her defenses. If she started seeing Joel again, even casually, she knew she'd lose herself to him.

She loved him. Then, and even now.

"I-I can't."

He exhaled through his nostrils. "Okay. I just wanted to—"

"I know."

CHAPTER SIX

"GOT ANY CHANGE, got change? Got any change, got change?" the fellow with the black toque and jacket said. He sat against the wall just outside the Grain Exchange building. Folks just passed him by, no doubt tired of seeing him day in and day out, night in and night out, begging for a handout.

"Get a job," a man in a gray business suit said as he passed.

"Yeah, yeah, but you know, I *am* working. Just don't do the nine-to-whatever like you. Or whatever shift you're on."

The man in the suit didn't reply and kept on walking.

"You'd think some people would have a heart," the beggar said, jingling the coins in his cup.

"I have some change."

The man turned toward the voice and let out a yelp when black-gloved fists hoisted him to his feet. Redsaw shot a hand over the man's mouth, muffling his cries.

A couple of women walking on the sidewalk across the street stopped their stride and pointed to one another, saying something. Redsaw couldn't make out what.

One of the women screamed.

The beggar's eyes went wide as Redsaw cupped him beneath the jaw, flew straight up and landed on the Grain Exchange's roof.

Redsaw threw the man down, watched him roll across the rooftop till friction stopped him. Cowering with one arm protecting his head, the other held out like a stop sign, the man said, "Don't hurt me. I didn't do nothing."

"Precisely," Redsaw said. "You didn't do anything. You don't do anything. You leech off society as if it owes you everything. You don't do anything for yourself. You don't get out there and try and improve yourself."

The man lowered his hand. "Hey, I do plenty. I'd have you know I make a really decent living doing what I do, all tax free."

"And you're not even honest with your taxes. Pity." Redsaw took a stride toward him; the man's hand shot up again.

"What're you gonna do?"

"Something."

———

Flying high above the heart of downtown, Axiom-man kept one arm stretched out before him, the other tucked in, fist balled at the waist, his elbow gently against his ribs. Flying wasn't too bad, almost like lying down. As long as he remained still, he felt fine.

"Quiet night," he said.

The streets below glowed yellow and red with head- and taillights, the people bustling up and down the sidewalks mere dots.

Gosh, the city's beautiful at night, he thought. The way the windows in the buildings were dotted with warm yellow squares, the soft glow of streetlights below—he couldn't wait for the Christmas season when the lighting decorations would go up, making Portage Avenue even more gorgeous.

A holler in the distance.

Axiom-man sped up, banked to the left, then went right.

A woman screaming. No, more than one. There! He dove downward and landed in front of two middle-aged women standing outside the parkade a block from the Richardson Building.

"Is everything all right?" Axiom-man asked.

"He just—he just—" one of the women said.

63

"He just what? Who?"

The other woman pointed toward the roof of the Grain Exchange building across the street. "Redsaw. At least, I'm sure it was him. He took some guy to the roof. Some guy, he . . . he didn't do anything! Redsaw just came down, picked the guy up and took him over there!" She shook her index finger in the air.

Redsaw? Axiom-man glanced toward the roof. "Do you know if he's still up there?"

Both women shook their heads.

"Thanks." He took off toward the roof.

Landing on the roof's edge, he paused and surveyed the area. Save for the light of the moon peeking out from behind a few lonely clouds, and a handful of stars, illumination was dim at best and the glow coming up from the streetlights below made the rooftop that much darker. Redsaw didn't appear to be up here.

He stepped off the ledge onto the roof proper and moved cautiously, paying careful attention to his stomach. If Redsaw *was* around, he'd soon be fighting nausea from the man's presence. So far, all he felt was a sense of unease, as if something bad happened here and he had been too late to stop it.

One of the clouds moved away from the moon, the increased light revealing a dark hump near the roof's far ledge.

Is this a trick? A trap? If Redsaw was playing possum, lying there, waiting for him to approach, he was going to be ready. Axiom-man filled his eyes with blue energy but kept the power at bay. Ready to let it loose at a half-second's notice, he approached the black hump. When he got close, he realized it *was* a body, face turned away from him. Whoever it was was wearing all black, but unless Redsaw had bulked up since this morning, it couldn't be him.

Crouching down beside the body, Axiom-man put a hand on its shoulder, hoping that this person was still alive and that his touch would rouse them. Nothing. It just lay still. Swallowing the lump in his throat, he rolled the body toward him and instantly powered down the energy in his eyes when he saw the man's face.

The man's mouth was agape, his toque pulled down over his nose similar to Redsaw's cowl.

Axiom-man peeled the lower lip of the toque back. "Oh no . . ."

The man's eyes were black holes, their rims puckered as if each had been burned through with a hot iron.

———

Dinner was awkward but by no means did the atmosphere between Valerie and Joel ruin the meal. More than once there was a lull in the conversation and Valerie feared they had run out of things to talk about, but Joel, being the slick conversationalist that he was, was able to bring up a new topic and gather her thoughts about it, ask her how her family was doing and what else she had been up to for the past two and a half years.

When it came time for the check, the waitress placed the little black book at the center of the table and immediately Joel reached for it.

"Can I see that when you're done?" Valerie asked.

With a wave of his hand, he said, "Don't worry about it. It's on me."

"You really don't have to. I don't mind paying. I'd actually feel more comfortable if I did."

Joel closed the little black book. "*I* mind and it's not open for discussion."

Valerie smiled. "Thank you. If you change your mind, let me know. It's really no trouble at all." Which was a lie. Her chicken and rice and drink probably ran just under thirty dollars and it would be thirty dollars she wasn't able to spare given her current month-to-month expenses.

But his offer stood and was followed through upon at the till.

With the bill paid—and Joel generously tipping the waitress—they went to the front doors, Valerie's heart picking up speed, wondering what was next. She checked her watch. It was 11:23. Had they really been there that long? It appeared so.

"How are you getting home?" Joel asked.

"Bus."

Joel put his hands in his pockets and looked off to the side. "It's late, Val. I'd like to give you a ride home, if it's all the same."

It wasn't "all the same" and she'd much rather part ways despite, admittedly, how pleasant their evening was.

"It's okay. I can manage," she said.

"Yeah, but by the time you get home, it'll be after twelve, most likely, and you gotta work tomorrow."

"So do you. Besides, I don't start till eleven so I'll be able to sleep in."

He sighed. "I'd feel much better if you let me drive you."

You don't need to baby-sit me. Besides, she hadn't lived in her current apartment when they originally dated and she didn't want him knowing where she lived. Not that he would constantly be hanging around outside her place, but by his not knowing where she lived, her apartment served as a sanctuary away from him, a kind of protection. "It's nice of you to offer but I'm fine." Yet she also kind of wished he would press the issue further.

"Okay, then," he said and took his hands out of his pockets. He opened the door for her.

Heart reluctantly sinking, she gave him a smile and stepped outside. They walked a few steps, then Joel brought his feet together. "At least let me wait with you at the bus stop."

"Okay," she said.

They went to the nearest bus shelter. Valerie thanked him again for the meal.

"No problem," he said. "We should do it again sometime."

Doesn't let up, does he? she thought though a part of her liked it. If he hadn't been such a jerk before, to be with him again . . . . She'd love to.

They waited for fifteen minutes, chatting. Not a single bus came by. Valerie left the shelter and checked the schedule on a post just outside. A bus should have come eight minutes ago. Probably running late. She rejoined Joel and when her bus still did not come, she found herself suddenly antsy.

If she asked him for a ride, she didn't trust herself to know when it would be time to stop. If he gave her a ride home, even just as "friends," there was something about getting dropped off after a one-on-one outing with a member of the opposite sex that suddenly put the label of "date" on it. She decided to wait for five more minutes and if the bus didn't come, more than likely it wasn't going to. There could be a million and one reasons as to why it hadn't shown—wouldn't have been the first time for her that a bus simply hadn't come—but why did it have to be tonight of all nights?

Never a break, she thought. She frowned at her own cynicism.

Seven minutes passed and they were still there. Several others in the bus shelter were with them, constantly glancing down the road, seeing if a bus was coming, as if somehow their checking for it would speed it along. A few grew restless and left. A couple others resigned to sitting on the benches, chins resting on their palms.

"Well, I guess I'll have to take you up on your offer," Valerie said.

Joel smiled.

———

Axiom-man had located a squad car a few blocks away from the Grain Exchange and told the two young officers inside what he found on the building's roof.

"Looks like Redsaw," he had told them, then filled them in on what happened—the women screaming, the flight to the roof and the discovery of the body, how the eyes were nothing but burnt holes in the corpse's head.

The cops had looked at each other dumbfounded, one conveying an expression of "Why us?" It was clear they didn't really know what to do or how the situation should be handled so Axiom-man suggested they head down there and radio in another car. He oversaw the cops—four of them now along with two paramedics—as they checked over the scene just in case Redsaw returned to clean up his own mess. Once the body was taken away and the police had his statement, Axiom-man flew home.

He entered his apartment via his balcony, paying careful attention that no one in the surrounding apartments saw him enter.

What a day, he thought and *shifted* his powers down.

Pulling down his mask, he headed for his bedroom, dreading having to get up in six short hours for work. He stopped walking when, out of the corner of his eye, he saw an envelope sliding underneath his door. Quickly, he ran to the door and, hiding behind it, opened it just enough to squeeze his head through.

The hallway was empty.

He hadn't heard any doors close so it couldn't have been one of his neighbors. They'd have needed to slip back inside their suite with lightning speed and gently close the door, and with his hallway known for echoing even the slightest of sounds, that possibility seemed unlikely.

Unless the guy is so careful he practiced moving silently about the hall before finally making his move on me.

Grimacing, he closed the door and picked up the envelope. Like the other, it contained a single sheet of white paper, the text typewritten.

It read:

Dear Mr. Garrison:

Once more I'm sorry for writing you. Please understand that I never wanted it to come to this. I honestly thought I could handle my own problems but things have gotten so bad that I have no place to turn. I know you're a good man and try to do what is right. My only concern was I wasn't sure if you'd be willing to help me given that, as of late, you've had your hands full with more "overpowering" matters.

I've never been one to exercise leverage over another. I view that as both cowardly and cruel. However, if you do not aid me in what I will shortly propose, you can rest assured that your secret will be revealed on the front page of every paper large and small in the country before the week is out.

As always, I'll be in touch.

Gabriel crumpled the paper in his hand, eyes wet with tears.

He didn't know what to do and there was no one who could tell him what needed to be done.

———

After driving around for a while—Valerie got the impression Joel was just killing time so as to spend more time with her; she wanted to tell him to take her straight home but couldn't find the strength—they pulled up outside her apartment block in his black, 2007 Mercedes-Benz. The moment she reached for the door handle, Joel was out of the car. He jogged around the front of the vehicle and opened the door for her.

It was a little forward of him to do so but she didn't mind.

"Thanks," she said and got out of the car. She closed the door behind her.

Joel looked the apartment block up and down. "Nice," he said.

"Yeah, they just did some remodeling on the inside and touch ups to the exterior. For a while there it was an obstacle course to get from the elevator to the front door."

Joel chuckled. He remained at her side as she advanced to the front doors.

"Oh, you don't have to walk me," she said.

"You kidding? In this town, you can't be too careful. Things have really . . . . Things have gotten strange. And dangerous."

"Maybe," she said, thinking back to Saturday and Axiom-man's battle with Redsaw. "But Axiom-man got a handle on it. He defeated Redsaw."

"He *stopped* him," he corrected. She looked up at him. "There's a difference. Remember, the guy reportedly fled after Axiom-man subdued him, and if you've seen today's paper, well, I just don't know what to think."

"Why? What happened?"

"Redsaw's been on a killing spree, Val. A couple of guys were murdered last night and you were there this morning, remember? All those dead cops?"

She had been so wrapped up thinking about her interview for Owen Tower, and so consumed by her "date" with Joel, that this morning seemed like it didn't even happen at all. She didn't know what to say. Redsaw was dangerous and the way he fought so viciously with Axiom-man—She hoped her knight in the blue cape would be able to hold his own the next time he collided with Redsaw.

"I have a feeling things are going to get a lot worse before they get better," Joel said.

"Oh?"

They reached the front doors.

"Don't get me wrong," he said. "I appreciate all that Axiom-man's done for the city, but his arriving here—from wherever he's from—it brings a sense of, I don't know, lack of control?" She must have looked at him quizzically because he began to explain. "You have this guy able to do things we've only read about in fantasy novels and comic books suddenly show up. He helps out, disappears once he's finished, puts a smile on all our faces. That's all fine and good, but we—and I'm referring to everyone who lives here—should have known better because, like in any of those stories, a powerful bad guy always shows up. I suppose it was only a matter of time but it's my feeling we got so enamored with the *idea* of having a

70

superhero of our very own that we completely forgot that there's always somebody out there to counter him. I'm afraid that his—Axiom-man's—presence in the city has opened the door to trouble. What if Redsaw's not the only one out there who can do things that puts us 'mere mortals' in a place where we don't know how to stop them?" Smirking, he added, "I've put a lot of thought into this. Between you, me and my car, lawyers citywide are talking. This whole thing is a lawyer's worst nightmare. We love our clients, but we do have a line. We don't want every single person bothering us. Too much to deal with. Even now, lawyers from firms across the country are putting in for either transfers or moving here. Saturday was just a taste of what might happen when two super-powered individuals butt heads and I strongly doubt what we witnessed was the fullest extent of the damage that can be done. People have already gotten hurt—many killed—due to super-powered acts. Injury isn't my specialty, but a few boys I know already have phones ringing off the hooks with people who've been hurt in these encounters, wondering if there's any legal recourse to the injuries they've sustained. The point is, I don't think this city understands exactly what's among them."

"Are you saying we should, what, arrange a citywide protest and run Axiom-man and Redsaw out of town?" *I hope not. Well, for Redsaw, yeah.*

"I don't know what we can do. I don't hate Axiom-man. Don't get me wrong, 'kay? What I *am* saying is that as much as his presence is a blessing, it's also a curse and, whether we like it or not, ordinary folks like you and me are caught in the crossfire between him and Redsaw, or him and someone else."

He had a point. No one was safe and with Redsaw still on the loose . . . . The air suddenly seemed colder.

Joel gave her a soft smile, one filled with warmth. She shivered and not from unease. Maybe Joel was right? Maybe life would be better without men in capes running around? She snapped herself out of it and reminded herself she had had a long day. Valerie wished she could talk to Axiom-man, see how he's doing and, perhaps, follow up on . . . well, she wasn't sure what there was *to* follow up on, but after his visit Sunday, she needed to know if there was something between them. Yet standing in Joel's presence, the rush of feelings from years past washing over her, blotting out the time spent apart—she wasn't sure what she should do or *who* might be in her future.

"Ready?" he said and nodded toward the door.

We're done already? she thought. She didn't want their night to end. "Yeah," she said quietly.

They stood there looking at each other, Valerie wondering who would be the first to say goodnight. As much as she didn't want to admit it, she was afraid to speak first.

His blue eyes, so piercing, so large, took her in—*drank* her in—and she felt the strength run from her legs.

Don't give in, she thought. But she couldn't help herself. Joel had been everything to her at one point in her life and, she knew, she had been the same to him despite what he had done. Even in the days following their break up, she had wanted to forgive him and take him back. Life without him seemed so empty, so lonely, so . . . not worth it. And now, those same feelings of need came over her. If this was their second chance, who was she to screw it up?

"Thanks for meeting me," he said.

"I'm sorry if I was difficult tonight. A lot on my mind. I had a wonderful time and it was . . ." *Don't say it!* But it was too late. The words were already half out of her mouth. "It was so good to see you again."

"Would you mind, um, seeing me again?"

Oh yes. "I'd love to, Joel. Really, I would."

His eyes glazed over and he took a step closer.

Trembling, Valerie bit her lower lip and cast her gaze downward.

When Joel spoke, his words were so tender, so careful. "I missed you so much, Val. Every day. All the time."

"Me, too," she whispered.

She glanced up, thinking her words might have scared him for some reason. Instead, she found him standing closer. He reached for her and she fell in to him. They looked into each other's eyes and drifted away.

Their lips found each other's.

The Past . . .

THIS COULDN'T BE *happening.*

Jeremiah's heart raced as he ascended higher and higher. His arms were stretched above his head, his fingers splayed, and any moment now he was certain he would touch the stars. Though his fingers clasped only air, only one thought—one name—*echoed in his mind: Rebekah. She had been floating, too. Were they possessed? What was this? There was no way to know and fear gripped him when he realized there was probably no way to know.*

Almost as if his mind was suddenly aware of his surroundings anew, he realized that the sky was in fact clear and that the strange collage of fluffy blue clouds was gone completely. No thunder. No lightning. Just sky.

His body rose and rose. Wanting nothing more than to be grounded again, he forced himself to flip over and face the earth, the ground drifting further and further away. The air grew cold and a chill swept through him.

Must go down, *he thought. And as if in answer to his inner plea, his body began floating downward, forward then back, like a feather on the wind. From this new vantage point, he was able to see he wasn't the only one airborne. Like silhouetted gingerbread men against the light of the moon, others were floating skyward. Some were screaming, others yipping for joy. One voice he was able to make out from this distance shouted, "At long last I am free!"*

Have to get over to them. Have to find out what has happened to us. *All* of us. *Once more, it seemed instinct and desire took over for he found himself gliding through the air, heading toward the mass of bodies ascending into the sky. Then an ear-piercing scream rattled him, and below he saw young Elishia in her nightgown spiraling upward, her arms and legs stretched out like a star.*

"Help me! Somebody help me, pleeaase!" she screamed.

74

"One moment!" Jeremiah shouted into the wind breathing at him. One moment? I do not even know what I am doing never mind what is happening to her!

Elishia seemed to be speeding skyward much faster than he had and if she didn't somehow regain control, she would surely reach the stars before dawn and be lost forever.

Jeremiah gathered his focus and acknowledged that he did have some control over this. How much control, he didn't know, but right now some would have to be enough.

"Go forward," he told himself and placed his arms at his side, his body now like an arrow.

As if in reply to his command, his body shot forward and picked up speed. He flew past Elishia and she cried out to him to "Help meeee!" as he zipped past.

"I am coming," he said though he didn't believe it.

Throwing his body back so he was now vertical to the ground, he slowed enough to flip around and try again.

Somewhere in the background the townspeople hollered and screamed. One exclaimed faintly, "I learned what to do!"

Jeremiah didn't pay him any heed and instead focused on reaching Elishia before she spun off the earth. He reached forward and willed himself to go higher and move toward her. Elishia, still spinning, stretched out her arms even more, her fingers already clenching and unclenching against the air in the hopes of soon catching onto his hands. Jeremiah flew toward her, slow at first, and when he wanted *to go faster, he suddenly picked up speed.*

The secret is to maintain calm and to maintain control, *he reasoned even though such a thought was only theory. Right now, all that mattered was getting Elishia to safety.*

He shoved all thoughts of his own distrust in himself to master this—flying?—and of his worry for Rebekah at home to the back of his mind.

As before, he shot like a spear through the air, this time heading straight for Elishia.

"I am coming. Hold on! Keep your hands out!" He hoped she heard him.

When the wind blew Elishia's long blonde hair off her face, her expression read pure panic.

"I am almost there!" he said. It looked like he was going to overshoot her again. "Not this time," he grunted and truly focused himself. He focused his attention on his arms, his legs—his whole being, internally grabbing hold of it like he would a sledgehammer with a heavy head. Control. That was the key.

He was upon her and took hold of her hands as he flew past, taking her with him. Elishia screamed and kicked her legs.

"Elishia, listen to me!" he shouted. "You have to stop struggling or we will both die." The sheer fright on her face told him she barely heard him. "Elishia!" This time he barked her name. He felt her hands jerk in his, telling him he had her attention. Jeremiah squeezed her hands hard enough to make her wince but not so hard as to crush her fingers (though he thought he might have felt something break). You tore the door clean off its hinges, *he reminded himself.* There is no telling what you might be able to do. *Then,* Use your strength.

Screams on the wind.

Was Rebekah all right? The baby! Was it all right, too? He prayed God would somehow let him know. Instead all he heard was Elishia's whimpering sobs less than a foot away.

He yanked up hard, jerking Elishia upward so her body—legs still kicking—was flush against his. He held her to him hard and firm like you would a toddler who was throwing a tantrum.

He did his best to keep his voice soothing and sure. "It is all right, Elishia. It is me, Jeremiah Garir. I have you. I need you to stay still."

Her tear-stained eyes pleaded with him to verify his promise that all would be fine. "Mr. . . . Mr. Garir?"

"I have you."

In all the commotion, Jeremiah failed to notice one thing.

They were still ascending, the earth becoming a dark blur of field below, Peraton Village no longer visible.

CHAPTER SEVEN

NOT TAKING ANY chances when it came to safeguarding his secret identity, Gabriel rose extra early Tuesday morning to ensure he'd have enough time to hit the drugstore before work. Payday was still three days away, four, including today, and he had never been one to use his credit card if it could be helped. But, alas, when things needed to be done, things needed to be done so he went to the drugstore, perused the reading glasses rack and picked a pair that were most similar to the ones that were broken Friday when he had been caught between the car and the gravel path at the Forks. Though the reading glasses were of the weakest strength, from past experience he knew that he'd have to have his friend, who was an assistant at an optometrist's office, change the lenses again otherwise the headaches he'd experienced when first using glasses as part of his "disguise" would return. What he'd say to his friend, he didn't know, as he'd already used the "my brother is going to a costume party and liked these frames better" excuse before.

Either that or maybe I'm just going to have to tough it out from now on. The thought frightened him because if there was one thing he hated most, it was a headache. His whole world ended when one hit. He couldn't think, couldn't focus, couldn't do much of anything and if Axiom-man were ever required while he had a headache, he couldn't risk running at only half-efficiency. The people of the city deserved better than that. They deserved his all, especially now after all the havoc Redsaw had wreaked, all the death.

The swelling anger rooted deep in his heart stayed with him as he took a bus to work. Try as he might, he couldn't shove his growing hatred for the man away. And *hating* was something he never wanted to do. No matter who the criminal was, no matter what they had done, four months ago when he had first donned his tights, he had decided that whomever he might encounter deserved a second chance and a shot at forgiveness. If he himself had been perfect, by all means, he'd be in a place to hand out judgment, but because his life was covered with many faults of his own, who was he to harbor ill will toward another? Granted, Redsaw was a killer, and if what the messenger told him about Redsaw and what he represented was true—well, Gabriel thought maybe it *was* okay to hold Redsaw in a different light and against a different standard.

But if I do that, he thought, *then I have to hold myself to that standard as well. Redsaw and I are the same, in a lot of ways, our powers coming from cosmic sources, just opposite sides. So far as I know, we're the only the ones on Earth with super-powered abilities. Besides, Redsaw's here because I am. If it wasn't for me . . .*

The bus stopped a few blocks from Dolla-card's office building. Though he had wanted to remain seated and think some more on this, he knew he couldn't. Gabriel Garrison had responsibilities as much as Axiom-man did.

He got off, checked his watch and was relieved to find he had eight minutes before his shift started.

Good, he thought. Eyes to the ground, he walked slowly toward the front entrance, forcing himself to forget the events of the weekend, Redsaw's slaughter of innocents yesterday, the letters revealing someone out there knew who he was—all of it—and changed gears inside. *Can't be preoccupied with this stuff right now. I'm on thin ice as it is and Rod's definitely going to fire me soon if I screw up again, and a busy head while trying to work will unquestionably cause me to slip.*

By the time he reached the front doors, he felt a little better. With each step toward the elevator, more and more he convinced himself that Axiom-man was indeed another person and those troubles were happening to *him* and not to himself.

Unzipping his jacket, he squeezed himself into the crowded elevator, giving a grin to the woman standing next to him.

She ignored him.

———

"This is Oscar Owen," Oscar said as he walked through the doors of the small office he leased as temporary headquarters for Owen Tower not far from the MTS Centre. "Yes. Mm-hm. No, I told him I wanted the lower level—Why? Think about it. Have you ever walked down Portage Avenue? Know how many punk kids hang around there at night? Better yet, have you read the paper lately? Since last week over a dozen cars have had their windows smashed. I don't want some juvenile trying to show off to his friends by smashing my windows. Yes, I know most other businesses along Portage only double up the glass, but—Listen, have you seen the renderings around town of Owen Tower? Do you know what it will look like when it's all done? Why, thank you. I think it's a gorgeous building, too, and that's exactly why I want my glass—Actually, know what, now that I think about it, I'm changing my order. Make it tempered or laminate glass for the lower level. I don't care what it costs. I'd rather outlay the money now than have to pay to fix it later. Yes, thank you. Good-bye." He mashed down on the END button on the phone and closed his eyes. When he opened them his new beautiful, young receptionist with dark brown hair looked back at him.

———

Between start-of-shift at 8:00 and 10:45, Gabriel's heart beat quickly. Valerie would start at 11:00. To see her again . . . . Though he knew everything he felt, everything he did would have to be done at a distance. Still, he couldn't wait for her to arrive. But what would he say? As Axiom-man he could easily walk up to her, pick her up and fly her away to some quiet place where they could spend time together. As Gabriel . . . *She won't even let you help her with her callback forms.* Still, throughout his shift he could glance her way now and then and think back to the tender moment shared on the viewing tower, the warmth of her touch through his mask while on her apartment balcony.

His headset beeped and he took a call. Once done, he was in the middle of wrapping up the customer's file when Rod stopped by his desk. His boss was dressed neat and tidy in a black suit, a crisp white button-down and black tie. Rod's black hair was even darker given the amount of gel that appeared to be in it and for a second Gabriel had to refrain a chuckle; the man looked like an Oreo.

Rod cleared his throat.

Gabriel ensured his After Call Task (ACT) button was activated. It was. "Uh, yes, sir?"

Leaning up against the small wall that bordered Gabriel's cubicle, Rod held out a palm. "You got that doctor's note for me?" A dramatic pause, then: "Again?"

Of course he has to make this difficult, Gabriel thought. "Sure. Um" —he dug around in the pocket of his brown dress pants then produced the note— "here." And handed it to him.

Rod unfolded it and checked it over, a skeptical look on his face.

"I was going to give it to you earlier but I couldn't find you," Gabriel said.

"I was in a meeting all morning. How long did you spend wandering around looking for me?" Rod folded the note back up and stuck it in his shirt pocket.

"Um, about five minutes. Eight or nine at most."

"It better not screw with your call stats, Garrison."

"I can work into my lunch or break if that'll help. I mean, I don't think it'll hurt my stats. At least the monthly ones."

Rod didn't seem too impressed.

Don't be careless, man, Gabriel told himself. *Some kissing up might help you right now.* "Uh, if you don't mind my saying so, I really like the suit you're wearing. Looks sharp." He gave a thumbs-up.

His boss twisted his lips to the side, eyes cold. "You better get back to work. You've been sitting in ACT for a few minutes now." He walked away.

Just like that, huh? No good-bye, no nothing. Sighing, Gabriel took another call, thinking that if he logged off right away in spite of it being his break time, Rod might get upset. *After this one, I'll only take five minutes for a break and it should help make up for the lost time while I tried to find Rod this morning.*

So that's what he did.

———

Gabriel was tempted to avoid going to the lunchroom on his break. The news channel was on and he didn't want to end up hearing something about some disaster in the city that would require his assistance. But if he didn't go into the lunchroom and if something was indeed happening that needed Axiom-man there—he could only imagine the guilt he'd feel if he found out folks were hurt as a result. The five minutes of his break ticked on by slow . . . slow . . . slow . . . as he watched the news, half-expecting the newscaster to relay some story of chaos that was happening *right now.*

Gabriel breathed a sigh of relief when nothing but the weather report seemed to be the event of the day. Returning to his desk, he glanced up at the clock. It was 11:02.

Valerie. She should be here any—

Where was she?

He logged in to his system and took the call that immediately beeped in his headset. Once done, he remained in ACT a moment, stood, and surveyed the calling floor, hoping to see her enter the office, perhaps late because of a missed bus or something. Valerie was nowhere to be seen.

Come on, he thought.

So badly did he want to see her. Not that there was anything he could really say to her. As far as things went, it would be "business as usual," she being somewhat cordial with him but having no clue that he was Axiom-man.

The morning wore on and the afternoon got underway. His stomach growled and he looked at the clock. It was 1:21. Lunch was at 1:30 today. That was the problem with shift work. Though he worked a set shift of 8:00 to 4:00, his breaks and lunchtime varied day-to-day, sometimes the variation only a five-to-ten-minute difference, sometimes as much as an hour.

At 1:30, Gabriel logged off his station and gazed longingly at Valerie's desk, which sat at an angle across from him. All her stuff was still there.

Maybe she's just sick? Then, *Hope not. She'd already been through enough this weekend, especially nearly getting killed by Redsaw as she and I were flying.* A pang struck his heart, one filled with a combination of anger and—painful nostalgia.

Heart heavy, he got up and went to Rod's office. *I can't believe I'm doing this.* But he couldn't help himself. He just needed to know if Valerie was okay. It was Tuesday and he was supposed to meet with Rod to go over call quality anyway, and that was at 3:00. Maybe he'd pretend he got the time mixed up as an excuse to talk to Rod then ask about Valerie?

While en route, a thought struck him: *Did Redsaw find out who Valerie was? Her name? Did he want some kind of revenge or want to finish the job and seek her out?* He hurried his pace.

Gently, he knocked on Rod's door. Through the window alongside the door, Gabriel saw Rod staring at his computer screen, chin on his palm, elbow on his desk. The man looked as if his thoughts were a million miles away. When Rod didn't acknowledge him, he knocked more forcefully. Rod glanced up and waved him in.

"What do you need, Gabriel?" he asked.

"Um . . ." He took a step into the office, one hand at his side, the other on the door. "I'm here for our stat review"

"That's not till 3:00, Garrison."

Gabriel snapped his fingers. "Oh, right. Sorry." He turned to leave then, heart beating quickly, turned back. "Um, have you seen Valerie? I, uh, need her for something. I didn't see her come in."

Rod kept his eyes on the screen. "You won't see her come in today."

"Real—"

"Or any other day for that matter." He looked at Gabriel. "She quit, Garrison. This morning."

It felt like someone smacked the flesh of his heart. "Q-quit?"

"Yeah. Bummer, too. She was a heck of a service rep. She called before I got here, left a message on my machine. Seems she got another job."

Another jo— "Do you, ah, do you know where?"

"Yeah. Not really your business, though, is it?"

Gabriel cast his gaze downward. "No, I guess not. Sorry." How could she just leave like that? Without warning . . . without even saying good-bye? *Snap out of it, Garrison. You don't own her and she doesn't even like you anyway.*

When he looked up, Rod gave him a tender smile. "I'll miss her, too, Gabriel."

The two men didn't say anything after that. Gabriel just stood there, hoping Rod would say more, say something about where Valerie now worked. Though he did feel kind of weird *wanting* to know, he knew his intentions were pure. He just needed to know how to find her aside from at her apartment. More so, how *Axiom-man* would be able to find her.

Rod glanced upward, his face long.

"Is everything all right?" Gabriel asked.

His boss didn't reply at first then said, gesturing to the chair across from him, "Here, close the door and have a seat."

Gabriel did and settled in across from him, no longer hungry.

"I guess you heard about Gene, huh?" Rod said.

How could I forget? "Yes, sir, I did. It's . . . it's a shame what happened. I'm not really sure what to think, actually."

A quizzical expression covered Rod's face.

"Wha—Well, what I mean is . . . is . . . it's so unfortunate that it happened. And it's the first time—*was* the first time, so far as I know—someone, um, passed on in the way he did."

"He was a good employee, as short-lived as his tenure here was. He was all gung ho about the job, much the same way I was when I first started."

Gabriel was surprised to hear that. He had always perceived Rod's job as call centre supervisor as the kind Rod only did because whatever Rod really wanted to be never came to pass.

"I really liked him, too," Gabriel said. Just then he felt terrible about judging Gene and thinking that the young man was Redsaw.

"He didn't say anything to you, did he?" Rod sighed. "Not sure what I mean. Just curious."

Gabriel thought a moment. "Not really. I just knew he thought Redsaw was something else. That is before Redsaw did what he did. One can only assume Gene was just a big fan and wanted to get close to him. In the end . . ." *In the end it cost him his life. "I just wanted an autograph," he had said. I got to him too late. Should have been more careful. Should have been more alert and more aware of who was around, someone I knew or otherwise.* He decided he'd check the obituaries everyday for Gene's remembrance. Most likely it wouldn't appear until later in the week.

"It seems my guys have a penchant for getting in to trouble," Rod said. The statement seemed to have been meant more as a thought than something said out loud.

"Sir?"

Rod leaned forward in his chair. "Just think about it. Gene was there Friday and got . . . was killed. You were around that Redsaw character yesterday and got hurt. It's just—and don't take this the wrong way—it's unfair that you only got hurt and Gene . . . Gene died. Who's next? You are okay, aren't you, Garrison?"

Not really, he thought. He also *did* wonder if Rod meant it would have been better if he and Gene had traded places. *Don't think like that. Rod didn't mean anything by it.* "I'm okay, um, yes, I'm fine. Banged up but not beaten." He forced a smile. He still couldn't believe Valerie was no longer with Dolla-card.

"I'm going to go to the funeral once I know when that is. You should come, too, seeing as how you trained him."

Gabriel nodded solemnly.

"I don't know, Gabriel. I, at least right now, am not so sure having these goofballs running around in tights is such a good idea. Redsaw, though still brand new to the city—well, it didn't take him long to reveal what he truly was. Who's to say Axiom-man won't be next? That the last few months have all been some kind of ruse and one day, bam! He'll hit us with the truth and team up with that other clown and take over the city?"

The sudden rise in Rod's voice caught Gabriel off guard. Was that how Rod truly felt about him, about Axiom-man? What if Rod wasn't the only one with suspicions? What then? What if no one trusted him?

Be careful what you say, he told himself. He made an extra effort to keep his voice light and insecure, the opposite of the low, confident tone he put forth as Axiom-man. Anything to keep Rod off his trail. He suddenly thought of those letters and whoever was out there that knew his secret. *It just keeps getting worse.* "Um, so far Axiom-man hasn't given us any reason to doubt him. I-I think—and I'm talking about me, too—we should all just wait and see what he does. He did face Redsaw yesterday, after all."

"Yeah, but like I said, it could all be a show. From what I hear, those two guys are very similar. Their powers are almost the same. Could be brothers so far as we know."

Brothers? The thought chilled him.

"I just think we should give him—Axiom-man—the benefit of a doubt for now and see what the future holds." *Because as of now, I don't even know what the future holds. At least, not for Axiom-man.*

CHAPTER EIGHT

IT WAS AROUND 1:40 P.M. when Oscar Owen returned from lunch. Valerie straightened herself in her chair, wanting to give the impression she was attentive and "on top" of the tasks at hand. So far, she felt, she was doing a great job even though it was only her first day. The job was simple: keep track of phone calls, sift and organize the email that came to the general inbox, answer inquires about Owen Tower with the aid of a white binder with an artist's rendition of the completed building on its cover filled with all sorts of organized information on the project, seat and assist those who had come in for meetings not only with Oscar Owen himself but others under his employ, and various other tasks. The receptionist who held the position before her had been placed there by a temp agency but, Mr. Owen told her earlier, that receptionist hadn't worked out and he was interested in hiring someone directly instead of going through an intermediary. Though Valerie wished she could have been trained by the previous receptionist, she soon discovered that Mr. Owen was so well-organized and such a good teacher, that learning the basics of her new position took only the majority of the morning. The rest, he said, would be learned hands-on.

Mr. Owen was sweet, she had to admit. He was well-spoken, carried a certain amount of charm and, what was most appealing, a confidence that she hadn't seen in anyone since Axiom-man. He also gave the impression that he cared about his employees and wasn't afraid to get in there with them and help them now and then.

"Welcome back, sir," she said. "How was your lunch?"

Mr. Owen gave her a warm smile then wiped the corners of his mouth with thumb and forefinger. "Not bad at all, actually. Had a hamburger today, something I rarely do." He came up to her desk and leaned against it on his knuckles, glancing side to side as if he were about to reveal a life-altering secret. "Between you and me, I'm getting tired of fancy dinners, steaks and pastas. Every time I have a business lunch, I'm always expected to take the client to the crème de la crème of Winnipeg's finest. Even on my own, I'm generally expected to be seen dining where the menu is prix fixe." Then, whispering, "Who's to say McDonald's can't be just as exquisite, right?" He winked at her.

"I hear you," she said. Then, with a whisper, added, "And your secret's safe with me."

Mr. Owen chuckled then headed toward his office. Where the hall met the waiting area, he stopped, put his hands in his pockets, and turned around. "What are you doing about a week and a half from today?"

"Me?"

"Ideally, yes. Yes, you." There was that charming smile again. Uh-oh. Was he going to ask her out?

"Um, nothing. I'll be working here, I mean."

"I meant in the evening hours."

The evening hours. She knew this job was too good to be true—the lack of pressure, the serenity that had been completely absent at Dolla-card. What should she say? She didn't want to lose her job. She needed it if she wanted to buy a house. But she also didn't want herself to turn into the classic lowly-secretary-who-gets-taken-advantage-of-by-her-boss type. "Home. Yeah, I'll be at home."

"No, you won't be," he said and came over to her. She must have given a worried look because he said with a soft laugh, "No, what I mean is I'm hosting a get together of sorts for the Owen Tower project at the Fort Garry Hotel. As my new receptionist, I'd very much like you to come. You can bring a date, of course." As an almost afterthought, he added, "I will be."

"Oh."

"Got anyone in mind?"

She smiled at the idea of bringing Joel, if he wasn't working late, that was. "Yes. Yes, I do."

"Good. I'll leave tickets in your inbox. You'll need them at the door. It's easier than crossing off names on a guest list. Don't ask me why but that's what the planner said." He turned and headed toward the hall. Calling back over his shoulder he said, "It's a formal affair so wear something nice. Just don't outshine my date, all right?"

"Sure," she said after him.

A few moments later, she heard Mr. Owen's door close.

The phone rang.

"Owen Tower. This is Valerie. How can I help you?"

"Hey, beautiful." It was Joel.

"Hi," she said, surprised at the enthusiasm in her voice. But after last night, who could blame her. It had been perfect.

"I won't take up much of your time. I'm sure you're busy. I just wanted to say hello and see how the first day at your new job was going? I got your message."

"Oh, it's great. Despite the very early call to get in here, Mr. Owen's really nice and so is everyone else working here. I don't see them as much. I'm pretty much confined to the front here, but that's okay. I got plenty to do and so far so good. I'm in charge of a lot but the way they work it here makes it easier for me. All system. No time for games. So far, anyway. He's even got me answering 'Owen Tower' even though the building's not all up yet." She recalled the day when Mr. Owen had called her up at Dolla-card, inquiring about an increase in credit. She never thought she'd one day be working for him, and so soon, too. Mr. Owen had no idea—or, at least, never let on that he knew—it was her he had talked to.

"That's great. I'm thrilled for you."

"How's your day been so far?"

"Agh, don't ask."

"Just did."

Joel laughed. "Yeah, I guess you did. Got a couple important cases I'm working on. The clients don't really have it together and one of them has changed their story twice now."

"Oh."

"Like I said, don't ask. Anyway, Val, just wanted to see how your day was going. I'll let you go."

"Wait!"

"Yes?"

"Mr. Owen just invited me to a party at the Fort Garry Hotel. He said I can bring someone and I was wondering, um . . ."

"Um . . . ?" he said playfully.

Why are you so shy? Because she seldom did the chasing, if at all. *Just ask. He'll say yes.* "Do you want to go?"

"As in an official outing, a date, you dressing up all pretty, me in my Sunday finest? I'd love to. When?"

"He didn't say other than about a week and a half from now. I'm assuming it's either a Friday or Saturday night. I can find out."

"Either way, sounds good. Besides, it'll be good for me to hang around with that crowd."

"Why?"

"You forget the game I'm in, Val. It's all about impressions and if Owen's current position is any indicator, it'll be good for me to represent my firm around him."

"It's not like he's Donald Trump or anything and is buddy-buddy with all the so-and-sos in the city."

"At the rate he's going, he'll surpass Trump and anyone else for that matter. The guy's come a long, long way in four years and he's still young. Late twenties, I think. Imagine where he's going to be when he's fifty, if he keeps it up. Never mind that. Even in ten years?"

"I see what you mean."

"Yeah, and you're in on the ground floor. If you keep it up, you'll have that house in no time and probably something a lot nicer than you ever dreamed."

She detected a hint of "I know something you don't" in his voice but couldn't be sure. Either way, Joel was right. Mr. Owen was going places and she was delighted she could be a part of the journey.

Line Two lit up.

"Joel, I gotta run. Someone's calling."

"Okay. I'll talk to you later, Val. I lo—um, I'll talk to you later."

"Okay, bye," she said. She switched lines. "Owen Tower. This is Valerie. How can I help you?"

———

Night was comfortable. Redsaw preferred it, reveled in it—enjoyed it. He didn't feel as *exposed* at night, and though he took comfort in the shadows that concealed his movements, the way his partially-black uniform blended him with the night sky, his kinship with dark, he knew, reflected the darkness growing within.

He stood on a building ledge in the Exchange District, surveying the street below. The sidewalks were relatively empty at one in the morning. A few cars went up the one-way, a couple of stray cats went about their business. It was a quiet night and the silence was what he needed right now. Heaviness weighed on his heart and his brow was constantly furrowed despite his efforts to lighten his expression.

You're falling apart, he thought. No, not falling apart . . . but losing himself to something. Maybe even to someone. The voice he heard in his head, the one telling him that if he built *it,* all would be revealed. His right hand began to shake. He used his left to still it. *This wasn't part of the plan. I was supposed to help people. I was supposed to be an example, someone everyone could look up to, both in and out of costume.* A part of him longed to go back in time and stop himself from killing that young man at the Forks. A piece of him wanted to stop himself from murdering all he'd killed since. But a larger part of him shuddered when, searching within, he didn't feel any regret. Not anymore.

The power. The way his powers jumped inside and surged with pleasurable energy every time he took a life. The way he caught a glimpse of something . . . beyond . . . a place, perhaps, of answers and, maybe, compassion.

But people aren't supposed to kill people. He knew that just like everyone else, but something inside told him what he was doing was *okay* and he had nothing to fear. He was chosen, but as to why he didn't know. If it was true, if he *was* indeed chosen, then there had to be a reason why he had these abilities. A reason *why* he felt somewhat indifferent to the robbing of another human life.

The craving had him. He crouched down, trying to stuff it away, tell himself that murder was wrong and he had no place doing it. But the freedom, the absolute freedom and ability to get away with it. No one could stop him. Not even Axiomman.

A young woman wearing a red overcoat with a black purse slung over her shoulder passed by below. Her high heels clicked on the pavement, quick and rhythmic. Her long, wavy brown hair reminded him of his new secretary. Valerie. Such a beautiful girl. There was something about her that got his attention. She didn't appear to be that much younger than him.

Movement below, off to the right. A guy with dark hair and a black jacket walking quickly behind the woman in red. The man picked up his pace, his brisk walk turning into a trot, then just as quickly into an all-out run. He rushed the woman from behind, ramming into her with his shoulder, tearing her purse away.

Redsaw stood. *Should I*—He was already in the air before he could reach a decision. Flying down, he landed in front of the man and held out his hand, ramming his palm into the man's mouth as the guy crashed in to him. The man fell to the ground with a grunt, covering his mouth. Blood seeped out through his fingers. Redsaw bent down, grabbed the guy by the jacket and yanked him to his feet. He tore the purse from the man's hand and whipped it to the ground. The woman, who was about twenty feet away, kept her distance, one hand over her mouth. She looked frantically side to side, presumably to see if there was anyone around she could call out to for help. There was none.

Redsaw pulled the man close; the fellow's eyes were wide with fear. "Didn't you know robbery is illegal?"

The man just stared at him.

Redsaw shook him. "Didn't you!"

The guy nodded weakly.

"Good." Redsaw set him down on wobbly legs. When the man's feet touched the pavement, Redsaw released him then locked his palms beneath the man's jaw, his fingers alongside the fellow's head. Squeezing hard, he shoved his arms upward, ripping the man's head from his body. The headless corpse fell to the sidewalk with a dull thud; blood squirted from the neck and dripped off the remains of the spine hanging from the dismembered skull. The sudden warm surge of power swept over him, causing him to rock back on his heels. Setting the balls of his feet back down, he closed his eyes and absorbed the moment and reveled in the swell of power that rose within.

Just beyond, the woman fell to all fours. Her mouth was open and her body convulsed as if she was throwing up. She probably wanted to scream but no sound came out.

Redsaw tossed the head in his palm like a basketball. When he caught it, he threw it to the ground like a melon. The skull shattered on the ground with a sloppy *splat*. Walking past the body, careful not get any brain matter on his boots, he picked up the woman's purse and brought it over to her.

The nearer he got, the more he could hear. Her voice was hardly a whisper: "Heellp. Heellp. Someone, I can't . . . can't breeaathe. Heellp."

"Here you go, ma'am," Redsaw said, handing her her purse.

She looked up at him with terrified blue eyes.

"Here, take it," he said and leaned down low.

She reached up with a shaking hand and clutched the purse as if she was drowning and the purse was a life-ring.

Offering her a warm smile, Redsaw said, "Be careful where you walk at night. Dangerous men are often about." He turned and reached for the sky, about to fly away.

Her, too, came the voice from within.

"I can't," he said softly. The craving hit him immediately. The need for the warmth of the kill, the glimpse of power. He had to build it.

He turned around. The woman was now on her knees, rocking back and forth, hugging the purse to her chest.

It looked like she was trying to speak but couldn't form the words though "Thank you" was what it appeared she was trying to say.

"You're welcome," He crouched down and, putting two fingers under her chin, lifted her bowed head. "Like I said, dangerous men are often about."

———

The police sirens echoed through the night air; Axiom-man's ears perked up beneath his mask. From this high up, he could clearly make out the glows of red and blue flashing off the tops of the buildings in the Exchange District. He banked to the left and flew over a street with four squad cars, cops and a couple of plain clothes officers. He spotted the brown leather coat of Sergeant Jack Gunn.

Great, Axiom-man thought. Last he spoke to him, they had parted on harsh words. The last thing he wanted was for the issue to be raised again but he knew it was his responsibility to check in and see if there was anything he could do to help.

He flew down and landed behind one of the squad cars. An officer, who was taping off the area, looked up from his work and gave him a nod. Axiom-man nodded back and made his way between the cars to the thick of the officers moving about. One gave him a dirty look, another offered him a smile and tip of the hat. Axiom-man didn't respond to either of them. He came up behind Gunn.

"Sergeant," he said.

Gunn turned around, his expression changing to a deep scowl. "Well, look who showed up to save the day."

Axiom-man didn't respond. *No sense getting into an argument.*

"Come to see what you missed?"

"I've come to see if there's anything I can do. What happened here?"

Jack moved to the side and like a doorman at an old-fashioned movie theatre, waved his hand out "welcoming him to the show." With a low voice he said, "See for yourself."

Axiom-man took a step forward as a few officers crouched over a body moved away. Lying on the ground, one leg at an odd angle, the other curled up beneath its buttocks, was a headless body. Beside it was . . . *Oh no.* It looked kind of like a shattered honeydew wearing a wig. A splattered ring of pink and gray and red brain matter and tissue surrounded it. A few shards of white poked out from the folds of hair and flesh. Bone. Lying not fifteen feet away was a mound of . . . . Axiom-man didn't quite know what it was. It looked like a bag of garbage covered in a red overcoat. Sticking out from one end of the overcoat was matted brown hair, red and gray flesh ringing it as well.

"This guy was obviously decapitated," Gunn said, coming up beside him. "The other" —he nodded toward the dead woman— "is congruent with a suicide, that is a jumper."

Axiom-man got a quick flash to the previous week and the woman who almost jumped off the catwalk running from Portage Place. But that woman had red hair. Not the same one, unless she dyed it. "What do you mean?"

"We checked her over. She fell, Axiom-man, from high up. At least ten or twelve stories if not more. Most likely more. Beneath that coat—I took a peek. Nothing but torn flesh, ripped and broken like a water balloon gone bust. Some of the head was still part of the body." Though it wasn't terribly warm out, Gunn wiped the sweat from his forehead. He pointed up, left then right. "The way she landed—there's no way she jumped off one of these buildings. She's nearly in the middle of the road. I strongly doubt she leaped off, and if she did, I strongly doubt she would have been able to turn her body in mid air so she was in line with the flow of the road, her face down. Besides, given the way she looks, she had fallen from much higher than these buildings."

"Theories?" Axiom-man knew all too well what Gunn was about to say. He just needed to hear it out loud, he supposed. Get it out in the open.

"Somebody threw her." He looked at Axiom-man in the eye. "Someone who can fly."

Axiom-man held his gaze. *Don't say anything. He's obviously insinuating that you—*

"Know anybody who could do that?"

"You tell me."

Jack eyed him a moment longer then shoved his hands in his pants pockets. "Where were you tonight?"

"Doing what I always do: seeing what I can do to help."

"And where were you thirty minutes ago?"

"Breaking up a fight outside one of the bars. Someone took out a gun."

"Anyone get hurt?"

"Only a few black eyes. I stopped it before it went any further."

"You get hurt?"

"No."

"Which bar?"

"The Hole."

"I see."

They didn't speak for several minutes. The cops moving around the scene seemed antsy, as if they wanted to talk to Gunn about something. Axiom-man decided not to suggest Gunn speak with his comrades in case Gunn mistook that as a sign of him hiding something. *The guy already suspects me enough as it is.*

"Seen Redsaw tonight?" Gunn asked. He pulled his hands out of his pockets and folded his arms across his chest.

"No. Have you?"

"We might have, if you or I got here sooner."

An ambulance pulled up.

"Finally," Gunn said.

A couple of emergency workers jumped out of the vehicle and one of the cops shouted at them for taking so long.

"You have no idea what tonight's been like," the medic said. "Calls all over the place. There's been at least six murders. Yours makes it eight."

"What? Six?" Gunn snapped.

"Yes, sir," the medic said.

Six. And these two. Redsaw.

Gunn turned toward Axiom-man and pointed at him. "You better tell me what's going on! Eight murders in one night is unheard of in Winnipeg. Eight murders in a month is unheard of. But what am I saying, right? You costumed nuts have got some kind of war going on. Redsaw went berserk Monday and slaughtered—" Gunn growled, turned away, spat, then turned back and faced him.

"I honestly don't know. But I intend to find out."

"Don't know, huh?"

"That's right."

"Well, you better start knowing because—I can't believe I'm saying this—because if you don't help us out with this, you and Redsaw are gonna find yourselves at the opposite end of a set of barrels. Got it?"

That was it. Axiom-man stepped right up to him and set his face an inch from Gunn's. The sergeant's hard-line expression didn't change. "Are you threatening me?"

"I don't deal in threats. Only promises."

"Same here. Now listen: I'm as eager as you to put a stop to this. I expect you to cooperate with—"

"Oh oh, *you* expect? Since when did you become a police officer? Who put you in charge?"

"I'm the only one you can count on to bring him down. I've stopped him before—"

"Yeah, yeah, you'll do it again."

Axiom-man turned and was about to fly away. Before he did, he said, "Sergeant, I'm sorry about your son." He looked back at Jack.

Gunn's face was sheer fury. "Don't you ever mention him to me again."

———

Eight murders. Redsaw . . . It was near 3:00 A.M. when Axiom-man landed at his balcony door. He made sure no one was up and looking out their windows before going in.

"This has got to stop," he said, his voice a whisper. He closed the door behind him, double-checked to make sure his blinds were drawn, then *shifted* his powers off. Pulling down his mask, he went over to the computer in the living room and turned it on. "I need answers."

The night he first received his powers, he'd been checking his email. That was when the messenger appeared. Same with the second time only a few days before. The messenger had come from the computer.

He sat down, loaded up his email, and waited. "You can't keep this from me any longer. You told me enough to get me started, to have an idea of what Redsaw was all about. Things have gone too far and I don't know what to do." *Is this what I have to face for the rest of my life? Me chasing after Redsaw night after night so he won't kill again? And if I do stop him, how can I be sure he will be stopped for good? I can't kill him. I won't. If I do, then I've become like him. Or, perhaps, I'll become him and whatever thing that gave him his power . . . . With Redsaw gone, it could very well come after me.* "I don't know enough about this to make a decision."

He leaned forward in his chair, folded his hands and placed them on his lap. "Okay, messenger, let's go. I'll wait here all night if I have to. I need your help."

The Past . . .

NO MATTER WHAT words of comfort Jeremiah tried to administer to Elishia, she wouldn't remain still, panic having fully taken her. There was only one alternative—one thing to do—and he knew he'd hate himself later for it. But if it meant saving her life, and his—he'd take that chance.

First, though, he'd try talking to her one more time. As the two continued their flight upward, Jeremiah unable to focus on slowing them down and arcing his body as such so they'd fly back toward the earth, he gripped her tightly to himself and said, "Elishia, listen to me."

"I do not want to die. I do not want to die!" she wailed.

"Stop shouting! You are not going to die, but you—we—will if you do not hold still." His words were lost to her. "Fine." Jeremiah adjusted his arms so one was wrapped around her waist. With the other, and not before a moment of hesitation, he raised it up and curled his fingers into a fist. "Forgive me," he said then let fly a quick punch to the side of her head. Her head and neck jerked to the side from the force of the blow. Her body went limp and Jeremiah thought he killed her. When he leaned his head against hers, he could make out the faint sound of breathing.

Thank the Lord, he thought. Finally.

He drew her in tightly to himself, like a child hugging a pillow. Dipping forward at the waist, Elishia's limp body bending backward, he forced the two of them forward until they had turned upside down. Ignoring the frigidness of the air and squinting against the wind blowing into his eyes, he kept himself alert for the ground now growing closer. He hadn't yet landed after this episode of floating into the heavens and had no idea how he'd be able to do it. His body told him to keep flying while his brain said he should go down and remain on the earth forever.

Closer and closer the ground came, at first the fields dark and blurry and charcoal black. As they neared, the more the ground came into focus

98

and soon he was able to make out the blades of grass in the fields and the few stocks of wheat lining the properties. As well, off to the north—at least Jeremiah thought it was toward the north—the few torches that burned the night long in the town became visible.

"No sense trying to get closer to Peraton," he said. Did Elishia hear him talking to himself? No. Her eyes were still closed and a bruise was forming on her left temple.

The ground suddenly rushed up to meet them as if it, too, had the gift of flight and was coming toward them. It was all an illusion, Jeremiah knew, but what an illusion. If he didn't slow them down, they'd plow straight into the earth like a spear.

Have to right myself before— *he thought. Using all of his strength, he pulled himself and Elishia back so that they were more or less vertical, his feet pointed toward the ground. There was a sudden jerk as he felt them stop then start to ascend again. No! "Go down!" His voice was a growl and even he, one never given to sudden outbursts or a hot temper, was shocked at how coarse the words sounded. His body obeyed and they began to lower, but still too quickly. Instinctively, he bent his legs at the knees so his feet wouldn't smash into the ground. This action somehow made him slow . . . but they were still falling too quickly.*

The ground was clear in view, perhaps only twenty or so feet away. It could have been a false impression from the shadows that graced the ground, but the grass seemed long here, almost plush.

"Oh Lord, help me," he said.

He pushed their bodies forward so they were horizontal and coming down at an angle. The ground came forward—quickly—and Jeremiah braced for impact.

When they hit, Jeremiah rolled to the side, taking the brunt of the impact on his right shoulder and hip. The two skipped along the ground like a stone across a lake, finally sliding to a stop some ways from where they landed.

Verifying Elishia was still unconscious lest she begin floating again, he let her go. Her body flopped onto its side and the two lay there.

Jeremiah half expected that at any moment, they'd return to the sky.

———

The next afternoon, Jeremiah sat with Rebekah at their kitchen table. For at least the fifth or sixth time, he recounted to her what happened when he left her the night before.

"You should have seen it," he said. "Hundreds of bodies floating up in the sky. It was both beautiful and terrifying. I will never forget it for as long as I live."

"You are safe now," she said, taking his hands in hers. "We both are."

"How is the baby?"

Rebekah shook her head. "I do not know. I have not felt it kick since early this morning. I am trusting God it is all right and is only sleeping."

"I pray so."

"What do we do now? Everything has changed." Her eyes conveyed a worry Jeremiah hadn't seen since their discussion on whether bringing a baby into the hard lives they led was a wise idea. Though they would never do the unthinkable once it was born, the thought of the baby growing up in less than ideal conditions still plagued them.

"I spoke to Isaac this morning. He said there is a town meeting after the evening meal." He grinned. "You should have seen him, Rebekah. I came by his property to see if he and his family were all right. His son, Daniel, was running around, and when that boy jumped, he must have ascended fifteen feet in the air before touching down again. The little guy then went up to a haystack and looked at it intently. Suddenly, a burst of blue fire came forth from his eyes and ignited the haystack in a rush of flame."

"And Isaac? Is he . . . different . . . too?"

"He and his whole family are, yes. Everyone is different. The whole town. We can now all do things we never thought possible. Isaac showed me by taking me into his barn. He said he had been fooling around all morning, unable to sleep since the blue clouds last night. In his barn, he had filled his wagon—you know the one, the one he likes to use for hauling lumber—with stones. Heavy ones, at least a hundred in all if not more. He went up to it and hoisted it above his head as if he were only lifting a hay bale. Then, he said I should try. Recalling last night when I tore the door off the frame—I fixed it, by the way—I decided why not. After Isaac set the wagon down, I came up along its side and set my hands

under it. I tell you, doubt and disbelief have never run through me so strongly. But I tried anyway. I must have thought it would be heavier than what it was because when I lifted it, I accidentally threw it upward. We both ran out from under it before it came crashing down. The wagon was destroyed. The rocks were fine." He smiled at the subtle joke. Rebekah did, too. *"And here is something else he showed me how to do before I left."*

Jeremiah stood from the table and went to the fireplace in the living room. Rebekah turned in her chair so she could see. The flame had gone out, he having forgotten to fuel the fire after last night. He took a couple of logs and set them in the fireplace, then took several steps back.

"Watch," he said. Eyeing the wood intently, he imagined them alive with fire. He imagined himself setting them ablaze.

As if someone had draped a blanket of light across his eyes, his vision became bright blue. He was barely able to make out the logs in the fireplace. Then, quickly, he released a blast of blue fire from his eyes. The logs burst into flame and Rebekah yelped. He turned to face her.

"Jeremiah, your eyes!"

He closed them quickly, afraid he'd accidentally shoot fire across the room and strike her. "Why? What is wrong?"

"I cannot see them anymore. They are completely blue. No white, no brown. Only blue."

CHAPTER NINE

GABRIEL AWOKE THE following Monday morning, angry, like every other morning since the night he waited until he had to go to work for the messenger to show up via his computer screen. The messenger never came nor did he come Thursday night when Gabriel tried waiting for him again.

The news was monopolized every single day with reports of terror and death. Each night there were seven to ten murders and each night Axiom-man was always too late to stop them. Not once did he see Redsaw. Only the flashing reds and blues of police lights alerted him something was amiss. Toward the latter part of the week, the streets were void of people by midnight. A few companies reportedly canceled their evening shifts for fear of their employees going home after dark. On the weekend, all of the eighteen murders took place in peoples' homes.

Winnipeg wasn't safe anymore. Not anywhere.

The police were at a loss. Gunn went on record vowing to take Redsaw down. He also wanted Axiom-man to turn himself in because as far as he knew, and since the damage done to the victims' bodies was consistent with what the public knew of Axiom-man's and Redsaw's powers, Axiom-man could have been the guilty party. Gunn went so far as to say that Axiom-man couldn't be trusted considering he'd ". . . only been playing hero for four months. He could very well have turned. Look at Redsaw. He tried playing superhero for less than a week and where has that left us?"

Work hadn't been any easier for Gabriel either. Aside from seeming to be the only employee who got all the irate customers, Rod had put up both the front page article from the Sunday after Gene's death, the headline reading SUPER DISASTER RESULTS IN LOSS OF LIFE, and also Gene's obituary which had come out Thursday morning. The obituary stated the funeral was for today.

When Gabriel was getting on his shoes to go to work, he saw another white envelope on his doormat after a week of silence. Heart heavy, he picked it up, opened it and unfolded the letter. Something dropped to the floor. He bent down, lifted it, and flipped it over. A picture of a little girl, perhaps seven or eight. Her brown hair in pigtails reminded him of Valerie.

The letter read:

Dear Mr. Garrison:

It's been seven days since you last heard from me. I have a job for you and I need you to report back to me before midnight tonight. If you don't, expect to see your identity revealed in every major newspaper and on every major network across the country beginning tomorrow morning. I'm pretty sure they'd "stop the presses" when they hear what I have to say. And I'm sure it will become worldwide news almost immediately.

There is a young girl that means the world to me. I've included her picture. When she was just a baby her father and mother divorced and the father received custody because at that time, he was the one who held a steady job. The mother couldn't find employment anywhere after maternity leave. There's a story as to why, but that's not important. In recent years, there's been evidence that the father hasn't been treating the girl well at all. She shows up to school with bruises and unexplainable scrapes and cuts. When asked what happened, she says, "I fell," which we all know is a cover up for something more. Something dark. This year, I contacted the police and was told there was nothing they could do about it because there was no proof. Child and Family Services were also contacted. They went to the father's house, checked things out, but he's a wily devil, you see. Covered everything up. Both he and the girl said nothing that would reveal what was going on. CFS didn't even take the kid, just in case.

But there is something, Mr. Garrison. Any fool would see that if they took a look at her.

The system that runs this world is inadequate. You above all people would know that otherwise you wouldn't do what you do. I need your help. She needs your help. I need you to get the girl out of that home (though "home" is hardly what I'd call it).

I need you to do this. Find out what you can, catch him in the act so she can go free. If you don't . . . well, I already told you what would happen and don't for a minute think you'd allow me to go public with the information I carry. Just imagine what Redsaw would do if he found out who you are?

The girl attends Emerson Elementary School. I trust you'll find out where that is.

Lastly, here's how you will report back to me:

Write me a letter detailing your findings. Put it in an unmarked white envelope, the same I use for my letters to you. Drop this envelope in the recycle bin by your lobby's front doors. Do not wait around for me to come. If I see you, your identity will be revealed. This will all go smoothly if you obey.

No police. This is between you and I.

As always, I'll keep in touch.

Gabriel re-read the letter. When he got to the words "Emerson Elementary School" again, the sharp pinch returned to his heart. That was where he'd attended school as a kid. Did this person know that? He doubted it.

That little girl . . .

It was a strange twist of fate. It was a little girl that first prompted him to put on the mask in the first place, a little girl whom he read about in the *Free Press* who was killed when gang members broke into her father's house looking for drugs. Now, it seemed, it'd be a little girl who could end his career as Axiom-man.

Unless he obeyed.

He studied the picture. The child—whoever she was—was smiling big and bright. The teeth beside her two front ones were missing. She had probably just received a big reward from the Tooth Fairy before the picture was taken. Then again, if what the letter said about her home environment was true, probably not.

What was he supposed to do? If he somehow did manage to catch something terrible happening to her, no problem. That would be enough to get the authorities involved. But what if the young one did have a *real* excuse for the bruises and all was really well? Would the person writing him the letters demand he kidnap her and take her to who knew where?

No police, the letter said so that ruled out going to Jack Gunn or anyone else at the station who would listen.

Could it be the mother who wrote the letters? No names had been given thus far but, Gabriel thought, finding out *who* the girl was wouldn't be that hard and a bit of digging would reveal the mother's identity as well.

He glanced behind himself and checked the clock on the wall. He was going to be late for work if he didn't hurry. Instead of bussing it, he'd have to fly.

Besides, today was an important day and he didn't want to be late.

———

The bell above the door to Owen Tower's temporary headquarters jingled when Valerie opened it. For the first time in the history of her working career, she had enjoyed coming in to work every day. It was so laid back here yet everything still ran with pinpoint precision. Efficiency was the name of the game yet Mr. Owen still knew how to make a person feel welcome and *belonging.* She got in behind her desk and set her purse down on the seat of her chair. As she was about to remove her brown jacket, she noticed the bouquet of roses sitting atop the ledge that bordered her desk. There was a tiny white card attached, with the painted portrait of a rose on one side and a message in black ink on the other.

Thought these'd bring some color into your day.

Love,

Joel

She felt her cheeks heat at the sentiment. Both hands on either side of the glass vase, she rotated it side to side as she examined the flowers. They were beautiful. No, not beautiful. Gorgeous! They were also already sitting in an adequate supply of water and one of the plant food packets already sat discarded just beside the vase.

"Awww," she said with a smile.

Mr. Owen came into the reception area from down the hall. Valerie was taken aback by his double-breasted beige suit that looked more to be made of silk than wool.

"Oh, good, you saw those," he said. "Your beau came not too long ago to drop them off. Fortunately I was here early otherwise he'd never have gotten in. Anyway . . ." He came beside her and held out his hand.

What does he . . . she thought.

"Your coat," he said.

"Oh, thanks." She removed her jacket and gave it to him. He went and hung it up in the little closet where the hall met the waiting area.

"He's the young man you're bringing this Friday?"

He sure is. "Yes," she said with a nod. "I wouldn't want to bring anyone else."

————

Oscar entered his office and closed the door behind him. *Finally. Alone.* As much as he knew he needed to maintain friendly chitchat with his employees for company morale, right now the very thought of having to "play nice" sickened him.

He took a step inward and squeezed his fingers into a fist. Closing his eyes, he relaxed a moment, *switched*, letting the power fill him. When he opened his eyes, he was pleased to see his balled-up right hand surrounded by a blood-red glow.

Almost there, he thought.

Opening his fingers, the red glow spread out even more and covered his wrist. The edge of the cuff of his shirt blackened as the red energy hit it. He made a fist again, stuck up the index finger . . . and focused. The red energy rolled like a wave, moving up his hand. The red power concentrated itself atop his index finger, snapped and crackled like red flame dancing atop a candle.

Slowly, Oscar reached forward and poked at the air with his finger. The air around the red power rippled then hazed over as if by a thin veil of smoke.

With a single forward thrust, he stabbed *into* the air, tearing it with a low, echoey *pop* rather than a ripping sound. Moving his finger, he tore the fabric of what he could only call *reality* in a small arc, leaving a trail of smoking black *nothingness* in its wake.

This *tear* was what he had been working for. He first discovered it last night but he could only make it so big. But with more power, he knew—and the voice later confirmed it in the shadows of the night—he could finally create a door to the knowledge he sought.

A black door. A shadowy door.

A doorway of darkness.

———

I hope my suit doesn't get wrinkled, Axiom-man thought, and he wasn't referring to his costume. Folded neatly in his backpack beneath his cape was a two-piece black suit, white button-down and black tie. Today, at 9:00 A.M., was Gene's funeral. The plan was get into work, take calls until 8:30 then go see Rod who had offered to give him a ride. It had been 7:42 when he left his apartment and work was only a short flight away.

Soon the Dolla-card building was almost below him. The back alley was clear; so would be the little alcove which had become a favorite place to change. If people were out back, he'd land on the roof and utilize the small, two-foot-square trap door that led to an unused room on the top floor.

The blare of sirens whirled up somewhere off to his right. He looked in that direction and couldn't see anything so flew a little higher, curving his flight until he passed the Dolla-card building and headed in the direction of the sound.

Main Street was packed with early-morning traffic. There, off in the distance, past where the road forked onto the Disraeli Overpass, were the sparkling lights of red and blue. There were three police cars, horns honking on top of their sirens, trying to get through the dense traffic heading north.

Grunting, Axiom-man thought, *I'm going to be late. Again!* But if this early morning distress had anything to do with Redsaw and the possible death of someone, or more, he wouldn't be able to live with himself knowing that his absence resulted in the murders of innocent people.

Axiom-man brought his arms to his sides, forcing his body to be more aerodynamic, and kicked on the speed. Up ahead, the traffic broke away from in front of the cops like a jigsaw puzzle, folks bringing their cars sharply over into the far right lane. The cop cars hit the gas and were off. Axiom-man trailed behind and was soon over them. At first he wasn't sure who they were pursuing but when the black TrailBlazer up ahead did a fishtail, he knew he had the quarry made.

Okay, think. You can only fly so fast. If they really nail it, you're going to fall behind and lose them. The best bet would be to not take his eyes off the vehicle even if that meant cutting straight on ahead when the TrailBlazer was forced to follow the curves of the road. The fastest way between any two points was always a straight line and flight gave him that advantage.

Horns blared below; people on the sidewalk cursed as the TrailBlazer tore down the street, its rear end bouncing when it hit the occasional pothole. The cops were about a dozen car lengths behind, trying to get around other vehicles that hadn't yet cleared the way.

Before Axiom-man knew it, he—who was about four car lengths behind the TrailBlazer—was already halfway between downtown and where Main Street would lead out of the city. Once those guys hit open road, they would accelerate to over one hundred kilometers per hour, and would be gone. It would truly be up to the cops then.

Have to stop them before then, he thought.

The wind whipped past his ears and a cold pocket of air zipped through the fabric of his uniform, sending a chill sweeping across his skin. He glanced back to see how far behind the cops were. They had lost some distance as two cars had tried crossing over to the median from a perpendicular street, no doubt hoping to evade the commotion so they could be on their way. Instead, they were adding to it. The cops honked their horns.

"They'll catch up," Axiom-man said and set his eyes anew on the TrailBlazer.

The black vehicle had already increased its speed. Axiom-man pressed on after it, straining his body forward, trying to increase his speed even if only by a few kilometers per hour. Sixty kliks was his limit; seventy, if he pushed himself. Already, he was fighting to keep up with everything he had and he was falling behind.

Come on, faster, man! He bent his head down and kept the TrailBlazer at the top left of his peripheral. He had to strain his eyes just to see it. "Go, go, go!" *Man, I'm late. So late. Rod's gonna fire me. I'm dead. It's over. Might as well start checking the classifieds when I get back. Gene's funeral!* He couldn't miss that. Wouldn't. He owed Gene that much. If he hadn't caught the car that killed him like he had, if he had been more alert or was able to somehow detect what Redsaw was going to do—Gene might still be alive. A burst of anger popped within and he felt himself fly a little faster. *That's it. Stay mad. If it can help you catch these guys then it's worth it.*

Main Street within the city limits was coming to an end. Traffic was thin and the TrailBlazer had plenty of room to move.

"Oh great!" he snapped and pressed himself forward.

The TrailBlazer nailed it. The sound of sirens grew louder behind him. *Good, they're behind me.* Soon, he knew, the cops would be past him. Did they know he was there or were they too busy focusing on the road to see the man in the blue tights flying high up beside them?

Altitude! I should be able to cover more ground if I fly higher. Axiom-man headed upward and though it could have only been the angle he was at, it appeared the TrailBlazer was now *under* him rather than ahead of him.

A large white semi turned onto Main just behind the speeding TrailBlazer. Axiom-man snapped his body forward and headed toward the semi like a dart. Flying as fast as he could, he stretched out his hands to grab hold of the front end of the semi's trailer.

Thankyouthankyouthankyou, he thought.

The white of the trailer was under him. He slowed his flight to match the speed of the semi and whipped out his arms. Like a magnet to metal, he latched firmly onto the front edge of the trailer and stopped flying completely. His body landed with a thunk from the few inches it was hovering over the top of the trailer. The driver didn't seem to notice he was there nor did the driver seem to hear the sound of his landing.

The behemoth of a vehicle picked up speed, gaining ground on the TrailBlazer.

Just need a rest. He glanced over his shoulder. The cop cars weren't far behind. Already one of them was closing in behind, the officer hitting the gas, speeding on past the semi. The other two cars quickly did the same.

The semi increased its speed from seventy to eighty, going ten kliks over the limit.

Axiom-man put his head down for a brief moment and caught his breath. A fleeting thought about what time it was quickly crossed his mind. *Don't think about that now. Just focus on what you need to do.* He looked up. The TrailBlazer was quickly becoming a black dot in the distance.

"I can't keep up," he whispered. "Ah! Why couldn't I have speed, too?" *Doesn't matter. You don't know what might happen. Things could slow down and you could catch up.* Though he doubted it. *Have to try.*

Centering himself, he rode the semi, hoping the TrailBlazer would slow down. A minute later, the TrailBlazer's break lights lit up red for a second. The cops were right behind them. That second of the vehicle slowing was enough for the semi to gain on them. The TrailBlazer and cops switched over to the right lane, the same as the semi. The semi quickly switched over to the left. *Shouldn't this guy slow down when he sees something like this?* No matter what was going through the driver's head, Axiom-man was thankful the guy was maintaining speed.

The TrailBlazer slowed a little more and someone was suddenly half hanging out of the vehicle's rear window.

Gunfire.

The semi driver must have had music on and not heard the shot because he showed no sign of slowing down. Nor did the driver seem to be paying attention to the man with the gun partly hanging out the back of the TrailBlazer.

A swell of energy welled up inside Axiom-man and, instinctively, he released the trailer and sped upward into the air. From behind him, what felt like a gust of wind drove him forward. He was flying so fast he could barely see against the wind blasting into his face.

The TrailBlazer was below him.

More shots. The cop cars swerved.

Axiom-man flew past the TrailBlazer, then—doing something he rarely did—brought his toes inward to slow himself. Right above the TrailBlazer, he flew down to its roof and landed on top of it. The vehicle swerved. Quickly, he wrapped his hand around the cargo rack on top. One of the sides of the rack snapped from the force but the other held and was enough to keep him from flying off. A bullet blasted through the roof just beside him. He moved to the side, the shock of the sound jolting his system.

Hurry.

Using all his strength, he spun his body around so he was facing the vehicle's back.

The semi finally backed off to a safe distance.

The fellow with the gun hanging out of the back caught sight of him. The man leaned against the TrailBlazer's trunk gate, his gun pointed at Axiom-man.

"Uh-oh," Axiom-man said.

As the man trained the automatic on Axiom-man's head, he shouted, "Shoot up! Shoot up!"

A shot blasted through the roof beside Axiom-man, punching a hole through his cape.

He knew his head would be next.

Wasting no time, he pooled crackling blue energy into his eyes and fired off a blast at the man's weapon. The gun fired off three successive shots as it went flying into the air, then hit the pavement and skipped across the concrete. The man retreated into the vehicle, no doubt going to rearm. Axiom-man leaped forward and grabbed hold of the edge of the vehicle's roof. Setting his body afloat, he used the edge as a pivot and spun his body around so he was hanging off the back of the vehicle. A split second later he flew forward, hooking his legs under him and swung in, nailing the man in the jaw. The man tumbled over the rear seat, landing on top of two of his comrades. Axiom-man's knees landed on two black duffle bags. Whatever was within them, it was slightly soft, presumably drugs.

No time to think about that now.

The guys on the rear seat scrambled to get their comrade off them. One produced an automatic and went to fire. Axiom-man lurched forward and grabbed the guy's hand, squeezed hard, and re-aimed the weapon so its barrel was now over his shoulder. With a powerful right hook, he knocked the guy out. Someone grabbed him from the side, twisted him, sending his tender ribs ablaze with hot pain. He grunted. The two guys in the front seat—clad in ski masks like the others—shouted to "Get rid of him!" and "Blow his head off!" The man's forearm locked in underneath Axiom-man's chin, pressing against his throat and driving his Adam's apple to the back of his windpipe, cutting off the air. With a hard elbow, Axiom-man snapped the guy's ribs. The man howled just as the guy in the passenger seat undid his seatbelt and spun around, pointing a pistol at him. Axiom-man blasted the gun from the man's hand, making the fellow scream. Knocking him back, Axiom-man drove the back of his skull into the guy who held his neck. Blood splattered onto Axiom-man's shoulders. The man eased his grip then released altogether. Quickly, Axiom-man turned around and punched the guy in the head, just to make sure he was unconscious.

Better safe than sorry.

The guy who had tumbled over the back seat and was now wedged in between the front two seats and the rear one had managed to turned himself over. His eyes were glassy and putting him out of the realm of consciousness was solved with a quick shot from the heel of Axiom-man's boot.

"Stop the car!" Axiom-man growled.

The guy in the passenger seat grabbed hold of him, one hand around Axiom-man's neck, the other clumsily trying to find purchase on his shoulder. Axiom-man socked the guy good in the chin then, grabbing the guy by the back of the head, drove the man's skull into that of the driver's. The TrailBlazer veered sharply to the left as the driver's weight pressed against the wheel. With everyone now unconscious, there was still a problem—the driver's foot was full-down on the gas, the speedometer already reaching one-hundred-forty kilometers per hour. Axiom-man grabbed the wheel and straightened the vehicle enough so it was straddling the left and right lanes. Cars that had been ahead of them had veered out of the way. In the rearview mirror he saw the cops were right behind them not twenty feet away.

It was too crowded to maneuver and get himself into the front seat and hit the brakes himself so instead, with one hand on the wheel, he reached down with the other hand and grabbed the driver's leg by his jeans. Yanking upward, he pulled the foot off the gas. The way the guy was situated, he couldn't then place the foot on the brake and press down.

The speedometer's needle began to descend, five kilometers, ten kilometers, slowly moving down so it was easier to control the vehicle.

Police cars were now on either side and one was in front. Cops from each were looking at him.

It seemed an eternity until the vehicle finally hit ten kliks an hour. Still unable to reach the brake, Axiom-man grabbed the gearshift and put the car in park. The TrailBlazer jerked forward as it slammed to a stop, sending Axiom-man between the front two seats, left shoulder first. He crashed into the dashboard. So did the passenger. The unconscious bodies behind him crashed into his legs, sending his heels against the roof.

It was finally over.

CHAPTER TEN

AXIOM-MAN FLEW TOWARD downtown as fast as he could. When he checked his watch moments after leaving the scene, it was already 9:20.

Gene's funeral had already started.

The last funeral he attended was for his grandfather and that was over eleven years ago. He couldn't remember how long such services lasted and, depending what became of Gene's body, if those in attendance would go to a cemetery for burial or not.

He also had no idea what he'd say to Rod. Rod, no doubt, was fuming on the inside, probably having a hard time contemplating why his once-star employee was suddenly always late, leaving work early and just making a plain mess of things. Adding to the already-building stress-induced headache, Axiom-man remembered the little girl in the photo he received this morning. Elementary schools let out just before four and his own personal work day ended at that time. By the time he flew over there, he'd miss her. What he was supposed to do when he found her, he hadn't a clue but he did have an idea as to how to find out *who* she was. And with that info, perhaps find out who was sending him the letters. But to do that, he'd have to leave work a half-hour early, something Rod would not tolerate.

Should I just quit and worry about it later? he thought. Where was the responsibility in that? *Man* . . . Already most of his paycheck would be used up in rent, a few bills and a new costume. Whatever was left over—if anything—wouldn't get him very far and he doubted he'd be able to find a new job before his next round of bills were due. He also didn't know how he'd manage to eat without a source of income either.

"Why does this have to be so hard?" he said and accelerated his speed.

His speed. What had happened earlier? It was as if he could suddenly fly faster than he had ever flown before and, he realized, this strange new development had occurred shortly after Redsaw made himself known to the city. Did Redsaw's— the black cloud's—presence have anything to do with this change in power? Was it merely a fluke? He had felt a gush of wind propel him forward. Maybe he hit an air pocket of some kind and it was *that* that made him fly quicker. But what "air pockets" would be that low?

"Where's the messenger when you need him?" he muttered. *Nowhere, that's where.* Either tonight or tomorrow night he'd wait up again for his glowing friend and see if he could learn anything.

Axiom-man hated being in the dark. It was as if the messenger—some cosmic force he could hardly understand— had singled him out, out of everyone in the universe and dumped every single responsibility in the world on him. Every single task. Every single demand to restore order and renew hope.

Ribs aching from the fight in the TrailBlazer, Axiom-man's heart lightened with relief when he saw he was finally over the city. If he remembered what Rod had told him last Friday correctly, Gene's funeral was at Cropo Funeral Chapel on Main.

What am I supposed to do? I'm late, I feel sick, my head . . . There was only one choice.

He had to be a man and take responsibility for his actions.

———

"Meet you at noon, right?" Joel asked on the other end of the receiver.

"Absolutely," Valerie said, her heart skipping a beat.

"Great. I'll see you around then."

Valerie hung up the phone then stood. Hands clasped behind her back, she bent at the waist and breathed in the sweet perfume scent of Joel's flowers.

———

After having changed into his civilian clothes in an alley near the funeral home, Gabriel walked to the side of the building, doubling checking his suit to ensure it sat on his frame smoothly without wrinkle. There were a few creases in the wool from being folded up in his backpack, but nothing that made it look too terrible.

As he rounded the front of the funeral home, he stopped his steps when he saw people exiting the front door.

"I missed it," he whispered.

Heart aching, a part of him wanted to cry for his carelessness. *No, not carelessness. You had to do what you had to do.* Then, *Yeah, but* they *don't know that.* He stood up against the light beige stone wall, formulating excuses, guilt already overtaking him because he knew he'd have to lie when he encountered Rod. And speaking to Rod was something he had to do. There was no way he could have just gone to work and pretended he "missed" Rod that morning and "forgot" where the funeral was supposed to take place.

Not too many people came out. One group—two women and two men, presumably aunts and uncles—went off to the side, each lighting up a cigarette. Another man, clad in an expensive-looking beige suit, black shirt and tie with dark shoes shiny enough to be mirrors, came out, head bowed low. When he straightened and brushed aside a few stray stands of jet black hair, Gabriel recognized him as Oscar Owen.

What's he doing here? he wondered. Oscar ran with a high profile crowd and if the appearance of the aunts and uncles was anything to go by, what he was looking at was the sharp contrast between high and low society.

Oscar made his way over to the small group of men and women, shook their hands and offered condolences, then went quickly on his way. He disappeared around the far side of the building.

Doesn't he have a car or a limo or something? He certainly wouldn't have bussed it over. A few moments later, Gabriel thought he heard a rush of wind somewhere on the air but could have been mistaken.

Rod emerged shortly afterward, hands in his pockets. When he saw Gabriel, he did a double take, then just stood there staring at him.

Gabriel offered a weak wave and, mustering his courage, went over to him.

"How—how was it?" Gabriel asked. *Not exactly the best way to open a conversation.*

Rod squinted, his brown eyes full of disdain. He seemed distant, though. "It was nice. Pleasant. Very formal." He glanced back at the doors.

Gabriel followed his gaze and, standing in the lobby speaking to the priest was a tall, lanky man who looked like Gene but twenty years older, a shorter, middle-aged woman at his side, and a young girl who, though wearing a plain black frock, had white, powdered skin and wore black lipstick.

"Is . . . is that his family?" Gabriel asked.

Rod nodded.

Gabriel's heart went out to them. If just the aunts and uncles, Rod and Oscar Owen and Gene's own family were all who were in attendance—it was so sad. There wasn't anybody there who could have been Gene's friends. If he had any.

"I should have been here." Gabriel said it before realizing he'd spoken.

Rod's eyes washed over with extreme disappointment, enough to cause Gabriel to flinch inside. "Yes, you should have. And you weren't. You weren't even at work this morning, were you?"

Bowing his head, Gabriel tried to lose himself in his shoes. More than anything he wished he could hide. More than anything he wished he could go back in time and stop himself from going after the TrailBlazer. More than anything . . .

. . . he wished he was someone else.

"No," Gabriel said. "I wasn't." He glanced up and Rod's face hardened.

"You're fired."

———

Valerie stood outside the Owen Tower office. It was noon, right on the dot. Heart pounding excitedly, she checked her reflection in the office's glass door, making sure she looked presentable. No, not presentable. Fabulous. She curled a lock of brown hair behind her ear, pressed a small poof of hair back against her head and was pleased with what she saw.

And so she waited.

At 12:12, she began to pace back and forth in front of the door and was tempted to go back in to see if Joel had called.

Maybe I should *wait inside?* she thought. *No, it's okay. He said around noon, not noon exactly.* But her lunch break was only a half hour and it was already half gone. *Well, at least I'll get to see him when he comes by.*

At 12:20, she went in, her feet seeming to drag beneath her. She checked the machine. The only message was from a Mr. Helberd who had leased in advance two offices in Owen Tower for when it was completed.

"So it's already come to this," she said softly. Joel stood her up. It was only a matter of time, she supposed. He'd done it to her before when they dated. Too many times. *Some things never change, I guess.* "Okay, you're overreacting. You've only been dating again for about a week." But what a week. Phone calls everyday (especially those tender good night calls), dinner, walks at Assiniboine Park, the constant expression on both their parts that this time they believed they had a chance of being together forever. And when he kissed her, it was as if she was the only girl he had ever kissed, the only girl he had ever *wanted* to kiss. Though neither had said "I love you," it was more than clear that that's how each of them felt. Sometimes you met someone who just *fit* you so completely, so fully, and even if life went on and you met someone else, they'd always be there in the corner of your heart, reminding you that *they* were the one meant for you. No one else. No substitutes.

Okay, just relax. I'm sure there's an explanation. He suddenly wouldn't dump me off. He's . . . different now. He's told me how much he hated treating me the way he did before. The memory of it . . . . It nearly killed him, he said. Joel had confided in her on the weekend that on a couple of dark nights after they had broken up, he had considered killing himself over what happened. The guilt and grief of loss, he said, consumed him.

"I just couldn't live with myself anymore," he said. "Every day was torture without you, Val. Every moment filled with pain and heartache. At work, I'd sometimes have to go into the bathroom and just . . . cry. I'd then have to stay in there until the puffiness around my eyes went down unless I wanted people constantly asking me what was wrong. I need you, Val. Always have."

Though at first she hadn't known what to make of it, the truth was she was touched by how much of an impact she had on him. Most women might think that a man who cried over them—longed for them—would be kind of creepy. Maybe. But not with Joel. Even though she had crammed down what had happened between them into the recesses of her heart and mind, she still missed him terribly. A part of her, even now, feared that if she never ended up marrying Joel, she'd never end up marrying anyone.

Joel was everything.

It was almost 12:30 and he hadn't called.

Heart breaking, Valerie waited a few more minutes by the door. When he didn't show up, she went into the ladies restroom . . . and cried.

The Past . . .

THE RESIDENTS OF *Peraton Village crammed into the town hall, one of the first buildings erected when the town was founded forty-nine years ago. The town's original population was two hundred-seventy-four, and the town hall seated three hundred. Now, the total town population was seven-hundred-eighty-two. Not once had its founders thought that at some point everybody would have to be in there nor had they the means to add to the structure for just such an occasion. Folks lined the walls, some sat on the floor in between the occupied seats. Others crowded into the entrance way so they could hear what needed to be said. For those who came late or could not find a place, they remained outside, gathered around the building, hoping that later someone would fill them in on all that had happened within.*

Inside, Jeremiah and Rebekah, having gotten there early, sat near the front on a wooden bench beside Isaac and his family.

While they waited for the meeting to begin, Isaac leaned over to Jeremiah and said, "I see your eyes are still blue."

"I was waiting to see if you would notice. They had not been earlier nor had been Rebekah's. Do you know why they are like this? I see others' are as well. Not everyone, but some. Likewise with your hair. Some, but not all."

Isaac grinned, as if he held some great secret in that brain of his. "From what my wife and I have been able to gather, the blue eyes or hair are a sign that you are using your abilities. A kind of 'permission,' if you will, to yourself that you intend to use them." He furrowed his brow. "You said that, as far as you were aware, that your eyes had not been blue earlier."

Jeremiah nodded.

"*That would mean,*" Isaac continued, "*that at some point you had learned, or had been able, to withdraw that permission from yourself. I have found that for myself—and so have said the other members of my family—that to withdraw said permission is to accept that you will not be needing your abilities for the time being. In other words, putting the knowledge that you have them and the need for them at the back of your mind. Simply stated: just not think about them.*"

How could Jeremiah not think about them? How many people did he know—present company excluded—who could fly? Who could lift heavy stones no different than hoisting a chicken? Could expel blue flame from their eyes and set items ablaze?

"*I will try,*" Jeremiah said.

He closed his eyes, hoping that he wouldn't accidentally let forth another burst of blue flame and burn through his eyelids. I do not need my gifts right now. I do not need my gifts right now. Do not think about them. *He opened his eyes and Isaac looked at him.*

"*I am sorry,*" his friend said. "*Still blue.*"

Rebekah groaned. Jeremiah turned to face her and saw she had a hand to her lower stomach. "*Are you all right?*" he asked. "*Is it the baby?*"

Her face was still pinched in discomfort. "*I felt it move, which is a good thing. But it hurts, my stomach. Well, not my stomach but, you know . . . down there.*"

Whatever excitement and vigor Jeremiah felt surging through him as a result of his abilities suddenly left him.

"*Jeremiah, your eyes are brown again,*" his wife said.

"*Really?*" He smiled. Isaac had been right. Not thinking about his gifts had made them go away. For now, anyway. "*The baby. Will you be okay? Do you need to lie down?*"

Rebekah forced a smile. "*I will be all right.*"

"*Let me know if I can do anything for you.*"

She nodded. "*I will.*"

He faced Isaac again.

"*See?*" Isaac said. "*You are learning.*"

Jeremiah turned all the way around in his seat and looked back at the sea of people. He couldn't help but laugh when he saw a few of the children hovering high up near the gray stone ceiling and others playing tag *along the stone walls of the town hall. Some sat with their eyes covered in blue light; others looked as normal as Jeremiah had ever known them.*

He faced front just as the two doors on either side of the front wall elicited the town's council members, and the town leader, Artemis Gailer, leading the way from the right. The council members took their seats at the long table at the front of the room, three on each side. The gray-haired Artemis took his seat on the wooden chair in the middle then quickly stood as if he couldn't stay still and approached the small podium on top of the table.

Artemis picked up the gavel on the podium's top and banged three times. "Order, please. Order." His eyes lit up blue.

The chatter in the room hushed. A few of the children floated down to their parents, conditioned to always obey an elder's command.

"Thank you." Artemis glanced around the room. "I call this meeting to order."

The room erupted in applause, something Artemis was clearly not expecting. He raised his hands and shook back the cuffs of the opened-faced brown robe he wore over a white shirt and black pants. "Silence!" He picked up the gavel and banged it three more times. The sound of wood banging on wood sent a jolt through Jeremiah's chest.

Despite the blue light covering his eyes, Artemis's icy expression was enough to quickly hush the room. "No more speaking. Not until we open the floor for questions. There are more bodies here than we have room for. Many of you are already sweating. The quicker you cooperate, the quicker we can leave to cooler dwellings. Now listen, all of you, for we have much to discuss." The blue light glazed over his eyes faded, revealing the aged gray eyes beneath. "I have been in chambers with the rest of Peraton Village's officials since late this afternoon, trying to discover what it is that has happened to us. Obviously, last night's strange storm is to blame. Each one of us have been granted—by whom or what, we will talk about in a moment—special abilities, all seemingly the same. Look around, folks." Many heads began turning as wide eyes glanced about the room. "How many children have you ever seen flying like a bird at a town meeting? How many wives do you know that before needed aid carrying a heavy load of dirty clothes that can now lift hay bales stacked ten high? How many of you men were once able to light your fire pits by a mere glance?"

The people murmured, a few saying, "Not any" or "None" or "Never before."

"Last night was a night that changed Peraton Village forever. Here is what we know: as mentioned, it seems we have all been given three special abilities. One is to fly. The other is strength that has yet to know bounds. The last is the ability to self-generate blue fire from our eyes. Where did these gifts come from? Who gave them? I now turn over the floor to the town priest. You all know Father Beltist quite well." Then, with a grin, "He has married all of you. Even some of your parents."

The crowd chuckled.

"Father Beltist, if you please," Artemis said.

Father Beltist stood from his place against the wall at the front of the room, clad in black, a Bible in his hands. When he came round the rear of the council members' table, he shook Artemis's hand, and approached the podium as Artemis stepped to the side. A grave and concerned look, yet with a hint of joy, overwhelmed his face. He ran his fingers over his short white hair before setting the Bible down on the podium. Artemis took his seat behind the aged priest.

"Ladies and gentlemen," Father Beltist said, "council members, Mr. Gailer, thank you for calling me forth. As our esteemed leader has said, it is warm in here so I will try and make it brief." Suddenly his eyes lit up bright blue. "As you can see, I, too, have been afflicted with the receipt of these abilities. I was sleeping last night when it happened. A flash of blue light, so bright it woke me from sleep, entered my room. I threw the covers back to see what was the matter but found that my feet would not touch the floor. They touched nothing. My heels hovered a good two feet from the floorboards. And, I discovered, so did the rest of my body hover above my bed. I was trapped in my room until morning, unable to make myself float to the floor whereas, I have been told, others had been able to discover how to do so relatively quickly. It was not until dawn that I slowly descended back upon my bed then ran out of my home to see if anyone else saw the strange flash of light. It turns out I was not alone."

"Absolutely not, Father!" someone called out.

Artemis stood from his seat behind Beltist and clapped his hands once. The strength he had used to slam his palms together made it sound as if a boom of thunder had gone off in the room.

Beltist's shoulders cringed from the noise. "Thank you, Mr. Gailer." Artemis sat back down. "I have spent the day in prayer and feel that what happened was an act of God. It had to be, for who else can control the skies? Who else can make the thunder roar and the lightning flash? Who else can control nature so it will or will not harm the earth below?"

A few of the people nodded, saying, "Amen." Jeremiah was one of them. He, too, had considered the idea that it was God Himself who had caused this. For what purpose, he had no idea, but who was he to question the Creator of everything?

"And so it stands," Father Beltist continued, "that now, as recipients of these gifts, we face a choice. What are we going to do with them? Will we learn from each other how to control them, how to hone them? Or will we allow the natural darkness of our hearts to misuse this power for evil?"

Rebekah stirred in her seat beside Jeremiah.

"Are you all right, dear?" he whispered.

"I do not know," she breathed.

When Jeremiah glanced back up toward the front, Father Beltist had stepped down and Artemis was back at the podium.

"Father Beltist poises an interesting question, and I am in agreement with him, both in that it was God who gave us these gifts and that also we now face a choice. At first, like many here, we were worried that these new abilities, namely the floating, were a sure sign of demonic possession. But from past instances, both recorded and otherwise, we cannot agree on that scenario given that we are still in control of ourselves and are capable of the want to be free of it. We are taking it on faith that we are all right though action will be taken should this be the work of the devil.

"I am not sure about the rest of you, but I and my fellow council members have a newfound urge deep within to do well with these gifts, to use them for the good of our community. One can only surmise this as further proof these abilities are from Almighty God. Only He can transform a life and change a heart. The great Jehovah has always been the cornerstone of our community. There is not a soul here who does not believe in both Him and His Son and trusted Him for their salvation. Perhaps what has happened is a great reward from above? Or perhaps it is a test, to see what we would do if given great power? I have sent out scouts to the neighboring towns to see if this phenomenon was localized or *not. Until they return home, let us assume that we as a village have been chosen, and since we have been chosen, let us be an example unto others and build our community as a shining symbol of hope and promise for all who might look upon it."*

The room erupted in applause, whistles and cheers.

Jeremiah moved to hug Rebekah but as he reached for her, he saw her head was bowed, her black hair hiding her face. Her hands were pressed firmly against her stomach. And there, between her heels, was a puddle of clear liquid.

CHAPTER ELEVEN

IT WAS TIME to take responsibility. That's what Gabriel told himself during the bus ride down Henderson Highway to Emerson Avenue. He could just as easily have flown there, but then he'd have to worry about a place to change and since Emerson was located in the North Kildonan suburbs, finding a secluded alleyway wasn't possible.

It had been his fault. As much as he hated Rod for firing him, he knew full well that he couldn't blame anyone but himself. It had been *his* choice to go after the TrailBlazer. It had been *his* choice each and every time Axiom-man was needed and he answered the call.

I knew becoming Axiom-man would cost a heavy price, he thought. *I just didn't realize how* much *it would cost.* It wasn't so much the losing of his job that bothered him and the inevitable stress of figuring out how he'd make ends meet. It was the fact that he had to *sacrifice,* seemingly, his whole life to be in the service of others. When he first started his crusade, he originally thought that it would only require a portion of his time and not all of it. And that had been the case up until Redsaw showed up on the scene. Now, with Redsaw an ever-present threat, Gabriel knew that his life had taken a turn. He knew that, more than likely, his life as Gabriel Garrison was over and from here on forth he would be Axiom-man both in and out of costume.

The fleeting thought of giving up the blue tights entered his mind only once. He immediately corrected himself by telling himself he had to finish what he started even if it took a lifetime to do so. No matter what the cost.

The seat behind him was empty save for today's newspaper. Gabriel picked it up and his stomach twisted at the headline: EVIL DOES NOT SLEEP. The subtitle read: MURDER PLAGUES CITY; CITIZENS IN FEAR. Upon reading the article, which continued in to two columns on the next page, he learned that the known death toll was sitting at one hundred-nine, more than what Gabriel had expected it to be. Winnipeg was already infamous for being the murder capital of Canada. Now, it seemed, it would hold that title indefinitely unless he did something about it.

Everything hinges on Redsaw, he thought. *I need the messenger.* Then, *Yeah, as if he would help. He hasn't shown up no matter how long you've waited for him.* There was, of course, the possibility that, as simple as it sounded, the messenger was busy. Gabriel didn't know *what* the messenger did with his time and it didn't seem reasonable to assume the messenger—a being with phenomenal cosmic power—would just sit around all day waiting for Gabriel's call. Below the article was another, a shorter one. The headline read: POLICE ASKING CITY FOR FUNDING TO CREATE SUPER-POWERED TASK FORCE. It seemed Jack Gunn's animosity toward Axiom-man knew no bounds. The police sergeant had petitioned the mayor for funds to create a special unit that would be armed and trained—*specialized*—in dealing with those who were, as the article labeled them, "empowered with unnatural abilities." The article didn't specify if the special unit was meant for Redsaw only, but knowing Sergeant Gunn, Axiom-man was in his sights as well.

Emerson Avenue was coming up on the right. Gabriel set the paper down, rang the stop cord, and got out when the bus stopped.

It was a fifteen minute walk to Emerson Elementary and each of those fifteen minutes was spent thinking about what his next move would be.

"I can't let whoever it is writing those letters win," he said to himself quietly. He kept his eyes to the ground, watching the lines in the sidewalk fall from his field of vision. "I can't let

Redsaw win." With discontentment, he added, "I can't even let myself win. No matter what I do . . ."

Finish what you started. Go till the end. This is your life now. You are Axiom-man. It's what you've been called to do. Finish it. He quickly ordered his thoughts. Once he finished up at the school, he'd find a hidden place in the forest that rimmed the schoolyard's backfield and change into his uniform. After that, Redsaw was his.

———

Joel hadn't called her all day thus far. Every time the phone rang at the Owen Tower office, Valerie hoped it was him wanting to provide some kind of explanation. Each time she answered, she was greeted by a voice she didn't know and someone she didn't want to talk to.

You have to get him out of your head right now, she told herself. *He might call you later.* Then with a smile, *And if he does, he has some serious explaining to do.*

Yet no matter what she did to keep her mind occupied or how hard she tried to shove Joel from her thoughts, he was always there, tugging at her heart, reminding her that he had nearly broken it.

———

Emerson Elementary hadn't changed all that much since Gabriel had gone there. When he opened the doors, though, he was surprised to see it didn't quite line up with how he remembered it. Everything seemed so much smaller now. He had been much shorter the last time he had been there at the end of grade six. It also seemed so much cleaner and more organized. Though jackets and backpacks lined the coat racks to the left and right just as you entered the door, they hung there symmetrically like shades in a kitchen instead of in a mishmash of fabric and straps. The floor was still tiled white and light gray, but bright and pristine instead of off-color like it was imprinted in his memory. The walls were still white but these, too, seemed brighter as if they had just received a fresh coat of paint.

From where he stood, he listened down the halls, checking to see if a class was heading to the music room or gym. His watch read 1:42. It had been so long since he'd been here he couldn't remember when one period ended and the next one began so he thought it best to keep moving. With the kids and teachers inside their classrooms, he could probably conduct most, if not all, of his visit unnoticed.

Pulling the girl's picture out of his inner suit jacket pocket, he studied it carefully, committing what she looked like to memory. Though he was hardly around any kids and wasn't one hundred percent clear about what kids looked like at any given age, he guessed her to be around seven or eight, which would place her in grade two or three. He turned right and followed the twists and turns of the halls. Just as he hoped, outside each classroom was a class picture. To the left of the image, as part of the light blue backboard imbedded in a black frame, was a list of who-was-who by row number. The first picture he set eyes on was for grade one. Just to be thorough, he scanned the smiling faces of kids for the little girl. Not finding her, he quickly moved on to the next classroom, careful not to be seen hanging outside the door. He didn't know what he'd say if a teacher suddenly opened the classroom door and asked, "Can I help you?"

Three classrooms later, he found a grade three picture. The girl was the first he saw.

Talk about a break, he thought.

He produced the picture of her just to be sure. This was definitely the girl. Though her hair wasn't in pigtails in the class photo, the soft smile and little dimples were definitely the same. According to the readout of children's names next to the picture, her name was Tina McGillary. *Not too many kids named Tina anymore,* he mused. As if he knew.

Just then, the classroom door opened and a stout woman with curly tufts of short gray hair asked, "Can I help you?"

———

Once more Oscar Owen found himself short of breath. His heart raced, pounding against the inside of his chest. He'd be going out again tonight, he knew. He *had* to. He needed more power. The door had to be opened.

Leaning back in his chair, he slid a finger in behind the button of his shirt and stroked the tight fabric of his Redsaw uniform. He sighed. "So many people." A sharp thrust of anger slugged him in the heart. His voice dropped an octave. "But it's worth it whether they know it or not. What I'll be able to do—" *—once I find out the truth. I have to be able to control this. Once I know why, why I have to live like this—I will turn it around.* He paused and took a deep breath, still touching his costume beneath his shirt. He thought back to the funeral earlier. Thanks to the paper, he was able to find out *who* it was he had killed. The death that started it all. The death that made his life turn a corner. He had to be there. He was a firm believer in *completion,* seeing something through from start to finish and never jumping into anything in the middle. Oscar was a ground-up kind of guy. It all began with the black cloud. It began anew with Gene Nemek. More than likely, it would end with one of them and since Gene was gone, that left only one possibility.

And Axiom-man. It was Oscar's desire to be like the man in the blue cape that, he presently felt, triggered this whole thing and was perhaps the reason the black cloud came to him to begin with.

But that couldn't be true, could it? There's gotta be thousands out there who'd give anything to be like him as well. There has to be something more. I need to find out. I'll do anything.

———

Gabriel recognized the teacher as Mrs. Balchitzky, a name he could never pronounce right when he went to school here.

Her hair had been brown when he knew her. Same hairdo, but brown. Now, it looked as if the brown had frozen over in silver gray.

"H-hi," Gabriel said.

Her eyebrows went down into a point. "Are you looking for someone?"

"Um, no, not really. I—"

"Gabriel Garrison?"

"Uh, yes?"

The sharp expression on her face melted away and was replaced by a lighthearted smile. She took his hands in hers and gave them a two-handed shake. "It's so good to see you. What brings you here? It's been, what, nearly fifteen years at least."

"Um, something like that. I always have to count backwards in my head when I try and think how long ago it was since I was in grade school." *It's also amazing that you recognize me.*

"So what *are* you doing here?" That was just like Mrs. Balchitzky, from what Gabriel remembered of her. She would never let a question go unless she got an answer.

"Well, it's, um, it's been so long and I was in the area so I thought I'd come by for a visit and see if anything's changed since I last was here." He stole a quick glance up and down the hall. "Yep, things have changed."

"For the better in some cases, for the worse in others. How's your brother? I had him in my class, too."

Gerry, he thought. "Oh, he's fine. He still lives at home with Mom and Pop."

"You don't?"

"No. I've been on my own for a while now. Trying out the whole" —he made quotation marks with his fingers— "'grown up' thing." He chuckled softly. *Some grownup I turned out to be. Can't even hold down a job.*

Mrs. Balchitzky looked in on her classroom. The young faces of her students were expectantly watching the door. Gabriel noticed Tina in the middle of the far row, the only one who wasn't looking at them. She sat there with her hands folded on her desk, eyes on her fingers.

Can it be true? He tried to see if there were any bruises on her but the little girl's hair hung over part of her face, obscuring the finer details of her skin.

"What are you doing now?" Mrs. Balchitzky asked.

Don't lie. "I'm, ah, standing here talking to you, Mrs. Balchitzky."

"Please, call me Verna. You're too old to be addressing me as 'Mrs. Balchitzky.'"

"I, uh, I don't think I'd ever get used to that."

The teacher laughed. "Anyway, what I meant was, what are you doing as a job, or are you going to school?"

"Oh, s-sorry. Um . . . I seem to have found my niche in the call centre industry so that's how I've been spending my days." It was a true enough statement though Gabriel chided himself for having to mislead her. *One lie will lead to another and the next thing you know . . .*

"Is there a future in that? I remember you being so bright. I may have thought you might consider, I don't know, law or medicine when you were old enough."

And there it is. Even now, "grownups" have to always say something about having a proper job. "Those things weren't really for me," he said with a goofy grin. "Um, anyway, I should probably be going."

"Yes," she said, glancing into the classroom again as a few of the kids began shouting. "They're getting restless."

"Well, it was very nice seeing you, Mrs. Balchitzky. Perhaps we'll bump into each other again?"

"That would be very nice." She gave him a warm smile before heading back into the classroom. Before she closed the door she said, "Take care now, *Mr.* Garrison."

Gabriel gave her a good-bye wave with his fingers then turned and walked away.

Less than a minute later, he was out the school doors, heading for the backfield.

Tina McGillary. Tina McGillary. At least now I have a name. School should let out just before four. He'd come back then and tail the little girl home and get the address. After that, he had a letter to write.

Approaching the backfield after all these years set him at unease. It wasn't so much that anything was wrong, but the feeling of déjà vu, the *idea* of having walked toward the backfield time and time again during his childhood and having not done so for so long but suddenly, and unexpectedly, finding himself doing it again made him stop and realize that *why* he was doing it was something he could have never imagined. As a kid, if you had told him that almost fifteen years later he'd be going to the backfield to hide and change into a superhero costume—well, any kid would have jumped at the chance. Who didn't want to grow up and fly around in a costume? But that sort of thing was always reserved for TV and daydreams and playing pretend. Never for real life. Now that he was *actually* doing it, actually doing something that as a kid he had wanted to do but then forgot about as the years went by—who would have known that's how life would really turn out?

"Wait a sec," he said. The backfield wasn't what he remembered it to be. The thick forest that once graced both sides of the property was thin and you could see through the gaps in the trees from one end to the other. *The forest was the coolest part about going here. How could they take that away?* What was left wasn't really a forest at all, but more the *memory* of a forest.

"Always something," he said with a huff. He entered what was left of the green and spotted a thick bush about three and a half feet high. There were a few trees around it; nothing super concealing. *It'll have to do.*

Glancing around to make sure no one was looking and no cars were passing by, he went up to the bush. Then, quickly, ducked behind it.

Changing lying down was a nightmare on its own and he could only wonder what kind of damage he was doing to the only dress suit he had. It was either this or take the bus but by the time he found some place downtown to change, he'd have to double back and find Tina.

And there was something he wanted to do first.

CHAPTER TWELVE

VALERIE NEEDED A break. It was already after 3:00 and she'd
be done work at 4:00. Though she was never one to take her
breaks so close to quitting time, she needed some air,
something to get her away from that desk and telephone and
thinking about Joel.

Not bothering to put on her jacket, she went outside, the
downtown air a welcomed embrace.

———

Axiom-man flew in between the buildings.

What am I doing this for? he wondered. *It's not like it's going to
work.* But he *needed* it to work or, at least, pan out as he hoped.

Deep within, a kind of tug in his heart drew his flight over
to the right. Keeping his eyes on the streets below, he debated
on turning around and heading back to the school so he could
find Tina.

"You can't confront her," he told himself. "You'll scare
the poor girl. She probably doesn't even know who you are so
seeing you, some guy in a mask and cape, she'd probably
scream or something."

Why did everything have to be so difficult? Just for once,
why couldn't something be handed to him?

Don't complain. Your powers were given to you free of charge. He
smirked. *Yeah, but you didn't ask for them. They were just dumped on
you.*

"This sucks," he said. "Never a break."

Suddenly a familiar feeling came over him, one of relief and one he had experienced not too long ago. There, below, was Valerie.

Unable to help but smile, Axiom-man realized he was already heading toward her. Below, Valerie walked down the sidewalk a few paces, turned around, then stepped back toward where she'd just been. As Axiom-man descended, he hoped she would look up and see him. Instead she turned again and moved up the sidewalk.

He flew down and landed behind her, those passing by on the street stopping their stride for a second at his presence before continuing on their way. A few gave him dirty looks, as if they didn't want to have anything to do with him. Axiom-man couldn't help but think it had something to do with Redsaw or at least what Redsaw represented: a man with super-powered abilities. A man who was now a bloodthirsty killer.

"Hello, Valerie," he said.

She stopped, turned, and her face went blank when she saw him.

"Sorry," he said, crossing his arms, "I didn't mean to intrude."

"No," she said, taking a step forward so they were only a couple of paces apart. "I just wasn't expecting to see you."

"To be honest, I wasn't expecting to see you either."

"I've mis—" She didn't finish.

"I'm sorry?"

"Nothing. It's good to see you though. I was wondering" —she came a step forward and whispered— "I was wondering if I would see you again. Up close, I mean."

"I know. I haven't been around much. Around you. I've been busy."

She nodded subtly, understanding. "I've seen the papers. It's everywhere. Redsaw's . . . . I don't know why he's doing it." She looked away to somewhere past him. "Even now there aren't as many people out as there used to be. We're scared, Axiom-man. I'm scared."

"I'm scared, too." *Shouldn't have said that.* Heroes never made their fears known. At least in the movies.

"You are?" Her eyes took in his.

He nodded. "But it'll be all right. I promise you." *And now here you are making a promise you're not sure you can keep. No, mustn't think like that. You have to stop him no matter what it takes.*

"Is . . . is there anything I can do?"

"I don't . . . . No, there's not. At least in regards to that. The truth is—" He stopped speaking when a middle-aged man in a business suit stopped by them and was obviously eavesdropping on their conversation. Axiom-man looked over at him, hardening his eyes. The man cleared his throat as if he hadn't been doing anything wrong and continued on his way. To Valerie, "Do you have a minute?"

"A few. I'm working right now."

Axiom-man looked at the sign hanging behind the door's glass: OWEN TOWER, HEAD OFFICE. "You work here now?"

"How'd you know I just changed jobs?"

Nice one. "I only assumed. So far as I'm aware, this is a new office for Mr. Owen. I can only presume that you just started here, too."

"Well, you're right. Anyway, you were saying?" Her eyes did a hopeful dance.

Good recovery. "You asked if there was anything you could do to help. There is, and I'm not sure how to say it so I'll ask instead and that's . . . can we talk?"

Valerie smiled; her face became radiant, sending the image of twilight's gold straight into his heart. "Sure."

"I'll be quick," he said and stepped up to her. Placing his hands on her waist, he added, "Hold on."

She put her palms against his shoulders.

Not caring what any passerby might think or wonder, Axiom-man rose off the ground and took her with him. A moment later they were on the roof, away from the crowd and the noise of the street. Valerie hadn't let go and he wasn't sure if he wanted her to, but at the same time knew this wasn't a time for intimacy (if *intimacy* was even something they could share right now; nothing had happened between them for anything more than mere friendship to be considered). He took his hands from her waist but kept his eyes on hers. When she didn't let go, he glanced at one of her arms.

"Oh. Sorry," she said and slid her hands down.

Stepping past her, he looked toward the sky and said, "Thanks for being with me now. Please understand that though you and I have never really had a chance to talk . . ." He turned and faced her. "I treasure every time I see you. And I don't mean to alarm you by saying that. I know we don't know each other that well and I honestly don't know how well we can get to know each other given what I am but I just needed to see you." *Okay, you've said way too much.* He just couldn't help himself though. Inside, his heart ached, his stomach swam, his head was full and heavy—too much pressure. Too much for one man to bear.

"I-I don't know what to say."

"You don't have to say anything. I just hope that—and please, don't take this the wrong way—I just hope that I can trust you."

She took a step closer so she was right up to him. "You can tell me anything, you know that, right?"

"I'd like to." Of all the times for his mixed feelings about her to surface, it had to be now. Yes, he adored her completely. Ever since working with her at Dolla-card, she had been all he could think about and that was *before* he became Axiom-man. But not too long ago she had been taken with Redsaw when he first appeared in the city. He honestly wasn't sure if he could trust her and that scared him. He desperately wanted to, desperately wanted someone he could confide in if he needed to. Desperately wanted someone to tell him it was going to be all right.

"Then tell me," she said reassuringly.

The way she looked at him, the way her deep brown eyes seemed like the beginning and end of forever—her tender expression, her lips pursed ever so slightly, ready to speak the words of comfort he so badly needed to hear—oh, how he cherished her. And here she was, ready to be what he needed.

But he couldn't tell her anything. Not yet. Perhaps in time.

Tenderly, he said, "I just needed to see you, Valerie. You've made everything all right whether you know it or not. Thank you."

A puzzled expression came over her face. "I didn't say anything."

"You didn't have to. Just being with me these few minutes made everything okay."

"Oh," she said, blushing.

"Here, let me take you down."

———

Valerie watched as the ground drew nearer. Thoughts of Joel, her doubts about him, about *them*, had vanished. More than anything she wished Axiom-man would change his mind and fly her elsewhere. She didn't care about work. Didn't care about anything. Though it had been a peculiar encounter with the man in the blue cape, it also warmed her in a way she never felt before, in a way that she needed.

When they touched down, she said without meaning to, "We can go somewhere if you want?"

He seemed to consider her suggestion before he answered. "Not right now. Besides, the last time I took you flying someone else showed up and you nearly died."

How could she forget? Redsaw had knocked her out of his arms. "Perhaps when this is over, then?" What was she doing? She was with Joel now. Axiom-man was a mere fantasy, nothing more. She hadn't even thought about him all that much since he flew from her balcony, leaving her alone with her thoughts and feelings. Now she was ready to just take off with him without regard for her job?

"Perhaps."

After an affectionate squeeze to her waist, Axiom-man took a step back, looked up, then ascended into the sky.

Valerie stared after him until he was out of view. When she re-entered the office, Mr. Owen was sitting at her desk, elbows on the table, hands folded together.

"So," he said. "It seems you have friends in high places."

The Past . . .

REBEKAH WAS QUICKLY *escorted out of the town hall and taken to a wagon outside, belonging to the village's doctor, Lucas. Jeremiah sat beside her the whole way home, holding her hand, assuring her everything was going to be all right.*

Groaning, Rebekah said, "I knew this was going to hurt. I just did not realize how much." She squealed and pressed her hands against her pelvis.

"You have to hurry," Jeremiah told Lucas.

With a quick snap of the reins, Lucas beckoned the two huge black horses hauling the wagon forward.

Each bump in the dirt road made Rebekah yelp. "Help me . . ."

"It will be all right, dear. I promise," Jeremiah said.

When they finally reached their home, Rebekah's face was coated with sweat, her breathing labored. The two men carried her inside and laid her on the bed.

"Jeremiah, go get me water and a cloth," Lucas told him.

Rebekah groaned so loudly that her cry sent a tremor coursing through Jeremiah's system. If only he could take his wife's pain away . . .

"Jeremiah!" Lucas snapped.

Jeremiah realized he had been standing there, staring, for the better part of a minute. "Sorry. I will be right back."

He ran to the kitchen and pulled a gray pottered bowl off the shelf above the stove and grabbed a cloth off a pile by the oven. As quick as he could, he darted for the door. The moment he flung it open, he jumped off the front step and soared high into the air, leaping the full distance to the well. Landing hard on his heels, he quickly drew water from the well. Once back inside, he rushed to his wife's side and handed the bowl and cloth to Lucas, who had one hand on Rebekah's forehead, the other on her bare belly. Jeremiah noticed his wife was already stripped from the waist down, her breathing erratic.

"Is this natural?" Jeremiah asked before acknowledging how insensitive such a question was.

Rebekah's eyes were closed, her face pinched in pain.

"No," Lucas said softly. "It seems there are further complications."

"From the blue storm last night?"

"There is no way of knowing."

Rebekah's hand snapped out, clutching Jeremiah's wrist. She grunted then wailed.

Jeremiah crouched down beside the bed and placed a gentle hand on her cheek. "What is the matter, dear? What do you feel?"

Between gasping breaths, Rebekah replied, "It will . . . not . . . come. I . . . can . . . not feel . . . anything . . . below . . . my waist."

Lucas leaned in and said quietly in her ear, "Mrs. Garir? I need to see if the baby is all right, okay? This may hurt, but I have to make sure all is well."

It appeared like she nodded but it was too hard to tell. Her head was sunken deep into the pillow like a stone. Even opening her mouth to pant seemed a chore.

After washing his hands in the bowl, Lucas reached down below Rebekah's belly, a look of concentration on his face. When he glanced up at Jeremiah with heavy blue-light eyes a minute later, Jeremiah knew the news wouldn't be good.

"What is it, Lucas!" he barked. "What is wrong with my wife?"

"Please, Jeremiah, you have to stay calm."

"How can I stay calm when she is—"

"Let me explain. Normally the baby has a chance to turn and get its head into the birth canal. From what I am able to tell, that has not yet happened. The child is sitting nearly sideways inside her."

Just then Rebekah's eyes shot open; she must have heard the news. The looks of worry seizing her once beautiful, caring brown eyes sent a sharp ache through Jeremiah's already ailing heart.

Panic taking over, Jeremiah asked, "What do we do?"

Lucas pressed his lips together. Judging by the way the crease lines easily formed by his mouth, Jeremiah guessed he had to deliver bad news often. After a moment, Lucas gestured for Jeremiah to stand and leave the room with him. Smiling warmly to Rebekah, Lucas said, "We will be right back."

"P-please . . . do not leave . . . do not leave me," she said, coughing.

"We will be right back."

Jeremiah couldn't bring himself to pull his arm away from his wife's grip. It wasn't until Lucas put a hand on his shoulder did he finally have the courage to. His eyes never left his wife's as he left the room. She looked back at him as if she would never see him again.

Concern pierced Lucas's expression. "We have only one option," the doctor said. "I can try turning the baby myself. It is a risky maneuver, one that I have seen performed with success."

"Is there no alternative?" Please, God, let there be one.

Lucas shook his head. "If I do not attempt this, your wife will die and so will the child. Given the position of the baby, there is also a chance the cord may be wrapped around its neck. From what I heard when I pressed my ear to her stomach, the heart is still beating. However, should its neck be wrapped . . ."

"Will she live if you do this?" Jeremiah's voice broke on the last word.

The doctor glanced down at his feet and shook his head. "There is no way to know unless we try. I wish I had better news; I wish there was a better way. I do know that if I do not act quickly, we will lose them both."

"Awwwhhhh!" Rebekah yelled.

Jeremiah and Lucas rushed into the room. Rebekah's arms were splayed out to the side, her back arched, her heels digging into the mattress. Lucas went to her side and felt below her belly.

"Jeremiah, you must decide and you must decide now!"

Oh Lord, why me? Why Rebekah? He had hoped he would receive an answer from On High, but instead received nothing but silence. There was no way out of this save one. Nothing to do but risk it all, risk the lives of the only two people he loved in all the world. His voice cracked when he spoke. "Do it."

"All right," Lucas said, placing a hand back on Rebekah's forehead. To her he said, "I am going to help you and the baby. Jeremiah is going to help me, too." With his free hand, he handed the bowl back to Jeremiah and instructed him to quickly rinse it and refill it.

Jeremiah took the bowl and left the room, overhearing Lucas explain to Rebekah what he was going to do.

With another leap off the steps, Jeremiah flew over to the well and landed beside it firmly. As he reached for the bucket, a blast of thunder startled him. He dropped the bowl against the well's stone ledge, shattering it.

Glancing up, his heart jumped when he saw smoky black clouds forming in the sky.

CHAPTER THIRTEEN

WHILE FLYING TO Emerson Elementary, Axiom-man felt somewhat of a fool after seeing Valerie. He also felt strange about opening up to her so suddenly. It wasn't that he *didn't* want to be completely honest with her—about *everything*—but he had never expected himself to do so today. He had just wanted to see her. There was something about Valerie that made the storm clouds go away, something *soft*, kind and gentle. Something that made him happy. Always had.

I wonder if she even thinks about me . . . Axiom-man. Or maybe even Gabriel. She was nice to me the week before she got her new job. At least, she looked my way now and then which was something she never used to do. What would she think if she knew Gabriel and Axiom-man was the same person? Whoa, slow down there, buddy. You know you're headed for trouble when you start to refer to yourself in the third person. Both *of "myselfs."* He shoved the thoughts from his mind and let the cool breeze rushing against him seep through the pores in the fabric of his mask like a cold shower.

"I have work to do," he said and flew onward.

Not long after, he saw the school in the distance. He arced upward, ascending high enough to be mistaken for a bird. Far, far below the schoolyard was empty. For a moment he thought he might be late but then, echoing off in the distance, were the three distinct chimes of the school bell, a sound he had heard day in and day out for the seven years he put in there. A few minutes afterward, the schoolyard was abuzz with life, the young students like ants swarming an anthill. One of them was Tina. He just didn't know which one.

Not wanting to miss her, he hovered high above the school then, as quickly as he could, dropped straight down so he landed at the center of the school's roof. Given a child's height, he doubted anyone could see him. But they *would* see him if he went closer to the roof's edge, which was something he'd have to do in order to pick Tina out of the crowd. The last thing he wanted to do was attract attention, both from the kids and from the parents picking them up. The kids probably wouldn't know who he was, but the parents would and would no doubt wonder why Axiom-man was at a schoolyard unless something was up.

Should have planned this better, he thought. *I should have changed and waited along the school fence. No one would have paid me any mind. And there's no time to go and change and come back.* Once more he wished he had been given a superhero handbook by the messenger, a handy go-to guide that he could consult when it came to the finer points of fighting crime and living a dual life.

Axiom-man flew straight up and away from the school before turning around. If someone saw him, so be it, but at the very least he could make it look like he was just flying by. No one would think anything of that beyond discussing an "Axiom-man sighting" at dinner time.

Kids joined their parents, others left the schoolyard. So far none of them was Tina. And so far no one seemed to have noticed him.

He was searching the right entrance, he was sure. K to three was on the right from where he hovered, four to six on the other side.

The moments passed by as the schoolyard quickly depleted of young ones excited to get home to afterschool television specials.

"Oh, great. If I missed her, I'm screwed," he muttered.

Kids now trickled out the doors, one here, a couple there. A few lingered in the schoolyard at the jungle-gym, getting in one last slide before heading home.

Then he saw her.

Tina McGillary.

Relief ran through him. He flew up and straight, moving past the school, feigning a flyby. Never letting her leave his sight, he stopped, turned and flew past the school again.

Tina, adorned in a light pink jacket, a dark pink backpack and bright white sneakers, left the schoolyard. She turned left and began walking down Emerson Avenue.

Axiom-man ascended high enough so Tina wouldn't notice him and watched her as she made her way down the long street, stopping now and then to adjust her pack or push her long brown hair out of her eyes.

Nearly at the end of the street, she stepped off the sidewalk and cut across the strip of grass alongside the road. After looking both ways, she waited for a car to pass before crossing to the other side. She went up the driveway of an older-looking house (older for this part of the city, anyway), one with brown paneling and a white door. Tina took the driveway slow, so slow that Axiom-man wondered if she'd ever go in. When she finally reached the door, she stood on the front steps for a few minutes before going in.

Here we go, he thought. He dove downward, arced right then flipped around so he could fly past the house at streetlight level, memorizing the house number.

It was time for step two.

When he got home, he logged onto the Internet and pulled up a 411 page. Typing in the address, he was surprised when he got a different homeowner name than McGillary. The address belonged to a Forrester Greene.

"How's that for a name," he said.

Had Tina gone to a sitter's? He didn't know but for now had to assume she lived there.

He pulled up MSWord and, gloves still on, typed up a brief message of his findings. Above all, he hoped he wasn't being played—or, at least, being *played* anymore than he already was—by handing out other people's information.

Well, it is on 411 for all the world to see. Just hate doing other people's detective work, he thought.

He wrote:

Her name is Tina McGillary, but I assume you already knew that. I tracked her to 484 Emerson, which, according to 411, belongs to a Forrester Greene. That's all I've been able to find out.

Please don't ask me to do anything illegal.

I won't.

He printed the message off and placed it in a blank white envelope. He ran the tip of his gloved finger under the tap so he could moisten the glue line then sealed it shut.

Now all he had to do was wait until later to drop it off in the recycling bin in the lobby.

———

"Man, I don't like this," the youth in the black toque said.

"What was that, Truck?" the other, a young fella in a blue baseball hat, said.

Truck, who got his name for favoring big vehicles, shifted back and forth on his feet. "I said, I don't like this, Hearty."

Hearty—in turn named for his barrel-like chest and burly laugh—pulled the crowbar back from the Monte Carlo's door lock. "Oh come on. Don't tell me you're scared."

"Scared? No, not me. Except that being out here at ten at night is no different than you and me covering ourselves in blood and swimming in a shark tank."

Hearty looked at him quizzically. "You been reading again? That almost sounded like a meta—meta-fur."

"Meta-*phor*," Truck said. Then, adding quietly, "Idiot."

"Huh?"

"Nothing."

"Look, the longer you stand there and babble, the longer this is gonna take. Gimme two secs to focus and we should be safe and sound inside this thing."

A.P. FUCHS

"Of all the cars to lift" —Truck glanced around the Impark lot— "there's a bunch of others here. Some with more class than this two-bit piece of junk."

"Yeah, and it's those high profile cars that attract attention. Now are you with me or are you not?"

"Fine. I'll wait."

"Atta boy."

Hearty crouched down and fit the straight end of the crowbar into the small space where the lock met the door. "This thing should just pop right out and—"

There was a loud *thunk* as something landed on the Monte Carlo's roof.

"Going for a ride?" said a cold voice.

———

Axiom-man took a deep breath as he flew over the city and allowed the cool night air to fill his lungs. So far tonight, everything was quiet. Folks were still heading indoors early, not wanting to be caught out and about with Redsaw on the loose.

Another pass over Portage then Main and then I gotta drop that envelope off, he thought.

He should have done it before going out on patrol, he mused. Would have saved time instead of breaking up his routine. *I could stay out later. Don't have to get up for work tomorrow.* The sharp pang of failure pierced his heart for the umpteenth time that day. He still had no idea what he was going to do aside from the traditional job hunt, but with bills due soon and his bank account hovering just above zero once rent was factored in—*Gonna have to cash out some RSPs or something. Why couldn't this crimefighter gig come with a wage of some kind?*

A siren went off in the distance, very faint, probably a good five or six kilometers away. He wondered what it was for. Despite being around them fairly regularly for the past four months, he still had a hard time distinguishing between police sirens and the drones of ambulances or fire trucks.

Have to look that up online or something. Now that I'm not working, might as well use every spare moment I can to be the man the messenger's called me to be. The messenger. He had to talk to that guy. And soon. Redsaw had to be stopped. Axiom-man just didn't know how. And, at present, there was nothing that could temporarily incarcerate Redsaw and keep him at bay.

Adjusting his course to the direction of the siren, Axiom-man paused mid flight when an explosion went off not far behind him. Doubling back, he increased his speed and headed straight for the flickering glow of orange and yellow in the parking lot below.

Landing near a white car in flames, he felt his heart stop then start beating again when he saw Redsaw holding a teen in a blue baseball cap by the collar of his jacket. The teen was on his knees, his posture like a man begging for his life. Held high above Redsaw's head with his other arm was another young fellow, one wearing a black toque even though it wasn't winter. Redsaw had this one by the neck.

"Let them go!" Axiom-man shouted and stepped toward them. After only two paces, his stomach went instantly nauseous, reacting to Redsaw's presence. *Ignore it. Shove it down. Deep down.*

Redsaw turned his head slowly toward him and glared.

"Redsaw, I'm telling you right now, let them go."

The fellow in the black toque said, "Yeah, listen to him. Let us g—" And was silenced when Redsaw squeezed the guy's neck good and hard.

"Redsaw!" Axiom-man growled and ran toward him.

The man in the black cape grinned and, with a powerful torque of his arm, hurled the one in the black toque high into the air as the young man made a choking sound. Axiom-man flew up after him and caught him. When he lowered him to the ground, he expected the young man to plant himself firmly on his feet. Instead the youth's legs were like noodles. And Axiom-man knew why.

The guy was dead, his windpipe jutting out of his throat.

151

Gently, Axiom-man lay the youth on the ground. If Redsaw harmed the other so help him he'd . . .

The car that was ablaze let off a high-pitched whistle and the windows blew out. Axiom-man noticed a crowbar stuck next to the lock on the driver's side. Immediately after, the entire vehicle exploded, sending the car nearly five feet from the ground. It crashed back down in a deafening metallic crunch, sending a wind of fiery heat against them all.

The young man in the blue cap, still on his knees before Redsaw, wailed in tear-choked screams, something Axiom-man didn't expect yet the outburst seemed natural all the same.

"Don't kill me, don't kill me," the guy said. Redsaw looked at him. "Don'tkillmedon'tkillmedon'tkillme . . ."

Axiom-man kicked off the ground, ignoring the want to throw up from Redsaw's presence, and plowed into the man in the black cape with both fists. Redsaw went flying back, taking the youth with him. Axiom-man tried to wrestle the young man free but Redsaw's hold on the fellow's collar was too strong.

Why isn't Redsaw saying anything? he wondered. The sudden sharp stench of smoke filled his nostrils. Redsaw's hand was aflame with red energy, the power burning the young man's jacket and searing the flesh beneath.

Quickly, Axiom-man powered up his eyes and let forth a blast at Redsaw's hand. Redsaw howled the second the energy pierced him, and let go. The young man fell backward but not before Redsaw twisted and hurled a ball of red energy from his other hand, straight at the young man's head. The youth's face instantly melted and his hair went ablaze.

"No!" Axiom-man screamed and went to grab the boy. He threw his cape over the youth's head, snuffing out the flame. When he pulled the material back, he saw he was too late. The boy's nose and mouth were seared shut; no air could possibly get in. The youth began to shake, his legs kicking and his arms pawing at Axiom-man for help.

"I-I can't . . ." Axiom-man started but couldn't think of anything to say. Moments passed, and he didn't know what to do. *Hospital! I have to get him to a hos—*

The youth twitched then arched his body, as if trying for one last gulp of air before the lights went out. The body relaxed and moved no more. Axiom-man checked the pulse. The young man was dead.

Redsaw looked on.

"Why?" Axiom-man asked, looking up at Redsaw.

"Because," he replied in that icy voice of his, "I have to know."

Have to know? "What do you—"

Suddenly Axiom-man's world turned bright red as Redsaw sent an explosion of fiery energy at him. The blast slammed into his chest, sending a shock wave of burning pain throughout his entire torso like a red-hot element forced upon his skin. He soared backward through the air and landed hard on his tailbone several feet away. Axiom-man wasn't sure what hurt more: the dull, throbbing ache in his tailbone that was now invading his lower back, or the stinging heat against his chest.

This isn't right, he thought and he wasn't referring to getting hit. The problem was, the blast from Redsaw actually hurt. Before, getting hit by Redsaw's energy was only a momentary discomfort. Now, it seemed, there were aftershocks. *Unless he was holding back the last time we fought.* He doubted it. The last time they fought, destroying a large portion of the intersection at Portage and Main, Redsaw had been out for blood.

No mercy, Axiom-man resolved as he got to his feet. He staggered a step to the right before regaining his balance.

Redsaw ran toward him, fists ablaze, that haunted red covering his gloved hands.

Losing himself to the moment, Axiom-man filled his eyes with blue energy, building and building it until he thought he could no longer restrain the power's awesome force. Through the bright haze of blue that covered his vision, he could barely make out Redsaw's form. The second Redsaw was about to hurl another fistful of red energy at him, Axiom-man shot forth a brilliant blue beam of raw power into Redsaw's middle. The man in the black cape howled as he flew backward into the air and onto the burning remains of the car.

Immediately, Axiom-man took off from the ground and flew into him, ignoring the heat of the burning vehicle. Fortunately, the fire wasn't so great as to be unapproachable. Redsaw clawed at him. With a quick swat of his right hand, he hit Redsaw's arms away and delivered a punch with his left to Redsaw's nose. Blood oozed out from beneath Redsaw's half-mask immediately. Axiom-man slugged him again, this time with his right hand, hoping that the force of the blows would be enough to render Redsaw unconscious.

With a loud scream, Redsaw rammed his fists into Axiom-man's chest and knocked him into the air. Axiom-man landed on his back and was thankful he managed to keep his head up enough so the back of his skull hadn't slammed into the pavement.

The sound of sirens whirred in the distance, their volume growing as they drew nearer. Axiom-man never thought he'd be so glad to hear the sound of the police.

But what are they gonna do when they get here? he wondered. *Nothing, that's what. Even I can barely get close to Redsaw without nearly getting killed.*

Back on his feet, Axiom-man grabbed onto Redsaw just as the man in the black cape was about to deliver another fiery blow. Axiom-man stopped Redsaw's fist mid-swing and delivered a kick to Redsaw's right knee. Redsaw's leg bent, causing his body to bend forward and to the side. Quickly, Axiom-man sent his foot against the side of Redsaw's head, sending his adversary spinning through the air and crashing into the wooden fence that bordered the Impark lot. The wood broke from the impact and it took a moment for Redsaw to get back on his feet.

Cop cars sped onto the scene but didn't come into the lot itself. Instead, the six cars Axiom-man could see surrounded the lot's border like an army preparing for a siege. Officers were out of their vehicles in no time, guns raised. Axiom-man wondered if Jack Gunn was among them.

An officer spoke through a bullhorn just as Redsaw came flying back to the battle. "Stop what you're doing. We have you surrounded. If you do not cease, we will open fire."

Before Axiom-man could say, "No, don't. You don't know what you're doing," Redsaw tackled him to the ground. The next thing he saw were green stars against a field of black when Redsaw delivered two fast, hard-knuckled punches to his head.

"You can't beat me," Redsaw growled. He sent another fist flying, this time to Axiom-man's jaw.

Axiom-man thought he felt his jaw dislocate then fall back into place but before he could be sure, another shot nailed him in the neck. Gasping for air, he powered up his eyes again and sent an energy beam into Redsaw with enough force to get the man off him. He didn't care where he hit him.

"This is Sergeant Jack Gunn, Winnipeg Police." Jack's voice rang from the bullhorn loud and clear. "You two are under arrest for murder. This is your last warning before we open fire. I repeat, stop immediately!"

Head swimming, stomach upside down and backwards from being so close to Redsaw, Axiom-man forced himself onto his side, gasping for air. His neck ached like nothing he'd ever felt, *more* than when his brother, Gerry, accidentally threw a softball into his windpipe while playing catch when they were kids. Wanting to puke, Axiom-man forced himself to focus. He was on his stomach now and suddenly dead weight landed on top of him, sending his face to the pavement.

"You have no idea what you're up against. I am *more* than what you've seen before. I'm stronger and faster and . . . more powerful," Redsaw said.

The dark tone of the man's voice sent a jolt of uneasy alarm through Axiom-man's body. The way Redsaw rasped the words it was if . . . it was as if it wasn't Redsaw speaking at all but something—or some*one*—more sinister, more evil than anything he'd ever encountered before.

"It . . . doesn't . . . matter . . ." Axiom-man said. He spat the blood out of his mouth. The wad landed against the inside of his mask and coated his lips. "You have to . . . stop . . ." He could kind of breathe, but not greatly. Just enough to keep him conscious.

With a grunt, Axiom-man did a push-up, lifting himself from the pavement. Redsaw sent him back down, sprawled out, right away.

"This is bigger than you could possibly imagine," Redsaw said. "And you're standing in my way. Tonight, Axiom-man, you die."

Shaking and oddly feeling cold, the thought of death suddenly became welcome. His life was in the sewer—no job, no girl, some stranger knew his secret identity; he was bleeding, hurt and his partially-healed ribs were now broken anew. Death seemed like a good idea.

Axiom-man felt heat somewhere behind him. Was it Redsaw's fist powering up for the fatal blow?

No, I can't give up. Can't stop. The messenger . . . the world . . . Winnipeg . . . Then, very clear: *Valerie—They need me.*

"Get up!" he commanded himself. With all the strength he could muster, he jerked his legs up underneath him so he was on his knees. At the same time he put his palms beside his shoulders to do another push-up. Redsaw rocked on his back. Not allowing Redsaw a chance to deliver the kill, he embedded his hands partly in the pavement as he pushed his body upward. Utilizing a strength he didn't know he had, his hands and knees left the ground and he soared up and up and up. Redsaw fell off and tumbled toward the ground before flipping his body over and flying upward. He knocked into Axiom-man just as the cops began emptying their pistols. The shots rang out; Redsaw sent three fiery blasts down to the squad cars below. The vehicles blew up in brilliant fire balls of orange and yellow, their flames engulfing the surrounding officers.

"No!" Axiom-man shouted and grabbed hold of Redsaw.

The two titans flew skyward, higher and higher until the carnage below was nothing but an orange dot lost in a maze of city streets.

Axiom-man drove fist after fist into every open spot he could find on Redsaw's body. Redsaw grunted as he received each blow then suddenly grinned maliciously before setting red, fiery hands to the sides of Axiom-man's head. Axiom-man's vision went a wild purple; he had been powering up his eyes in bright blue when the red surrounded him. Ignoring the pain not just in his head but in his whole body, he grabbed hold of Redsaw's wrists and tried to lower the man's hands.

"This . . . ends . . . now!" Axiom-man yelled and tugged Redsaw's hands away. A sudden swoon of dizziness engulfed him and the inside of his mask became immediately wet as he brought up the food in his stomach. The putrid stench of barf was enough to make him throw up again. He had to take his mask off, drain it, otherwise he wouldn't be able to breathe. Yet, if he did, Redsaw would know who he was. Wait a second . . .

The two of them were still rising. The air was frigid and getting thinner. Axiom-man arced his body backward, enough so he could get his legs up and under Redsaw and kick him off. Giving it all he had, he slammed his heels into Redsaw's ribs and sent the man in the black cape hurtling through the air. Momentarily safe, Axiom-man reached up and tore away the bottom of his mask. The puke blew out immediately and his wet lips froze when the cold air hit them.

They were so high up, at least thirty thousand feet if not more.

Barely able to breathe, Axiom-man searched the skies for Redsaw.

All he saw were the clouds of night, the stars and the moon.

He heard the faint cackle of laughter on the wind.

CHAPTER FOURTEEN

SERGEANT JACK GUNN ignored the teasing prods of his subordinate officers as he made his way to his office. No matter how many times the guys working the desk asked, "So, did you catch them yet?" he made a conscious effort to pretend he hadn't heard anything. To entertain their sarcastic remarks and rude questioning (especially to a superior officer) would only result in an upset he wouldn't want to have to explain to his bosses.

In his office, Jack draped his jacket over his chair, sighed and sat down. The ever-present cup of coffee he kept beside his keyboard was cold. He sipped on it anyway, too lazy to skirt the room outside to the coffee machine against the far wall.

The clock on the wall by the door read 11:56 P.M. If it hadn't been for the media circus after the "incident" at the Impark lot, he would have been back here a lot sooner. Also, if it hadn't been for shoving the microphone back in that reporter's face, he would have been back here sooner still.

"What a waste," he grumbled and slouched in his chair. Pinching the bridge of his nose, he couldn't believe that once again those costumed yahoos got away. Even worse, *Redsaw* got away. "What kind of a stupid name is that anyway?" he added. *So his costume's got jagged red marks all over it. So what? Whoever named these guys . . .*

Axiom-man had been there and from what Jack had been able to see, the man in blue had held his own, though he wasn't sure what became of him once the two guys took off into the air. As much as he hated to admit it, Jack hoped Axiom-man was all right. At least *he* was the lesser of two evils.

Face it. You hate them both but only Redsaw has given you enough cause. The guy's a murderer, pure and simple. That one's easy. Axiom-man, on the other hand . . .

Ever since that costumed do-gooder had come on the scene a little over four months ago, Jack had been hesitant about his arrival. Yes, Axiom-man had done a lot of good. A few of the regular perps who gave the Winnipeg Police a lot of grief over the years had suddenly stopped their dealings, presumably for fear of receiving a super-powered punch to the face. Yet others, it seemed, had come out of the woodwork, cocky guys who thought it might be interesting to take on the most powerful man in the city and, if they got away with it or came out on top, have something to brag about to their friends.

Redsaw was the root of his trepidation toward Axiom-man, he knew. Only days after appointing himself Winnipeg's newest protector had he gone ahead and killed someone. Axiom-man and Redsaw—those two guys, judging by what they could do, were more similar to each other than Jack cared to admit. If one could lose it and go on a mass killing spree, who was to say the other wouldn't be far behind? As far as he was aware, the two could have some elaborate scheme planned out: gain the public's trust, then break it and, when the time was right, unleash their wrath on the city.

Not while I'm in charge, Jack thought adamantly. But, he wasn't *really* in charge now, was he? He was just a police sergeant, worked the major crimes unit, and didn't have the same pull with the department the chief did and, given the rate things got done in the W.P.D., he wouldn't see the chief's badge for years. *I'd be fifty by then, past when I'm scheduled to retire.* Only if that old codger, Chief Boulette—the "bullet;" someone with a cop-like name worse than his own—had a heart attack or something would he actually have a shot.

Tonight had been a mess. Two more murders, destroyed vehicles, slaughtered cops, an embarrassed squad of survivors and, worse, an even more embarrassed police sergeant.

"Not anymore," he said and reached for the phone.

Mayor Charles Jones didn't sound too pleased when he picked up on the other end. "You got five seconds to get my attention or so help me you're fired for waking me up."

"Hey, Chuck, how's it going? It's your old friend Gunn here with a bit of disappointing news."

The mayor cleared his throat and Jack heard the creaking of bed springs in the background. "Don't tell me something happened and there isn't a certain man in jail."

"You're becoming a mind reader."

"Watch your tone, Sergeant. I'm still in charge despite our friendship. You told me after that debacle with your son that you had a plan to take these guys out. Both have cost me. Both. Especially Redsaw. You have no idea how that idiot in the red suit is making Winnipeg look nationally."

"And you have no idea how that schmuck is making me look locally." Jack straightened himself in his seat and leaned against his elbow on the desk. "I need resources, Charles. I have none. I got unseasoned cops looking for the big arrest and that's it. Zeal is fine but it's useless against guys who could level a whole city block if they wanted to."

"You can't come to me with this. You voice your concern upward first, the next rung on the ladder. They take it to the top."

"I need a favor, Chuck. I won't pretend to know how the city spends its dimes. What I'm asking for is for some of those dimes to be thrown my way. What I'm looking to create is a special task force specifically trained to take down these guys. If not—"

"You don't need to remind me. You already gave me the speech before. Twice, actually. Don't make it three."

"Then you already know what I'm going to say."

"Yes, and you already know what I'm going to tell you." Mayor Jones's voice grew stern. "Go through the proper channels."

"That could take weeks, if not longer!"

"If I give you a handout, you and I will both be out of a job."

"No one has to know. I've seen you close the curtains on some things and open them on others and no one's none the wiser."

"Watch it, Jack, or I'll have your badge."

What was the use? Charles wasn't going to budge. "Fine. Just don't blame me if you suddenly have a body count on your hands larger than anything you could have imagined."

Jack slammed down the phone, hoping the abrupt end to the conversation would give the mayor something to think about.

———

More than anything Axiom-man wanted to die. He hurt all over, his ribs screamed and his insides were still shaking with the nausea from Redsaw's presence. To just huddle up in a ball, drop from the sky and let the impact kill him—the thought was almost too tempting to ignore. But, deciding to be the man he had been called to be, he pressed on home, flying as fast as he could so he could make his midnight deadline.

Changing out of his costume was almost worse than getting slugged repeatedly by Redsaw. When he raised his arms, his ribs reminded him they weren't just broken, but likely shattered. Raising his knees to roll down the lower half of the one-piece dark blue tights forced his thighs to scream in objection.

He couldn't believe he threw up inside his mask. He also couldn't believe he had no choice but to rip it off his mouth so he could breathe. The idea that he now had to spend more money on a new outfit when he was out of work was just as revolting. It was either eat or conceal his identity and it looked

161

like he was going to have to starve unless he dipped into his savings, the little he had, and a habit he didn't want to get into.

Putting on a black pair of sweats and matching sweatshirt, Gabriel went to the hall closet, grabbed a pair of thin winter mitts, put them on then went and retrieved the envelope with his findings on Tina McGillary. He put on his glasses, took his keys and wallet and went out the door.

Slowly, he hobbled to the elevator. The little shake the elevator gave when he hit the bottom floor was enough to send his whole body into a series of sharp aches. He checked his watch: 11:58. He hoped that whoever was going to come and pick up the envelope wasn't early lest they should see him like this. He also didn't want to confirm for them, though they evidently knew about his dual life, that he was in fact Axiom-man.

Making sure the coast was clear, he went to the recycle bin, dropped the envelope in between the bin's inner wall and the newspapers within, then did a U-turn and made his way to the side door. He was tempted to hang around the corner by the front lobby and see who would come by. Then he remembered the warning: *Do not wait around for me to come. If I see you, your identity will be revealed. This will all go smoothly if you obey.*

Stepping out the side door into the night air was like being reborn. The cool wind blowing past the building was enough to refresh him and dull the pain that threatened to take him while he made his way to the emergency room.

He could only wonder what might happen once he got there and how he was going to have to explain his broken ribs and the bruises on his body.

———

The doctor hadn't been impressed and, it felt, had handled Gabriel roughly, like a dog that had again disobeyed its master. The excuse? The truth. Gabriel told him that Redsaw had come after him and nearly killed him, and if it hadn't been for Axiom-man, he would have been dead.

"If it wasn't for the headlines everyday, I wouldn't believe you," Dr. Carnen had said.

Gabriel's ribs hadn't been shattered, only re-broken, the places where the bones had begun to heal snapped anew. The bruises, he was told, were to be treated with ice regularly for the next twenty-four hours or until the swelling went down. The cuts were cleaned up and by the time Gabriel had left the E.R. hopped up on Tylenol 3s, the only question he couldn't give a solid answer to was why the police hadn't brought him in or an ambulance, considering the damage to his body. Fortunately a nurse had come into the examining room right then stating someone had just come in with a gunshot wound. Carnen left the room in a rush, leaving Gabriel sitting on the examining table for ten minutes until he guessed he was free to go.

Outside, Gabriel headed to the nearest bus stop. As was the habit tonight, he checked his watch. It was 2:13 A.M.

Have I been in there that long? he thought. "Great, the buses aren't running, not till morning."

The Past . . .

THE BLACK CLOUDS *covered the sky in a matter of seconds.*

Rebekah . . . *Jeremiah thought and ran toward the house, forgetting that he would have got their sooner had he merely taken the distance between him and the front steps in one leap. At the steps, he instinctively bent at the waist and covered his head when a loud* BOOM *shook the night air. Above, red light flashed behind the enormous puffs of charcoal-black.*

The clouds began to descend.

From inside the house, he heard Rebekah screaming, then Lucas say something to her loudly, something about her needing to "Stay still" and "Not worry."

Jeremiah jumped up onto the top step, the ball of his foot landing on the step's edge, not finding a foothold. He tumbled backward, his shoulder blades taking the brunt of the fall along with the back of his skull. Dizziness swept over him and his stomach twisted within, making him want to throw up. He lay there for a moment, trying to catch his breath and make sure he hadn't been injured. The nausea didn't pass and instead grew in intensity.

The sky looked down upon him, the black clouds roiling as if being spun by a wooden spoon in a bucket. More red flashes then a bright fiery one that stole the darkness from the sky for a split second. WHAM! *The thunder's crash shook the earth and echoed on the air for several seconds. Head spinning, he rolled over onto his side but not before catching sight of a series of small black clouds separating from their enormous counterparts above, speedily descending toward the earth.*

"Rebekah! Lucas! Help!" he shouted, his cries masked by another resounding boom of thunder.

His stomach swam, his insides ached. It was as if something within him was clashing with whatever was going on around him. Feeling the little he ate that day making its way up through his system and into his throat, he finished rolling onto his side and threw up. He grimaced when done and made another face when a putrid-tasting burp escaped through his lips.

Heart racing, he rolled onto his back. Jeremiah's arms shot out when a black cloud sped down toward him. Three more followed behind this first one and slammed into the front door, quickly seeping into the wood. Those three were no doubt inside, about to claim Rebekah and Lucas and . . . the baby.

"No!" he shouted. Just as he sat up, the first black cloud finished its race toward him and plunged into him.

Bright blue light covered his eyes and a fleeting thought of somehow blasting this cloud out of himself came to mind. Power surged within him and the blue faded from his vision. Still sitting, he glanced down at his hands when he felt his palms tingle with . . . something. Like water snaking its way along a table from a spilled mug, so did fiery red light travel along his skin, covering first his palms and then his fingers.

Jeremiah shot to his feet, feeling new, almost reborn.

Screams rang from the town not far away.

The baby . . . Rebekah . . . he thought. Then as if in counter to the desire to go in and see if his wife and child were all right, a sense of apathy came over him and a strong urge to take to the sky and explore what seemed to be a change in gifts. No, I cannot. I must not. "I have to know if they are alive." Those clouds! Three had gone into the house. His heart turned within him and a deep sense of calm washed over him. Rebekah, Lucas and the baby would be all right. Those clouds would take care of them. Those clouds would help them.

Unless . . .

Hands shaking, Jeremiah growled and sent forth a blast of red fire from his fingers, blowing through the heavy wooden door to his home like a wind through hay. If anything happened to his wife and child, he would kill . . . . His eyes grew wide when he finished the thought: I will kill Lucas. After all, Lucas, the great doctor, was responsible for them.

Jeremiah stormed into the house, his footfalls loud and firm. His brow furrowed, jaw set, he had to keep clenching and unclenching his fists

165

to keep this sudden rage at bay. He couldn't lose Rebekah. The baby, though he loved it, he didn't really know it. It was still a baby in name only. But Rebekah, his sweet wife, his lifelong companion and best friend—if anything happened to her, those responsible would surely pay. He would kill whatever killed her.

Even if it was the baby.

The whoosh of flame filled his ears; so did the sound of something hard smashing into wood, making it splinter.

In his peripheral he saw a red glow coming off his hands when he entered the room where Rebekah lay. The mattress was in tatters around her body, the straw within scattered about the room, bunches of them shriveled and burned. Where Rebekah's hands lay on the mattress, so were black scorch marks. Whatever had happened to himself had happened to her.

Lucas sat against the wall across from the bed, the wall above his head missing in places. In his arms he held a blood-soaked blanket, cradling something within.

When he glanced up at Jeremiah, his eyes were glazed over, the skin around them red and puffy. "I am sorry, Jeremiah. I could not help it."

CHAPTER FIFTEEN

MAGICAL MOMENTS RARELY came for Valerie Vaughan, but as she rode with Joel on the elevator up to his condo Thursday night, she knew this was one of them. Something was in the air; something good, something special. It reminded her of the eager anticipation for Christmas morning while growing up, that sense that something wonderful was awaiting her if only she'd hang on a little longer.

Joel had insisted on picking her up. After the newspapers devoted three pages to what had happened at the Impark lot, no one in the city felt safe. Joel even mentioned on the ride back to his place that it wouldn't have surprised him if Redsaw jumped on the roof of his car, tore it away and threw him to the pavement. Valerie's heart quickened at the thought of something happening to him. What they now had, though not utterly and completely perfect, to lose that . . . well, she was afraid she'd lose her heart completely if she lost him. It was already enough effort to let him in once more. She didn't think she'd be able to do it again, if it came to it. Not to him. Not to anybody.

They arrived at Joel's floor. With a sweeping hand, he gestured for her to get off the elevator first, holding the door back so it wouldn't close on her.

"How chivalrous," she said with a smile.

Stepping out into the hall, she quickly smoothed down her red dress beneath her open ivory overcoat, the wavy fabric cut off at the knees. The ornate, dark wood-framed mirror across from the elevator allowed her to check her hair, something that she had spent nearly an hour making to look *just right*. She only

167

hoped Joel would comment on it, or at least her dress. He hadn't so far. Yet.

The two made their way to his condo and went in. Joel took her jacket ever so delicately. She reveled in the way it slid off her shoulders. For a second she thought that when she turned around, he would kiss her. Instead, when she did, he was hanging her coat up in the hall closet, and then hung up his own.

"I'll be right back then I'll give you the tour," he said and disappeared into the kitchen that ran off the main hallway.

No sooner did she remove her shoes than he reappeared, his white collared shirt beneath a slightly fuzzy dark gray sweater partly hidden behind a stark white chef's apron. Valerie couldn't help herself but laugh.

"Yeah, I know, I look like a goof," he said, bowing slightly at the waist, "but it's either this or I get dinner all over myself."

She chuckled some more. "I think it looks cute."

He came up beside her, arm bowed; she placed her arm in his and he led her down the hall, pointing out his office and the bedroom at the end.

"Then there's the linen closet, the one where I keep odds and ends instead of 'linens' like my mom would like," he said with a smile, pointing to the door at the end of the hall. "Nothing to see there." They turned around. "And here, on your left, is the bathroom, if you need it."

They headed back in the direction of the kitchen and when they entered it, Valerie was taken aback by how spacious it actually was. She could fit two or even three of her own tiny apartment kitchens just in his. There was room for a table, chairs and an island with pots hanging over it in the middle.

"Nice," she said, though she wished she had said something more complimentary than "nice." It wasn't nice. It was *beautiful*.

"And here," he said, leading her into the front room, "is where I spend most of my time."

Valerie's breath caught in her throat. She had seen gorgeous homes before in magazines and on TV, but this—

this was just absolutely stunning. The living room had two levels, one about a foot higher than the other. To the right, the higher side, was the dining area, complete with a huge cedar table, a mini bar and a large mirror. Running alongside the table was an enormous window that opened up onto a balcony. From what she could see from where she stood, the city view was incredible, each building of Winnipeg's main downtown area clearly visible, the moon hovering in just the right place above the rooftops.

To the left in the sunken living room was two couches, both black leather and both full-sized (no loveseat), and a La-Z-Boy recliner chair. A glass table stood atop the dark beige carpeting in the middle, all the furniture before a big plasma-screen TV on the wall. In behind the couch on the left was an antique wall unit. From what she knew of Joel, it didn't seem his style.

He must have caught her looking at it because he said, "It's my mother's. She said I needed something to spruce the place up, make it feel 'more at home.'"

"I like it," she said.

"Really? Well, it's yours if you want it." He offered her a smile, which she returned in kind. "Anyway, why don't you nose around? I had something warming in the oven and I'd hate to have it burn on me."

———

Oscar Owen sat in his study, slumped in his chair. His original plan when coming home was to work on his latest ebook, but after turning his laptop on, he found himself suddenly drained, not so much of strength, but of the inner will to live.

How much longer? How many more did he have to kill before he'd be able to pierce the very fabric of reality and open the *door*?

He hadn't heard from the voice in a long time. He couldn't remember the last time he'd received instructions from it.

Despite the power the murders gave him . . . he hated having to do it. Looking at himself in the mirror every morning was becoming a task. More than anything—*anything*—he wanted this to end. Why couldn't the voice just tell him what he needed to know? Why did the voice insist on *showing* him instead? The regret, though having been partially absent for a time, came back full force.

"What's the difference?" he called out to an empty house. Then, quietly, "Why all the secrecy? Axiom-man . . . he has it so easy. He found his calling, it seems, and knows what his powers are for. And there's something . . . different . . . about him. There's—" He couldn't quite put his finger on it but Axiom-man seemed more . . . powerful . . . somehow. Certainly not in strength or speed. He knew that much. Axiom-man fought the same as he had the last time they exchanged blows. Whatever was different, it was deeper. It was his *powers*.

Oscar wished he could remember the exact moment when he sensed the change in Axiom-man. Well, he remembered the *moment*, the *feeling* of it, but not *when* he noticed it. There was a second there when a bright blue spark seemed to burst forth out of Axiom-man and just as quickly disappear, the spark something, he figured, that only he saw and Axiom-man didn't. Or, if Axiom-man did, didn't make anything out of it.

There's power in him, Oscar thought. *Strong power. For a second there, I felt . . . connected . . . to him somehow. As if we both came—or, at least, our abilities—from the same source.* What that source was, he didn't know. The voice, perhaps? But then why would the Redsaw side of him yearn for death and destruction, and Axiom-man not? *So far as you know, anyway. Perhaps he's able to keep the urge at bay, to suppress it somehow. Perhaps he's like me. I didn't know about the darkness until that day at the Forks. Perhaps Axiom-man's inner tendencies haven't been revealed to him for whatever reason.* It was questions like these and all these second guesses that made him long for the doorway—if that's what it was—to open. Then, and only then, would he finally get the answers he was searching for.

"I need more power," Oscar said. "And I can't wait. Not anymore. I've been patient enough."

Death was the only way for him to gain his strength. That much had been made abundantly clear. And with each murder, the easier it was to tear the fabric of Time and Space and peer into the dark.

I need to speed this along.

Maybe killing Axiom-man was the answer. With Axiom-man out of the way, perhaps whatever power that was in him would transfer over and Oscar would have both. Perhaps then the *light* and the *dark* of these powers would cancel each other out and finally—finally—he'd be able to control himself. He should have killed Axiom-man when he had the chance. Instead, he found himself flying off in the end, and not out of retreat. It was compassion and . . . fear, but not fear of Axiom-man. Fear of what might happen should Axiom-man die. They had fought hard in the air, exchanging blow after blow. If he had kept it up, he could have killed him. And if he had, where would he be now? Would he finally be balanced? Would he finally be able to master control over his urges or would he be, if the "canceling out" theory was true, completely powerless? He remembered their battle in CanWest Global Place and, for a moment there, the deep sense of loss when it felt like Axiom-man's energy beams were stealing his powers.

He shuddered.

"No," he breathed, "I can't lose this. I was chosen for a reason. I'm *needed* somehow. I've just lost my way. I can fix this. I can *beat* this."

Oscar sat in the dark of his study, a palm over his eyes, blocking out the light of the moon seeping in between the cracks in the wooden blinds. The minutes ticked by, though he wasn't paying careful attention to the passage of time. All he wanted was an answer, the knowledge of how he could become powerful enough to open the *door* and receive all that he'd been searching for.

Murder.

Anger.

Death.
Murder.
Axiom-man.
Rage.
Despair.
Murder.
Axiom-man.
Blood.
Destruction.
Murd—
He got an idea.

———

As girly as she knew it was, Valerie felt herself melting away in front of Joel. Together they descended the steps leading into the sunken living room, a glass of red wine in each of their hands, Valerie's stomach full from the dinner. Roast chicken, re-stuffed potatoes, corn niblets and Caesar salad—oh, so good. Even now, her heart was still aflutter from Joel's thoughtfulness and care in preparing the meal, his way of making it up to her for not showing up for lunch the other day. When he had set her plate before her, her breath caught in her throat when she saw, there, atop the potatoes, two strips of parsley in the shape of a heart. Did he really care that much? She knew he cared, but she hadn't been sure he really cared-*cared*. Now . . .

He led her in front of the leather sofa, his hand gently pulling hers along. Should she sit? Stay standing? Should she wait till he started to sit then follow his lead? Would it be like in those romance movies where their movements would match each other's and, after a moment of dreamy hesitation, they'd sit at the same time?

Joel smiled at her tenderly. Then his expression changed to one of puzzlement. "I didn't burn the chicken, did I?"

Valerie laughed softly. "No, it was perfect. Too perfect, actually. Just right."

His expression eased. He added, "There was something I didn't tell you during dinner."

"Uh-oh." Her thumb and first two fingers squeezed against her wine glass.

"I've" —he glanced away— "I've been keeping something from you." He looked back at her then down at his feet. "Oh, how should I say this?"

Valerie put a hand on his shoulder. "What?"

"It's just that" —his eyes met hers— "I know magic, you know?"

She smirked and put a hand on her hip. "Really."

"I really should have said something. I'm sorry. It's just that . . . it's just that I didn't want to ruin our evening by bringing up something of such magnitude."

She arched an eyebrow.

Joel set his wine glass down on the table then put both hands on her shoulders. "Careful now, stand just like that." He gently turned her so she was facing the wall with the plasma TV. Without taking his gaze from her face, he slowly lifted his hands then clapped them twice. A soft whirring filled Valerie's ears and the light beige wall beneath the TV separated. Rolling out on a small set of tracks came a steel-framed fireplace. Two distinct flames burst into being atop an ornamental log, bathing the room in a soft yellow glow.

Laughing, Valerie put her glass down and covered her mouth with both hands. For some reason her eyes watered. She said, "Too smooth." Then her eyes met his and in a sultry romantic voice added, "You have me captivated. I'm yours. Completely."

Joel grinned and together they sat down on the sofa.

The two watched the flames and the minutes melted away.

Joel broke the silence. "I'm really happy, Val. *More* than happy, actually. This . . . *you're* everything I—this is everything I could have ever wanted. I'm so sorry again for messing it up the first time."

"Don't . . . don't worry about it, okay? What's done is done. We're here now." She paused. "I'm really happy, too. I honestly wasn't sure where this would go but, it seems, it's going some place—oh, how can I say this?—warm? Good? Just simply some place better than the last time."

He adjusted himself so he was facing her head on. "So is it safe to say we're a—and this is only the lawyer side of me coming out, the me needing something 'on paper'—but is it safe to say we're a couple then? An item? Just you and me, like before?"

Adjusting herself, too, she said, "Yeah, just like before."

Joel drew himself closer and she did the same. Together, they leaned in close and their mouths lingered just before each other's.

"I don't want anything to change," he whispered.

"Don't worry," she said. "Nothing will."

Their lips came together and time became meaningless again.

———

Gabriel had remained in his front room all day, fixing up his costume as best he could. Reconstructing the mask—like the first time he created it—was a complete pain, the hardest part finding the right length for the thin elastic that ran through the forehead portion of the mask. It had to be tight enough to stay in place but not too tight as to leave a red crease along his skin afterward. What's more, he forgot how he had cut the eyeholes and did the trim inside them so the fabric wouldn't fray and had to keep going back to his damaged mask to see how he had done it. Home-Ec had never been his strong suit in junior high. He found himself constantly going to the Internet for aid—just like the first time he made his suit—hoping he'd learn something about sewing that would help him improve his skills and "upgrade" his costume somehow.

And when I can afford to make a few more, I'm gonna have to be extra sure these things remain sturdy and don't tear so easily. Maybe I should change fabrics? he thought.

He had kept the computer on, hoping that the messenger would somehow sense his plight and visit him and provide guidance.

Even at now at eleven at night, the messenger still had not come.

———

Around midnight Valerie asked Joel to take her home. As much as she didn't want to leave, she had work in the morning and Joel had also mentioned, while they spoke on the couch, that he had a 6 A.M. meeting.

Leaving his condo was the hardest part. When he helped her with her coat and it settled on her shoulders, it felt more as if he had heaped a sac of bricks on her instead.

The car ride went by so fast Valerie thought Joel had taken a short cut to her place. But, no, it had been the same route he took after coming to get her. Joel did seem strangely silent, however.

Is he scared? Did I *scare him?* She so badly wanted this commitment between them, this relationship and the decision to not let it fall apart like it had the last time, to work. *Maybe he's just tired? Yeah, that's it. Has to be.* Though she knew there was something more to his silence because she knew *him.*

Joel pulled the Mercedes-Benz up to the front of her building, paused a moment after setting the car in park, then got out and rounded the vehicle to open up the door for her. Valerie got out and Joel took her hand in his. She flashed back to the first time he walked her home and how now, like then, everything seemed so new yet *familiar* between them.

At the top of the steps, he asked, "Did you have a nice time?"

"Of course I did," she said. "Tonight was . . . . I'm just so glad that . . . . It was perfect, Joel. Really."

His face became fragile. "I, um . . ." He took a deep breath then said quietly to himself, "Okay, out with it."

"Uh-oh."

"You and your 'uh-ohs,'" he said, smiling.

"What is it?"

"Well, I . . . I just don't like waiting so I hate for this to be the first thing out of my mouth right after I took you home, but I figure I might as well say it and see what happens."

"I've said it once, and I'll say it again: uh-oh."

"Maybe." He took her hands in his. Her legs wobbled beneath her as an electric charge of affection raced through her hands, up her arms and flooded her whole body. Joel took another deep breath then said, "I can't make it tomorrow night."

"What?" She withdrew her hands from his. "Why?" She wasn't mad. Not yet.

"I got a call today from Mr. Gordon, one of my partners. They just acquired a huge case and tomorrow night he's taking the client out for dinner to go over the details. He wants me there."

"You said you'd come. I was really counting on you to be there, Joel."

"I know, it's just that this is such a huge deal, both the case and who this client is. The fact that Mr. Gordon and Mr. Fox want me there says how important this is. Normally, we just trust each other regarding what clients we take on; smaller ones, I mean. The big ones always require a joint decision."

"Can't you cancel it or say you have plans?"

He shook his head. "Not with Gordon."

Heart plummeting to her feet, Valerie turned away. Tears wet the corners of her eyes. If this was six months into their relationship, she would understand. She'd encourage him to go and make do going to Mr. Owen's party without him. But after tonight, after she and Joel decided to make it last this time, after walking on air this beautiful evening—She didn't want to let him see her cry. She forced herself to speak. "It's okay. Go."

"Really? I feel terrible, Val. Downright awful. I mean, after all I put you through before, I just don't want you thinking I'm doing it again. Pushing you away, I mean."

But isn't that what you're doing? "Just . . . just tell me one thing." She turned around and faced him. "Was tonight all a ruse? Something to soften me up before you . . . before you said—"

"No. Not at all. I just wanted to let you know how I felt about you. I mean, again, if I burned the bird, it's because—"

"I'm being serious for a second."

"Sorry. Honestly" —he held her arms in his strong hands— "I wanted to be with you tonight. I wanted to see you. I wanted to hold you. I just wanted . . . you."

Valerie bit her lower lip and she felt a tear slip out of the corner of her eye.

"I love you, Val," he said.

She smiled a little but wasn't sure what to think or feel. Moments passed then finally Joel pulled away.

"You'll be all right?" he asked.

Valerie wasn't sure.

CHAPTER SIXTEEN

VALERIE FELL AGAINST the inside of her door after she entered her apartment. Head spinning, she hit the light switch, turning on the landing's light, and slowly lowered herself onto the carpet lining the floor. She rested her forehead against her knees, her purse still wrapped around her arm.

Sniffling, she now wondered why she had even gone to Joel's in the first place. She had wanted to see him. More than anything. And it had been worth it. While she was there, she felt like Cinderella, someone who had been so alone, so hurt over the pain others had inflicted upon her, someone who had finally gotten a shot at happiness. But, like Cinderella, it was destined to be temporary and when midnight rolled around, it was all pumpkins and wishful thinking again.

It wasn't so much that Joel wasn't going with her to Mr. Owen's ball that got to her. Though she had desperately looked forward to spending a romantic evening with him and showing off the new dress she bought the other day, that wasn't the problem. It was the "set up for the fall" that Joel seemed to have instigated tonight. Despite his reassurance that the evening hadn't been a way to soften her up before he delivered the hurtful blow, she couldn't help but wonder if he had been honest with her about that. The thing with Joel was, he had a knack for telling people what they wanted to hear, had the ability to give them what they wanted so long as in the end he finally got his way. He had done the same thing to her back when they first dated and now it seemed he was doing it again.

Old habits die hard, she mused while wiping her eyes.

Leaning the back of her head against the door, she glanced up, the bright light from above her landing piercing her eyes, the tears amplifying it so she had to look away.

"What am I supposed to do?" she groaned. "I was so happy, and now . . ." She took in a sniffling breath. "I just want a guy who'll always be there for me, where it doesn't always have to be some soap opera where I never know when I'll be left hanging."

If she had been any other girl, she would have done what all girls did in a situation like this: change into her pajamas, pull out a tub of chocolate ice cream, then get on the phone with a friend and vent her frustrations. But she wasn't like any other girl. She had resolved not to be way back in junior high when she decided not to be like the other girls who had nothing better to do but look pretty for boys, travel in packs and set their individuality aside in the pursuit of teenybopper happiness. She had paid the price for that decision, however. Her friends list had been limited to two others, both of whom she lost contact with in high school. She then acquired a few new friends, ones who were friends in name only. The deep connection between them was nothing more than a dream. After high school, though she still talked to them once in awhile—well, once she started working, even those friendships fizzled and the closest thing she now had to a best friend was her mother, but even then, that relationship wasn't all that close either.

"Should I call Mom?" she asked. *Forget it. Mom never liked Joel to begin with. She doesn't even know that we're seeing each other again. She'll probably say, "See, told ya, Valerie. Guys like him always let you down. Why'd you even bother giving him a second chance in the first place?"*

For some strange reason, Mr. Owen's words from earlier that day came back to her. "I'm really happy you're coming tomorrow night. And I'm equally happy you're bringing a lawyer from Taylor, Fox and Gordon. They're high profile. Not to scare you, but this'll be quite a media circus. I hate them, but it's good for business." Valerie suspected that despite Mr. Owen's protests that the media would be there, he also relished in the attention. There was just something about him that said so.

So now I'm expected to bring a date even though my date canceled? Wonder if I told him at the office tomorrow that mine bailed on me if he'd understand?

"Couples make for healthy front pages," Mr. Owen had also said. "Individuals leave a feeling of wanting, like something's missing." Then, firmly, "And there's nothing *missing* regarding the Owen Tower project. Got it, Ms. Vaughan?"

"Yes, sir," she had said.

Valerie stood and paused a moment when her legs went rubbery beneath her. *So now I promised to bring someone. I am so screwed.* There was no one to bring. Not even a guy friend who could pose as her date. She needed this job and didn't know Mr. Owen well enough to know if he'd hold her coming alone against her.

Heart quickening, anger at Joel beginning to rise again, she set down her purse and removed her coat. Her makeup had probably run and she dreaded the idea of seeing herself in her bathroom mirror looking something like a zombie. Just another reminder of what Joel did to her this evening.

All smoke and mirrors, she thought, *and I don't care if I'm making something more out of it than it really is.*

"And I need someone to bring."

She took off her shoes and put them in the hall closet along with her coat. When she closed the closet's door, an idea hit her.

"If I do this, I'm never going to forgive myself," she said.

———

The pain had returned full force about ten minutes ago. Gabriel had popped back a couple more painkillers then lied down on the couch in the dark of his living room. Even now, just like it had been when he lived with his parents, he still preferred the couch to his bed. And his parents always had something to say about that. "Beds are for sleeping, couches are for sitting," his dad used to say. Gabriel never believed his dad's statement for a minute. If his dad had been correct, then why did lying on the couch feel *so* good?

Body sore, he forced himself to lie on his side. His thoughts drifted and when they came back, they came back as a single idea: *The caretaker! What if it's her? She has the key to my place. What if she's a snoop and was rummaging around in here while I wasn't around and found my costume? The person from the note said to leave the envelope for them in the recycling bin of my building.* It certainly made sense. But so did the idea that someone from the apartment block across the way saw Axiom-man repeatedly land on a balcony to this building and put two and two together.

If I get a job, I'm getting a house, he decided. *One outside the city without neighbors.* Then, *Yeah, right. I'd have better odds getting struck by lightning than getting a job that'd pay me enough to support a mortgage.* He took a slow, deep breath, careful to not aggravate his sore ribs. *Anyway, get some sleep. Tonight you'll stake out the Greene residence and see what else you can find. And today you're waiting for the messenger. That guy better show up.* Gabriel didn't care if the messenger heard the curt tone of his thoughts (if the messenger could read minds, that was). The messenger needed to know that he needed him. Now more than ever.

Gabriel had never been one to fall asleep the moment his head hit the pillow. Mind racing, he often had to wait till he thought every thought before he'd finally drift off to sleep. Now, since deciding to fully dedicate himself to being Axiom-man, he made an effort to quiet his mind and *not* think of anything.

A minute later the shrill ring of the telephone made his body jerk. He looked at the clock. It was almost 2:00 A.M.

"Who's calling so . . . ?" His midsection objected as he sat up.

The phone rang two more times before he was able to get to it.

Since losing his job, he hadn't had much contact with anybody (except for doctors), spending most of his time as Axiom-man. He cleared his throat and reminded himself that he was Gabriel Garrison now and he had to sound like him. "Um, h-hello?"

No one responded but the ambient noise in the background made it clear someone was listening.

"Hello?" he said again.

"Hi." The voice was female.

"Uh, hi. Um, how can I help you?"

"Gabriel, it's Valerie."

It was like someone had hurled a brick into his chest. His heart went into overdrive. *Oh no!* "Is something wrong? Is everything okay?"

Valerie grunted, annoyed, but softly enough to let him know it wasn't at him. "No. I am so, so sorry for calling so late. I hope you're not mad."

"N-no. Of course not. I'm just, um, concerned. You've never called here before. How do you, uh, how did you get my number?"

"The shift trade list from work, in case we needed to swap with someone last minute."

"Oh, right." He had never bothered to print the list out for fear he'd be tempted to call her for any reason *but* to trade shifts. "I thought you didn't work at Dolla-card anymore?"

"I don't, and that's not why I'm calling anyway. I, uh—I feel terrible for calling you so late. I honestly didn't mean to but I thought I'd call now instead of later this evening because by then it'd be too late. I was going to try you at Dolla-card early today but, as you know, you can't always get in touch with who you want to talk to. Again, I'm really sorry."

"Oh, please, stop apologizing. It's okay."

"Were you sleeping?"

"Yes." His heart ached from lying to her, and so easily, too.

"Anyway," she continued. Then she paused, as if her next words would be detrimental somehow. "I . . . I have a favor. A *huge* favor."

"Well . . . you . . . you are okay, aren't you?"

"I'm fine. I'll be better after you hear me out and hopefully you will—I mean, *can*—help."

"Okay."

"Okay," she breathed. "I'll just say it and we can go from there."

"All right."

She spoke so softly that he had to press the receiver hard against his ear to even catch half of what she said: ". . . metonight."

Met-o-night? What was—? "I, uh, didn't quite get that, Valerie. Can you repeat it, please?" he said.

There was that grunt again and this time it was at him. "I said, I need someone to come to a function for Owen Tower—I work there now—and I was wondering if you'd like to come with me tonight?"

Gabriel stopped breathing. His heart stopped beating, too. Mind blank, pain suddenly absent from his body, he couldn't do anything but stare at the blank wall in his kitchen.

Valerie jolted him back to reality. "Did you hear me? I know it's short notice but, like I said, calling later today wouldn't have worked and I'm really in a jam. I'm supposed to bring someone and the person I was going to bring bailed on me late tonight and I really need some help, and I figure since you've tried asking me out in the past you probably wouldn't object to me asking you for this now and . . . . Oh, I shouldn't have said that last part, now, should've I?"

Someone else? Who? As far as Gabriel knew, Valerie wasn't seeing anyone, and she never let on while he worked with her that she was. Or maybe it was just a guy friend who said he couldn't make it last minute?

"Gabriel! You're supposed to answer someone when they talk to you."

"S-sorry, Val. Um, Valerie. I'm just . . . um, honestly, I'm really surprised you called, that's all. Nothing personal, of course, it's just I always thought, you know, that I never mattered to you and . . . . I guess I shouldn't have said that last part, either."

"No, you shouldn't have. But what do you say? Wait, before you say anything—Look, first and foremost, we're going as friends, okay? I just really need your help."

Gabriel thought about Tina McGillary and how tonight had been meant for getting to the bottom of the mystery of the letter. But a date with Valerie? Even just as friends? For so long he'd wanted this and now that the opportunity was sitting right before him—though not the way he ever expected it to come about—he knew he couldn't say no. Axiom-man . . . . *He* had to come first, didn't he? Wasn't that all part of *getting serious* about this? Axiom-man first, Gabriel Garrison second. *I've played it that way. I'm out of a job to prove it. This could be my only shot with Valerie.* "O-okay."

"Great. Get a pen and I'll give you my address. You can pick me up at six."

"Um, Valerie? I, uh, don't have a car."

"Oh, you don't." She seemed disappointed. "Tell you what, I'll meet you there. Got that pen?"

The Past . . .

A HEADACHE BEAT against the inside of Jeremiah's forehead. His eyes were squinted so hard he could barely see Lucas sitting there, cradling the baby in his arms. There, on the bed, lay Rebekah, her eyes closed, her black hair matted and sweaty, her upper body peaceful above hips and legs coated in blood and torn flesh.

Hands flaring up with bright red fire, Jeremiah took two stomping steps over to Lucas and tore the baby from his arms, tossing the swaddled infant onto the bed near its mother. The baby wailed and Jeremiah blocked out its cries. He didn't even care if it was a boy or a girl. With one powerful hand, he grabbed Lucas by the collar of his shirt and yanked the doctor to his feet. At first, Lucas didn't struggle, but when the doctor was slammed up against the half-destroyed wall, suddenly two strong hands planted themselves on Jeremiah's wrists and began to push down.

"You killed her!" Jeremiah screamed so harshly that his voice scraped against the back of his throat. He lost his breath.

Lucas applied intense pressure on Jeremiah's wrists, forcing Jeremiah to lower him so his toes touched the floor. "The baby would not come. She would not follow my instructions, would not let me attempt to turn the baby."

"Liar! She wanted that baby more than anything. She would have given her life for it. She—" The realization that Rebekah was dead struck him anew. Growling, Jeremiah set both hands around Lucas's neck then pushed upward with all his might, throwing Lucas straight up and into the ceiling. Lucas's body broke through the wooden beams as though they were twigs and landed with a thud somewhere on the roof.

With a shout, Lucas reappeared by the hole in the roof then jumped, the force of his weight crashing down sending pieces of floorboard up in the air.

Operating solely on instinct, Jeremiah thrust out his glowing hands and let loose a blast of red fire into his friend. Lucas reacted just before the flame hit and jerked up his forearms, creating a field of fire of his own, blocking the onslaught of flame.

Jumping off the floor, once more choosing to ignore the wailing cries of his child on the bed, Jeremiah dove into him. Both men somersaulted through the air and crashed into the wall. The roof above came tumbling down, showering the men in shards of wood and tiny splinters.

Lucas delivered a swift hook to Jeremiah's jaw, sending his head craning back and to the side. Ignoring the sharp pain racing up and down his neck, Jeremiah punched down with both fists into the other man's face.

"I will kill you!" Jeremiah screamed.

The baby cried. Jeremiah almost hated himself for being thankful that it was still alive. If the baby hadn't been in his wife's womb, she would not be dead and none of this would have happened. Instead, she had been cursed with a complicated labor and now lay in a pool of her own blood and flesh on the bed that was once their haven after a hard day on the field.

The two men wrestled and began floating upward to the hole in the roof. Jeremiah didn't care if they ascended to the stars themselves as long as Lucas paid for what he'd done. The beat up and broken floor of his once heartfelt bedroom began to sink away. Just past Lucas's growling glare, was the baby, lying with its mother, its tiny face scrunched and coated with tears, its little mouth wide, letting forth all the sadness it had within.

Up they rose until they were just above his home.

Lucas struck him again and Jeremiah returned the punch in kind with one of his own.

Head throbbing, chest rumbling with an anger he had never known nor ever felt, Jeremiah decided to end this now instead of continuing to rise. He came in with both fists to either side of Lucas's head; his knuckles blazed with pain the second bone struck bone. The doctor's eyes rolled in their sockets . . . but he was still breathing.

Just as Jeremiah was about to repeat the same skull-crushing blow, his ears picked up shouts and angry screams from the town beyond.

His breath caught in his throat when a crash of thunder resounded on the air, silencing all.

186

Blue clouds faded into existence over them, covering the entire night sky with their amazing blue brilliance.

The lightning came down.

Bright beams of spiky blue ripped through the sky and shot at the earth below. Screams filled the air.

Distracted, Jeremiah didn't notice Lucas reposition his hands and quickly found himself now underneath the doctor. A fist connected with his face and another with his neck. Gasping for breath, Jeremiah let this new power he had been given flood into his hands, igniting them bright and red. About to blast the head off his former friend's body, a spear of bright blue lightning shot toward them, coating them with unearthly radiance. Whatever vigor and enthusiasm this new power gave him was quickly silenced and the fire on Jeremiah's hands extinguished.

Feeling as if the very life of his soul was oozing out of him, Jeremiah fell with Lucas down through the hole in the roof just as another spike of blue lightning raced passed them and struck somewhere below.

The baby. The lightning must have hit it.

"No!" Jeremiah screamed as he and Lucas hit the floor with a body-numbing thud.

Back crying out in pain, head spinning and headache full blown, Jeremiah tried to glance up toward the bed to see if the child was all right. From the angle he was at, he couldn't see. He didn't even have the strength to roll Lucas's unconscious body off of him.

As blackness began to encase his field of vision, Jeremiah saw something else fall from the sky as the bright blue clouds faded away.

A man made of pale blue light.

CHAPTER SEVENTEEN

AXIOM-MAN YAWNED BENEATH his mask as he soared over the city. It was Friday afternoon and he had been up since just past five that morning. Try as he might, he couldn't get his mind and racing heart to slow down after Valerie's phone call. Why she had called him—more so, why she had *invited* him to Mr. Owen's gala—he had no idea. As far as he was aware, Gabriel Garrison, to her, was just another schlub who worked at Dolla-card. Yes, they had been friends, though *friends* wasn't exactly what he would have called it. More like daily acquaintances, if there was such a thing. During the last week she had worked there, she had glanced to where he sat several times throughout the day. The most he ever thought of it— given the fact she ignored him ninety-nine percent of the time—was that perhaps she had a question for him or needed something or, very, very remotely, wanted to be friends at *work*. Her calling him had previously only existed in his dreams where he fantasized about her calling him up and asking him out.

Is it possible dreams come true? I mean, look at me. As a kid I dreamed about flying around in a pair of tights saving the day and, here I am, doing it, able to do things no one else except one can. The thought was comforting and encouraging. But the idea of Valerie, the only girl he couldn't help but adore, actually being interested in him—Gabriel—seemed too farfetched, even for someone like him.

He could easily envision Valerie swooning over Axiom-man, who in and of himself was a kind of "real life fantasy," but for someone like her—so pretty, so forthright, so . . .

unbelievably terrific—to be interested in a call centre geek like Gabriel Garrison . . .

"Stranger things have happened," he said to himself.

After having been unable to quiet his mind that morning, he forced himself out of bed, made coffee and drank it while double checking his repair work on his uniform. The suit looked as good as new.

Deciding to make the most of his day—and avoid hitting the online job listings (job-searching had never been his strength and the idea of sending out résumé after résumé made him shudder)—he suited up then put on a sweat suit over his uniform. Thinking that perhaps it *was* someone from the apartment block across the way who knew his secret identity, he resolved to no longer enter his suite via his balcony as Axiom-man. At least until the mystery was solved.

He changed in an alleyway not far from his home and hit the skies, hoping that an over-the-city flight would calm his nerves and burn off the excess energy surging through his system that seemed to be constantly replenishing itself. After being in the air for only five minutes, he considered going back home and *not* seeing if Axiom-man was needed. If Redsaw also happened to be about and they got into another scuffle, he could only imagine the selfish regret he'd feel if he had to miss out on being with Valerie tonight because he was in the hospital yet again. But reminding himself of his private vow, the promise that it was now time to become responsible regarding his abilities and the path he chose for them, he pressed on.

The morning hadn't been quiet, but it had been simple. There had been a car accident on the Midtown Bridge and the drivers involved—two stocky men with thick arms—got into a fist fight. Axiom-man broke it up and remained with them until they cooled down and the cops showed. A woman had had her gift bag swiped by some punk in a bandana. The punk—who really wasn't a punk but was actually a guy who appeared to be in his mid-thirties—had been stopped and the gift bag returned to its owner. The bandana-wearer then got a quick flight courtesy of Air Axiom-man to the police station. A blind man's dog had broken free of its leash. The dog, too, was returned to its owner. The biggest event had been a convenience store robbery. Axiom-man had heard the alarm from the air and swooped down just as three young teens fled the store. Subduing them and getting them to the police hadn't been a problem.

All in all, a pretty uneventful day in comparison to everything else that had been going on.

He considered looking into Tina McGillary's house on Emerson. The little girl would be at school so there was nothing he could do about her, but perhaps her father would be out and he could peek in the windows and see if anything stood out. The idea of breaking in and looking for anything suspicious did cross his mind, but the thought quickly left him when he realized that he *couldn't* break in even if he wanted to.

Axiom-man couldn't break the law.

He banked right and did a quick survey of the Exchange District below, his mind flashing back to the dead man found on the roof of the Grain Exchange building. He searched the skies, envisioning Redsaw flying around somewhere in the distance. He wasn't. Axiom-man wasn't sure what he'd do if he'd seen him. The man in the black cape . . . . Anger burned like a fire of blue flame deep within Axiom-man's heart and soul. Jaw set hard, eyes tensed around their edges, he wished for Redsaw to show up so they *could* have it out.

Instead, the skies remained clear.

Around 3:00 P.M., fatigue from last night's absence of sleep slugged him in the head like a pair of boxing gloves filled with sand. He headed toward home, wanting to nap before heading out to see Valerie.

After changing back into his sweat suit in the same alleyway as earlier, Gabriel briskly walked home. He checked his mailbox, half-expecting another letter from his mysterious "fan."

Nothing, he thought. *Besides, they slip their letters under the door.*

He headed straight for his answering machine upon entering his suite, not even bothering to take off his shoes. Hopefully, Valerie had called. *Why* she would call, he couldn't think of a reason, but one could dream, couldn't they?

There was only one message.

It was from Rod Hunter.

———

Oscar got into his car around 4:00 P.M., happy not to linger at the office any longer than he had to. Being the workaholic that he was, tearing himself away when there was still "just one more thing to do before the day was out" was always difficult. The way he saw it: if he let that one final task remain incomplete, then the next day he'd have two "one final tasks" to deal with. If he let those slide, then there'd be three and so forth. After a six-day work week, which he always put in, sometimes seven, that would be at least six things he could have gotten done, six more steps toward growing his company.

Today will be the only exception, he thought. *You need this thing to go off without a hitch.*

If the media, who would no doubt attend tonight's ball, gave it nothing but praise in the pages of the papers tomorrow, the publicity that could buy for him and his firm would be worth shirking "one final task." It would be worth that step backward in exchange for going who knew how many steps forward.

Oscar turned on the ignition then turned it back off. *I could leave the car here and fly home. I'd get there fast in turn allowing me more time to oversee things before tonight's ball begins.* He reached for the door handle then stopped himself. He knew that if he stepped out of the car and donned Redsaw's black mask, he'd open a door within himself, a pathway that would almost certainly lead to murder. *Exercise control. Take a deep breath.* But the power within called to him, begged him to be switched on so Redsaw could soar. Whatever beast had been awakened, whatever savage creature that had been fed with each murder—it

191

yearned for another kill. Its appetite for death and power—who could satisfy it? Oscar wasn't even sure if he'd be able to control it much longer. The desire to split open the fabric of Space and Time was so strong—so *overpowering*—he knew he had to act fast and satisfy the darkness's hunger. He had to open the doorway and discover why he was chosen and what his purpose was.

"After tonight's event, you can go out," he told himself. He glanced in the rearview mirror and was shocked to see a film of sweat shining on his forehead. He wiped it away.

Hoping to distract himself, he reached for the copy of today's *Winnipeg Free Press* on the seat beside him and began to thumb through it.

It wasn't long before he found an opportunity to open the Doorway of Darkness on one of its pages.

———

Gabriel chose to take the bus to the Fort Garry Hotel, not wanting to fly there, which would mean stuffing his freshly ironed black suit into the backpack he wore beneath his Axiom-man uniform. As he approached the stone steps leading up to the hotel, he took a deep breath and waited for his speeding heart to slow. He checked his dress shoes for any scuffs, bent over, and with a bit of spit on his thumb, wiped a mark away. After he stood, he straightened his shiny purple and gray-striped tie and double checked the collar to his off-white button-down, ensuring his costume was safely beneath and out of sight. Adjusting his glasses so they sat more comfortably on his nose, he went up the steps and prepared himself for an evening with the girl he adored.

According to Valerie, he was to meet her in the front lobby, where she would give him his ticket and together they would make their way to the ballroom. No sooner did he enter the main doors and push through the revolving door than he stumbled over his feet on a corner of rolled up carpet. Arms flailing out to the sides, he caught his balance and in his peripheral saw Valerie standing in the middle of the lobby, rolling her eyes. She turned away, pretending she didn't know him

Talk about a grand entrance, he thought.

He had to do a quick dance to the right when a couple of people pushed their way through the revolving doors, nearly knocking him over.

"Uh, sorry," he said, raising his hand, index finger poised as if asking a question. He adjusted his suit—the same one he wore to Gene's funeral—and went over to Valerie.

When she turned to face him, his heart stilled and a rushing calm swept over him, the type of serenity one could only feel in the presence of the only person who could steal their heart.

So badly he wanted to say how beautiful she looked, her dark brown hair done up in gorgeous swirls above her head, with a few loose strands hanging down in ringlets in front of her ears, forming to the contours of her soft jaw, accenting her face in such a way he'd never seen on any woman before. She wore an ivory overcoat, which was open, revealing a black, form-fitting dress underneath. Her legs were clad in black pantyhose that flowed smoothly into a pair of shiny black high heels with straps around her ankles. Over her shoulder hung a long-strapped, matching black purse. His mind felt like it was melting away and he forgot where he was . . . and even who *she* was. Whoever she was, she was stunning, beautiful, utterly and completely amazing. He wanted to tell her how magnificent she looked. He yearned to compliment her in a way that would make her blush just so he could see her smile softly and her cheeks flush red.

He said, "Jeepers, you look like my mom did when she and my dad got married."

The room went silent and Gabriel thought he heard crickets chirp somewhere in the background.

Valerie gave him a cross look. "Excuse me?"

Nice one, Doofus, he thought. *Your mom looked terrible when she got married.* "What I meant was . . . um, you look—you look great."

"Thanks. Now let's go." She took him by the arm and led him to the dining room/ballroom off the lobby. "I do appreciate you coming—"

"Sure thing, um—"

"—and if you do anything to embarrass me, you're a dead man."

CHAPTER EIGHTEEN

JUST OUTSIDE THE ballroom was a coat check. Gabriel fumbled for his wallet but the young lady working the counter said coat check was free, courtesy of Oscar Owen.

Still reeling over that stupid comment about how Valerie looked like his mom on her wedding day, he tried to be a gentleman and help her take off her coat. She handed him her purse and he nearly dropped it on purpose. She rolled her eyes again. He could tell by the ridgedness of her arms that she was uncomfortable with him helping her take her coat off, but his father had made it clear during his pep talk on dating that you were to *always* be a gentleman when out with a woman. You helped her with her coat, you opened doors, you pulled the chair out for her when she was about to seat herself at a restaurant.

He watched as Valerie's overcoat slid off her smooth, bare arms. Her dress was open in the back, held to her small body by a pair of black straps that sat equidistant from her neck on her shoulders.

Wow.

Gabriel took her coat and handed it to the young lady at the counter. After he got the hanger number, he offered the little slip of paper to Valerie. "Or do you want me to hang onto it?"

"No, I got it," she said and took the paper from him and slid it into her purse. "Here's your ticket." And handed it to him.

Before he could even read the ticket printed on the heavy stock, die-cut, embossed paper, Valerie was already making her way to the ballroom doors.

She glanced over her shoulder and said, "Are you coming?"

"Uh, yeah," he said and caught up to her.

Just outside the doors, she said, "Now listen: I don't mean to be rude by saying this because, again, I appreciate you coming, but please let us try and have a nice night. I've been doing nothing but creating a good impression for Mr. Owen since I started working for him and I'd really like to maintain that. I'm not saying you'll ruin anything, but I have to make it clear we're here as friends. Deal?"

His heart ached at hearing that last part. Though he knew full well Valerie didn't think of him as anything more than a friend, he still wished she would give him a chance, Axiom-man abilities aside.

But, if all else fails, he thought, *you can always sweep her off her feet while wearing the cape.* He made a mental note to ask her about how she felt about Axiom-man, just in general, before the evening was out. He just hoped there'd be an opportunity somewhere in the conversation for that to happen.

Putting on his best smile, Gabriel came up beside her and bowed out his arm, hoping she'd take it. His body gave a soft shudder when she did, one of utter contentment.

"Okay, here we go," she said. And they entered.

———

For the first half hour, Gabriel spent his time admiring the antique ceiling and the huge chandeliers hanging in the middle of the room while Valerie wandered about, he at her side, finding who she knew and saying hello to them. Each time she found someone, she always introduced Gabriel at the end of the conversation, as if his presence there didn't matter at all. If he didn't feel the way he did about her, he would be appalled at how rude she was being to him. But knowing that he as

Axiom-man had spent some pleasant moments with her drove those thoughts away and brought him some comfort. He just wished she didn't constantly try so hard to make it clear she wasn't interested in a relationship with Gabriel Garrison. He already knew that.

Once the rounds around the room were done, Valerie checked her ticket and together they went to the table they had been assigned. When Gabriel sat down, he counted the silverware twice, finding it somewhat silly he had three forks, two knives and three spoons.

"They're not all for the meal," Valerie pointed out.

"One salad, one dinner, one dessert—all forks," he said with a grin.

"Charming," she said. "But you're right and I'm surprised you knew that."

"What does that me—"

The room erupted into applause when a man in a tailored dark navy suit with thin white stripes approached the podium at the front of the hall. His black hair was neatly combed and gelled, his gaze piercing. Remembering him from outside the funeral chapel and countless news articles, Gabriel recognized him as Oscar Owen.

"That's him," Valerie whispered, leaning over to him. "My boss, Mr. Owen."

Gabriel nodded. "Sharp looking lad."

Valerie made a face at the dumb comment.

Careful, buddy, he thought. *You don't want to be too much of a goof in front of her. Don't overdo it!*

Mr. Owen tapped the microphone once, checking to see if it was on. It was. "Ladies and gentlemen," he said with a charming smile, "the press and those I work with each and every day, thank you all for coming. I won't bore you with a lengthy speech but before we have our meal, I just want to say that tonight marks a historic event for my company, Owen Enterprises. Owen Tower has been under construction for sometime now, and tonight is the opportunity not to honor just my company, but rather what Owen Tower stands for and what it'll do for our great city once it is complete. More details are to come, but first let me thank the kitchen staff here at the Fort Garry Hotel for cooking up what I hear will be a terrific meal." Hands came together and everyone applauded. Mr. Owen then hushed them by a raise of his hand. "Before we begin, let us take a moment to bow our heads and be thankful in our own way for the meal that has been prepared for us."

Gabriel shifted in his seat at the idea of this "politically correct" prayer. He was thankful that he was here and for the meal, but he had never known someone not to say a prayer to God. Even at Dolla-card's Christmas party last year, someone had come up and said grace.

Maybe Mr. Owen doesn't believe in God? he wondered.

Mr. Owen raised his head, as did everyone else in the room. "Ladies and gentlemen, enjoy the meal and I'll be back up here shortly afterward to explain *why* we're all here tonight. Thank you."

Valerie, along with everyone else, clapped as Mr. Owen took his seat at the table nearest the podium.

———

Later, after the Caesar salad, the server brought Oscar the main course. He thanked the server even at the risk of his natural aversion to unnecessary physical contact, then adjusted the red cloth napkin tucked into his collar. The others at his table—his date, a blonde bombshell whose name he could hardly pronounce, the mayor, Charles Jones (there on special invite), higher-ups who were his most trusted managers at Pay-Me-Loan now working managerial positions for the Owen Tower project, and a few select members of the press—dug into the main course of steak, mashed potatoes, side corn and sour cream and onion noodles. Oscar only stared at his plate, the rare steak staring back at him.

He suddenly lost his appetite.

Here he was in a room of over two hundred people . . . with the power to destroy them all. So easily could he slip off to the bathroom, change into Redsaw, then come back in fiery glory and decapitate each one in a magnificent blood bath. The power that would create . . .

Perhaps tonight, ahead of schedule, he might even be powerful enough to open up the doorway. Perhaps tonight he could finally have his answers and find peace.

He surveyed the room, his eyes darting from table to table, taking in all those under him. They were working-class people, nobodies. Not a soul would be missed by the city at large should they not come home.

He saw Valerie. Ah, his new receptionist, eager and attentive and a wizard at client care. Oscar was pleased he had hired her and though at times he found her a little *too* eager to "get everything right,"—though there was no shame in excellence—he was happy that tonight she'd be tied to her date at the table, who, by the way, didn't seem like he *matched* her at all.

Thought she was dating a lawyer. Thought she was in love. But by the way she sat nearly an arm's length away from the poorly-postured buffoon in glasses, they'd either had a fight and weren't speaking or this wasn't the lawyer and was some kind of B-card. Still, he was glad she brought him. He had insisted she bring her lawyer boyfriend as he was always on the look out for a new soldier in his growing army of legal representation, someone who could be swayed by the dollar sign and not by the letter of the law. Though he planned, as Oscar Owen, to do everything above board, you never knew when you might need somebody ready to bend a few rules for you. He hoped she would introduce this fellow with the badly parted hair to her afterward. Though he might look harmless, this guy might be the toughest bulldog in the pen when unleashed in the courtroom.

The smell of his steak was reinvigorating his hunger, and once more he found himself trading glances with it. A small pool of blood rimmed the tender meat, exciting him. Once more the thought of annihilating over two hundred people in a river of red invaded his mind.

Someone nudged his arm. "Oscar, are you all right?"

Keeping his eyes fixated on his food, he replied to the mayor, "Yes, just fine. Just drifted off there for a moment. Had a busy day."

"Tell me about it. I'm having it out with the police sergeant over a particular issue and the guy wouldn't get off the horn with me all day. Can't go into specifics of course, but my head is so full it feels about to burst."

Oscar nodded ever so slightly. "Uh-huh."

"By the way, compliments to the chef, whoever that might be. This steak is terrific."

"Uh-huh."

Mayor Jones went back to eating.

Two hundred people, maybe a few more. Oscar had to control himself to not switch his powers on and attempt cutting through the air and taking a peek into the darkness.

I could do it tonight and no one would know it was me. The sympathy it would bring to my enterprise would be staggering. Then, as if another voice, a more reasonable one: *Or it could become a PR nightmare and Owen Tower would forever be remembered as the enterprise that almost was.*

He needed tonight to work. He needed the good reviews in the paper, radio, TV. He needed to let the people of Winnipeg know that Oscar Owen was here to rejuvenate businesses, both established and new alike, citywide.

No, he would wait, and when he did have his way and ignite the already-growing power within him, it was going to be fantastic.

———

"Boy, this corn is really something, isn't it?" Gabriel said between mouthfuls.

"Yes, Gabriel, it's just dandy, isn't it?" Valerie said condescendingly.

"I mean, really, who would have thought to put the butter in *while* it was cooking instead of afterward. At least, that's what it tastes like."

"Yes, very fascinating."

Okay, just did my part to keep up appearances. Now I get to lay off it for a while, Gabriel thought.

As much as he hated making a fool of himself in front of her, he knew it had to be done. Valerie had met both Gabriel Garrison *and* Axiom-man. All that separated the two men was a thin layer of material and a change of voice. Fundamentally, anyway. The other stuff, like powers, personality and attitude, seemed *extra* somehow. She had been the first person who had met both sides of him. He wasn't sure if she'd eventually recognize they were one and the same. Case in point, he knew that if, say, his own brother were to put on a costume, mask and all, then suddenly come up to him, he'd know straight away it was him. After you really got to know someone, after years of spending time together, no disguise would hide you.

In theory, anyway, Gabriel thought.

He took a sip of his ginger ale and wondered if there would be another letter waiting for him when he got home. As much as he dreaded—and hated—dealing with someone at a distance like that, a part of him wished there *would* be something there on his doorstep so he could get to the bottom of this and get it over with. He glanced around. Anyone here could be the one who knew his secret. It could be that woman over there with the poofy hair and bright red lipstick. Could be the older gentleman with the gray shirt and bowtie. Could be—

"How's things at Dolla-card?" Valerie asked.

Gabriel cleared his throat. "Um, well . . ." How could he tell her he was fired? He thought of Rod and of the message his former boss left on his answering machine. Maybe he had left something on his desk at work he had to come and pick up? Maybe that's why Rod had called? "You know, it's, ah, Dolla-card and—" He didn't want to tell her he was fired. Not that she'd care or anything, but somehow being fired and being a goodie-two-shoes didn't seem to jive. "When I last to spoke to Mr. Hunter, things had changed around there since Gene, um, died. It seems he—Mr. Hunter—was taking it very hard. I guess you, ah, you heard about it, too?"

She nodded slowly and set her fork down but still had her knife in the other hand. "I was there."

He already knew that, of course, as he had saved her that day from falling off the Main Street Bridge as Axiom-man. He feigned surprise. "You were? Really?"

"Mm-hm. I saw it all, the way Redsaw just hurled that car at the crowd as if he didn't care about who it might hit. I've never seen a temper like that. His whole body just went rigid, like someone in the midst of a tantrum and he just chucked it" —she jerked the hand holding the knife— "in pure anger. Axiom-man tried to stop it and . . ." She hesitated a moment, as if she wasn't sure whether to continue with her story or not. "I almost died, too."

Gabriel felt his eyes widen and though he also knew that as well, it still surprised him that she almost died that day, too.

"Axiom-man caught me. Saved me."

"He did?" She looked at him with furrowed brow. "I mean, yes, of course he did. You're here. Are you, um, were you okay?"

"Just shaken up more than anything. I was bombarded by the media afterward, too."

"F-first, I'm glad you're all right. I could only imagine what that must have been like." *Though not too hard.* "Were . . . what did you say about what happened?"

She squinted her eyes slightly, as if she didn't understand.

"I mean, to the reporters."

"What?"

"Well, I just would have thought they'd make sure you were all right, see if you needed emergency assistance or something instead of asking you questions."

"I told them the truth. I told them what happened."

"And Axiom-man?"

"He flew away after we landed on the viewing deck of the tower at the Forks."

"Is he a nice guy?" What was he doing? Prying into her about himself?

She smiled softly; his heart suddenly warmed at the sight. When she spoke, her voice was soft, tender. "'Nice' isn't the right word. Gentle, kind. Most of all—comforting. There was a moment there, after he rescued me, where I've never felt safer."

Gabriel bowed his head, reminiscing. They had held one another, looking into each other's eyes. During that moment, there, high up on the viewing deck, he had felt utterly safe, too, as if the chaotic world that kept on bringing up new challenges never existed. She had calmed his heart, soul and mind that day. He had lost himself in her.

She was his shelter, if only for a moment.

When Gabriel looked up, he saw the others at the table were staring at them, mouths slightly open. They had heard everything.

——

Dessert, coffee and tea were served promptly after dinner. When the healthy-sized slice of Swiss velvet chocolate cake was placed before Valerie, she quivered with anticipation. She could use a good dose of chocolate right about now. She looked over to her left and watched as Gabriel dove into his own piece, smearing spots of chocolate at the corners of his lips after he took a bite.

She noticed he opted for tea when the server asked him.

"Coffee for me, please," she said when it was her turn.

As she added cream to her coffee, once more she felt herself eager to get the chocolate cake into her system. Chocolate always calmed her nerves and right now she needed all the serenity she could get.

Joel was supposed to be here. He promised he would be. He had been eager to come and told her how good it would be for his firm if he attended. Instead he was at another meeting. She couldn't blame him completely, she supposed. Though she had never held such a demanding job as being a lawyer, she could see how such a career could take up so much of his time. Lawyers were known to bill sixty to even eighty hours a week instead of your average forty.

Still. Joel was supposed to be here.

She carved out a sizable chunk of her cake with her fork and savored it. Rich and smooth, the piece melted in her mouth and already she could feel its soothing effects.

Gabriel dabbed at his mouth with his napkin then offered her a chocolate-toothed smile when he saw her looking his way.

And now I'm here with him, she thought. She smiled weakly in return then focused back on her cake. The second bite she took was even more pleasant than the first.

It wasn't that Gabriel's company was all that bad. He was a nice enough guy, caring, thoughtful, perhaps even ideal if she had a thing for guys with glasses. One thing she did admire about him, though, was his authenticity. He didn't seem to care what others thought of him. He was just Gabriel Garrison and if you liked him, great. If you didn't, he seemed to get along just fine anyway. It was the *idea* of him that bothered her. He liked her, she knew. *Really* liked her and constantly showed it. When she first thought of inviting him here tonight, she quickly tucked the thought away. Then it bounced back, as if something put the idea of bringing him along in her head. And it was either him or come alone.

Joel. Oh, how she missed him. Things had been going so great save that one bump when he didn't meet her for lunch.

Oh well. No relationship is perfect, she had resolved sometime later. Now, like it had been two and a half years ago, Joel was letting her down again.

Or am I being selfish? she wondered. Relationships were give and take. It couldn't be all about her. Yet with Joel—and she hated to admit this because then it would mean that she *was* selfish—she felt that it *should* be all about her. At least at first. He had burned her so bad before that the least he could do would be to be everything to her. *That's the definition of selfish,* she thought as she took in another mouthful of chocolate cake. *I just can't believe he screwed me again. Why? What did I do? Why do I have to be so into a guy who'll treat me bad? Relax. Get a grip. It's not like he's canceling dates left, right and center. It's just*—And she knew that if she let the thought trail continue any further, she'd admit something to herself that she didn't want to. At least, not right now.

She'd admit that she loved him.

Boomph, boomph, boomph. Someone was tapping on the microphone up at the front of the room. There was the shuffling of feet as the media took up the space in front of the podium.

Valerie took the handle of her cup of coffee and glanced up. Mr. Owen was at the mic.

He cleared his throat. "I hope everyone's had a pleasant evening so far. How about that dinner?" He clapped and with a smile nodded in the directions of the various servers about the floor. "Thank you, guys, truly. It was delicious. And this cake. Wow! Where'd did that come from? Too good. Truly excellent." The comment was followed by a round of applause.

When the clapping died down, Mr. Owen took a sip of his coffee. "Thank you again, everyone, for coming. It truly means a lot to both me and my company." He smiled. "I know that everyone here is good and full and are getting even fuller by enjoying this great dessert. I've been to enough business luncheons and dinners to know that listening to some guy in a suit talk with a full stomach can be daunting so I promise to keep it brief." Everyone laughed. Mr. Owen chuckled. "Before I begin—to the press here tonight, please note that I'll take a round of questions after I say what I have to say, should you have any. Should there be any more, I'd be more than happy to speak with you one at a time once I step down from here." A few in the room looked puzzled by what he was implying. He said, "I've done enough press functions to know that Q and As can run long and I'd rather my guests enjoy themselves than watch me field questions." The room was quiet. "Okay, then. Onto the main event."

Mr. Owen undid the button of his suit jacket and let it hang open. "You were all invited here for one reason: to get a glimpse of the future, not just for Owen Enterprises, but for Winnipeg as a city. Ladies and gentlemen, members of the press, I give you Owen Tower." He stepped down from the microphone to a small table just on the other side of it and pulled away the white cloth concealing the model building beneath. The miniature not only showed the sleek, glass-covered Owen Tower building, but also miniatures of the buildings surrounding it in the downtown area. Owen Tower stood there, tall, bright, modern. Something Winnipeg's older architecture had never seen before. The room erupted into applause and a few members of the press went forward with their cameras and took snapshots of the miniature.

The pleasant thought of working there flashed through Valerie's mind and she suddenly felt freshly excited about her new job. Even just simply working in such a wonderfully-designed building would outdo all of her previous jobs combined. She could actually have a real career on her hands.

Mr. Owen stepped back up to the mic. "Thank you, thank you." The applause quieted. "Ladies and gentlemen, Owen Tower isn't just a fantastic business idea or a chance for me to dabble in the real estate market. The OT Project—as I've come to call it and as it's been known throughout my office—is a chance for Winnipeg to truly grow and prosper as a city. Up until now, businesses large and small alike have been forced to take office in lesser-equipped facilities, buildings that have been around for decades, some for a hundred years. Of course, there's nothing wrong with that, but progress demands that one move ahead, that one upgrade their position so they can grow. Owen Tower is the answer to that. Already my office has been flooded with inquiries from expanding businesses in regards to leasing office space, their owners wishing to not only put a different face on their company, but also wishing to motivate their troops by placing them in an environment free from plumbing problems and crumbling drywall." A few folks chuckled. Mr. Owen did, too. "We have other high-rises in the city, but up until now, if you owned a business and wished to work in such a splendid environment, the leasing fees alone would be enough to drag you under. Not so with the OT Project. I have brochures available here at the front, but if you compare what Owen Enterprises charges compared to the competitor, you will see quite a difference, one that won't drain your bottom line should you decide to hang your hat at Owen Tower. Furthermore, the current floor plan is arranged as such to link like-minded or 'like-industry' companies together by placing their offices on the same floor or floors to enhance networking. I've also instituted a Common Goal committee, which consists of twelve board members who aid your business at a distance by keeping your company up to date with industry news and functions specific to your business and by also making arrangements, should you so choose, for your company to attend said functions with like-minded individuals and companies." He took another sip of his coffee. "The idea here, folks, is growth. Winnipeg has such great potential to become a major powerhouse in Canada, nay, North America, business-wise. We just need the environment and motivation to do it. That's where my company and I hope to come in—to help nurture enterprises both great and small and get them to where they want to be by providing them with one of the main resources they need, and that is state-of-the-art office space. This is more than just real estate, ladies and gentlemen. This is the future." After a pause, he said, "I'll take your questions now."

Immediately reporters raised their hands and called out to him. Mr. Owen pointed to one and took their question.

Valerie turned to Gabriel. "Sounds pretty good, doesn't it."

"I'll say. Very nicely delivered."

"Do you actually think it'll work?"

"His plan?"

She nodded.

"Well, I won't pretend to know the ins and outs of all this, but it sounds like he knows what he's talking about and that he's thought this through. Truthfully, I don't know Winnipeg's business climate all that well—not really well at all, actually— but if someone like Mr. Owen says that what he's about to do will rejuvenate Winnipeg business, then I believe him."

"Um, Gabriel?"

"Yes?"

"You have chocolate on your face."

The Past . . .

WHEN JEREMIAH CAME to, *his body was wracked with numbness. Barely able to feel his arms and legs, he grimaced when a tingly feeling covered his skin. Stomach queasy, more than anything he wanted to roll over onto his side and throw up. As he tried to turn onto his side, the sickening realization that he couldn't move made his stomach feel even worse. The most he could do was turn his head slightly so he was facing the foot of the bed. The rest of his body just lay there, still, as though dead. Vision blurry, his breathing short and quick, a slap struck his heart when he saw a man made of dim blue light, standing beside the bed, cradling the baby in his arms. He had completely forgotten about the man until now and under any other circumstances he would have been alarmed at seeing such a being, but after what had happened to the town and their newfound supernatural abilities, the man of blue light seemed almost normal in a way.*

When Jeremiah tried to speak, his words were quiet and not fully formed. "Leabe . . . leabe my baby . . . alode."

The man glanced from the baby, who wasn't making a sound, to him then back to the baby again.

"I saib—" *Jeremiah choked on that last word.*

"Please, be still," *the man told him, still not taking his eyes off the child.*

"My baby . . ."

"Is sleeping."

Jeremiah closed his eyes a moment; a rush of fatigue swept over him and if he hadn't opened his eyes immediately, he was sure he would have fallen asleep. "Put . . . put my baby bown." *He tried to get up . . . but couldn't.*

"Do not be afraid," the man said. "It will be all right." The man's voice was soothing and though it dripped with firm masculinity, it was laced with compassion, like an aged grandfather assuring you that though you were going through a hard time, it would pass. Jeremiah felt compelled to listen to him.

His heart slowed and his breathing became calm. He just wished he could move so he could get up and take the child away from this bizarre stranger who had invaded his home. Not taking his eyes off the man, his heart leapt in his chest once more when the man seemed to swoon and almost drop the child.

"No . . ." Jeremiah breathed.

The man regained his balance, paused a moment, then slowly ambled over to where Jeremiah lay, his footsteps soft like an old man with a limp. The man then carefully knelt near Jeremiah's head, holding the baby swathed in a fresh blanket tight to his chest.

"My baby . . ." His words were clearer now though speaking was difficult. He could barely muster the strength to breathe let alone speak.

Now, closer, Jeremiah was able to get a good look at this stranger. The man's body was made of dim blue light, like a burning hot ember about to go out. This strange being's facial features were muted, like someone pressing their face through a cloth. Though it was hard to be sure from the angle he was at, the man appeared to be ailing in some way, tired and sore and . . . something else.

"My baby," Jeremiah said again.

"I will hand him over to you once you are well."

Him, *Jeremiah thought.* It was a boy. If only Rebekah could— Rebekah! How could he have forgotten about her? His dear wife, there, on the bed, dead. He had wanted to kill her for— No, do not think about it. It is different now, something is . . . *It was hard to explain but whatever rage he had felt toward her dying on him had faded. Lucas. His friend and doctor.*

As if the man could read his mind, he said, "Lucas is all right. He is merely unconscious. Do not worry about him."

Jeremiah's heart lightened at the knowledge that his friend had not died from their crash through the ceiling.

The tingling sensation racing across and up and down his skin began to subside. He also felt . . . tired . . . the intensity and vigor and enthusiasm to go-go-go no longer with him. So badly he wanted to sleep but not without seeing the child he nearly killed earlier. His heart ached at the thought of what he had been willing to do, of the anger that had inexplicably burned within. How could he have thought such a thing? How could he have felt such a thing? Shame became his only consciousness. Tears wet his eyes.

The man swooned again and he lowered the baby into his lap.

"Do not . . . drop him," Jeremiah said.

"I will not. In a few moments you will be well enough to move and I will hand him to you." The man smiled softly.

"What are you?"

"I am a messenger come with news, Jeremiah."

"And what is your message? How did you know" —Jeremiah swallowed the spit building up in his throat— "my name? Lucas's name?"

"There is little I do not know about those I have chosen."

"Chosen?"

"Please, rest. I will reveal all in time."

Jeremiah wanted "all" to be revealed now. Instead, he heeded the man's wishes, too overwhelmed emotionally and mentally to take any more in.

The moments passed, the two men remaining in silence. Stomach settling, Jeremiah attempted to move again and was able to finally wiggle his fingers and toes. The tingling on his skin was completely gone and he had this feeling that something else was also missing though he couldn't quite place what it was.

The baby sighed in his sleep. The messenger bowed his head, as if to fall asleep himself (if such a being did sleep).

"How is it that . . . that you are not dead?" Jeremiah asked. The man raised his head. "I saw you fall from the sky. That would" —he took a deep breath— "kill anyone."

"I was able to slow my fall before I hit the earth. The impact still shook me through and through—but I lived."

"What are you?"

The messenger smiled. "You already asked that, Jeremiah. Like I said, I am a messenger."

"That is not an answer."

"Do not question me, man of the earth!"

The *command forced Jeremiah to clamp his mouth shut.* Man of the earth. *The name sat on Jeremiah's mind for a moment.* "Are you an angel?"

"No, I am not. But I do serve the One True God."

So it *was God who had given the town's people their powers. How else could it be explained that this man of light was here now?*

Once more it was as though the messenger had read his thoughts because he said, "It was not He who gave you your abilities. It was I."

"But do you not come from Him?"

"All things do, but that is a discussion for another time." The man glanced at the baby; the child was still asleep.

Jeremiah rolled his head and eyes toward the ceiling, and tried to sit up. Slowly, he was able to raise himself so he supported himself on his elbows. Dizziness came over him and he fought the urge to lie back down.

Push yourself, *he thought.*

Summoning all his strength, he grimaced and forced himself forward and sat up. He allowed himself a moment to rest and to regroup within before turning his head over his shoulder toward the messenger.

It was then the tears came, memories of Rebekah flooding his mind. If only he hadn't left her with Lucas, she might still be alive. It was his fault. He should have been there. Jeremiah gazed longingly at her still form on the bed then turned his face away when he saw the blood and flesh by her legs, the crimson stained mattress, the scorch marks.

Rebekah.

A sharp pang pierced his heart and he brought his left hand to his face to catch the tears.

The messenger remained silent as Jeremiah sat there, grieving, willing to give his own life if somehow hers would be returned. After a time, he asked, "Can you bring her back?"

The man of dim light didn't answer until Jeremiah looked at him. "No, my friend. It is not up to me to decide who lives and who dies. But there is something you can do for me."

CHAPTER NINETEEN

GABRIEL FELT LIKE a child hanging off the arm of a parent while he followed Valerie in between the people standing about on the ballroom floor. More than once did he bump shoulders with someone (sometimes intentional, sometimes not) and had to apologize. The sound of soft classical piano music trailed through the air, a style he had been fond of ever since he was a kid.

"Oh, there, I see him," Valerie said, coming down off her tip-toes.

"You sure you want me to meet him?" Gabriel said.

"Why not? Mr. Owen's an amazing man, from what I've seen."

The two weaved through a few more people and came upon Oscar Owen, who was just finishing up a series of questions with a reporter off to the side. Valerie and Gabriel waited until he was done and when Mr. Owen turned his back to them, Valerie went up to him and tapped him on the shoulder.

Mr. Owen glanced over his shoulder to see who it was. "Oh, Ms. Vaughan, so glad you could come," he said, that charming smile of his gracing his face.

"Glad to be here," she said and offered her hand in greeting.

Mr. Owen clasped his own over it. His gray eyes flicked to Gabriel. "Is this your lawyer friend?"

She gently pulled her hand away. "Friend? Um . . . yes. Lawyer? No."

"Oh." Mr. Owen seemed disappointed.

Gabriel bowed his head shyly then straightened when Valerie suddenly jerked him forward so he was closer to Mr. Owen.

"This is Gabriel Garrison," she said. "I used to work with him back at Dolla-card."

"Please to meet you, sir," Gabriel said meekly, offering his hand.

Mr. Owen immediately took it and gave it a firm shake. "A pleasure, of course." He released Gabriel's hand and stuck both of his in his pockets. "So, you used to work with Valerie at Dolla-card?"

"Yes, sir, I did. She was the best customer service rep they had there. You did well to hire her, if I may say so."

"Well, you may say so," Mr. Owen said, his tone suddenly making Gabriel feel small.

"Um . . ."

"Relax. I'm just fooling around."

"Oh." *Seems like a cool enough guy,* he thought. *Not nearly as overbearing as the papers make him out to be.*

"I just want to say congratulations on all you accomplished here tonight, Mr. Owen. It was very nice of you to arrange all this," Valerie said.

Mr. Owen nodded, keeping his eyes on Gabriel.

Why is he looking at me like that?

"So you say Ms. Vaughan was the best Dolla-card had to offer by way of service to their customers?" Mr. Owen said.

"Absolutely. It was an honor to work with her day in and day out," Gabriel said.

Valerie shot him a hot look, as if he was overdoing the flattery.

"Excellent. I wish to hire no one but the best for my company and if you say she was the best, then I believe you."

"Gee, um, thanks." Gabriel grinned.

"Please forgive me for asking, and nothing against you, Mr. Garrison," he said then turned his eyes on Valerie, "but didn't you say you were bringing a lawyer friend as a date?"

Lawyer friend?

Valerie suddenly looked uncomfortable. "I was going to but he had to work so had to cancel last minute."

Right. I'm a B-plan. Forgot.

"Pity. But no worries. What firm does he work for, again?"

"Taylor, Fox and Gordon."

"One of the best. Here." He produced an off-white business card from a small black case from his inner suit jacket pocket. He handed it to Valerie. "Please pass this on to him."

"Oh, he'll be thrilled," she said, taking the card then slipping it into her purse.

There was a moment of silence among the three and Gabriel wondered who would blink first. *He's still looking at me strangely. Quick! Don't look at him. Um . . . eyes to the floor!* Gabriel took in a healthy gaze of his own dress shoes.

Mr. Owen checked his watch. "I only have a moment. I promised a reporter from the *Sun* I'd do a quick one-on-one, but, here, did you see the miniature up close?"

"Not yet," Gabriel said, looking up, "but I was going to. Looks splendid. Real tall, and big and—"

Valerie shot him a look again. He stopped talking.

A shorter man with graying hair came up to them. "Excuse me, Mr. Owen? Carl Gringert is waiting for you."

"Tell him I'll be there in a moment," Mr. Owen said. To Valerie and Gabriel, "Ah, duty calls. Anyway, please, check out the display. As well, a snack table will be spread out shortly so please help yourself to as much as you'd like. It was a pleasure meeting you, Mr. Garrison." He offered his hand. Gabriel took it. Mr. Owen gave his hand a squeeze. Gabriel feigned wincing. "And Ms. Vaughan, I'll see you bright and early Monday morning if we don't speak again tonight."

"You got it," she said.

Gabriel got the impression that her efforts to butter up the boss fell through. Mr. Owen released his hand, and to the both of them said, "Enjoy the rest of the party." And he left them.

Valerie stared off after her boss like a starry-eyed cheerleader.

"Seems like a swell guy," Gabriel said from just behind her.

———

The evening wore on, most of Gabriel's time spent hovering around Valerie as she moved about, saying hello to the coworkers she knew and meeting ones she didn't. Most took to her right away, others just offered frozen smiles and courtesy handshakes. Ah, office life.

The floor began to clear as guests returned to their seats. As several couples moved to dance to the soft ballad that increased in volume over the speakers, Gabriel found himself standing beside Valerie on the sidelines, wondering why she held a look of longing on her face.

"Everything all right?" he said, leaning in.

It took a moment for her to reply. "Mm-hm." She kept her eyes forward, seemingly lost, gazing at the middle-aged couple moving in a slow waltz.

Anxiety overtook Gabriel and butterflies crept into his stomach. *Should I ask her to dance? This might be my only shot. Ever. I'm sure I could hold her again as Axiom-man—hopefully—but I'd much rather do so as me. It'd seem kind of artificial otherwise.*

He leaned close to her again and the words caught in his throat. "Um . . . uh . . . um . . ." he said quietly.

Valerie snapped around to face him. "What?"

He took a step back.

She must have seen the look of surprise on his face because she said, "Sorry. What is it?"

"I, uh, I . . . I was just wondering . . ."

Valerie rolled her eyes . . . then smiled. "Okay, Garrison. You get one. If do you well, you might get two. Here." She held out her hand.

The whirlwind of bats swirling through his stomach immediately melted into oblivion. *Is she asking me to dance? Me? Don't read too much into it.* "I'd be delighted," he said and gave a prince's bow.

"Forget it." She crossed her arms and turned away.

He came up to her. "Did I miss something?"

When she faced him, an incredulous expression was on her face. "Why can't you ask me to dance like a normal person?"

Because I'm not normal, he wanted to say but kept his mouth shut. "I'm sorry, Valerie. Just trying to be chivalrous."

"That's not chivalry. That's just . . . goofy."

"Sorry."

"I have to do everything myself, don't I?" she grumbled.

"Sorry?"

"Nothing. Here. Take my hand . . . that's it . . . and lead me out to the floor."

He did so and they found a spot not too far from the middle and not too far from where they just were.

Let's see how she handles this, he thought and took a quick step up to her. She didn't back away from his closeness. Gently, he drew her hand up to chest level and with the other tenderly took her waist.

You can thank my grandma for this, Val, he thought. Then, *Thanks, Grandma, for saving me tonight.* The ballad ended before he could even take the lead. *Just my luck. No sooner did we get out here does the song end. She'll probably want to sit down.* But Valerie didn't. Instead, she remained with him as another song came on, this one featuring the soothing melody of a violin.

Carefully, he drew her in closer and wondered why she didn't resist. She gave off so many mixed signals. One moment she seemed to be his worst enemy, the next a cool companion he'd known all his life. He was sure she had good reason for it—hopefully—but more than anything he wished she'd be straight with him and let him know where he stood.

Or maybe she just needs a friend right now? he thought. *Whatever she needs, I'll be there for her.* He drew her in even closer, just enough to let her know he cared but not too much as to scare her away.

They didn't talk, didn't exchange glances, though Gabriel yearned to look into her rich brown eyes. A man could lose his heart in those eyes . . . and then some. He simply held her, gently. Though he couldn't be sure from the angle her head was at, he thought he saw a tear roll down her cheek.

———

Great, now you're crying, Valerie thought. As casually as possible, she raised a finger to her cheeked and wiped the tear away. It was silly, she knew, but dancing with Gabriel reminded her of what this night could have been and *who* she could have been with. Despite her ribbing and harsh looks, Gabriel still remained loyal to her. She knew he'd never leave her side even if she asked him to and she wasn't just talking about here, tonight. Gabriel Garrison was about as loyal as you could get in regards to friends. Friends? Yes, she supposed that's what they were. *Why can't I let myself be friends with him? What's holding me back?* She was tired of constantly defending herself to him in her mind, always reminding herself that she wanted nothing to do with him romantically. What was she afraid of? Yet . . . she knew the answer and it wasn't to do with Gabriel specifically. *It's Joel. You're afraid of getting hurt again. And you're with him* again! *Why do you keep setting yourself up for a fall?*

Gabriel led her gently in a slow circle. Every so often he'd readjust his soft grip on her hand. Though it was subtle, she felt an affectionate squeeze every time he reclasped his fingers around hers. *He cares for me so much and I can't reciprocate. Not romantically, of course, but even just platonically? Has Joel screwed me up that bad? You shouldn't think that way. You and Joel have a good thing going right now. Don't ruin it by dragging the past into it.* But she couldn't shake the idea that *Joel* was the one doing the dragging, albeit this time in a way different than before.

Gabriel's embrace was comfortable, soothing and . . . just what she needed. She closed her eyes and tried her best to enjoy the moment even if it was with a man she didn't particularly want to enjoy it with.

Suddenly, an electric charge permeated her waist when Gabriel adjusted his hand. She'd felt that same charge before.

The song came to an end and she took a step back, something about how Gabriel's height compared to hers seemed familiar.

Her heart began to gallop.

CHAPTER TWENTY

WHEN THE EVENING came to an end, Gabriel double checked with Valerie to make sure she had everything before they joined the line in front of the coat check. Seeing all was in order the two left the hotel, Valerie waving good-bye to any coworkers she saw.

Once outside the main doors, Gabriel wondered if this was the end of his evening with her or if she would be up for going somewhere for a bite to eat. *Then again, you really should get out there and do a sweep of the city,* he thought. *Axiom-man cannot afford a night off, especially with Redsaw on a rampage.* His heart beat quickly at his indecision. Never had he felt so torn; never had he felt so much like *two* people. *You had decided to see this through—be Axiom-man at all costs. Live it out.*

Valerie adjusted the collar of her coat and set the strap of her purse more firmly on her shoulder. Her lips were pressed together, as if she had something to say but was keeping it all in. The look in her eyes didn't help anything either.

Gabriel broke the silence as they descended down the steps in front of the hotel. "Um, thanks for inviting me, Valerie. I had an utterly terrific time."

"I'm glad you did," she said, her tone flat.

"No, really, I thought it was great. And the food? Wow! Not since Mom's cooking have I had a meal so delicious." *Okay, that was lame. At the very least maybe my dorky dialogue will be enough for this to end quickly and I can get into my uniform.*

Her heel caught on the edge of the last step and she lost her balance. Gabriel snapped out his hand and grabbed her by the arm.

"Are you okay?" he asked.

"Fine," she said, bringing her feet together and giving a cool stare to the step that nearly made her trip.

"Um, do you want me to walk you home or ride with you on the bus or—" *What did I just say? I need to go home and see if there's any mail.*

"No, I'm all right." She walked past him to the curb and peered down the street.

Did I do something? he thought and came up beside her. "Everything okay?"

"You already asked that, Garrison. I'm fine." She turned and faced him, squinting her eyes as if studying him. Then her expression grew soft. "I'm sorry. I'm just tired."

Gabriel flipped up both hands. "No problem. I understand. I'm tired myself." Then he added with a grin, "Past my bedtime."

She smirked then looked back down the street. A cab turned onto Broadway a moment afterward and she flagged it down.

"Thanks again for inviting me, Valerie. I" —he swallowed— "I don't get out much so I appreciate this."

"You're welcome, Gabriel."

She opened the rear door to the cab and was about to get in, when he stopped her.

"Um, Valerie?"

"Yes?"

"I know we don't work at the same place anymore, but do you think, um, do you think we could still keep in touch?"

Hand on the top of the door, she stood there for a moment, pondering the question. "Don't take this the wrong way, but let's see what the future brings."

Gabriel beamed. "Sounds good to me." He waved. "Goodnight."

"Bye." And she got in. He watched as she leaned between the cab's two front seats and spoke to the driver. Then the cab was off, Gabriel staring after it until it turned the corner.

"And so it ends," he breathed and stuck his hands in his pockets. He debated if he should simply fly home now that he didn't have to worry about creasing his suit, but opted for hoofing it.

He tried not to lose himself in his thoughts too much as he made his way home and kept alert, just in case he came across something where Axiom-man was needed. He would have donned the mask right away after seeing Valerie off but he was concerned about not having heard from whoever it was that wanted him to check up on Tina McGillary, and he knew he'd rush his patrol if he didn't see if there was a letter waiting for him.

As he walked, he mulled over the evening—the dinner, Mr. Owen's speech, dancing with Valerie, her sudden curtness with him once the festivities were over.

Why does she have to be nice to me off and on? When we left, it was like she was a different person again. He thought for a moment. *Maybe she was mad because that guy she was supposed to come with didn't show.* His heart ached at her seeing someone else and though he knew that he didn't have any claim on her, it still pained him. It was as if now he had someone to compete against and with them not working together at all—he couldn't believe he let her remain under the impression he still worked at Dolla-card—it was going to be even more difficult to try and get her attention. He caught himself wondering if Axiom-man should pay her another visit. At least that way she would talk to him.

The walk home was quiet. Not even a single siren sounding anywhere in the distance.

The night's still young, he thought.

He arrived at his building, went in, and stood with eyes downcast in the elevator as he rode up to his floor. When the door opened, he didn't feel like stepping out.

"Why do I have to love her so much?" He leaned his head back against the wall. He pushed away from it when the elevator door began to close and he stopped it from doing so just in time.

When Gabriel got to his apartment, he paused before sticking his key in the lock. There could be a letter waiting for him behind the door and once more he would be swept back to reality where his life was a mess and the almost-fairytale of this evening would have been nothing but a dream.

"Suck it up," he grumbled to himself and stuck the key in the lock. He unlocked the door and went in.

Flicking on the light, he clenched his jaw when he saw a white envelope sticking out from underneath the toe of his shoe.

———

Valerie didn't talk to the cab driver the whole ride home, something she usually did because she often felt sorry for those lonely guys who spent twelve hours a day away from their family, dropping off strangers. When the cab pulled up to her apartment, she paid the fare and wished the cabbie a goodnight. The guy said the same, though judging by the subtle disdain in his voice, was unhappy she didn't tip him.

She kept her emotions at bay until she entered her apartment. Once inside the safe confines of her suite, she finally let it all out. A swell of anger bubbled deep within, one rooted in frustration and fear. She still couldn't believe Joel hadn't come out tonight and why she couldn't let it go, she had no idea. As she removed her coat and shoes, she debated calling him but decided it was too late. She'd let him have it tomorrow, if she talked to him.

No, you won't, she fought back. *You'll just cower before him like a puppy and lick his hand and assure him that his skipping out on you was A-okay.* "Man, I'm such a suck."

Besides, she had more on her mind than just this latest upset with Joel.

She was frustrated with herself for being so unpredictable with Gabriel. He had never done anything wrong to her except maybe make it *too* plain that he cared for her. Other than that, he was the kind of guy that most girls would drop whoever they were seeing just to date. He was caring, affectionate, always placed the lady first.

"But he's such a goof!" she screamed, then covered her mouth as if to prevent any more outbursts from streaming forth.

Grunting, she went to the bedroom with the mind to change into her pajamas before flipping on the TV to wind down. Instead, she sat on the edge of the bed and considered what had been plaguing her mind since she and Gabriel danced together.

"The way he held you," she said softly. "The way he looked down into your eyes . . ." *His touch. I know it.* She stared at her dark nylon-covered feet. The tight material against her skin reminded her of a certain someone else with a penchant for form-fitting clothing. Her chuckling came out of nowhere and soon the brief chortles became all out laughter. "Gabriel? Him? Yeah, right."

———

Being around all those people tonight made Oscar Owen's blood curdle into heated lumps of hate, and he didn't care if that loathing came directly from him or from the black cloud that infested his body.

He had hung around after the ball to thank those of importance for coming and willed himself to keep the darkness within at bay long enough to offer endearing smiles and happy handshakes to his employees and the media. Once the ballroom was near clear of late-stayers, he discreetly made his way out and into the elevator, and rode it to the top floor of the hotel.

Finally, he was alone. No cameras, no constant questions, no showboating. When he got off the elevator, he leaned against the wall next to it and sighed. Head bowed, it felt as if a monster were caged inside him, banging against the inner walls of his body with heavy paws, scratching at his sanity with razor-sharp claws.

All those people. Half of him was delighted that so many showed up and he was able to portray Owen Enterprises as the next big thing to hit the city, for the betterment of all. The other half burned with malice against them. They were nothing more than pawns, bearers of pleasant word-of-mouth for his upcoming glory. Through them, he would be able to attain a position of extreme prominence in Winnipeg and, eventually, the world. If only somehow he could couple his powers with his business counterpart. If only somehow the two could work together. Only once, so far, had Redsaw served him. The man in red and black had aided in speeding up the construction of Owen Tower not too long ago. But that was only a building and a building was only a shell for what was within. If only somehow Redsaw could help him with what really mattered—a re-shaping of the world.

Oscar's thoughts paused at that last sentiment. The desire to change humanity had never surfaced before. Was he equipped for such a task? If history had shown anything, he could never take the path of a dictator. Dictators always fell, if not immediately then eventually. The world resisted rigid structure. Yet . . . what about order? He took a deep breath and let it out slowly. Such an undertaking would be nigh impossible, at least where he was currently at station-wise and right now the idea of running for office in whatever capacity made him cringe. There was probably an alternative but if Oscar had learned one thing since beginning his ever-increasing empire, he knew that the old saying of patience being a virtue was irrefutably true. Something like that would have to be planned and planned meticulously. Perhaps after opening the doorway. Maybe after discovering the purpose of his powers and why he had them. Maybe then.

The doorway.

He was so close. He sensed it everywhere within. Already his power had grown exponentially and so had his ability to open the door. But more death was needed. A glow of red caught his eyes' attention. Glancing down, he saw his fists glowing. He had switched inside without knowing it, calling forth his abilities. Soon, he would use them to understand the gifts he had been given and what he was placed on this earth to do.

The thought of increasing his power taking him, Oscar scanned the hall of the hotel's floor for any sign of overnighters. The dark chocolate brown doors were all closed, everyone in bed after a long day.

At the end of the hall was a stairwell and window and Oscar marched toward it, loosening his tie and unbuttoning his shirt, revealing his Redsaw costume underneath. Each step forward increased the urge to go out and amplify his ever-growing power. Once through the glass doors leading to the stairwell and at the window, he thrust out his hands and sent forth a stream of red energy, blowing out the window in a rain of glass. He leapt over the stair's railing and landed on the window sill just as he heard one of the doors being unlocked behind him. Pushing off from the ledge, he took off into the sky, clawing at his thousand-dollar suit, ripping it to shreds, revealing Redsaw in full. He pulled on his mask and lost himself to the night.

The streets below were quiet, with only a few cars and even fewer people occupying the city sidewalks. He had seen the papers. No one wanted to be outside after dark for fear of his attacks. Scowling at their fear, frustrated anger building inside because there was no one he could use to help him boost his power, he flew fast and hard away from the city in search of an outlet for his rage.

There had to be something he could do to let out the malice bottled up within. There had to be *someone* whom he could destroy, a small sacrifice in the steps toward establishing his purpose. There had to be—

Redsaw got an idea.

Yes, that would do nicely.

———

Gabriel's hands shook as he read the letter. It said:

Dear Mr. Garrison:

Excellent work on your findings. Unfortunately, the information you provided was information I already knew. Your job was to find out if Tina was being abused, not just merely find out her name.

Now tell me, do I need to go public with your secret? Is that the incentive you need to do something about that poor girl's situation?

You have one more chance to get things moving otherwise your face will be plastered on the front page of every major newspaper across the country, perhaps even the world.

Get things done.

As added incentive, I have a date in mind and I'm keeping it to myself. From here on in you won't know when I will come forth and reveal to the world who you are. It could be tomorrow, for all you know. But I assure you, you have less than a week to save Tina.

Go.

Gabriel re-read the letter several times just to make sure he had read it correctly. A part of him *wanted* whomever this was to reveal him to the world. At least that way this would all be over with and he wouldn't have to worry any longer.

But I would worry, wouldn't I? If anyone knew my secret, if Redsaw knew who I was—He couldn't fathom the consequences but it would be a safe bet that not only would the lives of those he loved be in jeopardy, his own life would be in danger, too. His life as Gabriel Garrison was his only haven, a safe house against those who would love to see Axiom-man dead. If all of a sudden people knew who he was—especially those with a grudge against him—he would never be safe. Never. They could even come in at night and murder him in his sleep and there would be nothing he could do to stop them.

Something had to be done and he had to do it quickly.

Gabriel went to the bedroom and didn't bother turning on the light. Heart heavy, he removed his glasses, thankful that he wouldn't be wearing them for a bit (a headache was already forming from having not yet switched the magnifying lenses to plain glass ones), and stripped off his clothes, unveiling the

227

bright and dark blue of his Axiom-man uniform underneath. Once the pants were off, he tossed them on the bed with the rest of his suit, pausing for a moment as he thought back to Valerie and his evening with her. She, too, would be in danger if anyone ever found out who he really was.

Is it even worth it pursuing something with her? he thought. There was really no way to know and even if he planned for every eventuality, there was still the question of what if. He guessed he wouldn't really know until when or if he got there. Yet if something ever happened to her . . . . His heart ached at the thought.

"I need to talk to the messenger," he said quietly.

He removed his gloves from the backpack beneath his cape and slowly slipped them on. Raising his hands to the mask bunched up around his neck, he paused a moment before tugging it upward and setting it on his face.

You need to focus. One thing at a time. It could have been his knowing that he was about to step outside and fly into the night, but for the first time since donning the costume, he noticed a drastic shift in his thinking, a kind of transfer of consciousness and awareness from Gabriel Garrison to Axiom-man. *One more step to truly becoming two people,* he mused. He pulled on the masked and *shifted,* letting the glorious power of the messenger's gift fill him through and through. It wasn't until he reached the door to his apartment's balcony that he remembered he decided *not* to enter and exit his suite that way for the time being.

"There's always something," he said and turned around. He threw on a pair of sweats, old shoes one size too big, and a long coat. He stuffed his gloves in the coat's pockets and pulled down the mask. *Shifting* again, he let the power leave him.

He left his apartment and triple-checked the door lock to make sure his home base was secure. The last thing he wanted was for the person sending him the letters to come barging in because a simple thing like locking the door had slipped his mind.

Outside, he rounded to the rear of the building and found a shadowed corner in which to quickly change. After checking to make sure no one was around and no one was peering out any windows, he quickly pulled up the mask, put on the gloves, and *shifted*, then proceeded to do away with the coat, sweatpants and shoes. Folding the clothes nice and flat, he stuffed them in his backpack and did up the light blue diagonal portion at the front of his uniform, concealing the backpack's strap on the one side.

He gazed toward the heavens and floated upward. Stretching his arms out before him, he embraced the night air and left gravity behind.

The city was quiet. No screams, no calls for help. No car accidents and no alarms. There wasn't even a siren.

I can't be this lucky, he thought.

He patrolled the streets for a while and still nothing happened.

"One more round and I guess that's it."

A part of him was relieved that it appeared there wouldn't be any confrontations tonight. Yet another part hoped for some action to take his mind off of little Tina McGillary and her secret protector.

Just after he banked right and was about to do one more sweep, he saw a faint orange glow in the distance. Though he couldn't be sure from this far away, it also looked like billows of smoke were rising from it, obscuring what had been a clear night.

"No, not that lucky," he said and flew on toward the glowing light of what could only be destruction.

The Past . . .

THE MESSENGER GUIDED Jeremiah out of the house to get away from the blood and images of devastation. There was so much to know and it didn't appear the messenger was all too willing to share. He still hadn't explained what he meant by wanting Jeremiah to do something for him.

When the messenger walked, his movements were slow. At times he dragged his feet, other times he stumbled and fell onto his knees. Thankfully, he had handed Jeremiah the baby before they went outside.

Now, out here in the night air, the sky black and dotted with bright yellow stars, it was as if the calamities of tonight had never happened. Jeremiah held his newborn son close to his chest and smiled every so often as he watched the child sleep. So beautiful, so precious. So completely his, nay, his and Rebekah's despite her no longer being with them. His heart overflowed with joy at this tiny new arrival, yet it also sucked itself deep within his chest, aching for the woman he had loved so long. If only these two events could have happened separately. If only . . . if only she could have lived.

The two men were about fifteen or so feet from the house when the messenger collapsed again.

"Are you all right?" Jeremiah asked. He didn't know what to do or how to even help someone such as this.

"I just need to rest." The messenger's body glowed blue then faded to a dark blue without any light circulating beneath his skin (if skin was what it was; he wasn't wearing any clothes yet nothing was revealed either).

So Jeremiah waited a long time, gently rocking the sleeping babe in his arms. Finally, the messenger was able to get to his feet though, on and off, his body still flared dim blue then went dark again. Out here in the night, the only light came from the moon and stars above. When the messenger's body went dark, Jeremiah could barely see him.

"I had come to try and help this earth, to aid its people, but instead" —the messenger looked off to somewhere past Jeremiah— "my plan was thwarted. I had thought it wise to do your people a service, to give them a gift they could use to help each other and build a world without war, without famine. Perhaps, one day, without disease. Instead, it was taken from me. Taken from you."

"I do not understand."

"I do not think you ever will, dear Jeremiah. But please listen to me because this part is very important. You hold in your hands the only hope for this planet. What happened—to you, to your wife, to Lucas, the town and the world over—it was my doing. I had tried to bring enlightenment to men but instead that was taken by another who saw my work. And so I undid what I had wrought." The messenger paused, as if the next words out of his mouth would break Jeremiah's heart. Jeremiah wished he could see him but instead the messenger's face was cloaked in darkness, the dim blue light having faded completely again. "You no longer have your abilities, my friend. No one does. Not here, not anywhere. Except for your son."

Jeremiah's brow furrowed and he looked down upon the sleeping babe in his arms. "My son?"

"Yes, your son, yet even he is not as he once was. I had to take back what had been given but I was only able to take back so much lest I lose my own life, and though I would gladly give it for the betterment of this world, I must remain alive to ensure that the darkness which countered my work does not return."

He wasn't making sense; frustration set Jeremiah's mind racing.

"It is best this remain simple instead of confusing you with facts. Your son, though like you in almost every way, still has within him a portion of the gift that I brought. He will be stronger than most. That is all that is still within him. He will not fly, will not be able to bring forth blue flame from his eyes. But he will be different and it is up to you to raise him to use the remnant of his gift responsibly."

Jeremiah shook his head. It was all too much. How was he supposed to follow through with this when he didn't even understand it himself? Why him? Why the baby? Why . . . Rebekah? "I almost killed him," he said before realizing he said it.

"You were not yourself. You had been given over to a darkness you could not possibly comprehend. That was why I had to do what I did. Humanity was not ready for what I had to offer and did not counter the forces that changed what I had done. You could not control yourself under his influence."

"Who's?"

"Do not burden yourself with questions. It is best that you only focus on the task at hand, and that is ensuring you raise your son well so that he, too, will raise his children well."

"You are incredibly unfair. How can you expect to show up as you did, bring to light certain details yet keep others in darkness, namely details that affect my child and I?"

"Do you not think I know more than you based on the display of my power?" He had Jeremiah there. *"If so, then you must also trust my judgment. I have told you what you need to know. Put this day behind you. The entire world will forget the day they were able to touch the sky."*

"I very much doubt that."

"Then you underestimate what it is that I am able to accomplish, for it is already done. You must never speak of this day again. You were only allowed to retain the memory so you remember the legacy your son carries. And one day, at the appointed time, another will arise to finish what I started."

CHAPTER TWENTY-ONE

AXIOM-MAN SOARED THROUGH the sky. The closer he got to what revealed itself as an out-of-control fire in a suburban neighborhood, the more he poured on the speed. Red and blue flashing dots spackled the suburban streets like neon paint as the lights from four fire trucks, three police cars and two ambulances sped toward the mass of fiery disaster.

It happened in an instant. One moment the carnage was just a flaming orange and yellow glow in the distance, the next it was a raging inferno, as if the Apocalypse itself had decided to touch down on the once quiet bay off a friendly street. Axiom-man slowed on instinct and wondered what he had just gotten himself into. The next he tore through the sky again, speeding toward it as fast as he could, not even considering how he would handle it once he was there. The emergency vehicles' lights fell behind him as he flew on past; in the back of his mind, he took comfort they would soon be joining him and the experts in such carnage would take leadership over this catastrophe.

He came up nearly right over the furnace of burning homes—yes, *homes*—and hovered a moment, then began to float down into the midst of the chaos. Quickly, the heat from the fifty-foot-tall flames began to permeate his uniform and for a moment he doubted if he'd be able to set down in the middle of the bay—which was now a ring of fire—at all. Consciously ignoring the heat, he descended into the inferno and touched down in the bay's center.

Bringing a hand to his mouth to stifle the asphyxiating smoke, he surveyed his surroundings. There were ten houses on this bay, all probably around fifteen hundred square feet. This was a middle-class neighborhood and in the light of day, he supposed, the homes were probably quite beautiful. Now, all he saw were shadowy outlines of houses hidden behind walls of fire. The flames roared so loud he couldn't hear the sirens anymore.

BOOM!

Axiom-man bent at the waist and covered his ears as a car to the left of him exploded and shot off a driveway and landed onto a nearby lawn.

Another deafening *BOOM* signaled the same had happened to a car on his right.

The inside of his mouth tasted like cotton, the heat from the smoke flooding the air having already dried out his mouth and tongue. Swallowing was like trying to swallow woodchips.

Shielding his eyes from the brightness of the fire all around, Axiom-man took a quick glance in each direction, hoping to see a fire hydrant. He couldn't see any though he was sure that all bays had one.

Righting himself so he was standing tall, he ignored his racing heart which had now given way to panic. Roughly thirty feet away, behind a sheet of flame, he saw a figure come forth.

Half of Redsaw's cape had been burned away, the charred ends still aflame in some places, smoking in others.

Redsaw came up to him, immediately sending Axiom-man's stomach into an uneasy spin.

"Admiring my handiwork?" he said.

"What did you do?" Axiom-man shouted above the roaring fire. It was only until after he asked the question did he realize how unnecessary it was.

"Quite interesting, isn't it? You could have prevented all of this, you know. You could have stopped me every other time we met. But you didn't."

Why was he talking to him? Why didn't Redsaw attempt to take him out?

Redsaw put up a hand. "Don't try to answer. You are obviously at a loss for words. You're a coward, Axiom-man.

You try and play hero and instead you play it safe." His hand lit up with red energy. He brought it near Axiom-man as if showing it to him, then swept his hand past Axiom-man's face and sent a blast of red power through a wall of flame and into the house beyond.

The sound of the explosion shook Axiom-man's insides. "Stop it! Help me put it out. You've tried to help others in the past. Go back to the way you were. You have to! The people!" Yet the messenger had warned about Redsaw, had made it clear that what the man in the black cape represented was a counterbalance to Axiom-man's presence in the world.

Should Axiom-man end it tonight? Should he throw Redsaw into the flame and burn him alive? Even if he had to go into the fire with him and lose his own life in the process?

WA-BOOOM! Another car blew off a driveway, skipped along a lawn and landed on the street, its remains only ten feet from where the two titans stood.

Faintly, very faintly, Axiom-man thought he heard sirens. *Finally.* But what good would the police or firemen do?

Screams poured out from behind the roar and crackling of flame.

Axiom-man searched quickly for a fire hydrant and finally saw it.

No time to waste, he thought and in the span of a second, powered up his eyes and let fly a blast of blue energy into Redsaw. The force of the beam sent Redsaw flying back into a wall of fire beyond. Axiom-man took to the air and leapt over to the fire hydrant. He slammed his fist down over the spout, knocking off the cap and smiled as a glorious rush of cold water exploded from the spout and sprayed the house beyond. A billow of hot steam raced toward him and he jumped back so he wouldn't get singed.

That's a start, he thought. But there were still nine other houses. He couldn't let the people trapped inside die, if they weren't dead already.

Redsaw growled as he dove out from behind the wall of fire and tried to tackle Axiom-man. Using the sudden queasiness of his stomach as a kind of alert, Axiom-man shot into the air, Redsaw's body skimming the bottom of his boots as the man in the black cape missed him.

Racing high and fast, Axiom-man left the ring of flame then landed just outside of it on the street that ran parallel. People were on the lawns of nearly every household to either side, families huddled together as parents kept their children back. An elderly couple held each other in horror as they watched their neighbors about to perish.

In front of one of the houses off-center from the bay was another fire hydrant. Axiom-man straightened his fingers and made them rigid, as hard as board, and swiped at the top of the hydrant. A thick beam of water shot upward. He rounded to its rear and bent the hydrant's iron casing slowly toward the flame. The water's spray went along with it and shot forth from the hydrant in an arc of relief. The fire's light blended with the powerful stream of water and a rainbow bathed the sky.

Steam sprang forth from one of the houses at the corner of the bay as the water began to extinguish the flame.

But that was it. There were no other hydrants close enough to contribute further. At least this way, perhaps the emergency vehicles, which were finally coming down the street, would be able to get a little closer.

A sickening thought paralyzed him. Despite the good intentions of his efforts, the firemen now had nothing to hook their hoses to since both hydrants were preoccupied.

"Great!" Axiom-man growled and flew off back into the fire.

Redsaw was in the air, too, and grabbed hold of him while he was in the sky. The two zoomed toward the pavement below. Axiom-man steered the two of them to the ground in a less-body-shattering thud than if they had simply fallen. His shoulder hit first and numbed his arm, making him think he might have broken it. On top of him, Redsaw pummeled a fist into his face; stars burst before his vision. A blast of pain raced through his still-sensitive ribs as Redsaw struck him somewhere in the chest, the force of the blow echoing throughout his torso.

Redsaw's words from moments before played themselves over in Axiom-man's mind. *You could have stopped me every other time we met. But you didn't.* As much as he hated to admit it, Redsaw was right. He could have stopped him or at least tried harder. Whatever uncertainty Axiom-man had about his position here in the city, whatever questions he had about what the messenger called him to do—they were gone. Axiom-man knew that the man he was seconds before had just perished in the flame and a new man, one refined through the fire of pain and experience, was born.

Blue light filled his eyes, brighter and brighter—all his pain, all his hate toward what Redsaw had become, all his frustration and guilt over what being a hero meant—pooled into his eyes in a roiling mass of pulsating energy. With a shout, Axiom-man sent the beam forth into Redsaw's face with more force than he had ever sent it before.

Howling, Redsaw flew backward off of him.

Getting to his feet quickly, Axiom-man dove into the air and rose above the flame. The sudden change in air temperature refreshed him. Newly invigorated, he did a quick sweep around the outer rim of the fiery homes and located in two yards what he was looking for.

I can do this, he thought as a quick flash to that night in the Impark lot burst across his mind.

He sped down into one of the yards and approached the above ground swimming pool. Steam was already spinning off the water's surface. Stepping up to the pool's sides, Axiom-man squatted and put out of his mind any thoughts of his thousand-pound lifting limit. Shoving his hands deep beneath the pool's base, he began to lift up, separating the pool's bottom from the earth. Water spilled over the sides as the pool went suddenly off balance. Trying to keep it from wiggling as much as possible, Axiom-man focused his strength and pushed his arms further and further beneath the pool's bottom so its outer edge was soon part way up his biceps.

The weight of the pool suddenly pressed against him, as if the pool itself was aware and was offering resistance.

You can't lift this. You can't. It's too heavy. It's—No! I was *lifting it.* I can *do it.*

Beneath the mask his face was hard with determination. He fought against the sheer mass of the pool and recalled his sudden burst of speed the day he chased the TrailBlazer. He had suddenly flown faster than he ever had before. It had been as if a gust of wind had propelled him forward like a dart. It was almost as if he had tapped into something that had always been there but was never made known to him. He had to tap into it now, whatever it was.

Grunting, Axiom-man pushed up against the bottom of the pool enough so he was able to squat beneath it. He repositioned his hands so his palms were flat, his elbows at his sides. Water spilled out from the edges, the liquid's momentum still rocking the pool from his readjustment. With a guttural screech, he pressed his heels into the earth, digging them into the ground, his thighs screaming in hot pain as he exerted himself beyond what he thought he was capable of. When he was finally standing, the underside of the pool pressing down against the base of his neck and shoulders, he screamed and pushed against the pool's bottom, fearing that his hands would burst through the liner to the other side and he'd lose whatever water was left. He was surprised the liner had held out as long as it did.

The pool's bottom rose off his shoulders and the back of his neck.

His ribs begged for relief as searing pain beat against the bones. Axiom-man would not relent and would not give in. He would not let Redsaw's evil destroy innocent lives.

Please, God, let them be alive. Let those people—The prayer—the first he ever recalled praying in a long, long time—was cut short with a burst of power when he set his flight in motion. He rose from the ground; the pool pressed against his hands, obeying gravity more than him. *I can do this. I can do this. I have to do this.*

His breaths short and labored, he ascended above the flames of the house whose occupants owned the pool. Leaning forward, careful to not let the pool fall, Axiom-man poured the water upon it. The pool's weight grew lighter as the water cascaded down in brilliant liquid sheets onto the home below. Steam exploded upward, filling his lungs with fiery air.

He bit back the searing hot pain and dumped out the rest of the water. Though the house was still ablaze in some areas, the majority of the flames were out.

Sirens. A multitude of them.

Axiom-man dropped the empty pool and let it crash to the backyard below, welcoming the relief of weightlessness on his arms.

Lights danced up and down the street. From where he floated, he saw firemen running to and fro, attaching hoses to their trucks, then hoses to other hoses and, eventually, to another hydrant further down the street.

Hopefully it'll be long enough to reach the bay and they can put out at least one of the other houses. Heart heavy, he wondered if anyone was even alive and if his efforts were worth it. So far, he hadn't seen a single soul. Had some managed to run out of the house and gather with the people lining the street?

Where was Redsaw?

WA-BOOOM!

"Oh no," Axiom-man said quietly. There was nothing he could do about the car that had just gone off, but there was something he could do in regards to putting out another house.

Swiftly, he flew over to a yard at the middle of the bay, the only other one that had a pool. When he landed beside it, his mouth dropped and tears wet his eyes.

The pool was *inground*. And massive.

"Help!" he shouted. To who or what he was calling to, he didn't know.

You can do this, Axiom-man, came a voice in his head. *Trust me.*

Axiom-man would recognize that voice anywhere.

It belonged to the messenger.

CHAPTER TWENTY-TWO

NOT FAR DOWN the street someone was walking. It had been a habit of this person's to leave the news on quietly while they slept in case anything came across the wire. The news of the fire infested all channels and radio waves. And when word came that Axiom-man *and* Redsaw had been spotted on the scene, this person just had to be there.

And this fire was near Tina's house.

———

"You got to be kidding me," Axiom-man said.

I never "kid," the messenger said within him.

"And Redsaw?"

No longer here. Now hurry.

Whatever *presence* Axiom-man felt, it was now gone.

"Sure, no problem," he said.

The now familiar sound of water crashing against fire greeted him. The firemen must have had enough hose to reach the bay. Where those hoses were aimed, however, he didn't know and he knew it didn't really matter. As long as help was here, it was better than nothing.

Axiom-man surveyed the poolside one more time and realized there was only one way to do this.

"This is going to hurt," he said and flew upward a couple hundred feet. Once at the apex of his climb, he flipped his body over and sped toward the earth, fists cocked, ready to pummel. Mere feet from the ground, he began shooting his fists out with all he had—left then right, left then right, like a dual-pronged jack hammer. His fists slammed into the grass outside the pool's edge. Grass and mud exploded around him as he punched through it like dynamite. He kept digging deep into the earth until he felt he was far enough below, then adjusted his course so he was punching horizontally instead of vertically.

It was sheer darkness under here.

Gonna have to do this blind, he thought and not for the first time mused that the messenger should have also bestowed upon him some kind of enhanced vision.

Keeping in mind he had to do this in the span of less than a minute, he powered up his eyes and blasted a beam of energy upward. He smiled when it struck something and a fine spray of water cooled his sweating face beneath his mask.

Here we go.

He positioned himself so he felt he was relatively square beneath the pool and the layer of earth around its cement casing—though there was no way to know if he was indeed beneath it at its center—and set his hands against the mud lining its bottom. He gave a quick zap from his eyes to the thin packs of mud between the inside of his palms and the bottom of the pool, drying it to dirt so his hands wouldn't slip.

The messenger said I could do this so I must *be able to, right? Don't think about* what *you're doing. Just* do *it.*

Taking a deep breath and not paying mind to the fine particles of dirt that he breathed in through the mask's fabric, he pressed up against the bottom of the pool. For the first portion of the lift, he pushed his heels into the clay beneath him, doing a power squat like he had before. Letting loose a low, droning growl, his heart raced at the realization that something was moving up above him. He just hoped it was the pool.

Clenching his teeth and jaw and pressing his tongue against the roof of his mouth, he executed flight, using its force and speed to aid him in the lifting of this gargantuan tank of water.

The horrendous weight of the pool pushed against him and his arms immediately bent beneath its profound mass. Though his palms were sturdy, he had to also bear the weight along the tops of his shoulders, trapezius muscles and the base of his neck. Grunting, he pressed upward, the sound of the pool's cement casing breaking free of the earth rumbling in his ears.

Slowly, he ascended from the earth and grinned when he saw the base of the pool clear the ground. Orange light from the flames of the nearby burning house spilled in and it took his eyes a moment to adjust from the total darkness. Newly invigorated by this incredible feat, Axiom-man kept onward, keeping the focus of his intent clearly in his mind.

The insides of his palms ached and a sharp pain dug its way through the inside of his hands and filled his wrists and forearms.

Don't let go. Don't drop it, he told himself.

The ground dropped below and so did the burning house. The other homes on the bay, still burning, came into view, but he was relieved to see that the firemen had made some headway in extinguishing the flames from now two of the houses, the second ones in from the mouth of the bay.

Roughly sixty feet or so from roof level, Axiom-man readied himself for what would come next.

That's when he saw him.

Redsaw, speeding toward him like a torpedo.

"No!" Axiom-man shouted and sent off a blast of blue power into his adversary.

The impact from the beam of energy knocked Redsaw off his flight path and forced him to slow down—but not stop the collision. Redsaw smacked into him, grabbing hold of either side of him in a gigantic bear hug. The crushing weight of the pool above Axiom-man's head was sent off balance and the two men's bodies swayed as the pool threatened to tip off of Axiom-man's hands and shoulders.

"Let go!" Axiom-man screamed.

The pool beat down on him, its awesome weight begging to tumble to the ground.

Redsaw persisted and for a brief second, Axiom-man thought he caught a glimmer of disbelief in Redsaw's eyes at what it was he had lifted.

No time, Axiom-man thought and let blue energy flood his eyes. Redsaw disappeared before him in a haze of blue as the power covered his vision. Then, with all he had, he let a blast fly, smoking Redsaw off his body and sending him into a mass of burning house below.

Quickly, Axiom-man looked up to the bottom of the pool and shot a half dozen holes into its bottom. Water shot forth from the holes, bright steely rods of liquid, dousing the flames below.

Steam soared up, each gray misty beam like a spear piercing his legs and sides. He fought the scorching pain and raised his body so he was more horizontal beneath the pool. Axiom-man flew the enormous tank of water slowly over the burning homes, letting the water do its work. As each torrential beam of water went crashing down into the flames below, Axiom-man fought against each blast of searing hot steam that sped upward to meet him in the air, but also reveled in the pool's lessening weight. After doing one half of the bay, Axiom-man turned the pool and himself and flew to the other side, bringing the pool over the remaining houses, draining the water and putting out most of the fires.

The pool weighing nearly a quarter of what it once did when he first started, Axiom-man had to remember to adjust his strength accordingly to keep it above his head; for a moment there, he had still been pressing against it as hard as he could and almost tossed it off his shoulders.

The houses below went out save for a few spots and he heard cheers from the crowd below as they applauded him for ridding the bay of most of the fire.

The water stopped pouring out of the holes in the bottom of the pool and began to trickle out.

Just as he was deciding how he was going to put the pool back—or where he was going to put it at all—a shrill scream came from his left. Redsaw sped toward him through the steam-filled air. Axiom-man flew the pool so it was over the center of the bay. Redsaw smashed into him and he lost his grip. The pool tipped forward and went spiking downward. It plowed into the pavement below, landing on its edge, the pool standing vertical. Spiky shards of concrete sprayed up and out around its edge.

Redsaw still had his powerful hands around Axiom-man's waist and in Axiom-man's confusion, sent him hurtling to the bay. Axiom-man managed to kick on the flight just before he was going to hit the ground, slowing his descent enough so when he hit, it felt as if he had just fallen backward off a chair. He lay on his back, at first unable to move, his arms and shoulder muscles thanking him for this reprieve. Redsaw flew down and landed firmly on his feet before him. Behind the man in the black mask, the pool stood on end, its bowl facing them.

Redsaw, the lower half of his face covered with soot, grinned then put his hands before him and covered his fists with bright red energy. About to fire up his eyes with blue power, Axiom-man was put on alert when he heard a creaking groan come from just behind his foe. The pool teetered on its edge, causing Redsaw to turn his head to see the source of the sound.

The murmuring crowd on the sidelines fell silent.

The pool, the liner cracked and punctured with bowling-ball-sized holes, the cement casing broken in places, just hung there.

As if this were a moment of victory for him, Redsaw turned back around and aimed his fists at Axiom-man.

"Finally, it's over," Redsaw said.

Axiom-man couldn't be sure, but it appeared as if something else was crossing Redsaw's mind at that very moment, a look that conveyed that his death would give Redsaw something he had yearned for for a long time.

CROOM! The pool snapped in its middle and toppled forward, coming down so fast neither Axiom-man nor Redsaw had time to move.

The smoke and steam from the aftermath of the fire quickly vanished as the two men were encased in blackness, the only light the fiery red glow coming off Redsaw's fists. *WHAM!* The sides of the pool came crashing down, slamming into the pavement, sending out speeding shards of cement and pool liner.

Axiom-man rolled to the side, curled up and covered his head to protect himself from the onslaught.

A low, echoey rumble droned on and on as the hulking mammoth of half the pool settled into the ground. Whatever faint glow of red light that was in his peripheral faded.

There's no telling if he's alive or dead, Axiom-man thought. He got to his feet, hands raised above his head, not knowing if it was the shallow end or deep end above him. Of course, it had to be the shallow end and he was forced to crouch. *Can't stay here. He'll kill me if I do.*

Beyond the cement wall of the overturned pool, he heard footfalls on the pavement. In his mind he pictured nearly everyone who had watched the spectacle try and come to their aid. But they couldn't, not with all the hot smoke and steam.

Stay back. Just. Stay. Back. Someone was going to get killed, if they weren't careful.

Pure dark. One half of the pool upside down around him, the other acting as a wall before him, both halves tucked up together, creating a cement prison.

A blast of red light zipped past him, just missing him. The energy beam tore a hole through the cement wall beyond, letting in what little streetlight there was. Axiom-man could barely see Redsaw somewhere there, in the dark, near the deep end of the pool. To show him he wasn't afraid, Axiom-man sent a blast of his own and the underside of the pool lit up blue for an instant as the beam flashed and blew a hole through the other side. Redsaw must have moved because he didn't hear anything that would indicate a direct hit.

A.P. FUCHS

I have to get out of here. I don't want to kill him, but maybe . . . maybe that's the best option. One death to save many. My job is to stop him. The messenger said as much. The messenger. How now Axiom-man would love to hear his soothing voice and counsel. But he doubted the messenger would come to his aid. This wasn't his fight. Besides, the messenger had *lied* to him! He had said Redsaw had gone from the scene of the fire when Axiom-man was about to lift the pool. It was that hope that was the final clincher in him even attempting such a feat. And *how* he succeeded in lifting the thing, he didn't know. Perhaps one day. Was he still that powerful now? Why not just lift the pool off them and fly it up into the sky and—

Axiom-man couldn't risk it. Besides, his arms felt like jelly and he barely had the strength to keep his legs beneath him. Hot spikes of pain darted up and down his ribs.

Just go, he resolved and powered up his eyes as fast as he could, not wanting to tip Redsaw off as to where he was here in the murky underbelly of what was once a place to swim and play games. Letting off a quick succession of energy blasts, Axiom-man punctured holes in the opposite side of the pool's wall, weakening the wall so much that huge chunks of it broke off and fell to the ground in a pile of rubble. He kicked off from the ground and sped forward, straight for the opening. As he left the broken, overturned pool, a smack of raw tingling heat nailed him in his insteps. He glanced back and saw Redsaw hurtling blast after blast of red power. Then the man in the black cape took off after him.

"I can't outfly him," Axiom-man said. "He's too fast." *But so am I, aren't I?* Once more he remembered the gust of speed when giving chase to the TrailBlazer. *How did that happen?* He tried to will himself to go faster as he flew higher but to no avail.

A gun shot went off below and behind him Redsaw howled.

Still speeding ahead, Axiom-man looked back long enough to see Redsaw, now only a black dot against a matte of gray smoke below, change his course and fly off into the night.

246

Letting out a sigh of relief, Axiom-man kept on and headed upward until he was over a thousand feet up. He slowed and hovered and it was then that tonight's ordeal caught up to him. The muscles in his arms pounded from their exertion, his head ached, his ribs hurt even more and he assumed he had broken them. Again.

Throat dry, he kept his place in the sky, catching his breath and willing himself to stay alert in case Redsaw decided to pursue another round with him.

There has to be a way to beat him, he thought. "I have to. I just can't keep fighting him like this only to have him go free after each battle. I'm sick and tired of it."

He wanted to go, and when he thought of doing so, an image of a white envelope sat crisply in the fore of his mind. There was still that matter to attend to and he was tired of it hanging over him.

It had to be dealt with now.

Dawn was approaching. He checked his watch. It was already near 4:30 A.M. and he couldn't recall where the time had gone. Had he been hovering here that long? Despite his exhaustion, despite the pain that filled every bone and muscle in his body, he changed his mind, not wanting to go home only to have to get up in a few hours to resolve this Tina McGillary problem once and for all.

With one final breath, he stretched out his arms and flew toward her place.

CHAPTER TWENTY-THREE

YOU GOT TO get back to reality, man, Axiom-man thought. In all the excitement, after barely escaping with his life, he had momentarily forgotten about those poor souls in the fiery homes. He flipped himself over in the air and flew back to the bay, keeping a keen eye out for Redsaw.

If Redsaw was still alive.

I don't know where he was shot, he thought, a part of him hoping that Redsaw was off somewhere, bleeding to death. *Stop it. You're tired. I hope . . .* A sharp twist of discomfort bent his heart. *I hope he's all right. Or, at least, alive.*

A minute later he touched down in between two fire trucks parked on the street just outside the bay. Most of the crowd, from what he could remember, still seemed to be there though a few may have gone inside. Police milled about, helping out where they could. The emergency workers were busy, a few of them working quickly to get people up onto gurneys. One of the people lying on a gurney was a small child, her face black with soot. From where Axiom-man stood, it appeared a portion of her face had been burned pretty badly. A woman who appeared to be her mother stood beside the gurney, both hands grasping the rail as if it was the last thing she'd ever hold on to.

"Just hang on, Sweetie. Just hang on," the mother said.

The emergency worker handling the gurney adjusted the oxygen mask over the child's face then told the mother to take a step back while he loaded the gurney into the back of the ambulance.

Axiom-man's heart ached and he wanted to go over there and apologize. In fact, he was already stepping forward to do so when a fireman, still decked out in heavy coat and helmet, came over to him. "Thank you."

Not taking his eyes off the child, Axiom-man replied softly, "For what?"

"If you hadn't did what you did, we would have lost everyone."

Axiom-man surveyed the bay. Most of the houses seemed to be extinguished, smoke and steam rising from the wreckage. He couldn't see over the overturned pool in the middle of the bay so didn't know the status of the houses on the other side. There was no flicker of flames though. He could barely find the strength to speak. "How many . . ."

The fireman, a stocky African Canadian fellow with bold eyes, puffed his cheeks and blew a sigh slowly from his lips. He rubbed his gloved hands together. "From what we can gather so far, there were ten families on the bay, averaging three kids per household." His dark eyes turned toward him. "They're being tended to; others are being taken to the hospital. These . . . . They were fortunate enough to find protection in their basements. All the exits were blocked. One guy said his basement flooded last night. He even laughed and said the foot of water in his basement was probably what saved his family's lives. But . . ." The fireman wiped the sweat from his face. "A little under half survived, all told. We won't really know till we go through everything."

"Only half." Axiom-man spoke so softly he had trouble hearing his own voice.

The two men stood there silently, letting it sink in.

The fireman broke the silence. "What about you? Are you all right?" He glanced Axiom-man up and down.

Axiom-man's body hurt all over; his uniform clung to his sweat-soaked skin. His heart hurt so much from the grief that he feared it might stop beating. "I'll be okay."

"Thank you," the man said and stuck out his hand.

Axiom-man shook it, but his heart wasn't in it.

249

The fireman looked around, then waved at somebody that Axiom-man couldn't see on the other side of the fire truck. "I'm sure the police would like to talk to you. I know our department would, too."

He shook his head. "I'm sorry, but I can't right now. I'm needed . . . elsewhere."

The fireman nodded, as if he understood though Axiom-man doubted he even had a clue. Interviews with the police and firemen, never mind the media circus once the police tape blocking off the end of the street was removed—it could take hours.

"I have to go," Axiom-man said. "Whoever you talk to, tell them I'll drop by the downtown police station later. Maybe have someone from your department hang around there as well. Right now . . . I need to go."

"Fair enough. I won't pry. I can only assume that you're busy."

You have no idea. "Thanks." He put a hand on the man's shoulder. "Take care . . ."

"Oh, um, George. George Stelankton."

"Be careful, George. Sound the sirens if you guys need anything. I might be nearby."

"Will do."

He gave George a friendly tap on the shoulder then looked up and left the ground behind.

"They died," Axiom-man said softly as he flew away. He did some quick math in his head. "That's about twenty-five people. All dead. I took too long." *The pool. Both of them. They were too heavy.* "I may have lifted them but I took too long." *I'm no hero. I'm a murderer.*

Feeling empty inside and void of self-worth, he flew over to Emerson Avenue and located the Greene household. *I don't know what's going on in there or if Tina really is in trouble. But if she is, I won't let anything happen to her. Too many have already fallen on account of me.*

It was just after 5:00 A.M. and once more Axiom-man marveled at how quickly the time passed, especially when the circumstances were grave.

Landing on the Greene's roof, he stepped along the shingles and settled near the chimney. Leaning up against it, he felt his ribs and winced when his fingers grazed over them. Fatigue beat against the backs of his eyes and his knees no longer felt like they could hold him up.

The sky grew lighter, revealing the band of smoke rising just above the once-aflame houses in the distance.

Twenty-five. Gone. How could Redsaw do such a thing? "He's not himself. He can't be. The black cloud must really be doing something to him." He needed the messenger. And soon. No more did he want to handle this on his own. No more *could* he handle this on his own without some help. And not even physical help—though he'd gladly welcome it—but *insight* into why things were the way they were.

He straightened, the act enough to make him more alert. He cursed himself for almost dozing off for a second.

Lungs aching from inhaling all that smoke, he thought maybe he should have asked George for an oxygen tank. Something to help him out before staying up till who knew when, trying to solve the mystery of the white envelopes.

The neighborhood was quiet. People were sleeping in this Saturday morning.

All that changed when he heard shouting coming from under the roof beneath his feet.

Someone was angry.

———

Redsaw landed in his backyard just outside the city, collapsing onto his knees. He removed a blood-soaked gloved hand from his left shoulder and grimaced at the sight of the bullet wound. He reached over his shoulder and felt from behind. The bullet had gone clean through.

But he was still bleeding.

251

Knowing he couldn't go to a hospital as Oscar Owen—and certainly not as Redsaw—without raising suspicion, there was only one thing he'd be able to do to stop the blood.

Red energy covered his right hand. He pointed his finger as if it were the barrel of a gun . . .

. . . and plunged it into the hole.

———

The person had got as near to the area of the fire as they could. For a long time they had pretended to be one of the people who lived down the street, staying within the confines of the police tape. They had seen Axiom-man take off into the sky, Redsaw on his tail. They had heard the gunshot that made Redsaw turn away. They had also seen Axiom-man return and talk to the fireman.

This person's heart lightened when they had seen Axiom-man fly off again, this time seemingly in the direction of Tina McGillary's house.

Finally, the man in the blue cape was about to do something.

Casually, this person walked away from the scene though a part of them ached when they had heard the mother of the burned child crying. They only wondered if one day Tina would be that child if Axiom-man didn't do something.

Perhaps today he would.

———

Axiom-man hopped off the roof and landed in the backyard near the kitchen's glass sliding door. Keeping out of sight, he stayed up against the wall and inched along it so he could hear what was going on within. The sound was muffled because of the walls and glass, but he could still make out the gist of what was happening.

"I said go back to bed! Daddy's trying to sleep. It's not even six in the morning yet!" The man's voice was strained, raw sounding, as if he was an expert at screaming.

The shrill cry of a little girl pierced even Axiom-man's ears. "I'm hungry," she whined.

"Go back to bed and we'll eat in the morning."

"Daaaad, I'm—"

"Tiiinnnaaa!"

Brow furrowed, Axiom-man considered barging in but so far he didn't have the grounds to do so. It was just a dispute—albeit a loud one—but still only a minor argument. And in light of the fire, this didn't seem significant at all.

Yet.

The sounds within faded. Pressing his ear against the wall, Axiom-man heard light stomping coming from within, presumably Tina storming off to her room in a huff. Then faint whimpering. His heart broke for her. All she wanted was something to eat. What parent didn't feed their child?

The whimpering continued for a few moments until the thundering voice of Daddy Greene shouted, "Shuuut uuup!"

Tina wailed.

"Quiiieeettt!"

She just wants some food. Come on, man, Axiom-man thought. Tina's cry for something to eat reminded him of his own hunger. He hadn't had anything since the dinner with Valerie and soon, if this were a normal morning, he'd be getting up to have breakfast.

The little girl continued to ball, her cries abruptly silenced when booming footsteps raged from within.

"Uh-oh," Axiom-man breathed.

CRAM BOOM! Something smacked something hard. Tina was no longer heard.

Heart racing, Axiom-man's feet left the ground and he quickly flew to the rear of the house and surveyed the row of windows. The one with the butterfly glass decal in the window had to be Tina's. He rose up to it and felt his eyes widen when he saw Daddy pulling his foot out of a hole in the girl's

A.P. FUCHS

bedroom door. Once his foot was yanked out, Daddy stomped it down and straightened his bulky arms. Fists closed, his barrel-like chest heaved beneath a tight gray T-shirt as he stared Tina down from beneath a bird's nest of graying black hair. Tina sat on her bed, hiding behind her pillow, her face a picture of glassy-eyed terror. Axiom-man could tell she wanted to cry but her father's gaze was holding her back.

Daddy pointed at her. "One more whimper out of you and it's to the basement."

Tina buried her head in her pillow, her shoulders jerking up and down.

"That's it," Daddy growled and marched over to her. He slammed a beefy hand down on her shoulder and yanked her off the bed.

Screaming, trying to get away, Tina begged him to stop.

Axiom-man drew himself back from the window, snapped out his arms before him and clenched his fists hard. An instant later, he flew through the window, the jolt of the glass breaking against his knuckles encouraging the anger bubbling within.

Daddy Greene and Tina froze their positions as Axiom-man brought his legs down beneath him, his boots crunching the shattered glass on the carpet.

"Let her go," Axiom-man said, his eyes digging deep into Tina's father.

Daddy paused and just stood there, staring at him, as if deciding what to do. He then took his hand off the girl and kept it hovering there a few inches above her shoulder.

"Take a step back and leave her be."

The man didn't move.

"I'm telling you," Axiom-man said firmly, "take a step back and leave her alone."

The bulky man in the torn gray T-shirt and black boxers finally complied. Tina stood there, her tiny body shaking beneath her white and blue jammies.

With as gentle a gaze as he could muster, Axiom-man looked at her and held out his hand. "Tina, come here. I won't hurt you."

254

"How do you know her name?" Greene asked.

Axiom-man ignored him. "It's all right, Tina. I'm here to help." The girl stood there, her fingers entwined just below her chin. "Please? It'll be all right. He can't hurt you as long as I'm here."

Daddy Greene was on him in a flash, grabbing hold of him and tackling him onto the bed. "I said, how do you know her name!"

Knowing he didn't need to answer, Axiom-man jerked Greene's arms and hands to the side, loosening his hold. Quickly, he grabbed the man by the shoulders and tossed him to the floor. A quick flash of relief came over him when Daddy only landed with a *thud*. For a moment there, he thought that maybe the tremendous amount of strength he used to hoist *both* pools was still with him. Whatever that surge of power had been, it seemed to have left him and his strength was at its normal level again.

Crying, Tina ran over to Axiom-man just as he was getting off the bed. Her tiny fists railed against his thigh. "Don't hurt my daddy. Don't hurt him. He's a nice man. Don't hurt him."

Trying his best to calm her, he put his hands on her shoulders and said, "I won't hurt him, Tina. Don't worry."

"Don't touch her," Greene said on his hands and knees.

Axiom-man pulled his hands away; Tina kept beating against his leg. "Tina, stop it." She kept hitting him. "Stop it." Her tiny fists didn't give up. He grabbed her hands gently. "Stop. It."

Greene pounced on him again, tearing his hands from Tina's, throwing him half on the bed and half on the floor. The little girl fell on all fours off to the side.

The fists came out and a huge hand pummeled into Axiom-man's face. When the next fist came, he blocked it with his left hand and took hold of it. With his right, he pressed under Greene's jaw and he pulled the hand and pushed the jaw in opposite directions, as if opening a tent door. Hopefully the strain would force the man to stop. Growling like a wild man, Greene managed to get a heavy knee on top of Axiom-man's chest, sending bursts of hot pain into his ribs and an immense pressure into his stomach. Tina was on her feet and stood right near them. She moved to get closer, to help her father. If he threw Greene off, he had nowhere to go but right through her. The only option was to—

Gripping Daddy's wrist and taking hold of his neck, Axiom-man lifted himself and the man off the floor till they almost touched the ceiling. Tina gazed upward in amazement. Greene's face turning red from the pressure against his neck, Axiom-man knew he had to let go or this guy wouldn't be able to breathe. Ensuring Tina was out of the way, he hurled Greene through the bedroom's open door and into the hall beyond. The large man hit the floor with a wild thud. The force of the landing jolted him enough to lay still. He was still conscious and breathing, his large back rising and falling slowly.

Tina screamed and Axiom-man landed beside her and crouched down to her level.

"Shhh, it's okay," he said. "Your daddy was going to hurt me."

"No! He was trying to protect me."

Had he made the wrong choice? Should he really have barged in? Maybe Daddy Greene wasn't really going to do anything to her and the broken door was just the result of a temper gone out of hand. Maybe the same thing with his threats.

No, I couldn't risk it, he decided. *And if whoever has been writing me is correct, Tina would have been in trouble.*

When he glanced into the hall beyond, Greene was gone.

"Where'd—"

Tina turned to look into the hall as well. "Daddy?"

"Let's go find him," Axiom-man said, standing.

Sniffling, she wiped the tears from her eyes. "O-okay . . ."

Axiom-man followed her out into the hall then down the stairs to the front room. The place was a mess. Not a dump, but a mess. The couch and chair were covered with magazines, napkins and a couple dirty dishes. The coffee table had one leg missing and three cans of beer stood prominently on its top. The off-white walls were void of any pictures or sense of home. A lone TV was on a brass stand off in the corner, the volume off but the weather channel playing proud. The front door was off to the left.

"Daddy?" Tina said.

"Right here, baby," Greene said from behind them.

They turned around only to be greeted by a rifle aimed squarely at Axiom-man's head.

"Come here. Come to Daddy. This guy won't hurt you or me anymore."

"Mr. Greene," Axiom-man said. His courteousness seemed to have worked because Greene's eyes did a little dance, as if he was willing to pay attention. "Please, it's okay. Nothing's going to happen. Let's talk about this."

Daddy Greene snarled. "Get away from my daughter."

Tina slowly stepped over to near her father.

Axiom-man raised his hands shoulder height in a gesture of goodwill. "Put down the rifle. Let's talk."

"Get out of my house."

He almost conceded, his fatigued mind momentarily forgetting why he was here. Then, "I can't. Not until you explain what you intended to do to her after destroying her door."

"That's none of your business."

"It *is* the second an argument turns to the destruction of property."

"Oh, what, you think you waltz in and out of people's lives just because they get a little mad?"

"Breaking a door isn't 'a little mad,' Mr. Greene."

The man raised the rifle and set his sights down the barrel. "Get. Out. Now."

"I'm not leaving."

"I mean it!" Greene boomed.

"Then shoot."

Squinting his eyes, Daddy Greene readjusted the rifle in his hands slightly. Axiom-man saw the man's finger tense, about to fire. Axiom-man ducked just as the rifle went off, blasting a hole through the front door. Tina shrieked from the sudden noise. He dove forward, grabbed hold of the rifle with both hands and tore it away. Before the rifle hit the floor and slid along the ground, Axiom-man took hold of either side of Greene's body and spun him around, sending him flying into the door.

Whampf!

Fear widening the man's eyes, Greene shakily scrambled to his feet, unlocked the front door and ran outside, knocking over someone who was coming up the front steps.

"Daddy!" Tina screamed.

Axiom-man ran to the door only to find Greene and what looked like a woman tumbling down the steps, past the sidewalk at its bottom, and onto the front lawn.

The two lay there, catching their breath. Axiom-man took the distance between the front door and lawn in one leap and threw Greene off the woman.

Greene landed about seven feet away.

The woman lay there, staring up at him with fuming eyes.

What felt like an open-palm slap smacked Axiom-man in the heart. "You."

CHAPTER TWENTY-FOUR

SHE LAY THERE and stared back at him. "Hello, Mr. Garrison."

Axiom-man hadn't thought of her in the four months since he received his powers, but seeing her again sent the same sense of panic that came over him when he saw her standing there at that bus stop, a wide-eyed look upon her face. The look she gave him—before he noticed it later when looking in the mirror up in his apartment—when she saw the man with the blue hair and glowing blue eyes. He was surprised at himself for not thinking it could have been her. Who gave second thought to someone they saw briefly in passing? She obviously had. She had kept track of him, probably after he made the paper the day after his first heroic exploit, the night he saved another woman from two hoods. This woman must have put two and two together and decided to use that knowledge to her advantage when the time was right.

"What are you doing here?" Axiom-man asked firmly. Though he knew—at least he thought he knew—he had to hear it from her. Had to have her admit that she was the one who threatened him with her knowledge of his true identity.

The woman got to her feet.

"Hi, Marcy!" Tina said.

Axiom-man turned to see the little girl standing in the doorway, waving a small hand.

Daddy Greene got to his feet and, though shakily, stormed over to them, waving his finger like a gun. "You were told never to come here, girl."

"And you have no right to pretend to be Tina's father." To the little girl, "Tina, honey, you okay?"

"This man" —she pointed at Axiom-man— "came in when Daddy was yelling."

"Tina, quiet!" Daddy Greene snapped.

Marcy looked to Axiom-man as if for confirmation.

"It's true," he said. "Mr. Greene was yelling. He grabbed her and looked about to hurt her. I intervened."

Marcy nodded and her eyes grew soft. "Now do you believe me?"

"Believe what?" Greene said and jabbed a fat finger into Axiom-man's chest. His tone went grave. "You think I abuse my daughter?"

"You tell me," Axiom-man said.

"I oughtta rip your head off for saying such a thing."

"You oughtta rip his head off?" Marcy said, hands on her hips. She eyed Greene coolly. "You're the one who brought this on yourself. You're the one who sends Tina to school with bruises. You're the one who'd rather spend his money on beer than for food. You're the one who barely works and leaves Tina all night at the neighbors so you can go out partying with your friends."

"Shut up," Greene growled.

Axiom-man looked to the little girl. She was still in the doorway. He wondered if he should let Daddy Greene and Marcy work this out for themselves, but he knew he couldn't. Not only could things turn ugly, but he was also finally face to face with someone who knew who he really was.

"Is this true?" Axiom-man asked him.

Greene shot him a hot scowl. "What business is it of yours, you little goof? Or, should I say, Mr. *Garrison*?"

Axiom-man's throat went dry.

"Yeah, I may have been down but I heard what she called you. How she knows, it doesn't matter. But now I know. You're a dead man, you hear me? A dead man!"

"Forrester, stop it!" Marcy said.

"You still didn't answer my question," Axiom-man said. "What are you doing with Tina?"

Before Greene could answer, Marcy spoke for him. "He's her dad. I'm her sister."

"Then why is the name dif—Where's Mrs.—"

"Long story and it doesn't matter." To Greene, "I'm calling the police." She dug into her pocket and pulled out her cell phone.

As she began dialing 911, Greene knocked the phone from her hand. "Oh no you're not!"

"Hey!" Axiom-man said and shoved Daddy Greene back.

The man faltered back a couple of steps and put a hand to his chest where Axiom-man had struck him. "You're gonna pay for that."

"No, he's not," Marcy said and reached down for her phone.

"Put that down," Greene said firmly.

"Yeah, right," Marcy said and completed dialing the number. Greene charged her just as she hit SEND, his large arms engulfing her and taking her down to the lawn. Marcy landed flat on her back and her face lit up in panic when she tried to breathe. He must have knocked the wind out of her.

Axiom-man took a stride forward and grabbed Greene by the collar. With a powerful pull, he yanked the man off her, the T-shirt stretching, and hurtled him near the front steps.

Tina screeched.

Now on his knees beside her, Axiom-man eased Marcy up and gently tapped her on the back. "Go slow. Breathe slowly. Let a little bit of air in at a time. The rest will follow."

Marcy's hands waved frantically in front of her face as if she were cooling herself. She no longer had the phone and Axiom-man couldn't see where it had gone.

"Don't panic. I promise you, you will start breathing. You have to relax."

Marcy closed her eyes in an effort to calm herself. Tears leaked from the corners of her eyes. A few moments later she was able to gain a sip of air. A few moments more and that sip

261

became a gulp. Axiom-man kept tapping her back and eventually she was able to get enough air in to breathe somewhat normally.

When Axiom-man checked behind them, Tina was still standing in the door, worry and fear covering her small face. Greene was gone.

"Thank . . . thank you . . . Gabriel . . ." Marcy said weakly.

"You're welcome. Here." He offered his hands. She took them and he helped her up. Steadying her, Axiom-man asked, "Where'd he go?"

No sooner did the words come from his mouth than Greene reappeared in the doorway, one hand behind his back. With the other he urged Tina to the side so he could get by. Walking quickly, he came down the front steps and stood before them.

"If there's one thing I have going for me," he said, "it's excellent hearing. *Gabriel.*"

Axiom-man's heart leapt into overdrive. Now this fella knew his full name. Everything was falling apart.

"You trespass onto my property, break into my home, wreck my belongings and assault me. Marcy, maybe you *should* call the police. I'm sure they'd be very interested to know what this clown was doing."

"Quiet, Forrester. You know what you did. And you know the police side with him."

They do? Kinda. Axiom-man's heart still beat rapidly. He didn't how he'd be able to manage from here on in knowing these two knew who he really was.

"Shut up!" Greene shouted and whipped the rifle out from behind his back, swinging the butt-end across Marcy's jaw. The woman twirled with the blow, spun around and landed on all fours, facing away from them.

Axiom-man instinctively reached out a hand to her then a second later went to take Greene out. Daddy Greene cocked the rifle and aimed it squarely at him. "Don't."

"Daddy?" came Tina's small voice.

"Daddy's all right, darling," he said, not taking his eyes off Axiom-man. "Just go to your room and I'll be there in a moment."

Tina remained there.

"Go on, honey, it'll be fine." Greene's all-knowing grin made Axiom-man's stomach turn. "How does it feel, hero? How does it feel when someone else intrudes on your life, huh? I know who you are. You are no longer safe. You will pay for what you've done. I'm going to tell everybody. Gonna tell the whole world."

Jaw clenched, Axiom-man ground his teeth, not knowing how to respond. This guy would make good on his word.

"But first," Greene continued, "let's see if you're bulletproof." He fixed his eyes along the top of the barrel.

"No!" Marcy screamed. In a blur she was on him, grabbing onto the gun, her body in between the two men. Before she and Greene spun around, she had somehow managed to get the rifle behind Daddy Greene's back.

Axiom-man took a step toward them to break them up and . . .

. . . the shot rang out and Marcy and Greene fell backward to either side.

Tina screamed.

Marcy lay on her back, a circle of blood growing in diameter just beneath her heart, the red soaking through the light powdered blue of her shirt.

Axiom-man was at her side just like before when she had lost her breath. "Marcy . . ."

She coughed and blood bubbled between her lips. "I'm . . . I'm sorry . . . Gabri . . . Gabriel . . ." She swallowed and gazed off to somewhere past him. "I thought I was . . . was doing the right thing."

"I'll go get help," he said. "Tina!" He looked to the doorway and the little girl was gone. Instead she was by her father's side, her tiny voice repeating, "Daddy, Daddy, Daddy."

Greene lay still, a red hole blown through his stomach from the rear. His chest neither rose nor fell.

"Go to her," Marcy said. "She . . . needs you."

WhatdoIdowhatdoIdo . . . Panicking, he scanned around for the phone and saw it lying on the grass several feet away. He went over to it, picked it up, and returned to Marcy's side. The tiny digital screen showed 911 had been dialed. He put the phone to his ear and heard someone breathing on the other end. "Hello?"

"Is everything all right? I heard gunfire."

"You better get an ambulance over here quick."

"Can I have your name, sir?"

"Axiom-man. I—"

Tina's shrill shriek cut him off. The little girl had her head tilted back, tears streaming from her eyes.

"Go to her . . ." Marcy whispered. Her head fell to the side and her eyes partially closed.

"Sir?" came the operator's voice.

Axiom-man put two fingers to Marcy's neck and checked for a pulse. Nothing. He pulled his glove off and checked again. She was gone.

Tina howled.

"I'm going to need police, too," he said into the phone.

"Already on their way. A call came in a few moments ago from one of the neighbors. You better stay where you are as I'm sure you'll have some explaining to do."

Axiom-man stood, leaving Marcy's body behind. Tina was on her knees beside Greene, her small body folded in half over her father. Gently, Axiom-man put a hand to her back.

She raised her head and with large brown eyes said, "Where did my daddy go?"

———

The phone rang; Valerie groaned. She rolled over onto her side, the untouched, cool edge of the pillow making her want to go back to sleep. The phone rang a second time then a third. She opened her eyes and brushed the strands of dark brown hair off her face. The clock read 9:42. Having been so tired the night before, she had forgotten to set her alarm so she could go for her Saturday morning run. Thoughts of the Saturday two weeks ago zipped through her mind, the Saturday Axiom-man had found her at the Legislative grounds and taken her into the sky. The Saturday she nearly lost her life when Redsaw knocked her from Axiom-man's arms. The phone rang again. She reached over and grabbed the receiver off the nightstand.

"Hello?" she said softly, her voice laden with sleep.

"Val? Hey, good morning."

Eyes closed again, she rolled onto her back. "Who is this?"

"Val, it's Joel. Did I wake you?"

With her free hand she rubbed her eyes with thumb and forefingers. "Yeah."

It could have just been the sleepy haze of morning, but she wasn't as mad at him anymore.

"Sorry. Do you want me to call back?"

"No, it's okay. I need to get up anyway."

"Okay," he said, then after a pause added, "I, um, feel bad about last night. About not going to your dinner."

"Uh-huh." She opened her eyes; the morning light coming in to the room through the window alongside the bed made her squint. "How was *your* dinner last night?"

"Let's not talk about that right now. I'll fill you in later, but it went well."

She just lay there and listened.

"I was hoping to make it up to you," he said, "my not going with you yesterday."

"I don't know," she said. "You're gonna have to try real hard. I wasn't impressed, Joel."

"I know."

"Just like old times, huh?"

"What?"

"Never mind."

Silence hung between the two of them.

After clearing his throat, Joel said, "What are you doing this Wednesday?"

"Um . . ." She thought for a moment. As much as she liked to think her schedule was chock full of things to do and places to go, aside from work, she really didn't have all that much going on. She had hoped Joel would change that, but so far, this horse hadn't changed its trot. "I'm open, I think. Why?"

"Got a couple of tickets to Screamer Eyes."

"Dreamer?"

"*Scream*-er, with a S. And 'eyes,' too."

"Oh, them. Cool. How'd you manage those? Last I heard they sold out pretty much right after tickets went on sale."

"You'd be surprised what a little charm and a credit card can do," he said, the smile evident in his voice.

Valerie chuckled. "And?"

"*And*, I was wondering if you'd like to go? Seven rows back from the stage, center, loud and big and, well, you know."

You really shouldn't go. How many more times are you gonna set yourself up for a fall? But this was Joel offering her the tickets. More so, a night out with him. Her will crumbled. Saying no to Joel was a like a dog saying no to a bowl full of meat. "Sure."

"Awesome. I was hoping you wouldn't be too mad to say yes."

"I'm still mad, Joel, but this helps. I used to listen to Screamer Eyes when I went to high school."

"And you stopped because . . . ?"

"Who said I stopped?"

"You did. You said 'used to.'"

"Don't play semantics with me," she said playfully.

"Wanna do lunch Monday?"

"You buying?"

"You bet."

———

By the time Gabriel got home, it was a little after 10:00 A.M. Entering his apartment after such an eventful night, the feeling of detachment from the place was almost surreal.

As much as he thought of his apartment as a safe house for him—especially ever since donning the blue tights—this morning it seemed as if the place belonged to someone else. He leaned back in the doorway and double checked the suite number just to be sure his tired mind hadn't misled him to a place that wasn't his own. And just because his key opened the door didn't mean that he had the right place. Twice since moving into the building he had overheard others talking about how their keys had opened others' doors. So far, the caretaker hadn't done anything about it. Probably still wanted to snoop around if she could. But the suite number checked out and he was in the right place. He locked the door behind him, mulling over Jack Gunn's words from earlier that morning as he kicked off his shoes.

The police sergeant had showed up at the Greene home along with two other squad cars. When he got out of the cruiser, he made a bee-line for Axiom-man.

"Well, well, well," he had said. "Looks like you're everywhere tonight."

Axiom-man didn't reply.

Hands in his pockets, Gunn surveyed the front lawn. He sniffled, no doubt from the cool morning air, as he did a circle around Axiom-man, his eyes surveying the bodies lying on the ground. One of the officers had taken Tina off to the side. She didn't make too much of a fuss but kept looking his way.

Gunn must have noticed him glancing in her direction because he said, "Leave her. She'll be fine."

Biting his tongue, Axiom-man complied.

The other officers began taping the place off; another was advising a few of the neighbors who had come out to see what was going on to stay back.

"Care to tell me what went on here? More importantly, why these two are dead?" Gunn asked, bushy eyebrows raised.

Axiom-man folded his arms across his chest. "I don't know how you can say that so coldly."

Gunn raised a finger, pointing it at Axiom-man's face. "Don't start with me, Wise-guy. I'm not interested in this hero-for-hire nonsense you got going on." He pointed to the bodies. "Look around. You're at the scene of a double murder here. Aside from the little girl over there, you're the only one left standing. You expect me to believe you had nothing to do with this?"

"I didn't," Axiom-man said firmly.

The police sergeant rolled his eyes. "Then what happened? And don't think for a moment that just because you helped with that fire you're getting some lee-way. Good deeds don't cancel out the bad ones, got it?"

Axiom-man stepped right up to him; Gunn's eyes wavered a little in their sockets from his sudden advance. "What's your problem, Gunn? You barge in here accusing me without even attempting to hear my side of the story."

"Hey," he said, his voice carrying an undertone of steel, "I asked you what happened."

"By insinuating I'm somehow responsible for this."

"Are you gonna co-operate or not? I'd love to take you in on obstruction of justice. You're lucky, so lucky, you got the majority of the force behind you." Gunn shoved a finger into his chest. "If it weren't for that, I would have put you away a long time ago."

Axiom-man pushed back, sending Gunn stumbling back a couple of steps. "Lay off."

A couple of officers started coming over.

"Is everything all right?" asked one of the officers with lengthy blond hair sticking out from under his cap. He had a hand on the butt of his gun. Another officer, a bald one, came up beside his comrade, same pose.

Their eyes still locked on each other, Axiom-man and Gunn stood there, seeing who would make the first move. Finally, Gunn relented. "Everything's fine. I'll be with you in a moment."

The blond officer lingered a moment before turning away. His partner followed his lead.

Gunn stepped forward. "You have five seconds to get on with your side of the story or things will get ugly."

Grimacing beneath his mask, Axiom-man wanted to smack this guy upside the head. It may not have been the "hero" thing to do, but right now, he was too sore and too tired to care. Gunn was a jerk, plain and simple. Yet, if he were able to win the major crimes unit police sergeant over somehow, it would make his job much easier and would ease any possible tension in the force his presence in the city brought on.

"Fine," Axiom-man said. "Here's what happened."

He filled Gunn in on the details; more than once throughout his speech Gunn gave him a quizzical look. Since Gunn hadn't been there, there was nothing the police sergeant could do to disprove his story. At least, not until the case was studied and documented. And even then his story would check out.

Once Axiom-man was done filling him in, he firmly told Gunn he had to get going in case he was needed elsewhere. Further, Tina was now sitting in the back of a police cruiser, balling her eyes out, the officers not even having the decency to comfort her.

Winnipeg's finest, Axiom-man thought. Despite some of the good cops out there, the apathy of the force still got to him. *Thankfully, I'm around to help balance things a little.* It was a shameful thought, one he regretted thinking right afterward. Yet he also knew deep down there was some truth to it as well.

He opened the rear door of the police car, one of the officers eyeing him all the while as if he was going to abduct the poor girl. The second he opened the door, Tina stopped crying and peered up at him with tear-stained eyes.

"Tina?" he said softly.

She didn't reply.

He crouched down just outside the door so he was at her level. "These nice people are going to take care of you for a little while, okay?"

She wiped at the tears leaking out of the corners of her eyes. Despite even this young one's efforts to compose herself,

Axiom-man could see her heart breaking over and over again beneath the surface.

"I know it's hard sitting here in this stupid car," he said. "It's boring. There's nothing to do and no one to talk to. But you know what? At least here you'll be safe and sound. This is a safe place. A good place. All that messiness from earlier is all over now."

She looked at him intently. He hoped she understood what he meant.

"Are my daddy and Marcy going to be okay?" she asked.

"They—" Axiom-man started but stopped when he felt a hand on his shoulder. He glanced up and a female officer with her hair tied back in a tight, long sandy-brown-haired ponytail beneath her cap look down on him with gentle eyes.

"I can take it from here, if you want," she said gently.

He stood. "That might be a good idea. I really should get going. But . . ."

"You'd hate to leave her like this."

He nodded. "Please find out if she has anybody aside from, well, you know."

The officer nodded then glanced over Axiom-man's shoulder to her comrades beyond. "I will, and pay no mind to them. It's a long story and Gunn has them all worked up about you over nothing. I appreciate what you do."

"Are there others?" he said.

"On the force?"

"Yeah."

"Many others. Despite some of the garbage, please know that your efforts don't go unnoticed."

He nodded again. "Thanks." He pointed at Tina. "Take care of her, all right?" He crouched down beside the little girl again. "Tina, this nice lady" —he glanced up at the officer— "what's your name?"

"Judy."

"Judy," he said. He took Tina's small hand in his. Tina tugged it away. "She'll take care of you. But if you ever need me, you ask Judy here and she'll try and get in touch with me, okay?"

Tina nodded but not before the tears began pouring again.

"Take care of her," he said to Judy.

"You got it," she said and winked at Tina.

Axiom-man lingered there a moment.

"It'll be all right," Judy said.

"Thanks." He put a hand to her shoulder then walked away.

Before he rose into the sky, he gave Gunn one more hard look. Gunn's stare back said it all: he wasn't done with him. Not by a long shot.

By the time Axiom-man was back in his area, he had to force himself to focus and stay alert lest he fly past his destination and wound up who knew where. And by the time he found a place to change and throw on the sweats, coat and shoes, and shift his powers off, he was even more tired. The idea of going home never felt so good.

Now, in the front landing of his apartment, the feeling that this wasn't really his home still hung over him. It would pass, he knew. He just wanted to take off his street clothes and costume and lay in a hot bath. If he passed out in there, he didn't care. His body would thank him for it later—at least till the water cooled and he froze. Groaning, he went to the bedroom and threw the coat onto the bed. He removed the pants and undid the belt of his uniform. Unfastening the light blue front piece that ran diagonally across his chest so he could take off the cape, he was stopped when he thought he heard something coming from the front room. *Shifting* inside, he switched his powers on and quickly re-did up the chest piece and locked his belt into place. Putting on the gloves and pulling up the mask quickly, he then carefully stepped toward the front room and stopped his stride when he heard what sounded like a static *SNAP!*

Redsaw? Here? Can't be, he thought. He peeked around the corner. His front room was empty.

"That's weird," he said.

Just as he was about to turn around to go back into the bedroom, he spun on his heels at the sound of the blinds in front of the balcony window sliding across and flipping flat, the curtain drawing closed, too, blocking out the sun and any view from the outside world inward.

His computer monitor flashed bright blue.

CHAPTER TWENTY-FIVE

THE BRIGHT BLUE flashes on the computer screen increased in speed until the snap-snap-snapping of static electricity fired off in rapid succession. Axiom-man shielded his eyes as the room strobed from bright blue to pitch black in time with the snaps.

Snap-snap-snap-snap-snapsnapsnapsnapsnap—SNAP!

The screen radiated a brilliant blue glow, its luminance hanging there, its awesome light bathing the room so bright that even the details of the edges of his furniture were softened.

SNAP!

Two blue beams of light shot forth from the monitor, hitting the air like a pair of snakes zipping away from a hunter. The beams softened and became liquid-like, as though the beams themselves had changed to water but still carried awe-inspiring light within their waves. They swirled and twirled around the room, the beams licking every corner, zooming past him, bending around his body before shooting back out again. They did another lap around then connected at the center of the room in a loud clap, spiraling together until they took on the form of a man made of pure blue light. The man was featureless save for his face which, though no clear-cut eyes or nose or mouth could be seen, clearly resembled that of a human face, like one pressed up against a thin cloth.

The messenger had arrived.

Still fighting his fatigue, Axiom-man didn't pay any mind to his own feelings. He stormed over to the messenger, his arms straight at his sides. "What took you so long?"

The messenger's body shone bright when he spoke. "You dare question me?" He raised a hand and zapped forth a beam of light, lifting Axiom-man off his feet, quickly and firmly, setting him back down further away.

Axiom-man didn't care. "You bet I'm questioning you. I've called and called, waited and waited, and you took your sweet time getting here."

"Quiet!"

Another blast of bright blue flew from his hand, slamming Axiom-man in the chest, sending him in a back flip through the air and onto the carpet where his front hall met his living room. He landed on his face, arms beside his head. It took a moment for it to register that his head was ringing. A sharp sting zipped through the bridge of his nose.

Mental note: don't question him. Shaking the cobwebs from his brain, he raised himself so he was on his knees.

"Get. Up," the messenger said, his normally comforting voice firm and hard, like a parent's whose patience had been tested beyond its limit.

Axiom-man complied, hating the way the messenger made it crystal clear that *he* was the one in charge and not him. Though deep down Axiom-man knew it stood to reason that this wielder of awesome cosmic power *should* be the one to call the shots—he still hated it. Especially after all he'd been through. "I'm sorry."

"Remember it for next time, then."

"So there will be a 'next time'?" He put a hand to his head then brushed his finger along his nose, testing it to see if it was broken or bleeding from the fall. It seemed all right though he'd have to double check later when there was an opportunity. For some reason he dreaded what might happen should he remove his mask now, in the messenger's presence.

"You're seeking me for encouragement so, yes, there will be a next time. I'm not finished with you yet, Axiom-man."

He wished he knew what that meant, but now wasn't the time to worry about it. There were more pressing matters at hand. Matters with a capital R.

"I need your help," Axiom-man said.

"I know. Remember, you and I are entwined, your abilities relating to me where you are in your journey."

Journey?

Only now did the messenger lower his hand. "From here on out, you must not question my timing. Do you not think I pay attention to what goes on in the battlefield I placed you in? Do you not think I am aware of what is transpiring?"

"Um . . ."

"You have come a long way since we last met. I know you have many questions and there will be time for those, but you must also first learn that what you have been given and the task you have been charged with are things you must carry on your own. I will be near to guide you, but I cannot do it for you." His voice softened. "I know this can be intimidating. I know that on certain days you feel lost and wish this burden can be taken from you. But, it cannot. You and you alone are the one who must see this through. You and you alone are the bearer of light in a very dark world. It is you who must keep evil at bay lest it overrun the globe."

Axiom-man took a step forward, his legs shaky beneath him. "I am grateful for all you've done for me and in hindsight I'm glad that, for whatever reason, you found me worthy to this calling—but I honestly don't know if I can do it. Since . . ." He cleared his throat and fought the tears pricking at the corners of his eyes. "Since we last spoke, everything's gone wrong, both for me personally and for Axiom-man. I'm sure you know that already but I had to say it. I don't like what's happened and, worse, I don't like what's become of me."

"What is not to like?"

Did he need to spell it out for him? Did he not know that since their last encounter countless lives had been ruthlessly stolen on account of Redsaw, that he lost his job, that he'd been beaten up and broken, that his mind and emotions had been stretched and pulled and flat out torn apart? "My world is ending," he said without meaning to. But it was the truth.

Whatever control he once had in his life had been ripped away from him and all that was left was the shell of the man he once was.

"Your world is not ending," the messenger shot back, his voice cold. "It is beginning. You have been brought to a place where you've been forced to let go, where you have no choice but to face your responsibility head on." Gently, he added, "This is a good thing, my friend."

Friend?

"I just can't believe more people died again on account of me," Axiom-man said.

"It's the cost of what you do," the messenger replied.

"Was there any way to stop it? Marcy, Mr. Greene?"

"We are all victims of the choices we make. It is our duty to not complain of their consequences. To do so and to second guess only leads to disaster. Human history has dictated as much."

"What . . . what do you know of us . . . humans?"

"More than you realize. Which is why I specifically chose you, Gabriel Garrison, to become an axiom man for this planet."

"You have yet to tell me why. Unless I'm missing something, I cannot figure out why me out of all you could have picked. Surely there are others better. There has to be someone else out there who is a better person than me, who is more good, more decent."

"It was not a question of who was good or who deserved it more. It was a question of *who* was the rightful heir to inherit the abilities you now possess."

What? "Rightful heir? To whom? In case you don't know my family's history, we're plain and ordinary people. Probably average if you compared us to everybody else. Especially me. I didn't ask for this, and you're implying it's my birthright."

"Excellent choice of words. Now listen closely." The messenger lit up bright blue, sending a shiver through Axiom-man's body. When the messenger's body dimmed, he took a step forward, his eyes never leaving Axiom-man's. "Long ago I visited this earth, a little over five hundred years it has been since I made my presence known."

"You've been here before?"

"Let me finish."

Axiom-man pressed his lips together to keep from speaking. So far as he knew, there was nothing recorded in history about a being of blue light descending from the sky. Unless, of course, this prior visitation was a one-on-one experience between the messenger and someone else and such an encounter had been sworn to secrecy.

The messenger continued. "Long ago, I came with the plan to bring hope to mankind. There once was a place named Peraton Village. One night, I gifted all there with powers similar to your own. Every person in the town received the gifts and received them well. They planned to begin using them for not only the betterment of themselves, but for the world. They desired in their hearts to become an example unto others to show what humanity could be if given the chance and the proper tools. But just as it has been recently with Redsaw, so it was back then. The evil one of who I spoke last we talked came and reversed what I had done, robbing all of the abilities I had given them. As soon as this dark power was placed within them, so their hearts turned immediately. They did not need a murder to trigger the change, instead of how it has been with Redsaw. Hate and anger followed and quickly grew volatile. I did not have a choice but to restore things to what they once were . . . but at great cost." His illuminated body dimmed even more. "It nearly killed me in the process. I searched the flesh of every person of Peraton Village, pulling from them the darkness that gripped them. I was able to restore all to what they were before their abilities save one: a baby, son of Jeremiah Garir, your ancestor. Though the child could not fly nor shoot blue flame from his eyes, he had been left with incredible strength. If I had chosen to remove even that from him, I would have died. I debated it, killing myself in an effort to leave God's creation as He intended it. But I relented because I could not help but think that at some future time, I might be needed again."

Was he serious? An entire town of, what, axiom men and . . . women? "But what of this . . . evil presence you keep mentioning. Couldn't he or it or whatever it is or was, um, come and then reverse your, uh, reversal?"

"No. What he did—and it is a he—when he undid what I had wrought, that, too, nearly killed him. How I still wish for evil to have been destroyed that day, but like myself, he employs foresight and sensed that at some future time he would rise to interfere with my plans again."

I hate how he never mentions names when it comes to these cosmic forces at work. Despite the frustration for lack of details, Axiom-man knew he had to trust him. Or get another blast of energy to his chest for asking for an explanation.

"If I may ask," Axiom-man said, "when this . . . power . . . was weak, why didn't you destroy him then? It would have prevented Redsaw now."

The messenger illuminated bright and bold and Axiom-man feared he had overstepped his bounds. His heart leaped into overdrive and he braced himself for the impact of another blast. Instead of firing, the messenger said, "At the time, after I had restored order, I was too weak to even attempt it. Later, when I tried seeking him out, he had fled and taken refuge in the cosmos. Until recently, that is, with the birth of Redsaw."

The messenger, weak? It was hard to imagine but who was he to question it? Everyone had limits even, apparently, cosmic beings made of light and incredible power.

Axiom-man ran his fingers through his blue-sheened hair, trying to take it all in. "My birthright, huh?"

"That child grew up, keeping his power a secret. For at that time, since his ability had sprung from me, I was able to keep track of him and sense what he was doing, his needs—the same as I do for you. But with each generation, the gift dwindled and, eventually, faded to a state of dormancy. This seed of power had grown so weak that it took me years to find you, Axiom-man. Once I did, I knew that if I did not act with you, I would not have the chance again. It was because of that special deposit within you that you were chosen. It was because of a promise made to Jeremiah Garir that I selected you above all others. I am sorry if you expected any other reason."

Axiom-man's heart ached at that last statement. For a time, he thought he was special, somehow chosen from the rest of humanity because of who he was or for some outstanding character trait. Instead, it could have been anybody, really, as long as they were Jeremiah's descendant. Whatever confidence he just had in himself shattered. He wanted to strip away the mask and toss down the cape and walk away from them for good. Now, though, he knew he couldn't in spite of how worthless he felt.

"I wish you hadn't told me that," Axiom-man said.

"But it was the truth. And it needed to be shared if things are to progress from here. The evil force knew as well as I did what our previous visit to Earth cost us personally. That is why now, it has come down to only two—you and Redsaw. To use our power upon others, to each raise up an army—it would kill us both and it's a risk neither one of us are willing to take."

Progress from here? Will that evil presence return and deal with me personally? Undo what the messenger has done? He dreaded the thought and the very idea made his stomach swim. "I hate it when you talk like that." He didn't care if such a forthright statement would land him on his face again, this time with a broken nose.

The messenger's light glowed so bright its luminance covered the entire room. Axiom-man stood there in spite of it, resolving not to back down but willing to take any abuse, should an energy blast be dealt to him. The messenger's light remained, almost blinding. After several minutes, each second that ticked by matching time with Axiom-man's thudding heart, it finally subsided.

"So what I am supposed to do now? Do you truly know what is going on? Do you know what Redsaw is doing?"

The messenger just stood there; Axiom-man wasn't sure if the man of blue light knew the answer or not.

Not wanting to play any more games, Axiom-man said, "He's killing innocent people. I have no idea how many have died at his hands, but he's not stopping. The city is terrified of him. *I'm* terrified of him, of what he might do. And I don't know if I can take him down. Except . . ." He looked down at the toes of his boots. His feet hurt from being on the move all night; his muscles and joints were sore all over. His ribs begged to be tended to. "There's been a change in my powers. At least, I think there has been."

"I know."

"You know?"

"You and I are connected, remember?"

"Right. I keep forgetting."

"Start remembering."

"Fine." He braced himself for another blast. None came. After a moment's pause, he said, "My powers have changed or, at least, I'm capable of doing things I haven't been able to do before."

"Your speed and strength."

"How did you—oh, right."

"What you experienced was a *surge,* a boost akin to what you would call adrenaline, but unlike adrenaline, a surge cannot be called upon by simply getting worked up in a given situation." He shone bright then dimmed. "This is the simplest way to explain it: the more you use your powers, the stronger you get, the increase in power manifesting itself in a surge, a sudden increase in whatever ability you happen to be using at the time. However, that surge subsides and your powers return close to normal. I say 'close' because, though they do decrease again, they decrease to a level a little above what they were previously. Yet you must also understand this: should a period of time come where you do not utilize your abilities, you will grow weaker and they will return to what they originally were when you first received them."

"So the idea is keep using them. Like working out?"

"More or less."

"How strong will I get? Is there a limit?"

"Questions like that can lead you to a place you do not wish to go."

Absolute power corrupts absolutely, he thought absentmindedly. "Will I be strong enough to stop Redsaw?"

"Only time will tell, but now you have incentive to use your gifts and use them well."

Silence hung between them for a moment. "Do you know why he's killing everyone?"

"With each death, his power grows. Redsaw's ultimate goal is to open the Doorway of Darkness, a portal which would allow him to connect with the evil force that gave him his abilities. Should this happen, he will become unstoppable and you will fall before him."

"Then how can we stop him?"

"We?"

"You and me."

The messenger glowed bright blue and shot forth a beam, taking out Axiom-man's legs from under him. He hit the floor with a hard smack; his knee caps screamed in pain. "I know what you meant. Must you always make useless statements?"

"Why do you keep doing that?" Another blast struck him in the chest, sending him rocking back then falling flat on his stomach. His nose bumped the floor and a burst of stars flashed before his vision. "ARRRGHH!" Throat dry, he swallowed the lump in his throat. "Fine," he said, catching his breath. "I'll stay down. Why can't you, I don't know, join with me so we can stop him?"

"This is *your* journey, Axiom-man. I cannot interfere. Find Redsaw and put an end to the evil that threatens to overtake your world."

In his peripheral, blue light grew brighter and brighter, followed by a loud *SNAP!* A hot, tingly sensation came over him as what felt like rubbery tubes made of electricity snaked around him. With each pass, a warm fuzzy sensation gripped his insides, at first painfully then soothingly. The ache

drumming against the inside of his head began to subside as did the sharp pain in his ribs. His muscles rejoiced as they were massaged through and through, even to his bones. The light then pulled away and zipped around once more before—
SNAP!

Only darkness remained.

When Axiom-man pushed himself onto his knees, his eyes not used to the dark, he smiled in spite of being alone on the floor.

He was healed.

CHAPTER TWENTY-SIX

AFTER THE MESSENGER left, Gabriel went to his bedroom and sat on the edge of his bed, mask pulled down . . . and just sat there, letting the events of the past twenty-four hours seep into him. The moments bled into hours and only a few times during his reverie did he notice he had been staring at the same spot in the carpet the whole time. His body was . . . fine . . . at least, from what he could tell. Though fatigue banged against the inside of his head and soon gave way to a headache, he had a hard time grasping that, so far as he was aware, his ribs no longer hurt and what should have been sore and bruised muscles and bones were healthy. How powerful was the messenger? Were there any limits to his power? If the story the messenger had relayed was true—and he had no reason to doubt him; the messenger had been nothing but forthright with him since the beginning—for a being to transform an entire community not once but twice—he could not help but sit there in dumbfounded wonder at the marvel that was his mentor.

Around 4:00 P.M., Gabriel finally stood and removed his costume and put it away in the box in his closet. He'd give it a wash when he had a chance but right now sleep was all he cared about. Wearing only his boxers, he crawled into bed, sleep immediately sucking him in the moment his head hit the pillow. He was drawn from his slumber only once when the phone rang, but he didn't answer it.

The sleep was a black sleep, one void of dream or of any conscious awareness that his body was getting the rest it so desperately needed. He woke once around 6:00 Sunday morning, just barely conscious enough to rollover and crash again. This time, when he went back under, he dreamed. Valerie was there, wearing the same black dress as Friday night. She said something to him, something about how she couldn't find her shoes and feared she left them out on the dance floor. In the dream, as Gabriel went in between the other couples dancing a slow waltz, there was the haunting feeling that Valerie losing her shoes meant the barrier dividing him as Gabriel and him as Axiom-man had faded and she knew who he was. He scanned the dance floor, searching in between the slowly moving feet of the couples, trying desperately to find her shoes. If only he could find them, their recovery would protect his secret anew and Valerie would be none the wiser about his second life. But the shoes were never found. Panicking, he fought the urge to just get up and leave, but knew that if he did, he would surely give himself away. So he went looking for her. Valerie was gone.

When he turned to ask a portly gentleman dancing with his equally stout wife, he found that he and the couple were now outside, and all the others who had been on the dance floor were gone. Soon after, the short chubby couple was gone, too, and he was alone, standing in an open parking lot in his Axiom-man costume. The night was clear save for three spirals of thick smoke snaking back and forth through the air.

Marcy came up to him. "Have you seen my dad?"

Thank goodness she was there. He had been trying to find Mr. Greene all evening. He had been looking for Tina because he had promised her to take her flying. "No, I haven't seen him," he replied, the memory of where he had just been with Valerie gone.

"Oh," she said. "He has something of mine. I, um . . . I have a picture of it. Do you want to see?" Her eyes flashed the hope that he would say yes.

"Sure."

Marcy dug in the pocket of her jeans and pulled out not a picture but a tiny porcelain doll. "Here," she said and showed him the doll standing upright on her palm.

The tiny doll had little brown pigtails and Tina's smile.

"I'm trying to find its mommy and I think he has it," she said.

Axiom-man took the doll and looked it over. The doll's straight-mouthed expression curled up into a smile. "Hi, Tina," he said.

"Hi," the doll spoke back, its voice small and squeaky.

"Do you know where your dad is?" he asked.

"I think he has me at home. The fridge doesn't open from this side."

"The fridge?"

"I was hungry so he said I could go to the fridge and help myself. But when I opened the door, it was empty. Now I'm inside it 'cause something pushed me in. It's dark in here. Do you have light?"

Axiom-man let the power fill his eyes, just enough to offer a subtle blue glow. "I sure do. I can help you see in the dark."

"Will Marcy take you? She likes walking. Do you like walking?"

He glanced up to where Marcy stood no more than a foot away, but instead of standing there, she was lying on the ground and her skin was a deep red.

"She can take me," he said then closed his hand around the tiny doll.

"It's warm in here," came Tina's voice through his curled fingers.

Axiom-man knelt down beside Marcy, happy they were about to leave and he'd finally get to see Tina and take her for a flight. "Marcy?" He shook her shoulder. "Marcy, we have to go." Thankfully, it was night and the sun wouldn't be out for several hours so it wouldn't add to Marcy's sunburn. "Marcy, come on, we have to go."

She gazed up at him and opened her mouth to speak. Blood pooled up in her mouth and oozed out the sides, thick, like pudding.

"I told you not to eat that," he said.

"Sthoorr-ee," she replied.

When he touched her shoulder again, he jerked his hand back as the flesh beneath her powder blue sweater became wet to the touch. Her skin shone with the dampness of blood and then began to run like wax trickling down a candle. Her body melting, Axiom-man moved to pick her up so he could fly her to the fridge Tina was in and cool her off, then realized he couldn't because in order to use both his hands to do so, he'd have to set the Tina doll down. He couldn't leave her. Not Tina. If he left Little Tina here, he wouldn't be able to find the fridge Big Tina was in.

"Leave them there," said someone behind him.

He looked over his shoulder to see Daddy Greene on one knee, his right hand balancing a rifle on his palm, as if proposing.

"We have to get her to the fridge," Axiom-man said. "She'll die if we don't and Tina won't have anything to eat."

"Tina's fine," Greene said. "Here, hold this." And he passed the rifle to him.

Axiom-man took the gun and Greene scurried on all fours toward where Marcy lay. Axiom-man didn't remember doing it, but he must have set the Tina doll down. It lay there, in Greene's path and before he could say anything to stop him, Greene's knee came crashing down on the doll, crushing it.

"No!" Axiom-man shouted and aimed the rifle at the man's back.

Greene didn't pay him any mind nor did he seem to have noticed that he had just crushed the only way Axiom-man could find Big Tina.

"Do you realize what you've done? You've—" He raised the rifle and stared down its barrel.

Greene scooped Marcy up in his arms and when he stood with her, Marcy's body broke and splashed all over in pools of crimson red.

"What're you gonna do?" Greene said.

Axiom-man didn't know. Then all became clear. He wrapped his finger around the trigger and squeezed. Instead of a resounding *BANG*, the sound of ringing poured forth from the barrel.

Of course, he thought. *Always something.* He flipped the rifle around and put it to the side of his head like a telephone. No one answered when he said hello.

———

The phone droned on and on. Gabriel opened one eye and then the other. The clock read 9:43. Had he slept the day away? It didn't feel like it; felt only like a few hours. He pulled the quilt over his head, hoping the machine would kick in and the incessant ringing would stop puncturing nails of sound into his brain.

It finally stopped. Ten seconds later, the phone rang again. And again. And again.

"Grugh!" He threw back the covers. He stormed to the doorway of his room and had to stop to let his eyes adjust between the darkness of his bedroom and the light coming from in between the cracks in the blinds in the front room.

"Wait . . ." he said.

The phone rang. And rang. And rang.

He marched over to it and picked it up. "H-hello?" His mouth was drier than he expected. He cleared his throat. "Hello?"

"Garrison?"

"Um, this is. Who's speaking?"

"This is Rod Hunter."

Rod Hunter? "Oh, um, good evening."

"Evening? Garrison, it's Monday morning."

"Monday mor—Really?"

"What's going on? Are you okay?"

"Um . . ." He put a hand to his head and checked the stove clock. It read 9:44. He glanced across the way and the streaks of light coming in through the cracks in the blinds signaled more time had passed than he realized. "I'm-I'm fine. Sorry. Had a rough night."

"Sounds like it." He paused. "Did you get my message Friday?"

"Um . . . yes, yes I did. Is everything all right? Did I forget something at the office or . . . ?"

"You didn't forget anything other than your record of doing a splendid job here." Was that a smile he detected in Rod's voice? "Listen, I'm sorry for blowing up at you on the day of Gene's funeral. I really don't know what to say other than I was out of sorts myself and edgier than usual."

"It's okay. I understand. It's my fault. I—"

"Have you found another job yet?"

"I, um, I've been looking but—No, no I haven't. I was going to hit that pavement today though."

"Well, you don't have to if you don't want to. I've reconsidered and if you want to come back, you can. You in?"

He had to think for a moment. Mind still racing from that dream—would he, in real life, actually pull that trigger?—the idea of working at Dolla-card again didn't really appeal to him. And with Valerie gone, there didn't seem much point in going anymore aside from simply making money. Money. Yeah, he needed that. His account was pretty much tapped out and soon another batch of bills would arrive never mind his next rent payment. "I, uh, I can do that. Sure. Thank you. When do you, ah, when do you want me to come in?"

"Can you be here by twelve? Pull a half day today then start your regular eight-to-four tomorrow?"

He checked the clock again, half-expecting a huge chunk of time to have passed during this phone call and that he wouldn't somehow make it to the office on time. The clock read 9:47. "Um, sure. Yes, sir. I'll be there. Thank you."

"Okay. Look, I gotta go but come see me when you come in and we'll go from there."

"O-okay."

Rod's voice went quiet and something rubbed up against the phone. "Yes, just put that there. I'll look at it later." His voice louder again: "Sorry. Someone just came in. Okay, great. I'll see you later."

"Thanks again, um, Mr. Hunter."

"Don't mention it."

"Thanks."

"I said don't mention it. Bye." He hung up before Gabriel could say anything.

Gabriel set the phone back in its cradle then pulled out a chair from under the kitchen table. "So," he said, "back to work."

———

Valerie stood outside the Owen Tower office, both hands folded across her thighs, gently swinging her purse side to side, waiting. She jumped when a soothing voice spoke over her shoulder: "Hey, Beautiful."

"Hi," she said and wrapped her arms around Joel's neck. She still liked the way she had to get up on her tippy-toes to hug him.

He pecked her cheek and she set her heels back down, her arms still around his neck. "All set?"

"Yup." She pulled away, hoping for that feeling she had many times prior after hugging him, the feeling that she couldn't wait to put her arms around him again. Now, when she lowered her arms, that longing was absent.

Disappointed, she moved alongside him and hand-in-hand they walked down the sidewalk, Joel stating the quickest and easiest place for them to eat would be one of the places in Winnipeg Square.

They walked briskly, both on a clock, and both barely speaking.

The sun was behind a series of clouds overhead but still warm enough that she felt its warmth on the back of her neck.

"Something wrong?" Joel asked as they weaved in and around the people on the crowded sidewalk.

She shook her head. "No. Just waiting till we get inside to sit down and talk."

"Uh-oh," he said.

Valerie smiled. "No, it's not *that*. Just don't want to get all our talking done before we even have a chance to visit, is all."

"Oh, it's that exciting, eh? Only enough to say to last the two-minute jaunt to the Square and that's it?" His tone conveyed he was clearly joking, but Valerie couldn't help but wonder if—in light of the absence of the desire to hold him again—there might be some truth to it.

You're probably just still mad, she reasoned. *And if you are still mad, then you've got some things to work on.* It pained her heart to think it, but people screwed up in relationships all the time and if she was going to hold Joel's bailing on her against him, then this relationship really wasn't worth pursuing. *If he means that much to me, this'll pass and we'll move on.* I'll *move on.*

They reached the entrance to the Square via the doors at the Royal Bank Building and went down the escalator.

"Did you come down here often when you worked at Dolla-card?" Joel asked.

"Not really. Now and then. Had a coworker who did though." Knowing her luck, Gabriel might even be down here now. How would that be for awkward? He didn't seem too happy Friday night when it became evident Mr. Owen's quip about a "lawyer friend" was in reference to something more. *He probably also wouldn't have ever left you hanging either,* she thought. *Grrr, get over it already!*

They got a booth at the restaurant near the drugstore, and both laid their jackets on the seats before heading up to the counter to order their lunch. After they placed their order—pea soup and chicken Caesar salad pita for her, a BLT with tomato soup for him—they approached the till together, and got a couple of canned drinks. Joel reminded her he was picking up the bill.

"You sure?" she said.

He brushed the question off with a wave of his hand. "Don't worry about it." He dug into his wallet for the cash and though she didn't normally do it, she snuck a peek and couldn't help but notice a couple hundred-dollar bills, a few fifties and a couple of twenties. Maybe he was more well-off than she thought? It would explain how he could afford the Screamer Eyes tickets. Last she heard, they were going for eighty bucks a pop. And that was just for mediocre seats. She couldn't imagine what seventh row, center, would go for.

They sat back down and waited for the waitress to bring out their food.

"So?" he breathed.

"So?" she mimicked.

He smiled. "So you did manage okay Friday night?"

"Yeah. Was nice—wasn't the greatest—but it was nice. Went with a friend."

"Really? Who?"

She glanced off to the fork and knife on the serviette beside her Orange Crush. "Just some guy I worked with at Dolla-card."

"Anyone I know?"

She looked at him pointedly. "You don't know anyone there, Joel."

"Thought I'd ask anyway."

She chuckled and popped open her drink. "His name is Gabriel. I worked in the cubicle diagonally across from him. Nice guy just a little . . ."

"A little . . . ?"

"Pushy."

"Ah, I see."

"What do you mean 'you see'?" She took a sip of her drink.

"Well, beautiful girl like you working in a place known for hiring guys who live by themselves and read comic books and watch cartoons—what's a guy like him to do?"

She snorted in her drink; some of it sprayed onto her fingers when she moved to cover her mouth. "Gabriel? Comic books and cartoons? I think he's too much of a nerd for even those. Naw, knowing him, he probably comes home and hangs out on his computer all night, trying to solve the secrets of the Internet or something." At least, she hoped she was right in that assessment. Gabriel hadn't ever really expressed interest in cartoon type stuff. Only once, that she could recall. The day Redsaw's picture was in the paper and Gabriel said he didn't like the man in the black cape's costume.

"Sounds like the man of your dreams." Joel opened his own drink.

The waitress came by and set a tray in front of each of them. They thanked her and she retreated back to the counter.

"Bon appétit," he said.

"Ditto."

As they ate, Valerie checked her watch periodically, not wanting to be late in returning to work, even though, she figured, she could probably get away with being a few minutes tardy if it came to it. Mr. Owen hadn't shown up for work today, but she assumed he was probably busy having meetings or getting things done for Owen Tower that could not be done at the office. She had expected him to call, however. She counted on him in regards to her job, someone to answer questions, if she had any. *As if he needs to let* me *know where he is. The guy's in charge of the company, for crying out loud. I'm just his receptionist.* Still, it would have been nice to know what's going on especially if any clients called that needed his immediate attention.

"Aren't you going to ask me about my dinner on Friday?" Joel said.

"Huh? Oh, sorry. Um, how was dinner?"

"Don't act so excited," he said with a grin. After dipping his sandwich in his soup then taking a bite, he continued. "It actually went quite well. Had dinner with my partners and that client. A lot of it was legal mumbo-jumbo, nothing too exciting. What *is* exciting was that I was asked to head up that new case."

The crumbs on his chin stood out even more as he sat there beaming. Valerie didn't want to ruin the moment by telling him to wipe his face. "Really? What kind of case or can't you talk about it?"

"I can talk about it, just can't get into specifics like names or anything. But remember I had mentioned that most of the law firms in the city were on edge due to Redsaw's current rampage?"

She nodded and took a large bite of her pita.

"Well, it was for good reason. And especially down at our firm. We just got a dozen cases in from families affected by the deaths of loved ones. A few of them—and this is fast, mind you, even in the law world—from that fire Redsaw caused late Friday night-Saturday morning."

She didn't say anything.

"You didn't hear?" he asked.

"Haven't seen a paper yet."

"It was all over TV on the weekend, front page Saturday, second page Sunday. Heavy duty stuff. Redsaw nearly fried an entire bay in an N.K. suburb."

What was Redsaw after? Why was he doing this? What was the point? And to think she had been interested in him in the past. "Was anybody hurt? Wait, I think you already answered that."

"Dead and injured. Axiom-man helped in putting out the flames then it erupted in he and Redsaw duking it out on the bay before he flew off and Redsaw gave chase. I think I have a paper in my office I can give you when I see you next, if you want to read the whole story. Point is, this is serious stuff and a lot of people were affected by it. My firm is now handling a few of the cases. The victims want us to nail Redsaw and garner financial compensation from him. That client I told you about? In short, they own a recently-founded institution designed to be a kind of 'go to' place for victims of super-powered crime and incidents. The owner has deep pockets, hence why it's a big deal."

"And this is good news how? Aside from what it can do for your firm. There's no way the police can stop Redsaw and even if they could, it's not like he has the money to pay these families."

"I know. The only 'good news,' for lack of a better term, aside from the bucks, is that it means long hours at the office for me, a special arrangement for overtime on top of my salary, and a shot at a very healthy bonus should this thing ever get to court. To be honest, I know the futility of these cases as much as you do, but I also know that if my firm goes in smiling, it'll boost my career tenfold. Gordon's one of those guys that, though he does care about himself and his firm winning all the time, he also rewards effort, strangely, and places trust on anyone willing to go all out by rewarding them with referrals to some of the zillion influential people he knows. As much as we are friends, he approaches our co-ownership strictly 'business only' and treats our relationship as such when it comes to things work-related."

She took a sip of her drink and finished off her pita. Joel was just finishing up his sandwich, too, and a part of her yipped for joy that they each still had some soup left. That meant more time together.

"Isn't it, I don't know, dangerous for you guys if word got out that you'll be aiding these families? I mean, what if Redsaw finds out that you're out to get him? Aren't you afraid he'll nail you guys, too, maybe even . . . kill you?" It hit her then. If something happened to Joel . . .

"We talked about it. We decided no press and we'll make the families and the client sign an agreement on the utmost confidentiality for the case. If something leaks, well, we won't be able to help it but at least we tried."

"I don't think you should this."

"Why not?"

"Why not? Does the word 'suicide' mean anything to you?"

He frowned and finally got around to wiping his chin. "It does, but that's not what this is."

"Why isn't it? You even said yourself you guys talked about the possibility of this getting out of hand."

"Valerie, do you have any idea how important this is? Not just for me, but for us?"

"What are you talking about?"

He folded the napkin and set it down, casting his gaze onto the tops of his hands. "I'm doing my best for you, for . . .

for our future." He hesitantly looked up. His expression conveyed that he thought she was going to reach across the table and slap him.

"Our future?" she said softly and leaned back in her seat. Her stomach suddenly filled with butterflies.

"Yes, our future." He reached across the table and held open her hands. She placed her fingers in his palms and he gently closed his fingers around hers. "If I do a good job with this, it could really establish some things for my company. For you and I."

Oh no. Already? "What . . ." Her voice caught and there was a pinch at the back of her throat. She swallowed. "What do you mean by that?"

———

The elevator door opened on the seventh floor of Dollacard and Gabriel stepped out. Taking a deep breath, he straightened his glasses—he still hadn't done anything about the magnifying lenses he was wearing and was happy it was only going to be a half-day—and walked down the hall toward the door. As much as he was looking forward to rejoining the workforce and receiving the promise of a bi-weekly paycheck, he dreaded the inevitable awkwardness that would come with his return, especially if those he worked with had caught wind he had been fired. He padded the pockets of his dress pants when he reached the door, searching for his pass card, then sighed when he remembered he had turned it in upon his dismissal.

About to knock on the door, hoping that the woman working at the cubicle nearest the door would hear him and let him in, he took a step back when the handle clicked and someone came out.

Gabriel took hold of the handle and held the door open as Robert came out. Raising a finger in a "hello" gesture, Gabriel said, "Um, good afternoon."

Robert walked past him to the elevators, not even signaling he heard him.

Just like old times, Gabriel thought and went in.

He surveyed the calling floor. Folks sat hunched over keyboards, immersed in their calls, a few others stood at their cubicles with forearms draped over the partitions that separated each one, chatting away to a customer. A part of him hoped some of his coworkers would take notice and give him a "welcome back" smile or nod or wave. None did. It was like he wasn't even there or had even been gone altogether.

He touched his black tie, which he wore with a white collared shirt beneath a gray sweater, adjusting it slightly so it wasn't so tight around his neck. He hadn't pressed his mask as far beneath the neckline as he should have and already he could feel the heat from wearing several layers of clothes. He removed his jacket and draped it over his arm then strolled on in, remembering to slouch his shoulders slightly so as to further conceal what he wore beneath his clothes. Gabriel only hoped that folks wouldn't notice the smoky scent of his uniform, as he hadn't even had a chance to wash it over the weekend.

Barbara walked past him, callback papers in hand. Gabriel waved at the short brunette but she was too busy looking over the forms to notice him.

He checked the clock on the wall and saw it was 11:58. Two minutes to spare. As he walked over to the lunchroom, he smiled, waved and nodded at whoever was looking in his direction. Only one guy—"Old Tom," as he was known throughout the office, the only guy in his forties who worked the phones—gave a wave of acknowledgement before hunkering back down in front of his computer to assist a customer.

The lunchroom was void of people, but that would only be for another few minutes and then the lunch crowd would pile in for a bite to eat and watch TV. On the bulletin board near the coffee maker was Rod's newspaper clipping. The headline read: SUPER DISASTER RESULTS IN LOSS OF LIFE.

Gene . . . A sharp sting pierced his heart. He verified the date. If only he had been strong enough to stop that car *without* being hurled along with it, Gene Nemek would still be alive. Wanting to look the article over again but knowing he didn't have the time, he forced himself to turn away. Before he left, though, he glanced at the television, knowing he wouldn't be settled unless he checked to see what was on. Commercials. Relieved that that was the case instead of some news-related disaster, he turned on his heels and moseyed on out of the lunchroom, making a straight line for Rod's office.

Gabriel passed his old workstation, which was now occupied by a blonde in a black blazer and skirt who he didn't recognize. The cubicle that used to be Valerie's diagonally across from his also had a new face, a young man with red hair and freckles who looked to be less than twenty years old. Too often had Gabriel gazed into that cubicle, watching Valerie work, dreaming of ways to come up to her and just say hello. Sometimes she'd even look back at him. If only to be able to do that once more . . .

But that would never happen again.

Rod's door was closed. Gabriel peeked in the small window beside the door; his boss stared intently at his computer screen, fingers poised above the keyboard, as if about to type a letter of the utmost importance.

Well, no turning back now, he thought. He gently knocked on the door.

"Come in," came Rod from the other side.

Gabriel opened the door. "Well, Boss," he said, making a thumbs-up, "I'm ready, willing and able."

CHAPTER TWENTY-SEVEN

REDSAW THREW HIS cable motion gym unit across the gymnasium in Oscar Owen's basement; the unit smashed into the drywall thirty feet away, the wall crumbling in places, the twenty-five-pound plates from the leg press breaking loose and tumbling across the floor. It took several moments for their metallic ringing to stop.

He growled, spun on his heels and slammed his fists into the wall behind him, bringing down the wall in broken sheets of drywall.

Almost. So close.

He tried his best to relax and let the power fill him through and through. He had to try again.

Hands aglow in pulsing red energy, he kept all his fingers tucked into his palm except his forefinger, and pointed at the air.

Careful now. Don't rush it. But he almost couldn't help himself *but* do it quickly. The excitement of opening the *door*, to gaining a glimpse into the realm where all his questions would be answered—ah, he could hardly wait. His glowing red finger pierced the air. Carefully, he trailed it upward past his head then swooped it back down in a subtle arc, as if creating the top of a rounded doorframe. He dragged his finger down the one side, the energy cutting through the air, leaving a smoky black line in its wake. He brought this side of the "doorframe" to the floor, then pulled his finger across back to the left then drew it upward, connecting with the thin and misty black cloud that was already there. A dark frame was now before him. If this worked anything like last time—like it had all day—he should be able to stick four of his fingers into the right side of the frame and begin pulling the fabric of Space and Time open, like parting a tent door.

Redsaw opened his hand and brought his fingers together. Digging his fingers into the line of smoky blackness, he braced for the soothing yet-at-the-same-time jarring electric charge to penetrate his hand.

The jolt hit and he pulled.

The air around the door grew warm and as this air began to peel back a few inches, the loud *whoomph fwoomph* of the essence of the fabric of what made up the realm and reality of Earth being torn away resounded in his ears. Air sucked into the cracks in the doorframe like it was being sucked out of an open plane door in mid flight.

Grunting, he pulled against this sheet of broken reality, revealing slowly but surely an ever-growing doorway of utter blackness. Snakes of soft dark smoke slithered out of the door from this alternate place, funking up the room in the stench of rotten fish.

"Puuulll," he said through gritted teeth.

Growling, he reached over with his other arm, holding onto the edge of this door firmly with both hands.

"PULL!"

The door opened an inch further.

Whoomph! Fwoomph!

And budged no further.

The door pushed back, as if someone or something were on the other side, closing it. Redsaw fought against it with all he had and the moment he made just a bit of headway, the door banged shut, air slamming against air.

SHBAM!

When his hand snapped back from the slamming door, he flew backward from his own momentum and crashed into the damaged wall behind him. Drywall rained down upon him when his bottom hit the floor.

As the fine white dust began to settle, he looked to where the doorway had almost been opened.

"I'm not strong enough," he breathed. "Too much. Can't . . . can't do it."

Tears wetted his eyes, but none trickled out.

His suit was matted with white dust, turning nearly all of the black of his uniform gray, the red almost pink. The room around him was a mess.

"Too much," he said, and closed his eyes.

———

The phone rang and Gabriel answered.

"Hey, guy."

"Oh, um, hi, Dad."

"I know it's kind of late but thought I'd give you a call since your mother and I haven't heard from you in a while."

"Sorry about that. Just been kind of busy."

"Been doing lots of overtime, or . . ."

"Um . . . yeah. Lots going on, taking up a bunch of my time." It wasn't a complete lie. Life as Axiom-man had been taking up most of his spare time. Especially this past weekend. And now with going back to work . . . . He could never tell his father what happened. Couldn't let him know he'd been let go only to be rehired later. Despite having to hear the disappointment in his dad's voice at the news (his father had never been one to endorse working at a call centre as a career; he was more insistent on finding corporate or government jobs and this recent upset would somehow prove his father right because, in his dad's mind, it was easier to get fired from a "so-so" job than from a "real" one), the biggest problem, as simple as it was, was not coming across as one of those people who *did* get fired.

Ever since donning the tights, Gabriel had made a grand effort to portray himself as an all-round good guy, trustworthy and polite, even a wimp, in some cases. And part of that portrayal came from the idea that all-round trustworthy wimpy guys *never* got fired and were always on their boss's good side.

Though he hated the term "company suck-up," it was also the role he was now playing as best he could.

I just hope I don't play the role so intensely that I become too much of Axiom-man's opposite and that in and of itself begins to tip people off. Don't want to come across as a fake.

He just hoped he hadn't reached that point already.

"Gabriel, you there?" his dad asked.

"Yes, I am. Sorry. My mind wandered."

"Well, it's late." He paused. "You missed coming over for dinner a couple weeks back and didn't let us know you had a change in plans."

"I know and I'm real sorry about that."

"What happened?"

"Well . . ." Did he have to lie to him again? To lie to his dad . . . . Prior to gaining his abilities, he and his father had been enjoying a season of openness and honesty, a camaraderie that he hadn't enjoyed growing up. To lose that . . . . Maybe he could change the subject instead? "Um, well, how about this weekend? So far as I know I'm not doing anything and I'm not working so maybe that would be good?"

His dad spoke off-phone to his mother. "Honey, we doing anything this—" To Gabriel, "This Saturday?"

"Yeah."

To his mother, "This Saturday?"

She spoke in the background. "Let me check the calendar. Um . . . no. Not that I can tell."

Back to Gabriel, "Saturday's clear. Let's say evening, around six-ish?"

"Sure," Gabriel said. "I'll mark it down, too, and let you know if there's any change in plans. Is Gerry going to be there?"

"Should be, though I don't know if he's working or not."

"Haven't seen him in a while."

"I know. He misses you."

Gabriel smiled. "Tell him I say hi, okay?"

"Okay."

The phone line grew quiet, a signal his dad had run out of things to say but didn't want to hang up. It was always up to Gabriel to end the conversation.

"Well, okay, then, Dad. I should go. Got a big day ahead of me tomorrow. Besides, you got to get up early for work, too, right?"

"That I do."

"Okay. Um, good night."

"Night, Son."

Gabriel hung up the phone.

Still tired from such a trying weekend, he decided it best to hit the hay.

But not before making a trip downstairs to the laundry room first. He had a uniform to wash and now was the perfect time because most of the other tenants were inside and winding down for the night.

———

At a little after 1:00 A.M., Oscar finally shed his Redsaw costume and went upstairs wearing only his boxers.

Entering the kitchen, he went to the steel-finished fridge and opened the door in search of something to drink. The fridge was almost bare, him having eaten out so much on business over the past several weeks that he had hardly been at home enough to cook his own meals. The only items left that hadn't expired were condiments and an old Tupperware container full of rice. And even the rice was questionable. All there was to drink was a pitcher of water that had been sitting there since who knew when. No matter. He'd make do.

He reached himself a glass from the cupboard across from the fridge, ran the tap and drank two glasses worth before setting the glass on the counter. Leaning against the countertop, he shivered when his palms touched its cool surface. Hair soaked with sweat, body trembling, he couldn't believe he had remained in his home gym for so long, stewing over what happened.

The doorway . . . . He knew he could open it, if given just a little more power. Maybe a lot more. As was his habit in the business world to always plan ahead, he also had to consider what was *beyond* the door and what kind of strength might be needed to withstand whatever was there. He needed a surge of power, a supercharge, as it were, if he was going to see this through. And of that he had no doubt. He had to finish this. Too much power and energy had been expended in seeking the unknown, too much blood had been spilled on his journey to what he hoped was glory, too much had been lost personally and too many nights he had gone without sleep in his pursuit of answers.

And answers he better receive. Whoever or whatever was behind the black cloud owed him that much.

The fire on the weekend, the deaths of over twenty-five people—it had tremendously increased his power. Their demises had awoken within what he could only describe, and feel, as a warring beast yearning to lash out and unleash its fury on any who dared to stand in its way. But anger was only a part of it. The other was exhilaration at a complete and utter surge of control and ability, something he had not felt since first gaining his powers in what seemed a lifetime ago. He could do this. He knew he could. He just needed the means.

On the kitchen table was Saturday's paper, the news of the fire on the front page. Hoping to take his mind off what happened in the basement, he went over to it and began thumbing through it, quickly flipping past the front page and shoving the story of Redsaw's fiery rampage far away.

Nothing the paper reported was of interest, and besides, the news was already two days old.

However, he stopped a few pages toward the end and saw the ad for the Screamer Eyes concert this coming Wednesday.

CHAPTER TWENTY-EIGHT

AFTER LUNCH WEDNESDAY, Valerie plopped back down on her chair and stared at the computer screen. Try as she might to put tonight's date with Joel out of her head, she couldn't stop thinking about him. More specifically, couldn't stop thinking about what this date would *mean*.

Time had run out on their lunch date Monday quicker than she had wished. Though Joel never had come out and said it, she knew what he had been thinking.

Marriage.

A life together.

Establishment.

If all went to plan, he had said, handling this Redsaw case could catapult his firm to one of the most in-demand law firms in the city, maybe even the country. That is, only if he pulled it off and though he said he had ideas as to how he was going to, he didn't say what they were. Yet, knowing his current reputation and talent in the matters of law, Valerie doubted things would backfire on him.

She opened up the first of a dozen or so emails that had come in during her lunch break and scanned the first one, not really focusing on it though.

Do I really want to spend the rest of my life with him? We've only been dating for two and a half weeks. Her fingers tapped the tops of the keys, but she didn't write anything down. *No, it's too much, too soon. Besides . . .* She chose not to finish the thought, however. Despite Joel letting her down as of late, she did realize that there were ups and downs in any relationship and that disappointment came with the territory. She just expected that those disappointments would come much later, not during the early cloud nine stage.

The phone rang. She answered it. Someone was looking for Mr. Owen. He hadn't been in all week—not even a phone call or email stating why—and, after much debate and hesitation, when she finally did try his home number, all she got was the answering machine. She didn't leave a message. Fortunately one of the managers had keys to the place so she was at least able to get into the building. The most she could do right now was take a message from the gentleman on the phone and let him know Mr. Owen would call him back as soon as he got in. The fellow on the other end of the line didn't seem too pleased with that but what else was she supposed to do?

Valerie hung up the phone and reread the email, this time thinking of an answer to the client's inquiry.

As she slowly typed up her response, and after she crosschecked her answer with a manila folder pertaining to the client, she still couldn't help herself but think ahead to what she would say if Joel popped the question tonight.

"As if he would do that," she said quietly to herself. "He knows it's too soon, too." Yet, knowing Joel and his ever-pressing habits of pushing himself onto her—in that good way—it wouldn't surprise her if he did pull out a ring after the concert. Knowing him, he wouldn't propose beforehand on the chance that, if she did say no, her denying him would ruin their evening and make the concert incredibly awkward.

Joel aside, she was anxious to check out Screamer Eyes. The group had been around ever since 1984, cranking out album after album, dominating the airwaves for the first decade or so of their career before fading into obscurity for a few years only to return in the late '90s as one of the greatest rock shows on the face of the earth. She was supposed to see them with a group of friends back in '99, but when that same night her friend Jill got dumped by her boyfriend the girls spent the night at home instead, eating chocolate ice cream, being there for Jill as she poured out her heart and let the waterworks fly. Screamer Eyes hadn't returned to do a show in Winnipeg since. Until tonight.

She sat back in her chair, not yet having hit SEND on the email. She wished she could get a flat answer out of Joel, not necessarily if he was going to propose to her or not, but just a clear statement on *what* his intentions were specifically. And if she did say yes, that would be it. She had promised herself long ago after she and Joel had first broken up that whoever came along later in life as her husband-to-be, once they did get married, she would stick with him till death despite any issues that might arise along the journey. It would be a locked-in deal, if she ended up with Joel.

"And no Axiom-man," she said softly. Upon hearing the words, she sat there in stunned silence, in awe that she would even say such a thing. Perhaps it had taken this pressing need to know the future to get it out of her, or perhaps it was her uncertainty with Joel that brought it to the surface. Regardless, it was only now that she realized she had feelings for him. *Real* feelings despite the brevity and scarcity of their encounters.

Get a grip, girl. You're not the only girl in the city who wouldn't mind taking a peek underneath that mask. You're in the dime-a-dozen category now. Besides, the whole city is enamored with him. Everyone. He'd never pick you, anyway. But she hoped that he would. And the moment *that* thought came into her mind, she quickly shoved it away and glanced at the clock.

Despite all this deep thinking, only six minutes had passed and she still had a few hundred more before the day would be over.

Evening couldn't arrive fast enough.

———

"I'm sorry you feel that way, Mr. Hannigan, but that's Dolla-card's policy in regards to your bill. All items must be paid for in full by the due date otherwise you will be charged interest on the full outstanding amount," Gabriel said into his headset. He had been on the phone with Trevor Hannigan for the better part of an hour, discussing the finer points of how the credit card system worked. It was now past 4:00 P.M. and he wasn't scheduled to leave till 7:00, Rod having offered overtime during the day for any who wanted it. Gabriel jumped at the chance, needing desperately to make up for the lost hours while he had been off work. Though Rod had apologized for canning him, he didn't offer to arrange for compensation for loss of time.

"That's ridiculous! I used roughly five hundred dollars *before* the due date and paid back a little over four hundred of it. I should only be charged for the eighty or so dollars I carried over. Other credit card companies don't do this. You guys are stealing from me!" This was the seventh or eighth time Mr. Hannigan was making his case.

"Sir, this policy is standard across the board. When a customer uses a portion or all of his or her credit limit, unless it is paid back in full by the due date, interest will be charged for the amount owing at the time the bill is printed."

"Let me speak to your supervisor."

"I can get her for you, but please note that she will tell you the same thing I have." He couldn't believe this guy. Gabriel stood from his chair and paced the four feet of walking room he had at his cubicle. *Just accept it and move on!* he wanted to say, but like any industry, regardless how uncooperative the customer might be, respect must still be given at all times.

"I don't care! I want to hear it from him!"

"Actually, it's a *her*, sir." *Agh, shouldn't have said that.*

"Excuse me? Are you correcting me?"

What do you think I've been doing for the past forty-five minutes. Man . . . "No, sir, not at all. Please hold a moment while I get her for you. Is that all right?"

"I guess it's going to have to be."

Gabriel pressed the hold button and surveyed the floor for Helen Brown, who worked the evening shift. Helen was off in the corner of the room, her stout form and neckless head looking up at a tall, lanky young man, yet another face Gabriel didn't recognize. Actually, he didn't recognize many of the people he found himself working with after 4:00. The evening shift was like a whole other world.

He removed his headset and set it down beside his keyboard then walked toward Helen. He checked his black tie, making sure it was still done up nice and tight, its job to conceal the thicker neckline of his uniform beneath his clothes. Actually, he felt, the tie worked with the white shirt and gray cardigan he wore today. The black dress pants and black dress shoes finished off the outfit nicely as well.

Yeah, okay, there, Mr. Fashion, he thought as he waited for Helen to finish speaking to, according to the name tag on his shirt, Jeremy.

Jeremy went back to his cubicle a row away; Helen turned and nearly bumped into Gabriel.

Gabriel raised his hands. "Oh, sorry, my fault."

"Can I help you?"

"Um, yes, you can, Ms. Brown."

"*Mrs.* Brown."

"Oh, uh, Mrs. Brown. S-sorry." He took note of the wedding band and engagement ring on her left hand.

For a short lady, *Mrs.* Brown was still intimidating. For some reason she reminded Gabriel of his mother though his mom was nearly as tall as he was.

"Uh, I have a customer on the phone asking to speak to a supervisor. I've been talking to him about an interest issue for about forty-five minutes."

"And does he owe interest?" She put her hands on her hips as if she didn't have time for this.

"Yes. Yes, he does."

The two went over to Gabriel's station and he filled her in on the rest of the details along the way.

Mrs. Brown sat down at his desk and looked over Mr. Hannigan's file before putting Gabriel's headset on her head.

"Okay, watch how it's done," she said as she pressed the LINE button, bringing Mr. Hannigan back on.

While Mrs. Brown took care of the call, Gabriel once more found himself glancing to where Valerie once sat.

Okay, you're pathetic. That's the zillionth time today you've looked over there. She's not there, dude. And she's not coming in either. Give it a rest.

Outside the large window on the other side of the calling floor, a fine layer of cloud covered the early evening sky. There was no Redsaw in sight.

He could be out there and I just can't see him, he thought.

So far this week, there hadn't been reports of any more murders. Still, the messenger had charged him to stop Redsaw. It had to be done, no matter what. And although he now made an effort to stay focused on his job during the day, Gabriel still found himself checking the TV in the lunchroom periodically for any reports of trouble. Only one had caught his attention yesterday afternoon after his break: a robbery at a convenience store not too far away. But the cops had caught the guys a few blocks from the store and they hadn't run into any trouble while making the arrests. So said the news report, anyway.

Mrs. Brown snapped her fingers, grabbing Gabriel's attention. He adjusted his glasses then put his palms on his knees and leaned down, peering over her shoulder.

". . . does that make sense, Mr. Hannigan?" she said. A pause. "Okay, then. Thank you for choosing Dolla-card. Have a pleasant evening."

She released the call then whipped off the headset, as if she couldn't stand to wear it any longer. Gabriel hopped back when she nearly struck him in the face with it.

"Be careful," she said.

Me? "S-sorry."

———

Joel picked up Valerie at her apartment at precisely 7:15 P.M., forty-five minutes before the concert was to start. She got in his Mercedes-Benz.

He leaned over, one hand still on the wheel, and pecked her on the cheek. "Hey, how're you doing?" he said softly.

"Hi," she said, then reached for the seatbelt and buckled up.

Joel pulled away from the curb and headed toward downtown. "All set?"

"Yep. And you?"

"How could I not be? I've been looking forward to this all day."

"Me, too." She gazed out the window; they left her neighborhood and were soon on the main roads, the MTS Centre not far away.

Traffic was steady and it took them about fifteen minutes to reach Portage Avenue. Folks lined the sidewalks on either side, heading up and down them, the crosswalk at the corner of Donald and Portage packed with those who seemed to be going to the concert as well.

"Good luck finding a parking spot," Valerie said.

"Yeah, no kidding. Sometimes I wish these things came with a hover device of some kind so I could just park on the roof."

"Yeah, but then how would *you* get down?"

Joel grinned. "Well, I'd have my hover boots as well, of course."

"Of course."

He took them on a detour around the building, going up one one-way, down another, Valerie not for the first time wishing Winnipeg's downtown was one-way free. They always made driving and getting to your destination difficult, traffic or no. He finally found a meter two streets over.

"Hope you don't mind walking," he said.

"Not at all. I could use the exercise," she said, once more hating herself for not being diligent on her morning runs.

"As if. I think you look great just the way you are."

"Uh-huh. And I think it's great how you're trying to score points right from the get-go."

Joel chuckled. "Okay, you caught me."

He parked the car, they got out, and Joel locked it via the electronic locking mechanism on his keychain. The Mercedes-Benz let off a shrilly chirp.

"Ready?" he said. He put his keys in the pocket of his jacket.

"Ready." Valerie had to admit he looked fantastic in his black leather jacket and deep blue jeans. She suddenly felt over-dressed in her black skirt, dark nylons, white T-shirt and suede black overcoat that came down to mid thigh.

The two walked arm-in-arm to the MTS Centre, alternating leading each other as they weaved through the busy sidewalks. When they reached the front door of the centre, there was a line up. Joel pulled his wallet out of his back pocket and dug the tickets out.

"Here ya go," he said, handing her one.

"Thanks." She checked the ticket over. Yep, seventh row, center, just like he said.

They stood in silence for most of the wait, Valerie glancing up at him every so often, wondering what was going through his mind. Was he formulating a way to pop the question or was he just as nervous as she was with high school giddiness at being here? Joel didn't convey either.

They showed their tickets, proceeded past the ticket-taker and emerged on the other side. Joel came up beside her and wrapped his arm around her shoulders, sending a warm shiver down her spine, the kind that filled her with a thankful joy. Maybe Joel was the *one* after all.

"Do you want anything to drink or eat or . . . ?" he asked.

"Naw, I'm okay. You?"

"I never eat at these things. Not that I go to a lot of them or anything. Just think it kind of takes away from it. The concert is supposed to get you good and hungry for going out afterward."

"Oooh, want to prolong the evening, do we?" she said with a smile.

"With you? You bet."

A.P. FUCHS

They found their seats and took off their jackets. When he turned to face her, Valerie found herself breathless. He wore a tight black Screamer Eyes T-shirt, the band's name written in white, bold lightning-stylized letters across his pecs, the shirt sleeves high enough on the arms so as to reveal bicep muscles that were bigger than she expected. She knew it was girly—even immature—to get all gushy over such a thing, but right then and there she wanted to reach over, run her hands up his arms and complete the motion by clasping her hands behind his neck. Follow up with a kiss and . . .

"Yeah, I know. It's a little tight. Had to dig it out of my closet," Joel said. "Had this thing since high school."

"Oh," she said quietly, the warm, electrifying moment gone.

"What?"

"I mean, um, yeah, looks good. Looks brand new."

"Might as well be. Only got to wear it once before my mother hid it on me when she thought rock 'n' roll was frying my brain. Long story. Besides . . ." He took hold of each of her hands and gently pulled them outward as he glanced her over. "I think we'd be better off spending our time complimenting you. You look gorgeous, Val." He smiled. "I mean, truly beautiful." He gave her hands an affectionate squeeze and Valerie felt her cheeks heat.

She stepped closer and hugged him and rested in his embrace.

After a while, they sat down and Valerie crossed her legs.

Seating over sixteen thousand people, the MTS Centre had a good way of hiding its potential capacity from the outside. When outdoors, the place looked like any other building, but once inside, it seemed to grow, as if the laws of space didn't apply here. Seats lined the place on four levels, the floor included, the seats so tight together that one had to be comfortable brushing someone's elbow.

The stage was enormous, speakers and monitors lining the front, with what looked like a dual drum set on a raised platform, the lightning-like stylized name SCREAMER EYES on

312

the fronts of both black bass drums. Gigantic speakers sat in pairs on either side of the drums, with red and blue and yellow electric and bass guitars on stands beside them. Three sets of mics ran equidistant along the front of the stage, one for front man Johnny Boss, the other two for guitar and bass players Tony Jewel and Mark Endear. The drummer, Hank Ripper, who made industry news at being a mute, didn't have a mic.

"And away we go," Valerie breathed.

———

Helen Brown stood beside Gabriel's cubicle and waited till he finished his call.

When he was done, he looked up at her. "Yes, Mrs. Brown?"

"Someone's just gone home sick. I'm a man short and was wondering if you could stay till 8:00?"

Trying not to show it, he sighed. About an hour ago the fatigue of a long day staring at a computer monitor finally hit him. He just wanted to get out of here, suit up and do a sweep of the city before heading home for a much-needed rest. He had already stayed later than he was supposed to as it was. To stay till 8:00 . . . . Then again, he needed the money, not only to play catch up but also to save up a little and craft a new Axiom-man suit.

"Sure," he said.

"Good. I'll mark it down for Rod so he can adjust your hours."

"No problem. Happy to do it."

Without so much as a blink, Mrs. Brown turned and walked away.

"Thanks for the thank you," he said quietly and got himself ready for another call.

———

The opening act came on at 8:00, a new band on the rise to fame (thanks to touring with Screamer Eyes) named The Tremoring. They were all right but nothing terribly exciting. For most of the set, Valerie and Joel remained sitting, exchanging playful small talk, all flirting. And throughout it all, Valerie couldn't help but feel like she was falling back into routine with him, like it had been at the beginning, that awesome and warm sensation of just being with someone you really liked with the hope of it turning into something more and, if it all went well, something permanent.

After a short intermission, folks returned to their seats and began screaming and cheering when the lights went out, the eager anticipation of their favorite band weaving through the air, permeating everything and everyone present.

The darkness became a glow when lighters were lit and cell phone displays held out; an indoor night sky, like being in space without aid of a spaceship.

On their feet, Valerie and Joel clapped with everyone else but held their tongues until . . .

. . . the low drumbeat of "Andrea" filled the arena, growing louder and louder, crescendoing into an explosion of bass drum, tom-toms, snare and cymbals. The stage exploded in red and blue and yellow lights, the Screamer Eyes front men holding their guitars high and proud like swords, then jerking them down across their fronts and hitting the strings in an orgy of sound.

The crowd roared and Johnny Boss took the mic from its stand and began hopping and running back and forth on the stage.

The drums swelled, the bass line along with it, the sweet distortion of Tony Jewel's guitar sending chilling chords through Valerie's bones.

She and Joel let loose and screamed cheers of encouragement at the top of their lungs.

Johnny came center stage and, one foot forward, one back, leaned toward the audience and in his trademark gravelly voice let it all out. "Coming home from Andrea, coated in a dream, I set my face up to the stars and I just got to—SCREEEAAAM!"

Fans cheered as the stage flashed white light.

After the first verse, Hank Ripper stole the show with a drum solo, the bass drums of the dual drum set beating quick and loud.

Valerie put a palm to her chest, feeling the thud-thud-thudding of the bass drums rattling her insides.

The drums subsided and the guitars kicked up again as Johnny began the second verse.

But something was wrong.

A puzzled look came over Hank's face as Tony glanced back at him, his face asking, "What're you doing?"

The thud-thud-thudding continued but Hank wasn't playing.

Thud. Thud! THUD!

Most everyone didn't seem to notice but Joel leaned over to Valerie and said loudly in her ear, "They're playing it differently. The beat's different and isn't supposed to come till after the third verse."

She was going to tell him that most bands played songs slightly differently live, but before she could, her shoulders jerked when a loud *THUD!* boomed throughout the arena, one not from a drum.

THUD! THUD! THUD!

Screamer Eyes stopped playing and all four band members glanced up toward the sound.

So did nearly everyone else.

It was coming from the roof.

THUD! THUD! THUD!
THUD! THUD! THUD!
THUD! THUD! THOOM!

Chunks of the ceiling came down, heavy pieces of metal beams and debris speeding toward the patrons below.

Screams resounded as people tried to clear the area. One of the large chunks of roof landed on someone, sending the whole place into panic.

A loud whistle screeched through the air and all within collectively gasped when a huge red and black pickup truck fell through the hole in the roof and landed in the center of the arena, its metal and plastic body creaking and clunking as it hit, crushing over a dozen people. One of its wheels spun off the axle and plowed into the person closest to it.

Everyone shouted and screamed.

A tattooed arm stretched out from beneath the vehicle, twitching.

Valerie's hands shot to her mouth. "Oh no, not again," she said into her fingers. This wasn't the first time she saw someone crushed by a vehicle.

Joel tapped her on the shoulder and shouted, "Valerie, look!"

She followed his pointing finger upward.

Redsaw appeared on the other side of the hole in the roof. The man in the black cape descended and the moment he was inside the arena, his black-gloved hands lit up with red energy.

Then he let that energy fly.

CHAPTER TWENTY-NINE

REDSAW DESCENDED SLOWLY, arms spread, legs together, his fists ablaze with red power. Bright fiery energy beams poured from his hands, penetrating all who were in their path. Valerie covered her ears from the blood-curdling screams that filled the arena as Redsaw lay into Screamer Eyes fans on the higher levels, those who had not been able to get to the crowded exits. The beams of raw power pierced the chests of men, women, young adults, and even from her low vantage point, Valerie could make out the wide-eyed looks of frozen panic on their faces as they met their end. Bodies tumbled over the seats, those on the lower rows somersaulting over each other once they were hit. Limp bodies plummeted over the balconies and crashed on top of the patrons below.

A pair of strong hands pulled her palms from her ears. "We have to get out of here!" Joel's face was white with fear.

Strength having run from her body, all she could do was nod.

Redsaw twirled his body around in a circle, the red energy beams cutting and spinning through the air like a blade in a dicer, bathing the dark arena in an eerie red glow, as if hell itself had just announced its arrival.

A handful of folks gathered around the pickup; two larger men crouched down, trying to pull out someone who was trapped underneath. A woman at their side shouted, "Leave him! He's dead. There's no point."

"No! He's alive. Just stuck. We have to—"

A low metallic *boom* jerked the men erect. They looked to the pickup's roof. Redsaw stood over them, his eyes cold, the exposed mouth area beneath his mask revealing a rock hard frown.

Redsaw brought his hands together and blasted red energy into each of the men's chests, their bodies flying backward from the blow. In one sweep of his arm, he cut down all those standing around the truck, the energy beam like a blade, removing the people's heads from their bodies.

Valerie yelped and fought against Joel's pull on her arm; she couldn't get her legs to move.

Joel rounded to her front and pushed her, sending her stumbling back a few steps.

About to yell at him for treating her that way, she stopped herself when she realized what he was trying to do.

People pushed against them as they tried to clear the area. Valerie glanced to the stage. Screamer Eyes was already gone.

A low metallic groan caused her to turn her head back toward Redsaw. The man in the black cape squatted down at the rear of the truck, his arms beneath the bumper. With one mighty heave, he picked up the rear of the vehicle so the truck was at a forty-or-so-degree angle. Then with one violent twist of his body, he hurled the truck into the air, sending it toward the exits at the front of the arena and the mass of people crowding to get out.

The truck came crashing down on a throng of concert-goers, squashing them, sending the other people outward like a ripple in a pond.

Redsaw rose into the air and flew above the crowd, his hands already fired-up. As he flew over them, he poured out red energy, killing at least forty people before adjusting his flight path straight up, directly over the vehicle. Once in position above everyone, he sent a fiery blast into the truck. The pickup exploded and a huge fireball wiped out all who were near it, pieces of the truck's red and black body slicing through the air like knives, bulldozing through the throng, sending splashes of blood and gore into the air.

Fire blazed all around; everywhere the flaming pieces of truck fell, burning. Black smoke filled the air, flickers of yellow and orange flame flashing behind the ever-growing cloud.

The exits at the front of the arena blocked by mounds of dead bodies and portions of a destroyed vehicle left those still alive with few options regarding an exit. From what Valerie could see through the smoke, only a handful of concert security personnel were present, having limited themselves to crowd control.

The next thing Valerie knew, she was in the air, Joel throwing her over his shoulder. He didn't say anything, and only carefully stepped around those who had fallen and the portions of partly destroyed seats. When they reached one of the side exits, he plopped her down. Just as they were about to head out into the large hallway on the other side, they jumped backward as a downpour of people fell before them from the balcony levels, creating a wall of smoking flesh, broken skulls and squashed bodies. A young man fell at their feet, his head striking the carpet-covered concrete floor with such force it split it open like a melon, brain matter and blood spurting onto their clothes.

Stomach swimming, heart racing, eyes teary from the smoke, Valerie glanced up to see Redsaw flying along the balconies of the arena, blasting away as many people as he could with each pass.

The screams and shouts were so thick that she could barely hear herself think.

Only one thought was clear: *Where is Axiom-man?*

———

About 8:40, Gabriel emerged from the front doors of Dolla-card, his shoulders sagging, weary from such a long day. He was supposed to have finished up at 8:00 but a long call with someone even more stubborn than Mr. Hannigan had kept him there till almost 8:30.

Well, at least it's an extra half hour of overtime, he thought. He yawned. *Man, I'm tired.*

He zipped up his jacket and put his hands in his pockets and headed down the sidewalk toward Winnipeg Square.

Head full, he decided to go for a short walk before changing into his costume and going on patrol.

So much had happened over such a short time.

Is this what it's all about then? Just non-stop action, non-stop drama, a complete sacrifice of who I am? Though in his mind he had surrendered to the truth that, because of the responsibility placed on him by the messenger, Gabriel Garrison had pretty much ceased to exist, he still had to give himself up completely in his heart. And who could blame him? For the past twenty-four years, he had just been Gabriel Garrison, nobody to the world and nobody to himself. He was used to living for himself, only worrying about what he wanted and how he would make it from day-to-day. Regardless of all that'd happened in the past four months, his heart was still locked into the old way of life, a part of it still believing that being Axiom-man was only temporary and one day the adventure would be over and he'd go back to just being Gabriel.

I suppose that's only a possibility if I defeat Redsaw, he reasoned. *Though the messenger told me my gift was to restore hope to all those looking on, to help motivate the world to create a better place to live, Redsaw seems to be a deciding factor in all this. I mean, what would happen if tomorrow Redsaw was suddenly no more? Would the messenger come to me and take away my powers just like he did to those other people over five hundred years ago? Or would I have to keep continuing on, striving to create peace in an unsettled world?*

As he approached the entrance to the Square, he considered what he might do if that scenario ever came to pass. (He hoped it would; Redsaw could not continue the bloodshed.) If the messenger did come to reclaim his powers, if eliminating Redsaw would be enough to undo what the man's darkness had wrought, should he go on being Axiom-man anyway?

He stopped his stride and glanced up at the starry sky.

The answer was clear: yes, he would go on. He would do whatever it took to wake up the people of Earth to a better way of life. He would continue being an example unto them of what humanity could be if only people would look past themselves.

Sirens filled the air, first a couple then a multitude, growing in volume. Gabriel turned his head in the direction of the sound and suddenly it was as if the whole street had become the interior of a night club with flashing red and blue lights. Cop cars streamed passed him on his right; fire trucks came from the opposite direction. Three ambulances went past on the street on the other side of the two-foot-high barricade, which blocked off the Square's entrance from Portage and Main.

He jogged a few steps forward and peered down Portage Avenue. Portage was loaded with emergency vehicles as well, the crowds of people as thick as ever, both they and the heavy traffic blocking the way for the emergency vehicles to get through.

Though he was several blocks away, he could make out a steady stream of smoke pouring out from the roof of the MTS Centre in a tight beam of black cloud. A fire? Maybe, but that seemed like an awful lot of emergency personnel for just one fire.

Gabriel doubled back and ran past the cars that had come to a stop, having made way for the police, firemen and ambulances. Not caring he was jaywalking, he ran over the median dividing the lanes and was on the sidewalk next to CanWest Global Place in no time. He turned the corner so he was walking quickly down Portage Avenue and had to come to an abrupt stop when the crowd of people was so thick it was like a wall.

From beyond the mass of people, screams and shouts of terror rose in the air. About thirty or forty people in, fights were breaking out and windows were being smashed as people let themselves go to rioting.

Just then a burst of flame shot forth from the roof of the MTS Centre along with a *boom*, like something had exploded within. He didn't know if anything was going on there tonight but if people were trapped within . . .

Flashes of lightning-like red energy beams shot forth from the roof in intermittent bursts.

Redsaw.

Immediately, Gabriel turned around and pushed himself through the people who had gathered behind him.

He rounded the other side of CanWest Global Place where the mammoth building was butted up against a parking lot. And beside that was a parkade.

His back to the busy street, Gabriel unzipped his jacket and unbuttoned his cardigan. In one fluid motion, he reached up and tugged at his tie, then trailed his fingers down the front of his shirt . . .

. . . and ripped it open, revealing the bright blue of his Axiom-man uniform beneath.

Hehe, always wanted to do that, he thought with a grin and ran up the stairway outside the parkade.

By the time he hit the third level, he was in full costume, powered up and ready to go. He sprinted along the parkade floor, dove over the railing . . .

. . . and tore into the sky.

———

Joel pointed past the bodies to the exit beside the one in front of them. "There, come on." He took Valerie by the hand and led her over to it.

Behind them, Redsaw alternated his hands, sending forth blasts of red energy into the chests, backs and heads of those trying to escape. They each dropped one at a time, like flies buzzing into a fly zapper.

It was difficult to see through the dark smoke; Valerie had to keep one hand by her eyes in an effort to shield them from the stinging haze. It made little difference. Her eyes watered; Joel's were glassy as well.

Coughing, the two got in behind the crowd cramming through this new exit. Joel hopped twice on the balls of his feet, trying to see over the heads of the people.

"The hallway's jammed. At this rate we'll never get out of here."

Valerie scanned the arena, hoping to see an exit that was more or less clear. Each was packed with people like sheep being herded through a narrow gate.

Redsaw growled and, flying over the crowd, began picking up people by the collars of their shirts, flying them up near the ceiling then dropping them to their doom. Arms and legs flailing, their bodies plummeted to the arena floor, bouncing off the seats and heads of those underneath, their broken flesh cooking in the flames.

This is crazy! she thought.

Redsaw zipped over to the stage and like he had moments before, went to another batch of tanks reserved for Screamer Eyes's pyrotechnics. Both hands held out before him, he shot a beam of energy into the tanks then flew off out of harm's way when they exploded in a brilliant fireball of orange and yellow. The rush of heat from the explosion bathed the whole place, sending most folks hunching over and covering their heads.

A pack of people shoved into Joel and Valerie from behind, slamming them into those before them. Valerie whacked her nose against a tall man's shoulder blade. She touched the sensitive tip and pulled her fingers away. Blood.

"Are you all right?" Joel asked, trying to straighten himself. He still held her hand firmly.

She dabbed at her bloody nose again. It hurt but not as much as she thought it would. "Yeah, I'll be fine."

"Where are the police?"

"Who knows?" She didn't think Joel heard her above the shouts of the crowd. *Axiom-man, where are you?*

———

323

The sweet warmth of the ever-escalating power within him made Redsaw shudder in ecstasy. This was how to do it. This was how he should have done it from the start. The rapid deaths of men and women, the quick succession of their demise pummeled him with surge after surge of raw power. The kind needed to open the Doorway of Darkness.

His fingers ached to try cutting through the fabric of Space and Time, a test to see how far down this energizing pathway he was.

"No, not yet," he said quietly to himself.

The top level balconies on either side held a few stragglers, those who hadn't yet made it to the lower levels in an effort to escape with their lives.

Redsaw flew upward and, hovering mid arena, held his arms out to either side and sent forth wave after wave of fiery energy into the people, killing them immediately.

A rush of warmth encompassed him and his fists glowed bright red.

Almost there, he thought, and swooped down over the now-empty arena floor, the only bodies there those of the dead. He glanced over his shoulder. Behind him a young couple was scrambling up onto the stage, most likely wanting to use the back exit. Above them hung one of several of Screamer Eyes's amplifiers.

Turning around mid air, he flew toward them and in a bright flash of red, sent a blast into the pair of chains suspending the amp above the stage, the couple below it. The chains snapped free instantly and the massive amp fell.

He hovered there, awaiting the awe-inspiring warmth of another rush of power to surge through his system, only to snap out of it when a blur of blue swept underneath the speaker, removing the couple from harm's way. The amp hit the stage with a loud crash, part of it puncturing the floorboards, part of it breaking in places, pieces of it skipping outward from the force of the fall.

Above the far end of the stage, Axiom-man flew the couple down to safety and exchanged a few words with them before turning toward him. "It ends here."

CHAPTER THIRTY

THE ARENA WAS a disaster. Bodies lined the floor, lying at odd angles over the seats, others in the rows between them. Smoldering corpses lined the seats beneath the balconies. Across the way, pieces of machinery sat ablaze, sending streams of smoke skyward with no place to go save for the hole in the roof.

The shouts and screams from those trying to escape rang in Axiom-man's ears, as did the pained wails of those hunched over fallen loved ones.

He wasn't ready for this. Who was?

Redsaw hovered before him, about twenty-five feet away. Even at that distance he could feel the man in the black cape's presence, the evil dripping off him, sending his stomach into a mass of swirling flesh. A headache formed at the back of his skull. Fists aglow bright red, Redsaw drifted toward him, sending his body on edge, nausea now fully setting in.

"Like what you see?" Redsaw said, his voice raspy and carrying a darker edge that Axiom-man hadn't yet heard from him.

"It stops. Now," he replied, his tone bathed in the upright anger that threatened to burst forth from within.

"Not today. Not tonight. Not ever." It appeared Redsaw was going to say more but the man didn't finish.

Redsaw grinned an all-knowing grin then turned toward those at the exits. The moment he took off toward the crowd, Axiom-man tore after him, filling his eyes with crackling blue energy.

The man in the black cape spun around and sent a red burst toward him; Axiom-man shot the attack down with a power blast of his own. The two energies merged in the air in a flash of purple before dissipating, the thunderclap from the merging blast echoing throughout the arena.

Leaving no time for Redsaw to orchestrate another fiery attack, Axiom-man powered up his eyes again and sent a shot at Redsaw's middle, knocking the man in the black cape back through the air into a section of seats just above the crowd.

Picking up speed, Axiom-man flew straight at him, arms set, fists clenched—and plowed right into him. Redsaw yelled from the impact, then brought a pair of fiery fists down on Axiom-man's back, dropping him to a section of floor in between two rows of seats.

Shoulder blades aflame with pain, Axiom-man got to his feet and backhanded Redsaw across the jaw. Redsaw came back immediately with a glowing red fist of his own, a straight shot into Axiom-man's nose. Blood gushed immediately from the force of the blow, saturating the fabric on the inside of his mask.

Axiom-man jumped on to him, eyes already bathed in blue. He let loose a blast into Redsaw's face, scorching not only the black fabric but the skin behind it. Redsaw looked at him with wide eyes. Despite portions of the mask ripped open, the charred skin around the man's eyes made it impossible to tell who he really was.

With a strong heave, Redsaw threw Axiom-man off him. Axiom-man tumbled back and lost his balance when the rears of his calves knocked into the back of a row of seats. He fell backward several rows before tumbling off the balcony's edge. Just before he would have slammed back first into the seats below, he kicked on his flight, stopped himself, then shot upward toward Redsaw.

Blue energy fired from his eyes. Redsaw countered with a blast of his own power, the force from the two energies colliding sending them both backward; Redsaw over the seats behind him, Axiom-man through the air so he finally settled hovering over the middle of the arena.

Redsaw came at him. Axiom-man flew to the side as the man zipped through the air passed him. Redsaw stopped his flight, turned, and headed straight for him again. This time when he went to dodge, Redsaw anticipated his attack and caught onto him when he moved to the right. The two men wrestled in the air.

With a quick thrust of his knee, Axiom-man slammed his kneecap into Redsaw's side. Redsaw retaliated with an elbow to the face, sending stars streaking across Axiom-man's vision.

"Almost," he heard Redsaw say faintly. He wasn't sure *what* Redsaw was referring to. His defeat, maybe?

In the span of an instant, Axiom-man thought back to his conversation with the messenger and wondered how strong he was right now. Would he be able to hold his own against the red-and-black-clad menace or would a miraculous power boost manifest itself while he was fighting thus enabling him to defeat Redsaw once and for all?

Axiom-man kicked outward, sending the ball of his foot into Redsaw's neck. The man grabbed his throat with black-gloved hands, gasping for air. Shoving the intense nausea deep into the pit of his being, Axiom-man came at him with a right hook to the side of the head then followed through with a left.

Redsaw dropped from the air and crashed into the seats below.

Off to the side, someone screamed.

Axiom-man turned his head in their direction, hoping to make out through the smoke who was in trouble. Suddenly, from the side, what felt like a semi slammed into him, sending him spiraling through the air onto the stage, crashing into the drum sets. The cymbals and drums banged all around, aggravating his already full-blown headache. He got to his feet immediately amidst the shattered drum sets, only to see Redsaw flying toward the crowd on the left, arms held out, fiery energy blasting from his hands.

———

This would be all it would take. There had to be over a hundred people there. To kill them all at once—oh, it made Redsaw quiver with delight. He set his aim on the support wall holding up the balcony, then smiled big when he noticed how many *more* people were lined up underneath it, trying to fit through the various exits along the side.

Over five hundred.

The red blast slammed into the support wall, blowing a hole through it. Already Redsaw could taste the surge of warmth that was about to course through him.

Those who were paying attention cried out in terror and pushed themselves back through and into the crowd with renewed vigor. Like a prisoner's riot, folks punched and clawed at each other as desperate panic took over.

They knew what was about to happen.

Redsaw shot another hole through the wall, then another and another.

The balcony shook and dropped a few inches.

"Almost there," Redsaw said.

Out of the mass of faces below, one suddenly stood out.

Valerie's.

Redsaw glanced back at Axiom-man, who was pushing the bass drum off his toes. "Friends in high places indeed."

———

The mammoth balcony overhang creaked above them, and with a loud *CROOM* the front portion dropped another six inches.

Valerie screeched and clutched Joel's arm. His bicep was coated in a film of sweat, so much so her fingers had a hard time finding purchase on his skin.

As if having singled them out, Redsaw raced straight for them, hands ablaze in fiery power. Throwing his whole body into it, he sent forth a thick energy beam not two feet from where they stood. The wave of power zipped over the heads of those around them, many ducking. The blast struck the wall, creating a four-foot-wide hole. The concrete crumbled in a brilliant display of rubble.

Joel dove over somebody behind them, got to his feet, then reached past the person, offering his hand to help Valerie over.

"Come on, it's coming down!" His fingers strained to reach her.

She stuck out her hand to grab hold of his, their fingers only touching a moment before a wave of people crashed into her, separating them. "Joel!"

"Val!"

"Help me!" The wave of people pushed her further away. "I can't reach you. Help!"

Joel eyed her intently then glanced at the creaking balcony above. Eyes suddenly growing soft, he looked at her one final time then turned away.

Heart breaking, Valerie tried to push past the people only to be met by equal force.

In front of the crowd, Valerie barely able to keep her feet under her, Redsaw sent another blast, this one over their heads, then another and another, the balls of red power disintegrating the only portion of the wall holding the balcony up.

Valerie looked up and gasped as the balcony collapsed, its huge and weighty expanse crashing down.

Swooomp!

Strong hands grabbed her under her shoulders and yanked her from the pull of the crowd.

A wall of blood and flesh splashed upward as the bodies were crushed beneath the balcony's massive weight. Shiny, liquid red all she could see, Valerie's only contact to the outside world was that of the deafening boom of the balcony completing its journey to the arena floor.

Wind breezed past her ears and light blue material came into focus. She glanced up from the length of blue fabric flapping in the air, then turned her head to see her rescuer.

Axiom-man kept his eyes forward, his mind clearly occupied.

Though she had meant to stay quiet so as not to disturb him, the words "So, that's two, huh?" slipped from her lips.

He set his penetrating blue gaze upon her, nodded, then flew her to the far side of the arena to an area less full of bodies, crushed seats and debris. Setting her down, his eyes searched the place; his gaze lingered on Redsaw, who had flown over to the stage and collapsed onto his knees.

Axiom-man placed his focus back on her, his strong hands gently holding her waist. She could have been mistaken—her body was already shaking with adrenaline as it was—but she swore she felt some kind of electrical energy flowing from his hands and into her, some kind of connection that she was the only one whom he held this way—gentle yet firm, caring yet careful.

"Try and get to an exit, but be careful. If you can't get out on your own, find a safe place to hide and wait for me," he said.

She ran her hands up his chest then held his face in her palms. "Promise you'll come back to me."

Blue eyes looked deep into hers. He didn't have to say anything.

He would be back for her and if not tonight, then sometime soon.

Axiom-man let go of her waist and lowered her hands from his cheeks. "Be careful." The man in the blue cape's feet left the ground and he flew hard and fast toward Redsaw, who seemed to be having problems of his own.

———

The wave of power that swept over him the second the balcony crushed the people in an awesome torrent of blood

331

and gore sent Redsaw's heart and mind reeling. The only thing he knew was that he had to find open space.

Something was coming.

Now on his knees on the stage, he brought hot, red glowing fists eye-level, his hands shaking from the power and energy he was keeping at bay.

This was it. If it wasn't . . .

He shot to his feet and took to the air just as Axiom-man was about to grab him from behind. He knew his adversary was there. He sensed him. Always had. Power and authority emanated from Axiom-man like cool breezes from a frozen lake.

Hands outstretched, he cut into the air with both sets of fingers, tearing the very fabric of reality that up until a second ago had held the universe together.

Pitch black smoke spilled from the gap in the air, billowing out, coating the stage in a screen of darkness. The stench of acrid smoke and rotten fish returned, but this time it no longer repulsed him.

It *excited* him.

Redsaw sensed Axiom-man was behind him, but so far over to the left that the man in blue didn't pose any danger. Not yet, anyway. And after tonight, never again.

Trailing both hands through the air, fingers outstretched, he continued to rip Space and Time apart. He dragged his hands to the side, then as fast as he could, brought them down. Changing course, he tore to the left, creating the underside of the door.

Axiom-man moved right past him, the smoke so thick that it was impossible to see.

Good. Let him take his time, Redsaw thought.

Trusting where this awesome newfound power was leading him, he stopped the bottom door line, sped upward, completing the fifty-foot-tall, thirty-foot-wide doorway. At the top corner of the door, he stuck his fingers into the gap and yanked at the flap of Space and pulled it diagonally downward, the soothing yet jarring electric energy from this alternate place penetrating his hands and forearms—his whole body.

It. Feels. So. Good! he thought.

The flap peeled away easily with zero resistance, unlike in his gym at home.

Smoke as dark as pitch poured out from the ever-growing opening, blanketing the stage and, presumably, the rest of the arena behind him.

"Yes, yes, yes!" he shouted, tearing the fabric of reality away, all the way to the bottom right hand corner.

He glanced down, expecting to see a giant flap of Space and Time draped over the stage and onto the arena floor, but instead found . . . nothing . . . as if such a flap never existed to begin with.

For a brief instant, a shock of fear hit him and he wondered if what he just did was irreparable. Then it didn't matter.

The door called to him.

He took a step back to admire his handiwork.

The Doorway of Darkness stood before him, its edges bright and red and aflame with raw power. Inside the door, massive black clouds twisted and turned and rolled over each other, with flashes of red-hot lightning beyond, in front and in behind the clouds. Thunder crashed, the lightning crackled.

Screams from those still alive beyond the murk behind him filled Redsaw's ears.

At last. At long last it had been created.

His insides jolted when he sensed Axiom-man behind him, probably not more than three or four feet away.

It was now or never lest that fool in blue try and destroy what he had made.

Pride swelling within, eyes set and jaw clenched, Redsaw reached out his hands—and flew into the dark.

CHAPTER THIRTY-ONE

JACK GUNN STOOD outside the MTS Centre, hands in the pockets of his brown leather overcoat, trying not to swallow the distaste in his mouth. "Ah, what a mess," he muttered.

More than anything he wanted to whip out his cell and call Mayor Jones and give him a big fat I-told-you-so. Yet knowing how the mayor liked to keep tabs on his city, he was no doubt already aware of what was transpiring. Besides, under such a tense situation, any curt words exchanged would only add to the stress of an already stressful problem.

Jack had seen this day coming. It was only a matter of time before Redsaw went completely berserk and brought thousands of people to their knees. The murders, as terrible as they were, were one thing. The mass slaughter of thousands, that was quite another. Yet even if Jones had conceded to creating an armed task force specially equipped to deal with people like Redsaw and Axiom-man, by the time the necessary funds were freed up and the deals were in place with a weapons manufacturer to create the required armament to subdue and hold these super-powered individuals, they'd still be where they were tonight. Things always took time. Especially in government.

It had taken awhile but the Winnipeg Police had managed to tape off the entire surrounding block of the MTS Centre and keep the crowds back far enough to allow the professionals to do their work. Police cars, fire trucks and ambulances, after finally having pushed through the thick crowd, now lined the front and sides of the building.

Jack took a step back as Simons held open the door for a wave of people who had managed to survive the ongoing holocaust inside. The crowd streamed out and was intercepted by a team of cops and emergency workers double checking everyone to make sure they were okay. Many who came out held either their heads or their arms or stomachs, wincing in pain. Others had black smudge marks on their faces. Nearly everyone was coughing.

A thin stream of smoke poured from the doors and wafted into the air, the smell of bonfire flooding the streets.

Gunn went up to Simons. "How's it look in there?"

Simons wiped the film of sweat from his forehead. "Like a bomb went off. Seems a car of some kind exploded." He took a deep breath and let it out through puffed cheeks. "I talked to one of the Hats." "Hats" was his name for fire folk. "It's like a furnace in there. For some reason the sprinklers didn't go off. They suspect sabotage but until they can get in there and investigate, there's no way to know. But I'll tell you this: Redsaw is one smart guy if he was behind it. The E.R.U.—"

Gunn raised a finger and shoved it beneath Simons's nose. "Don't. Don't say it. Redsaw's not some genius you can compliment. The guy's a cold-blooded killer, straight and simple." He peered past the officer through the Centre's glass doors. The crowd was slowly moving out, cops directing their way, firemen making their way into the arena area. One of the firemen carefully checked the door and, seemingly deciding it was safe to proceed, opened it. A huge cloud of black smoke poured out, blanketing the people. The smoke quickly filled the entrance and streamed out the front door. Jack grabbed Simons by the shoulder and pulled him back. From inside he heard, "Close it! Close it!"

"What was that?" Simons screeched.

"I have no id—" Jack's words were cut off when a stream of people poured toward him, a wave of panicking bodies crashing down.

———

A sudden blast of hot wind slammed into Axiom-man, sending him up in the air. He crashed face first onto the stage, his knees, shins and forearms absorbing most of the fall. Every muscle and bone in his body ringing from the impact, he stayed on elbows and knees for a moment, trying to shake the cobwebs out.

The gigantic . . . door . . . stood before him, gusting out plumes of black smoke smelling of rot and foul fish. All was black around him save for the shimmering red electric outline of the door and the jagged, bright red lines of lightning in the mass of clouds just beyond its entrance.

Redsaw's in there, he thought. *Maybe whatever this is killed him and my job is done. Aside from closing it, anyway.* And how he would do that, he hadn't a clue.

Body still vibrating from the fall, he forced himself to his feet. The wave of nausea overtaking him was so powerful that he tore down the front of his mask and threw up. Suddenly cold and feverish, he allowed himself a moment to focus, then put the mask back in place, the sharp taste of upchucked food assaulting him.

"Messenger, I need you," he groaned. His mentor didn't reply. Not that he expected him to. "It's up to me, then," he whispered and stepped toward the towering door. As if reacting to his presence, a bolt of red lightning shot out and struck him in the chest, knocking him straight back onto his shoulder blades.

Screeching from the sudden impact of bone on wood, Axiom-man lay there, his upper body numb.

I can't even get near it without it . . . . No, I have to do this. Grimacing, he got up despite the pain racing through him and powered up his eyes. The door reacted again, this time sending two bolts of red lightning toward him with laser-like precision. Axiom-man flew up and over the beams. They zipped past their target, their light disappearing into the black smoke that was everywhere.

Thunder resounded from within the doorway, its crash low and dark, and though it was only sound, Axiom-man got the clear impression it was telling him to stay away.

"Not today," he said and flew into the door.

Once he passed the threshold, his breath caught in his throat at the sight before him.

———

This was it. Finally.

Redsaw hovered in the black air through no effort of his own. It was as if a pair of invisible hands held him in place, cradling him as though a babe. Wicked and awesome energy coursed through him, filling every fiber of his being, calling to mind that night not too long ago when the black cloud visited him and bestowed upon him power beyond his imagining.

The massive unseen hands kept him in place, forbidding him to move even though he didn't want to. To rest here in this overwhelming power's embrace, oh, how he could for an eternity.

Arms relaxed and held slightly out to the sides, he noticed the bright red glow of his open hands in his peripheral, the glow pulsating with each surge of all-consuming strength that passed through him.

The vast expanse of black clouds all around roiled and turned, like waves on an open ocean at night. In the distance and also near, jagged streaks of red lightning crackled and flashed, as if so much power existed here that this place in and of itself was straining to hold it back.

He was here, finally, after all this time. Despite his questions, he couldn't find the will or strength to speak. Each effort to expel a breath, to say a word—his mouth wouldn't open nor could he form voice.

The hands held him, comforted him, assured him that it was all worth it and that the lives lost in the process were all part of a bigger picture soon to be revealed.

Time was lost in this place. Though he could count the seconds in his mind, he'd lose count after ten or eleven and need to start over, each re-start as though the first, no other thoughts having come before it.

"Redsaw." A low male voice on the wind, one heard both externally and in his mind. His heart skipped a beat at hearing his name spoken with adoration, not disdain. Finally, encouragement not condescension.

Thunder crashed, its sound vibrating through him. Lightning sparkled in the sky.

His fists pulsed bright red and his muscles energized, as if his strength had just been doubled, tripled, more.

"Redsaw. My son, my child. Welcome home."

Yes, I'm here. He could only think the words but what the voice said next confirmed it understood him perfectly.

"Redsaw, I have created you. You are my son. Of the world from which I chose you, only you belong here, with me, in this place of absolute power."

Master, I am yours. Reveal to me your ways, your secrets, all that you have for me.

"You have done well, my son. You have sought me in spite of the demanded price. The blood on your hands is now my own. This burden I lift from you."

Yes . . . Father.

"Lose yourself to me and I will share with you the splendor of the universe. All that I have built will be passed on to you. What is mine is yours. And what is yours I now make mine."

Take me. I'm yours.

Each word from his master's mouth was like a breath of fresh air. Never had he felt so *comforted* by something and . . . *someone.*

A rush of supernatural serenity encompassed him and the knowledge—in his mind and in his heart—finally hit him and was accepted.

He was home.

"The world was lost without you. I knew you from the moment you were born. I watched over you, I nurtured you, I revealed myself to you. You know this to be true."

It was as if the eyes of his heart and memory were suddenly opened. The master was right. He had been there, since the beginning. Regardless of where his life had taken him, this awesome cosmic force had been by his side, unseen and powerful, guiding him and motivating him to become . . . what?

Who am I?

"The ruler of the world."

———

Axiom-man forced his eyes to stay open despite the mind-numbing pain in his head trying to force them closed. Stomach swimming unlike anything he'd ever experienced before, he tried to ignore it, tried to push it from his mind. Before he could even absorb where he was, he threw up again, this time inside his mask. He didn't want to tear it away, unsure if somehow the fabric protected him from the strange and stench-filled atmosphere of this place. To risk it . . .

. . . but he had to. Unable to breathe, he clawed at the base of his mask and, bunching a small portion of it between his fingers, tore it away so his mouth was exposed. He went to look at the puke-covered fabric only to see his hand empty. He must have dropped it without realizing it. He glanced down and didn't see anything. Only darkness and black clouds and crackling red lightning.

He wiped his mouth and tried to process the enormity of this place. It appeared to go on forever. Body shaking from the nausea, he forced himself to search his surroundings for any sign of Redsaw. Nothing but tossing and turning black clouds swirled and moved before him. Red lightning flashed on either side. Then another streaked straight for him. The blast struck him in the shoulder and sent him backward through the air. Flesh stinging, a portion of his uniform burnt away from the zap, he slowed his fall backward then stopped altogether, hovering in the abysmal dark.

Fight it. You have to. Never had he been so sick. Being near Redsaw was nothing compared to this. Why did they have to clash so horrifically? Why the sickness every time he was near him?

It was the presence, he knew, the soul-sickening evil that he had never imagined until now. Being here was the complete opposite to being in the messenger's presence. Here he was at the opposite end of light, of all that was good and righteous and just.

The seriousness of his charge finally struck him deep and pure. If Redsaw wasn't stopped, if he didn't do something, the earth would fall prey to the darkness that ruled this place.

"Messenger," he whispered. Could the messenger even come here? If having reversed the evil's actions five hundred years ago nearly killed him, if he were to be in this place— would the very presence of this darkness consume him?

No, it couldn't. If *he* was still alive and still had his powers, then the messenger, someone much more powerful, would surely survive. Did the messenger even know he was here? Of course he did, if what the messenger said about sensing him through his powers was true, and Axiom-man had no reason to think it wasn't.

"Messenger," he said again.

No reply.

He was on his own.

Bringing his hands together, Axiom-man flew forward, pressing himself to go on despite the hard-hitting throbbing pain above his eyes and atop the center of his head, regardless of the stomach-twisting nausea that gripped his insides.

". . . ruler of the world." The voice came from all around, dark and foreboding yet one dripping with a strange comfort.

He waited for it to speak again. Perhaps if he could pinpoint its location, he could trace it to Redsaw.

"It was I who pushed you to become the epitome of human achievement. Though you have a long way to go, you were still chosen, for only I see the future of all things. I know where you are headed, my son."

It was useless. The sound came from everywhere at once, each direction as viable as the next for its source.

Axiom-man dipped in his flight, his eyes begging to be closed. Just a moment's rest, nothing more. Surely a few seconds couldn't hurt. His eyes closed but the moment his lids touched he snapped them back open. *No, don't fall asleep. Don't rest. Not until it's over.*

"You are the culmination of all desire. Your drive to exceed the standard call of man has set you apart. It is this passion, this need, which I have used and will use to create an empire of all of your heart's desires."

Scanning in all directions, Axiom-man's heart leapt in his chest when another bolt of red lightning cracked in the distance then streaked through the air toward him. He flew upward, the beam narrowly missing him.

I need to make this quick or I'm a dead man. He turned his mind even more to the task at hand, shoving any thought or acknowledgement of the near-consuming sickness out of his mind. *Entertain it and it will take you. What good are you dead?*

Two more lightning bolts came at him. He arced upward. The bolts collided beneath him in a loud, energized *CRACK!*

"You are my son. You belong to me. I will give you power beyond your greatest dreams as long as you swear to uphold all which I reveal to you."

Axiom-man zipped through a patch of black cloud. When he emerged on the other side, thunder crashed and rang in his ears. More rumbled in the distance.

Where is he?

———

The ruler of the world, Redsaw mused. Was it possible? Of course, it had to be. If such a being could grant him these incredible abilities, a being that lived in such an awesome and awe-inspiring place, surely he would make due on his promise.

But there was one obstacle which had and would prove a hindrance to the promise coming true: *Axiom-man*. The name produced a palpable distaste in Redsaw's mouth. From the beginning Axiom-man had always been there to counter him, to confront him, to slow him down. Like a shadow, the man in the blue cape's presence was constant, one that refused to let up and was determined to put an end to what was only the beginning of his reign.

Should he ask this powerful presence about his adversary? Was it not reasonable that this cosmic being already knew about him? He had to know if there was a way Axiom-man could be stopped. Permanently.

What of . . . He was going to think Axiom-man's name but just the mere thought of the man in the blue tights sickened him. *What of him? Do you know who I mean?*

"He came before you. It was his presence in the world which brought me to earth. Do not worry, my son, for his days are short, should you obey all I command."

How do I stop him?

"You already know."

He already knew? Redsaw searched himself for the answer. There was none.

"You dare to bring me shame? Are you not aware that your strength is double his own? Do you not know that you could have brought him to his knees shortly after you turned to me?"

When did he turn to him? The Forks! When he accidentally killed that young man. It was then his powers turned within and opened themselves up to him, made him who he was today.

He countered my every move. Even recently, when I sought this place with all my heart. He was there, refusing to back down. Circumstance forbade me from finishing him.

"And if the circumstances were in your favor?"

Once more Redsaw was at a loss for thought. Could he have killed Axiom-man if given the chance? He had certainly toyed with the idea. Had come close but it was the consequence he feared. If Axiom-man were destroyed, what might occur?

If I do kill him, what will happen?

"The day will come when you will bring him to his knees. When that day arrives, do not let him live. There is a power which resides in him, one which propels him to stop your rise to ultimate authority. Release that power from him and all that he has will be yours. Once his power is under your control, once it has turned to our ways, the world will fall, humanity will be at a ruin, leaving room for you and me to rebuild it in our likeness. In *my* likeness."

Yours?

"Mine! You are still my servant, Redsaw. Though an heir to the work I have begun in the world, and though the earth will one day be your throne, it is still I who will reign supreme."

Then it wouldn't turn out as Redsaw had hoped. To rule all who dwelt on the earth, to be their king, surely that had to be good enough, didn't it? No. It wouldn't be.

Redsaw wanted it all.

"I know your thoughts. Do not challenge me with them or you will be broken beyond restoration. All that you were is mine. All that you are is mine. All that you will be is mine. Do not threaten me with petty thoughts of conquest. Trust in me and you will become all that I have promised and more."

Yes, Master. A pause, and a mental image of Axiom-man entered his mind again. The very thought of him made Redsaw's heart contort in anger. *How can I destroy him, the one who stands in your way?*

No reply.

Was the being gone? No. The invisible hands still held him, still assured him with their comforting embrace.

Can you enter my—the—*world and bring him to his knees?*

"It is my desire to do so, but there is one who holds me back. One day his hold will be lifted and I will stand at your side and together we will watch the end of Axiom-man."

Do you know who—he had to force the name to surface in his mind—*Axiom-man is?*

"His identity is kept from me so I charge you with the task of discovering what man lies beneath the mask."

And if I find out?

"You will!"

———

Axiom-man flew on, body outstretched over the clouds. Several times he had to slow his flight, the uncomfortable effort of searching for Redsaw putting strain on his innards, making him feel worse and worse.

Thankfully, his stomach was empty, but his head still throbbed, the intense pain consuming his skull now also in his neck, making it difficult to move it from side to side, up and down.

His hands shook, and more than once did he find their quivering distracting as he flew.

It was impossible. This place was too big. The black clouds went on forever in all directions.

He was too weak.

What he wouldn't give for that surge of energy he felt when chasing after the TrailBlazer. How he yearned for the amazing onslaught of power that surged through him when he lifted those pools from the earth. But no wishful thinking would make him feel better and his powers were not responding.

Despair replaced whatever hope he had left of finding Redsaw in this murk of black cloud and crackling red light.

"Keep going," he told himself. Then, as an afterthought: "The messenger wouldn't give up. He hadn't on that day long ago. He risked it all to save the earth. You should do no less."

Thunder crashed, sending a shock wave of sound into his core, reverberating back out and echoing throughout his limbs. Far below, a flash of red burst behind a massive black cloud. The cloud's dark mist parted like gauze torn by two giant hands and three sharp red lines made of light shot forth from it, aimed at his head, body and feet.

Body aching from the evil presence's strain upon it, he forced himself to twist to the side. Two of the lightning bolts blasted past him. The third struck him in the knees, disintegrating the fabric and scorching the flesh.

Crying out, he shot his knees to his chest and wrapped both arms around them. Two holes the size of baseballs exposed charred flesh, the skin and meat still smoking from the impact.

Breathing slow and labored, he questioned if he could go on. Though the lightning attacks had been few, it was the very atmosphere of this place that weakened him and threatened to end his life.

"I can't go on," he said, his voice barely a whisper. Even speaking was an effort.

He had to continue. Had to find Redsaw. Once he found him, though, he didn't know what he'd do next. Should he end it here? *Could* he even . . . kill him?

"Only one way to find out," he said.

Brow furrowed, jaw clenched and lips pressed tightly together, he forced his body to straighten. Reaching out, he embraced the foul-smelling air and flew on.

Redsaw had to be around here somewhere.

As he flew, the voice's words played over and over in his mind, overlapping with the voice on the wind.

I will one day be killed, he thought.

"You are my herald on earth," the voice said from all around. Each time Axiom-man heard it, a chill raced up and down his spine. The malice and dark authority which dripped off every syllable made him want to shrink back and hide. Each time the voice had spoken, he had to resolve himself to continue on even at the cost of his own life.

Yet it seems something is stopping Redsaw from acting. Better, something is also holding back this . . . being . . . from coming through that portal or even just manifesting itself on earth. Could it be . . .

345

Thunder crashed. Axiom-man searched the skies for the inevitable sharp blasts of lightning.

A few seconds passed, then four thin and bright streaks of red, two from two opposite directions, came for him. He sharply arced upward with all he had, the tension on his muscles sending a sharp spike of pain into his lower back. Below his feet two of the lightning bolts hit, the impact firing off a spider-web of electric energy, its ends licking his feet like hot tongues. Screaming from the pain, he flew upward and zipped over to the left, the remaining two bolts just missing him. They, too, smacked together and sent out a web of hot electricity, their ends singeing the underside of his right arm.

"Redsaw!" he growled.

"He comes for you," the voice said.

Me? Wait, no, him. *Have to find Redsaw.*

"How much do you want it? Do you want it as badly as all else you've set your hands to? Are you willing to take the leap and step up the progress of my plan, in turn speeding up the day of your rule?" There was a long pause before the voice spoke again. "Very well."

Fwoosh! A wall of black cloud raced up from the misty abyss below, thick with darkness, the only light that of the faint flickering of lightning beyond its surface.

Axiom-man stopped his flight and brought his legs under him, hands at the ready should—

Redsaw, fists aglow, burst from the cloud, flying straight for him.

CHAPTER THIRTY-TWO

THE TWO TITANS collided, the thud from the impact sending a low and echoey drum beat through Axiom-man's core. Being this close to Redsaw made his insides lurch and his head swim.

Got to stay alert, he told himself.

Bodies entwined, Axiom-man looked for an opening for a clear shot. Before he could find one, Redsaw's fist came in from the side, the knuckles crashing into the side of his head. Neck craning to the left, Axiom-man tensed his shoulder muscles, slowing the momentum which otherwise would have sent his body into a spin. With both hands he pushed Redsaw in the chest, enough to gain a few inches of distance between himself and the man in the black cape. He followed through with a hook of his own and connected squarely with Redsaw's jaw.

Redsaw's eyes danced with fury; his fists recharged redder than before, setting Axiom-man en guard.

Blue light pooled into Axiom-man's eyes. Quickly, he jerked his knees up so his heels were aimed squarely at Redsaw's stomach. With a mighty double-legged kicked, he snapped out and sent Redsaw flying back behind a black cloud. Not wanting to be caught so close to him again, Axiom-man kept his body facing the black cloud but forced himself to drift through the air backward, opening the distance several meters at a time.

The wavy mists of the black cloud parted and Redsaw burst through, flying at him like he had before.

Bracing for impact, Axiom-man poured as much power as he was able to into his eyes and, just as Redsaw was a few feet away, let loose with a searing blast of blue energy, not caring *where* on Redsaw's body it hit, only that he *did* hit him.

Redsaw growled when the beam struck him.

Lightning flashed above and below Axiom-man, then two jagged beams of red electricity streamed at him. He flew backward, the two streaks of lightning colliding before him, sending out a web of energy, the crackling power zinging the surface of his legs, burning away the fabric along his thighs and shins, leaving dark singe marks in their wake.

Flesh burning, he knew he had to get out of here lest he face not only Redsaw but the hostility of this alien place.

Have to find that door, he thought.

He turned around and flew into the roiling masses of black clouds, keeping his eyes peeled for the hot red outline of the doorway that would lead him back to his world.

Shoulders tensed with unease, his mind partly focused on what was before him, partly focused on who was behind him, he searched the dark, hoping against hope that the door would reveal itself to him.

His flesh tingled, stung, vibrated—every cell in his body about to give under the intense pressure of this place. If he stayed here any longer . . . . He just didn't know *how* much longer he could hold out. Despite all his powers, he was still human. As he flew, his body reminded him over and over how much it was buckling under the strain of being in the presence of such evil.

Mind fuzzy, he hardly had time to recognize the intensified upset of his insides before a pair of strong hands grabbed hold of his boots. The next thing he knew, he was yanked backward, his flight suddenly reversed. A dark shadow zipped over him only to land on the other side and deliver a red-glowing fist to his face.

The blow sent his head knocking backward; a spike of pain raced down the back of his neck and into his spine. Red lit up all around him and violent electrical energy wracked his whole body, sending it into harsh tingling and numbing spasms.

Had the lightning struck him? Or . . .

No sooner did the hot tingling wave begin to pass than something grabbed him by the front of his uniform, jerking him upright.

Redsaw glared into his eyes. "I will kill you."

For a brief moment Axiom-man wished that he would. The sweet bliss of death would be a welcome relief from the turmoil that threatened him both outside and in.

Threatened to steal his powers.

No, he had to keep fighting, keep pressing on.

The doorway. He had to find the doorway.

Redsaw kept his hold on the front of his uniform with one hand, and with the other socked him one good in the face, then another in the throat.

Axiom-man's neck closed up; no air was getting through.

If I die, I die, he thought, *but not without bringing him down with me.*

He reached forward with both hands, grabbed either side of Redsaw's head and brought the man's face into his knee. There was a loud, wet *smack*, and though it could have been Axiom-man's imagination, he thought he felt blood splash onto his burnt skin.

Redsaw remained in a fetal position, hands clasped to his face. Seizing the opportunity, Axiom-man delivered a swift kick to Redsaw's side, his instep connecting hard and fast into the man's ribs. Redsaw rolled through the air several times.

This is where you pay for all you've done, Axiom-man thought, growling at the same time.

Blue energy filled his eyes; he blasted it out with all he had. The bright beam zapped through the air, striking Redsaw in the arm and side.

Anger and frustration at having not stopped him before, Axiom-man resolved that their struggle would end tonight, he the victor in spite of what that thundering voice had said about Redsaw one day conquering him.

Summoning all his speed and strength, Axiom-man tore through the air, the pain in his head and stomach now only serving to fuel his ever-growing rage at the man of darkness.

349

He plowed into Redsaw; the two caped men's bodies sped through the air, friction taking its sweet time to slow them down.

A sudden surge of heat nailed Axiom-man's sides, as did a sharp double-wham to his ribs. Redsaw pulled back his fiery fists and brought them together once more, digging them in hard and deep into Axiom-man's waist just below his ribs. Howling from the onslaught of pain, Axiom-man punched Redsaw in the nose and brought his fist down on Redsaw's chest. The two blows didn't seem to faze his opponent. If anything, it only increased Redsaw's rage and the next thing Axiom-man knew, he was being knocked downward. Gravity took over and he tumbled back, black clouds enclosing over him. Then utter blackness altogether.

When he came to, he was still falling. Redsaw was nowhere to be seen so he couldn't have been out that long, maybe a few seconds, maybe a minute, but no longer. He kicked on his flight and slowed his fall. What he might have fallen into, he didn't know. Only black clouds filled this place and if there was a land mass of some kind, it hadn't yet made itself known.

Lightning crackled in the sky and ten beams of red light streaked toward him from all directions. He evaded four of them but was nailed by six. The super charge of red electricity—if it was electricity—ransacked his whole body, sapping it of strength and filling his head with a sharp, pounding headache, the likes of which he had never known. The pain was so intense his vision left him. Were his eyes closed? They felt open but all he saw was utter blackness, the kind you see when you squeeze your eyes shut and lie face down in a pillow in a dark room.

Blazing agony swept through him the second a fierce hot tingle raged chaos throughout his body, the same pain he felt every time Redsaw belted him with his energy beams.

If only he could see . . .

He pawed the air, hoping to grab onto the man in the black cape and wallop him one good. His fingers grasped . . . nothing.

WHAM! A fist to his face.

THWAMP! What felt like the hard heel of a boot beneath his jaw.

The sound of the thunder ceased as did the electric crackle of the lightning.

The last thing he felt were energy-charged fingers around his neck.

———

In a moment, the world would be his.

Redsaw held Axiom-man's limp body by the throat, his fists aglow.

His master said one day Axiom-man would fall to his knees. Redsaw just hadn't figured that day would be today.

Or was it meant to be today? The notion gave him pause. The master never said; he only promised that it would happen.

"Doesn't matter," Redsaw grumbled through gritted teeth. "This fool has haunted me far too long. I no longer want any part of him."

He squeezed and vertebrae popped beneath his fingers. The intense joy of doing such damage thrilled him and reactively he hurtled Axiom-man through the air, then flew after him. Reaching his prey, he wrapped his arms around him and delivered blow after blow into Axiom-man's head, chest, stomach, sides, even his legs. Redsaw's heart thrilled at knowing so many bruises would be on his nemesis's body. Each one punishment for all the times he thwarted his plans.

After tonight, the world will fall into my hands. After tonight, I will rule along with my master. After tonight . . . His thoughts cut short when, off in the distance, he saw the energized red outline that was the Doorway of Darkness. Black smoke swirled beyond the door's threshold. No sign of the arena was evident. But . . . was it his imagination or did the door seem to be growing smaller?

"No!" he shouted and scooped an arm beneath Axiom-man's armpit. With all he had, he streaked through the air, dragging Axiom-man's body along with him, speeding toward the door.

I'm not ready for it to close. I need to know more. I need more power. I need everything!

He crossed through the doorway and emerged on the other side. With a quick spin, he slammed Axiom-man's body down onto the stage, which was hiding somewhere beneath the thick black smoke that filled the MTS Centre. Axiom-man's body hit with a loud and sickening *thud*, his body hidden beneath the murk.

I'll get to him in a second, Redsaw thought, then turned and faced the door. He checked it over and even from this side, he wasn't sure if it was closing or not. There was too much smoke and too many segments of the electrical red doorframe faded in and out along its top, sides and bottom.

There was only one way to ensure the door would remain open. It would be the same way he had opened it in the first place.

Redsaw focused all his energy into his hands; his palms and fingers shone bright red with crackling energy. He flew upward and began retracing the outline of the door.

———

Blackness was everything when Axiom-man came to. He was on his back (that much was certain), his arms and legs weighty and numb. Thick smoke covered his field of vision, enabling him to see nothing at all. His only signs of true consciousness were the frustrated grunts and snarls of what he recognized as Redsaw's voice somewhere on the other side of the smoke.

Head spinning, sharp pain filling the back of his neck, he tried to sit up. The most he was able to do was perhaps rise a few centimeters before having to lie back down. The moments ticked by, but as to how many, he didn't know. Time seemed to have ceased to exist and all he had was the awareness he was conscious and that was about it. His stomach ached and was sick with nausea. Time passed—if it really had at all—and he realized he didn't feel as ill as he had before he blacked out. Though still sick and wanting nothing more than to curl up and sleep it off, there was a marked difference in how his body felt. Was Redsaw still around? Sure he was. He could still hear him. What had changed? Something must have or—

Were they out? What—

Trying his best to focus his thoughts and jelly-like mind, Axiom-man coated his vision in blue light, using its luminance to help pierce the foul-smelling black smoke that covered him. The light didn't make a difference. It only turned the pitch black to a charcoal black.

Have to sit up, he told himself. However, thinking it and doing it were two separate things.

Concentrating on his arms, he managed to slowly get them tight beside him, then, with great effort, managed to get his arms bent and his elbows under him. Next were his legs, which seemed to refuse to move.

"Move," he whispered.

Thinking only of them, he rejoiced inside when he felt his feet twitch. *Okay, that's a start.* Taking a deep breath, he waited a moment—a *real* moment; Time seemed to be coming back into existence—then tried again. Slowly, he was able to pull his legs up so they were bent at the knees. *Thank goodness.* He forced himself partly on to his side, one palm to the floor, the other on his hip. *You're doing fine. Keep going.* As much as he hated this self-talk, he found it comforting right now. Head still aching, stomach still in a knot, he silently counted to three then pushed against the floor, hoping he still had enough strength to get to the job done. His arm fell off his hip and he rolled over, managing to get both legs under him, palms beside his knees. After getting the balls of his feet firmly planted on the ground, heels beneath his buttocks, he dug his feet into the floor and pushed with his legs. The second he stood, dizziness came in like a storm and he teetered a few steps before putting out his hands to either side to balance himself.

"Have to keep it open," Redsaw said behind him.

Axiom-man turned around and saw Redsaw in the air, coming down some thirty feet away. *The door!*

What was Redsaw doing? It didn't matter. There had to be a way to close the door and seal that evil place off from the rest of the world.

"Messenger, now would be a good time for some help," he said. Like always, the messenger didn't reply nor come to his aid. *How can I close it?*

He thought for a moment and put a palm to the side of his head when a spike of pain surged beneath his skin, over his ear and culminated above his eye. "Ow."

Redsaw didn't seem to hear him; the man in the black cape was too engrossed in doing whatever it was he was doing.

There had to be a way to cancel the power keeping the door open.

Axiom-man smiled when he realized there was. At least, he thought there was a way. Though he was no messenger, their powers still were connected and, dare he think it, even the same or similar.

The last time the messenger visited his energy full-out on this earth, it nearly cost that cosmic being his life. The thought of dying made Axiom-man shudder, but at the same time, the drive to finish what was started here tonight confirmed within him the need to do what he knew had to be done.

Taking a deep breath, he waited a moment to calm down, then with grim determination, stepped toward the bottom of the doorframe just as Redsaw flew an inch above the smoke hovering over the floor, his hand in the smoky murk, red light flashing beneath the darkness.

Axiom-man hoped for a super-powered surge of energy, but no surge came. Instead, he remained diligent, allowed blue light to fill his eyes, the energy growing brighter and brighter until all he saw was blue-white. The sound of the energy crackling around his eyes filled his ears. Though he couldn't see Redsaw, surely his opponent would have noticed him by now.

354

He crouched down, reached forward and felt around for the red line that made up the bottom of the doorway. At first he felt nothing, then a sudden hot electrical zing scorched his fingers.

Setting his sights where he thought his hand would be, he let the energy loose. A bright flash of purple lit up the air all around him with a loud *CRACK!*

His vision began to return as the energy poured forth from his eyes. All was coated in blue light, but at least now he could see.

Redsaw looked up at him with wild eyes. "What are you doing!"

"Closing the door," he said coolly. *At least, I hope my power cancels out the doorframe.*

"No!" Redsaw shoved him but Axiom-man wouldn't have it. He stood his ground then had to focus his eye-beams anew when he saw Redsaw blast red power from both hands to where he was attempting to seal the door.

Axiom-man brought his heel down on the back of Redsaw's head. Redsaw's body collapsed and disappeared beneath the smoke. The bright red energy of his hands faded, leaving only the flashing red line of the doorway's bottom.

With his eye-beams, Axiom-man flew along the bottom of the doorway. The electricity-laden red line crackled and smoked and transformed to bright purple everywhere the blue energy touched.

When he reached the far side of the door, he headed upward. About halfway up to the top, it was as if something was sucking the energy from his eyes, drawing it out like a vacuum. Sharp pain beat against his eyes and he was about to relent but instead re-doubled his efforts, coming back against the doorframe with all he had.

Purple light shone and snapped everywhere his eyes struck. It wasn't completely clear if the door was in fact closing, but in his peripheral it appeared the door was either getting smaller or the black clouds and red lightning beyond were fading away or the shadows of Screamer Eyes's equipment on the stage were coming into view. Either way, something was happening.

He hoped.

He reached the top. Flying along the top of the doorway, Axiom-man fought its pull against him, the agonizing pain which ripped at his eyes, drawing his power from him. About three quarters of the way across the top, the door—or whatever was behind it—kicked its efforts into high gear and a hot charge filled his body, burning his muscles and bones, setting his skin on fire.

"No . . . ignore it . . . keep . . . I have to . . ." The words barely came through panted breaths. Mind going blank, his only awareness the task at hand, he kept pouring on the power, moving—at least, he thought he was moving—along the remainder of the top of the door.

Something grabbed hold of him and pulled him downward.

Redsaw.

Axiom-man's eyes never left the top corner of the door. Once he felt it was sealed, he focused on its side and gave it everything he had.

Hot pain struck his side, sending his stomach and chest muscles into spasms. Heart beating rapidly, he kicked outward and to the sides, not caring where he hit Redsaw but that he *did* hit him. His foot struck something so he kicked again in the same place.

"Leave it!" Redsaw screamed.

"No!" Axiom-man shouted.

The door fought back, sending a streak of red light partly down Axiom-man's eye-beam. Focusing his power, he pushed back, coating the red beam in blue. Bright purple shone forth then exploded in a firework when it slammed up against the remainder of the side of the doorway.

Redsaw pulled him down, then raised a red-powered hand up in front of his eye beams; the clash of power created a spider web of purple electric light.

Axiom-man swung out wildly and knocked Redsaw's hand away. Redsaw tried swinging his hand back into place and Axiom-man met the effort head on, the two men's forearms colliding. A burst of pain filled the bone of Axiom-man's forearm, sending a shock wave of aching numbness through his entire left arm. Instinctively, he cradled it with his right while focusing hard and fast on sealing the rest of the door.

Redsaw pulled on him one more time and the two fell hard onto the stage, Axiom-man landing on his back, eyes still focusing their energy on the door. The final portion just before the door's corner crackled and smoked and emitted a high-pitched screech, like a thousand children screaming in agony.

Axiom-man moved so he was on all fours and scrambled toward the final section of doorframe that had not been covered with blue energy. The foot-long electrical red line grew smaller and smaller as he sealed it and when he reached its bottom, he thought it'd be over. Then the entire place rumbled, the stage shook, his whole body quaked.

Oh no. Is whatever that being was coming through from that place? Is the door even closed? he wondered.

A burst of red power zapped outward from that corner of the door just as Redsaw dug his fingers into it, seemingly trying to—

Axiom-man's eyes ignited in hot pain. He cried and had to force himself to keep himself from covering his eyes with his palms.

It hurt so bad. It felt like someone was sticking a screwdriver through each of his eyeballs, slowly, piercing the jelly-like substance of his eyes only to stab directly into his brain.

Searing pain filled his whole head.

He shot forth his power with all he had, feeling it gush from his eyes in torrential waves, the blue light growing blindingly bright then dimming then flashing bright then dimming then—

Whatever constant surge of energy that filled him and kept him energized while his powers were activated poured from

357

him, flowing from the core of his being and out through his eyes.

Bright purple flashed and crackled just beyond his field of vision.

Red energy surged forth from the corner of the door once more.

"No, no!" Redsaw growled, his gravelly voice carrying the undertone of despair.

Sudden fatigue hit Axiom-man like a slug to the brain, to the heart, to all that he was. He collapsed onto his stomach, the power from his eyes fading rapidly.

Don't . . . give . . . up . . .

Redsaw screamed.

The corner of the door flashed bright purple. A thunderous boom echoed throughout the arena.

Axiom-man focused his eyes even more and sent forth one last blast of raw blue energy. Then all went dark and his face hit the stage.

His heart trembled within him when he no longer felt the presence of his powers.

CHAPTER THIRTY-THREE

WITH A SHOUT, Redsaw whipped around to where Axiom-man had fallen.

"Fool!" he screamed and quickly shot his hands into the black smoke that was nearly knee height. His fingers found a bundle of material. He yanked Axiom-man up by the back of his cape and threw him back down again. Axiom-man's limp body slammed against the stage with a loud *thwump*. Once more, he shot his hands into the murk and pulled Axiom-man up. He ran his hand along Axiom-man's back then took hold of his adversary by the rear of the neck. After righting him, he socked Axiom-man in the face, caught his reeling body, then walloped him once more. Axiom-man's body fell. Redsaw kicked him in the stomach, in the chest, the sides of the arms, then pulled him up again. He held him steady and punched him in the face several times, Axiom-man's limp head snapping back with each blow.

Redsaw threw him back down then jumped on top of him. Though Axiom-man was concealed by the smoke, Redsaw knew where he was and delivered blow upon blow, smacking Axiom-man's head and face, neck and shoulders in an onslaught of raw anger.

"You will die for what you've done," he screeched.

He grabbed Axiom-man by the collar and lifted his head and neck up, then pushed him back down, the rear of Axiom-man's head banging into the stage's floor. Over and over he smashed his head against the stage until he was sure that Axiom-man would never wake again.

Adrenaline coursing through him, Redsaw shakily stood, turned and was about to walk away but instead whirled around and hoisted Axiom-man back up. He threw the man in the blue cape's body skyward into the smoke. A moment later a loud bang echoed throughout the arena when Axiom-man no doubt slammed against the roof. His limp body reappeared through the smoke. Redsaw caught it then flew it back down hard into the stage, smashing clear through the floorboards and into the concrete beyond. Amidst the splinters, Redsaw kneeled on his chest and let loose into him again, pummeling Axiom-man in the face over and over until all he heard was the moist smacking of bone against raw meat.

Fists lit anew, he eyed his adversary's bloody and smashed face in the red glow, Axiom-man's face nothing more than a mass of gnarled and shining flesh, whatever humanity that had been left of his visage now completely gone.

Gurgled breaths oozed from Axiom-man's lips and nose. Somehow he was still alive. Just barely.

And something else was missing, too.

Despite looking right at him, Redsaw could no longer *feel* his presence.

Finish him, he thought, the voice inside his head a mixture of his own and that of the thunderous voice of the cosmic being he had the privilege of meeting behind the Doorway of Darkness. *The ruler of the world*, the voice had promised. Now had to be the time.

Bitter rage his only conscious thought, Redsaw brought both glowing hands together above his head, fingers entwined, ready to bring them down with all his might and end Axiom-man once and for all.

"The power is mine," he rasped.

In his mind's eye, he could see his fists fly down into Axiom-man's head, the pure power of his might and energized hands removing Axiom-man's head from his body. He could see the blood gushing from the top of Axiom-man's neck as this once powerful being was finally brought to an end. He could envision tearing off the mask from Axiom-man's dismembered head and staring into the lifeless eyes of the one who had thwarted him for so long. It could all end here.

It could all *start* here.

Redsaw's hands remained poised above his head. His heart galloped in his chest. His moment of glory had come.

Finally.

It was time to rule.

His hands remained above his head, fists aglow.

Unmoving.

Bring them down and begin your reign! he told himself. "The power is mine!" he shouted.

Still his hands remained.

What was he waiting for? This was it. Finally it would all come to an end. The door had been opened. He had been given his charge. He had encountered the one who cared for him and who had predestined him to rule the earth.

His hands wouldn't budge . . . and the glow left them.

Arms beginning to shake, his lungs suddenly unable to inhale enough air, he slowly lowered his hands until they dropped into his lap.

"What's my problem?" His voice was barely a whisper. His heart sank into his stomach when he realized what it was: if he killed Axiom-man now, a new door would be opened. The voice spoke of one who was holding him back, one that prevented him from leaving the realm behind the door and entering the world. If Axiom-man died tonight, surely this awesome force would come looking for him and his master's promise of absolute rule would be compromised.

"I . . . can't . . ." he said. "At least . . . not now."

I can't die. Not yet. And I can't risk it either. Not until I know more. Whatever this power was, whatever was holding his master back, it was most certainly an awesome force to be reckoned with. If it could keep his master at bay, what chance did *he* have against it? Death would be inevitable.

With a heavy heart, Redsaw slowly stood and eyed Axiom-man's body. How he wanted to strike him once more, how he longed to watch this helpless man absorb another blow. But that could be the blow that killed him and, right now, Redsaw couldn't take that chance.

Not yet. Not until he was more powerful. Not until he felt himself ready to defend himself against a power that was perhaps even greater than his master's.

"One day," he said.

And with one final look at Axiom-man's body, he rose into the air and drifted into the smoke.

———

Blue light replaced the darkness, jolting Axiom-man back to awareness. Warmth filled him through and through, most notably in his head and face. Was he dead? Was this what happened when you died? Or would this only happen to him because of his gift from the messenger? His gift! Did he have it back? Had it left him completely?

The blue light pulsed bright white, soundless and pure. It flashed once more, blinding him, then was gone.

Black smoke—at least, he thought it was smoke—came back into focus and Axiom-man was aware he was on his back, his spine arched over what felt like metal poles and splintered wood. The putrid scent of rotten fish and filth filled his nostrils, making him gag.

There was a hole of some kind in front of him. When he checked the edges, he realized it was either a floor or a ceiling and he was on the other side. As consciousness crept back in even more, he decided it was the floor. How else would he explain the rubble pressed up against his back and legs and arms?

Groaning, he blinked several times, feeling like he hadn't slept in days. Throat dry, muscles sore, he tried to get up . . . but couldn't.

Redsaw. If he was still out there . . .

Quickly, Axiom-man summoned forth his power and was relieved to find he still had it. Slowly, he drifted off the smashed wood and bent metal, and rose through the hole in the stage, emerging into the darkness of the black smoke on the other side.

Was Redsaw still here?

"Redsaw?" he rasped, his voice barely audible enough to be picked up by even his own ears. As if the man in the black cape would answer anyway. He was probably waiting in ambush behind the smoke. He cleared his throat and forced out a shout: "Redsaw!"

No answer.

He adjusted his body so he was floating erect above the stage. The air seemed to be clearer somehow. Though virtually nothing could be seen, the smoke appeared . . . thinner.

Axiom-man glazed his eyes over with blue light and used its brightness to help him see in the dark. All he saw were the vague outlines of broken seats and mounds of bodies. In the distance, he saw many people moving about. One seemed to be carrying something. A few others were speaking.

He waited several minutes. If Redsaw was near, surely he'd be able to feel him. Instead, he felt nothing, at least as far as Redsaw's presence was concerned. His head and stomach only swooned a little, the black smoke from that evil place provoking a nauseating unsettledness.

Redsaw was gone and the doorway was closed.

Axiom-man's shoulders sagged with the realization that once more, the man in the black cape had escaped him.

What he did know, however, was that sometime soon another opportunity to stop him would arise. And when it did, he'd be ready.

Especially after tonight.

Axiom-man floated off the stage and touched down on the floor beyond. It could have been the knowledge that tonight's trouble was over—a kind of tension and apprehension release valve—but suddenly fatigue radiated from within, from the core of his power. His legs gave out and he collapsed onto his knees, wailing when his kneecaps struck the cement floor. He teetered forward and had to use his hands to stop himself from falling over completely. Palms stinging, he remained on all fours, catching his breath, wondering why he wasn't dead.

On the other side of the arena, the voices picked up, a multitude of men saying something he couldn't decipher.

Then someone said, "The bodies are over here! How in the world are we gonna get them out?"

It was either a cop or a fireman or an emergency worker of some kind.

Axiom-man wasn't in the mood to answer any questions and he certainly did want any of Winnipeg's finest to see him like this. With a grunt, he pushed himself onto his feet. His body rocked backward when a swell of dizziness threatened to overtake him. Fuzzy green danced before his vision and buzzing filled his ears. He wanted to throw up. Again.

When his vision cleared, he stumbled toward the side of the arena and found a door.

He didn't know how many more doors he passed through before he found himself outside, the crisp late night air shocking his system and cooling his lungs, reminding him that he was having a hard time breathing.

The city street was void of people. Good. He didn't want them to see him lean up against the side of the building to prevent himself from falling over.

Man, was he tired. Worse, each step reawakened his aching muscles in renewed bursts of pain. His skin was sensitive to the touch through the fabric of his uniform. He reached up to see if he was right in assuming the bottom of his mask was missing. His lips objected to the touch of his gloved fingers, proving him correct. How bad did he look? He wished he had a mirror, yet at the same time prayed he wouldn't find a reflective surface.

He wasn't ready to see himself yet, but judging by the way his face ached, he probably looked like someone had run a lawnmower over it.

"Oh, man . . ." he moaned. As he ambled down the sidewalk, a part of him expected Redsaw to come racing out of the sky and finish the job. Instead he found himself waiting for nothing.

He had to go home, get away from here.

His mind drifted back to the street. Where were all the emergency vehicles? He glanced over his shoulder. A cop car was parked at the intersection toward the front of the building, its lights flashing. Other red and blue and yellow lights bounced off the surface from what he could see of the building across the way. Perhaps some emergency vehicles had been here tonight but, as each did its job, cleared away.

Axiom-man felt compelled to turn around and check with the officers present and see if they needed any help. Yet, he couldn't find the strength to turn around never mind continue walking forward. He stopped and leaned against the wall, catching his breath.

What's wrong with me? he wondered.

He had his powers, that much he knew. He just felt . . . empty . . . somehow, as if something was missing. Maybe being in that other place had broken something within. Maybe he had pushed himself too hard and was now nothing more than the shell of the man he once was. Maybe his power would leave him and only enough of it was present to see him through the rest of the night. And if not that, then maybe just the flight home.

Barely able to keep standing, he contemplated sitting down on the sidewalk and just resting. But he couldn't do even that. To be out in the open—he'd be nothing but a target, if not for Redsaw, then for whoever else who might have it in for him.

Got to get home, he decided. He'd regroup there.

He leaned his head against his forearm and closed his eyes, catching his breath. His insides were hollow and any moment now he was going to pass out.

Closing his eyes, he welcomed the blessed relief of rest when he heard a familiar voice: "Axiom-man?"

He opened his eyes and pulled his head away from his arm.

Valerie stood beside him, her makeup running, her hair in disarray. Still, she was beautiful.

He smiled weakly, unable to manage anything more. Somewhere in the back of his mind he hoped she wouldn't recognize the lower exposed part of his face and put two and two together.

"Are . . . are you okay?" she asked.

He couldn't help but let out a soft chuckle. "No, I'm not," he said softly. "At least, not right now. Why are you . . ." Getting the words out was near impossible. "Why are you here? You shouldn't be here. You need to go h—" He coughed and was only able to bring his hand to his chest. His other hand slipped on the wall and he stumbled forward, bent at the waist.

Valerie caught him. "We need to get you to a hospital."

Still bent over, he waved her off. "No hospitals. Not right now."

"No, you need to go to one." She paused then yelled, "Hey, over here! We need help!"

Axiom-man pulled on her arm, jerking her down so her head was level with his. "Quiet!" A sharp pang struck his heart. He hadn't meant to yell. "I'm sorry. Please. Don't call them. I have to do this on my own."

"Why?"

"You wouldn't understand." He didn't feel like going into the details.

After a moment, she sniffled then said, "Okay. Here, at least let me help you up." She put his arm over her shoulder and pressed up against him. "One, two, three." And she straightened her body.

He tried to be careful about not putting all his weight on her. "Let's go around back." His voice had been so quiet he wasn't sure if she had heard him. "Let's go—"

"It's all right, I heard you," she said gently.

Slowly, they walked down the last few feet of sidewalk before they were at the back. Here, Axiom-man leaned against the wall and closed his eyes a moment, needing to rest.

"You need help." Her voice was so thick with concern Axiom-man couldn't help himself but agree with her. Still, he

366

couldn't go to the police. Gunn would surely show up, if he wasn't present already, and demand he be demasked.

"I know, but not from them."

"Then from who?"

"I just need to rest a moment. I'll be fine." Though he didn't believe his own words. As much as he tried not to think about it, he feared the worst. Something really had given way inside. Something from that place had tainted him or changed him somehow. In an effort to change subjects and take his mind off himself, he asked, "What are you . . . doing here?"

She didn't answer right away. She only looked at him when he opened his eyes. "I . . . I waited for you." She bit her lower lip, as if afraid that saying such a thing was a crime.

He exhaled slowly. She had waited for him. Valerie. The girl with the brown hair that smelled of vanilla, the girl with the smile that could change the world. "Thank you," was all he said.

Her eyes glassy, Valerie smiled subtly and reached for him. When she wrapped her arms around him, he did the same to her, not minding the bruises that objected to the embrace. Like she had the times they held each other before, she fit into his arms and up against his chest perfectly, as if she belonged there. Oh, how he hoped so. He was prepared to lose everything in this world, but he longed for the privilege of hanging onto her.

"Thanks for waiting for me," he said. Closing his eyes, he kissed the top of her head. She squeezed him gently, his gesture of affection obviously welcomed.

A cool breeze swept over them, but where their bodies met was only warmth.

When she pulled away, he looked at her with softness in his eyes. With his hand, he brushed a stray lock of hair from over her eyes. Deep down he knew it was because of her he pushed himself like he had tonight. To see her face again, if just for a moment, made staring death and darkness in the eyes all worth it. He leaned forward, kissed her forehead then brought her to himself once more.

A.P. FUCHS

They remained there, against the wall, for a long time, each moment filled with tenderness and adoration. She was healing him, reminding him of why was he was here, not just to protect her, but all people, those who, if given the chance and example, could change the world.

His strength began to return, at least enough that he knew he would be able to fly without falling and—

"Here," he said, "let me take you home."

EPILOGUE

OSCAR OWEN LOOMED over his bathroom sink, wearing only a red towel around his waist, his body laden with sweat. His gray eyes looked . . . old . . . as if he had aged ten years in a single night. He had expected to see a portion of his face burned away and could only chalk up his mysterious healing to being in his master's presence.

He glanced down to the running hot water and thought back to that night long ago when all this began and he killed those two cameramen.

Finally, the door had been opened. Finally, he had learned *why* he was chosen to bear the great and awesome gift of his abilities. Now he knew who was behind him.

And who was against him.

He ran his hands under the tap, ignoring the water's searing heat, and splashed some on his face.

Deep inside, he yearned to go back into his master's presence, to be held by those massive hands, to feel the love and warmth that emanated from them.

To find out what could be done to finally put an end to the force that held his master at bay.

One day he'd go back there. One day he'd spill enough blood to ensure that the door would remain open forever.

One day, but not today.

More needed to be done and if he donned the Redsaw uniform again, he feared he'd lose himself to it—to the power and drive it prompted within him—and never stop killing. He wouldn't be able to help himself but go after Axiom-man and put an end to the one who stood between him and his forthcoming reign.

No, he couldn't go after him, not until he knew for certain that his empire wouldn't be threatened by the cosmic power that forbade his master from setting foot on the earth.

One day, when he had the answers, he'd act.

And there would be no stopping him.

He only hoped that he'd be doing the right thing and wouldn't become a monster.

———

Leaving Valerie at her apartment the night before was one of the hardest things Gabriel had ever done.

Now, Thursday morning, he sat on the edge of his bed, elbows on his knees, face in his hands. Though he still felt weak, he sensed his powers more present this morning, more *whole*.

"Good," he said.

But last night . . . . How he had wanted to stay with her, to *live* in her comfort, to feel her heart and just simply *be* with her. While he stood on her balcony, about to say good-bye, he considered telling her *everything*. But with the way she looked at him, he could tell that she wasn't ready, that something else was going on behind those brown windows to her mind. He didn't know all she had gone through that evening, only the little bits she had told him on their flight to her place. She had said she was so scared when she thought she and her boyfriend wouldn't have been able to escape, yet at the same time, she said, she knew that no matter what happened, *he* would come to their rescue and stop Redsaw. When he had asked about her boyfriend, she glanced away and only said, "I'm not so sure about that anymore." Though the words gave him hope for himself, his heart still reached out to her because he knew what it was like to not be with the person he adored. To add to the confusion she was probably feeling by revealing his secret—he couldn't bring himself to do it.

One day, perhaps, when the time was right, he would.

Gabriel toyed with the idea of calling in sick so he could spend the day resting, but quickly dismissed the notion because if he did, he'd certainly be fired over the phone. Permanently.

He went to put on what was left of his Axiom-man costume, only to throw it to the floor in disgust, the material giving off the foul stench of rotten fish and garbage.

There's one more expense, he thought. *Had to be done anyway though.* He scooped the uniform up and put it at the bottom of his hamper, beneath a pile of clothes. He'd deal with it later.

Getting ready took longer than usual, each tug of his clothes over his limbs reminding him just what kind of a night he had. He checked his face in the mirror for anything that would give away he had been in a fight. Aside from his skin looking worn and his lips slightly puffy, everything seemed all right. Though his nose was sensitive to the touch, he didn't think it was broken. A part of him felt, however, that the damage should have been far more terrible than it was. Something inside told him that he had undergone something far worse than what he remembered about his fight with Redsaw. There had been that bright blue light when he came to beneath the stage. The messenger? Maybe. He'd have to ask him the next time they spoke.

When he was finally dressed in black dress pants, a white-collared shirt and brown sweater, he combed his hair and put on his glasses, reminding himself yet again he needed the lenses changed lest he be doomed to a working life filled with headaches.

While at the front door slipping on his shoes, jacket draped over his arm, he tried to shove the images of the night before out of his mind. Instead he kept thinking about that place beyond the doorway and the voice he heard and the promise to Redsaw that one day Redsaw would be ruler of the world.

I can't believe that though, he told himself. *If I do, I'll only be opening a doorway of my own, one leading to a world where Redsaw does rule. Valerie. Think about Valerie.*

Her beautiful face filled his mind, setting his heart at ease and curling his lips upward in a smile.

He nearly lost his life last night and any chance he might ever have had of being with her.

"Well, of Axiom-man ever being with her," he said softly. But he couldn't just be with her as Axiom-man, could he? It wouldn't work. It couldn't. "And to risk going down the same road again—I never want to do it. Life's too short and . . ." *I think it's time I say something. Really say something. I'll never know till I try. She asked me out to that gala. That's got to mean something. And maybe one day, when the time is right . . .* ". . . I'll tell her everything."

———

During the day, Valerie didn't return any of Joel's calls. She had considered giving in on her lunch break, but with Mr. Owen away again, the work kept piling up so she used that as an excuse not to talk to him. Of course she knew *why* she wouldn't speak to him. Not today. And probably not ever again.

The look on Joel's face when that balcony was about to come crashing down—behind his eyes she was able to see the selfishness, the concern only for himself. He didn't even come back for her last night. He was just . . . gone. All his words of love and kindness to her became worthless then. All the promises, all the feelings—everything.

You always pick the bad ones, she mused. "And they always pick you."

News of last night's massacre was all over the paper, radio, TV and Internet. In between emails, Valerie checked the reports online and after she read a few of the articles, the distinct notion that life here in the city was going to change forever hung over her. Especially since Mayor Jones was quoted as saying the city will be changing the way it does law enforcement, especially in how it deals with those with superhuman abilities. He said he had spoken with the police that morning and informed the chief that Sergeant Jack Gunn was to take the reins for a special task force designed specifically to deal with super-powered threats. No longer would the city fall prey to such a catastrophe, he said.

Well, at least Axiom-man will always be here to help out, she thought.

Valerie had been sorry to see him go last night despite the late hour. As silly as it was, she had wanted to ask him to call her when he got to wherever he went when not in costume just so she knew he was all right. She also considered inviting him to stay the night or at least until he got his strength back.

But you know why you really wanted him there, she thought. *You love being with him and not because of what he can do.*

There was something familiar about him and not just because they had spent some time together. It was as if she had known him for a long time.

———

Throughout the whole day Gabriel couldn't stop thinking about what he'd do come 4:00 P.M., and when the hour finally came, he logged off and ran his callback forms across the office as fast as he could.

Today could be the day that would change everything.

When he stood outside the front doors to Valerie's apartment, he didn't think he could go through with it. What if he told her how he felt—truly felt—and she brushed him off, like she always did? What if she said he could never speak to her again?

Heart beating rapidly, he really thought he could do this. In costume, he had gone up against far worse than just a girl. But Valerie . . . well, she posed a threat that nothing he had encountered as Axiom-man could ever pose. He honestly didn't know what he would do with himself if she shut him out of her life for good. At least right now they were still friends. That was better than nothing.

"Come on, you love her," he said. "That can't be a bad thing." *Can it?*

He put his hand on the door handle. *Doing this as Axiomman would be so much easier. At least she'd want to see him.*

His fingers remained on the handle, unmoving. Finding the strength to open the door and buzz her apartment was nigh impossible.

Maybe she's not home from work yet. He checked his watch. It was 4:33. If she walked, she probably wouldn't be here. If she bussed—the thought of her being there made his heart skip a beat. *I don't want to lose her and I don't want her to just like Axiomman. It wouldn't be fair to her and it wouldn't be fair to me. And right now, she's all that matters. It doesn't matter how I feel. I can't—*His thoughts stopped short when he realized he had already made up his mind about this. The zeal he felt this morning for coming here and confessing his feelings for her was absent. Too much was at stake. This wasn't some simple boy-girl thing. There was so much more to it and that *so much more* wore a blue cape.

"Who am I kidding?" he said. His fingers trailed off the door.

He stood there for a moment, thinking about giving it one more go, but decided not to. "Some other time," he said softly.

When he turned around, his breath caught in his throat. Valerie was coming up the front steps.

She looked up at him quizzically. "Gabriel?"

He took a deep breath and exhaled slowly. "I, uh . . . I have something to tell you."

Valerie smiled.

About the Author

A.P. Fuchs is the author of several novels and writes from Winnipeg, Manitoba. Among his most recent are *First Night Out*, *Axiom-man*, *The Way of the Fog*, and *April*, which was written under the pseudonym, Peter Fox. Visit his corner of the Web at **www.apfuchs.com**

Printed in the United States
84017LV00001B/1-75/A